Heaven Sent

BOOK ONE:
ATONEMENT

JL ROTHSTEIN

:

DEDICATION

I dedicate this book to my parents, Frank & Muriel, who always told me I could do anything I put my mind to. To Grace, who I am fortunate enough to be able to say is both my sister and my best friend. To my brother Frank who is an incredible listener and sounding board. To my amazing husband, Alan, thank you for all the plot debates, character discussions and hugs during editing

ACKNOWLEDGMENTS

I read an author's note once that expressed how no book is written in a vacuum, I could not agree more. I want to thank my editor, Beth Dorward. Brittany Huber for my first cover art. Thanks to Jeff Brown for the final cover art and promotional illustrations. To Michael Cannon for social media and website assistance so very early on. Special thanks to my husband, Alan, who read many iterations of this book and helped me work through many roadblocks

"Forgiveness is the fragrance that the violet sheds on the heel that
has crushed it"

Mark Twain

CHAPTER ONE

Strumming her fingers on the kitchen counter, Genevieve O'Mara waited for the soapy water to fill the last pot in the sink. Her bright blue eyes stared into the backyard, but her mind wandered to her husband.

I can't believe it's been forty years since I last saw you Gabe. A soft sigh escaped her unpolished lips. *I didn't think I'd make it two days, never mind forty years.*

At two hundred and thirty-two years of age, Genevieve vowed that no matter how long she lived she would never stop looking for her husband.

Memories of Gabriel haunted her, but never as vividly as on the anniversary of his disappearance. No day was harder to get through: not the anniversary of when they first met, not his birthday, not even their wedding day.

When I close my eyes, I can still see those dark blue eyes staring into mine. There are days I swear your scent lingers and your laughter echoes all around me. I wish I could still trace the small scar over your left eye and lose my hands in the jungle of your unruly brown hair. Turning the faucet off and drying her hands on the dish towel she grasped the wedding ring that hung from a silver chain around her neck. Sliding her finger along the inside of the band she could feel the engraved ivy branch that had been etched so long ago. She pictured her life back then and confessed aloud, "I miss you. I miss us. I can't stop, I need to know what happened to you."

Walking to the end of the cabinets she stretched upward to reach the potted plant that hung in front of the window. Its rambling branches outstretched toward the glass, while its variegated leaves curled upward seeking out the sun.

"You're going to need a trim soon, my friend," Gen muttered to the plant.

Thinking back to her previous time living in this area she lamented about how long it had been. Decades had long passed since she lived in this house and tended the garden she and her husband had planted together.

"Gabriel, somehow, I always felt you knew that I kept this house, even though I couldn't live in it after you were gone. I held it in trust and moved away, but I've been drawn back here. I asked my sisters to move in with me. Having Kelly and Deb here helps; it fills some of the emptiness."

Gen walked to the front windows and took in the hustle and bustle of the day.

"All the old neighbors have either passed away or sold their single-family homes for the payday of the real estate boom. It's quite a stunning change since you and I were last here. There isn't anyone left on this street that I recognize. I'm hoping that continues since my sudden re-appearance looking exactly as I did forty years ago would be impossible to explain." She went back to the plant by the sink and adjusted one of the branches taking a moment to survey the image of herself reflected in the windowpane. "Looks like the plant isn't the only one that needs a trim."

Ducking into the bathroom to use the mirror, she let her hair down and attempted to collect the wispy strands that had escaped her ponytail. Working to pull it back up she watched as small curls fought their way free and encircled her face. The brighter bands of blonde blended with her soft features and unmade face, while highlighting the blue in her eyes.

"Ugh, I don't know why I try." Giving up on taming her hair she left the room and heard the rattle of the front door open, then slam shut.

"Hey Gen, I'm locking myself in the office to get a head start on this case file!"

The clacking sound of heels on hardwood preceded the boom of toppling books dropping to the floor. This was her sister Kelly's typical boisterous entrance.

"Tom is coming over with food if you want to join us!" her sister hollered.

Shutting the kitchen lights off Gen wandered down the long hallway toward the library. The wall had a beautiful antique chair rail that Gen had been obsessed with restoring. Her fingertips lightly danced along the top of it as she walked. She was unfazed by all the opinions to tear it down and throw it away. Many a night she had spent painstakingly sanding the decorative wood by hand. Now that the old wallpaper above it had been stripped away, and the unvarnished cherry had finally shed its suffocating layers of paint, its intricate details had come to life. She wondered if her sisters had noticed the design. Even before she had begun working on it, she knew it was a trail of entwined ivy. Sometimes she felt like it was calling to her, its triangular tips beckoning to be saved from years of drowning neglect.

"Didn't you just come from dinner?" Gen stood in the large open doorway and surveyed the chaos with a smile. Kelly was feverishly unloading a multitude of books; her wavy dark brown hair swished across her shoulders. Her sister's narrow frame was nearly obliterated by the stacks of books on the floor that she continued to add to. Gen observed the pile of books as it grew ever taller by the second knowing their order would only make sense to Kelly.

"Yes, I met with several unhappy priests, though I had to leave early to help a charge. Gerry, my charge, nearly had a heart attack right in front of me. He's alright though, the ambulance came quickly."

"That's good, minimal interference for you," Gen remarked.

"Agreed, but you know who did have a heart attack?" Kelly asked rhetorically "Me! Those priests were so obstinate." Stopping to throw her shoulders back and puff out her chest, Kelly lowered her voice several octaves as she attempted to mimic one of her dinner companions. "Why are the O'Mara's always so insistent on combing through every little detail of every single case file?"

Gen smiled. "Yes, thoroughness is not exactly their favorite trait when it comes to demonic possession claims." Remaining in the doorway Gen continued. "I hate to ask, but do you need help in here, aside from a good cleaning I mean?"

Kelly ignored the swipe. "I think they would prefer we dig up dirt on the victim, so they can scare them away from making any more claims. I was good though, I didn't flinch. I just kept right on talking my way through. I mean I know I look like I'm only twenty-eight, but still, they should know by now I know what I'm talking about. I mean if I looked my actual age—"

"If you looked two hundred and twenty-eight years old you would scare them and us." Gen's attention was drawn to a soft glow that rippled across the glass and knew their brother Tom had arrived.

"Hello, sorry I'm late. Two pizzas take longer on a Thursday night." Tom must have switched out of human form after leaving the restaurant and used his powers to teleport to the house, as evidenced by the steam wafting from the pizza box.

Kelly, having finished arranging all her books, stared over at Tom. "One of those better have extra cheese and hamburger on it or I'm not helping you with this case file."

The room filled with the scent of warm bread and garlic. "What do you think this is, amateur hour?" Tom took hold of the paper plates that were jutting out of the top of the box and flipped the lid open to display proof. "I know which pizza to bring to properly bribe you," with a wink in Gen's direction Tom searched the chaos for a place to put the boxes down.

"Nicely done, Thomas!" Kelly reached over and plopped a slice down onto a paper plate. "Gen you better grab a slice before one of our five other brothers show up to help themselves."

"No thanks, I'm heading out. My mark has been irritating me for the last few minutes." Gen instinctively rubbed her wrist where a detailed impression of a crown of thorns marred her soft skin while emitting heat and light.

The glow was evident even with her hand covering part of the image.

Tom dropped the pizza boxes on a stack of books and quickly stepped toward her. His striking blue eyes and fair skin echoed her own. "Anything serious?" Tom turned her wrist over carefully while he examined the mark. "Do you know who it is? Are you going alone? Did Frankie sense a convergence of evil?"

"Now playing the role of Michael O'Mara." Kelly's sarcasm broke the tension and Tom's furrowed brows and tight shoulders gave way and relaxed.

"It's fine, Tom. I know who it is. This didn't come from Frankie and I have already told Xavier about it. I'm heading out to investigate this demon harassing a charge of mine. It's probably nothing but, just in case, I will keep my shield weakened and stay open, so Xavier can hear my thoughts and know where I am."

"That's a straight up solid plan right there. I would have just immediately gone after the demon." Kelly alternated bites as she flipped through the pages of a book.

"Why are you calling on Xavier? You have two siblings sitting right here," Tom asked.

"Xavier is familiar with this charge already from something we did together a few months back," Gen replied. "Besides, you two are busy, remember?"

"Hey, I would much rather track down a demon than research case files. Your call, Tom," Kelly tossed out.

"Gen's right," Tom said. "I did come here for help with this file and she's in good hands with Xav. Call us if you need us."

"Thanks, will do. I'll see you guys later." Gen used her powers to dematerialize and make her way to her charge Becky.

"Ron, I really don't think we should keep driving." Becky pleaded. "I mean it's nighttime and it's raining, and you must be exhausted with working a double at the hospital. It doesn't seem safe to continue. Why don't we get a room somewhere so you can sleep for a bit?" Gen felt Becky's anxiety grow with every passing second her husband didn't answer. "If you aren't willing to stop then you need to compromise with me and let me drive."

Gen was out of human view. Sitting with her legs crossed on the roof of Becky's car, Gen was vigilant as she waited for whatever was coming. She could see Ron turning to look at Becky quickly before his eyes went back to the road in front of them. The images were like watching a movie. As a Guardian, Gen couldn't see through the car, but being this close to her charge she could see through Becky's eyes, hear her thoughts, and physically feel what she felt. Gen mused that Guardians were endowed with such power so they could stay connected with humans in a way that other supernatural entities couldn't, such as Angels.

"You hate driving in the dark, in the rain, in an unfamiliar area." The words were clipped. Before Becky could retort Ron grabbed her hand and gave it a little squeeze "I'm sorry honey. That was unfair, I know you're doing your best to get past the accident and resume driving everywhere again. I'm just tired. I'm upset that my job at the ER has put us in this position once again. I'm seriously considering getting out this time, private practice maybe."

"You'd hate private practice. You love being an ER doc." She smiled at him.

"Yeah." He huffed. "But at least I wouldn't be forced into taking a double when I'm supposed to be leaving for vacation. My family living several states away makes these events more precious. Hopefully, we make my brother's wedding on time." Gen felt a cold wind whip up around her, it prodded the edges of her shield as if it were trying to penetrate her defenses.

Here we go, whatever is targeting her has just manifested itself inside the car.

Ron steered the car into the next available rest area off the highway.

"What are we doing? Are you going to sleep?" Becky asked.

He pulled into a space near the front door of the welcome center. "Yes, and if you are okay to drive then I'll sleep while you drive. If you aren't up for that, then I'll just sleep here at the rest stop for an hour or so. That should still allow us to get there on time, albeit smelly."

When Ron kissed Becky's hand, Gen's heart sank a little. *That's something you used to do, Gabe. Maybe this is going to be harder than I thought.*

Gen could hear her brother Xavier asking her if she needed anything. *No, I'm good for now. I'll be riding outside the car and using my shield so the demon that's just arrived won't detect me. My shield won't be full strength, that way you can still hear everything I do.* Gen thought more about her strategy. *I'm hoping if I counteract all the demonic interference, help Becky stay in a positive space, the demon will get bored or aggravated and just leave.*

Gen watched as Ron entered the front door of the facility and heard the strain of the passenger side door creak open. Becky got out of the car and made her way around to the driver's side. Since the accident, she'd only driven on a highway a few times, and they were short distances. She was able to get herself to work and around town by using backroads and side streets. The burden of driving any significant distance, however, still fell to her husband. Becky's therapist was helping her make strides, but getting past such a violent crash wasn't easy. Given that three years have passed, she worried she had missed her window to conquer her fear.

Becky was mumbling to herself as she settled in, "I can do this, I can do this. Breathe through the anxiety, lower your heart rate." Becky closed her eyes and Gen heard her breathing in and out, counting as she went. Becky believed if they could get there on time, they could make the entire wedding ceremony. Becky glanced at the clock and scanned the GPS, a little more than five hours to go.

"He doesn't ask for much. This is the least I can do." Becky's voice carried little confidence as Gen listened to her mantra. "I can do this. I need to do this. This is important to me and my family. The accident was years ago. I need to move forward."

"Becky, Becky, Becky." The demon in the backseat was there to cause chaos, while Gen was there to protect her charge. Thankfully, Becky wouldn't have to see either of them, but both could influence her thoughts and sway her emotions.

Gen could only catch glimpses of the demon whenever Becky would check the rearview mirror: bald head, pasty skin shimmered in sweat, beady black eyes the color of olives.

Ahh, the glamour of a demon, so Mad Max, Gen thought to herself.

Peaking over the back through the rear window she was able to gauge the bulk of him. Gen relayed an update to her brother. *"He's no slouch, Xav, but nothing I haven't encountered before. His stench is more bothersome than anything."*

Schlosser was splayed out in the back seat shaking his head as he surveyed his intended target. Gen knew Becky wouldn't see, nor hear the demon, but his presence would sway her. His husky tone rattled on as he began to taunt her. "Becky, it's been what, two, three years since your car accident? Doesn't matter, you're not better. The therapist didn't really help you, did she? She couldn't have. You're still having nightmares about it!"

The night of the accident Becky was speeding to get home. Gen could feel the demon lulling Becky back into the past with images of that horrible night.

"That's right, Becky, let's spend some time reminiscing back to that fateful day. I want you good and distraught by the time I finish you off tonight." Schlosser rapidly rubbed his hands together. He was delighting in the moment of demonic interference he was preparing to unleash on Becky.

Gen used her powers of influence to bring Becky's focus around to the present. Becky's eyes shifted from the dashboard to the side window, through which she saw Ron staring back at her. He got in the car and as he closed the door, she questioned, "What was that all about? How long have you been standing there watching me?"

Ron put his hand behind Becky's head and pulled her toward him for a kiss. Meeting in the middle they locked lips perfectly. She cooed, "Even after all this time you can still make me feel warm all over with one kiss."

Ron smiled "You amaze me Beck, I don't deserve you."

Gen heard Schlosser groan. "You two make me want to vomit."

"We deserve each other." Becky turned back to the wheel. "Now hunker down and get some sleep, no co-piloting tonight."

Gen's chest swelled with a tidal wave of Becky's emotions. The love and passion she held for her husband were both wonderful and heart wrenching to experience.

"Thank you for driving. I love you." Ron grabbed a sweatshirt from the back and rolled it up to use as a pillow. He pulled the lever on the side of the seat, reclined, and fell asleep instantly. Ron began lightly snoring immediately, and Gen knew Schlosser must have used his powers to put Ron into a deep sleep, but Becky was all smiles as she drove away.

"Oh, isn't this just all rainbows and lollipops in here!" The demon clapped giddily seeming to thoroughly enjoy the moment. "I can't have Ron interrupting us. We have important matters to attend to, you and I." Schlosser went to work immediately with his mind games. "Let's see how you deal with this one, Becky." The radio station went out, no static, no fading, nothing, just dead air. As Becky moved her hand to change stations on the wheel, the radio started scanning on its own. One at a time the stations flashed by until it stopped on one playing her wedding song.

Gen could feel Schlosser tugging Becky's memories around like pieces of a puzzle he was attempting to rip apart and reorder. Gen resisted the urge to push back, she was going to have to allow him some leeway if she wanted to learn what buttons he was going to push. As Becky's mind wandered Gen meandered alongside her. Becky was a new charge; Gen had spent only the past couple of months with her. Gen was eager to learn about her new charge's past, knowing what the demon might be targeting would help Gen mount a defense.

Memories of various people and places quickly flashed by until visions of the accident three years ago surfaced and became clear. Becky was trapped replaying her worst nightmare for Gen to witness. The afternoon of the accident Becky had been driving too fast on a quiet narrow road. Gen guessed it was springtime, she could smell the air filled with the scent of flowers and fresh cut grass. Gen could feel Becky struggle to free her mind from the onslaught, but Becky couldn't stop the images. On that late afternoon the darkness hadn't quite taken hold. The last of the sun cloaked everything Becky could see in a yellow haze that seemed to glow.

Gen nudged back against Schlosser's influence with some of her own. Before the accident, Becky began to fear that pregnancy was not in the cards for them. She remembered Ron's reaction and it made her smile. *"Try not to worry, luv. In the end, we'll always have each other and that's how we'll get through whatever comes."*

Gen knew that Schlosser was reading Becky's mind as she drifted in and out of the many years of her life. He could sense that the mantra she was repeating from her therapy sessions was working to keep her calm. It helped that Becky was thinking of Ron instead of the haunting memories of her past.

Gen could feel Becky's tension fade while her breathing steadied. She was helping her charge let go and enjoy the drive, but then her wedding song came out of the radio again. Gen quivered from the goose bumps Becky had running up and down her arms. She watched as Becky moved her hand to change the dial.

"It's a stupid thing to be superstitious about," Becky whispered. "Just because it was playing the night of the accident doesn't mean I can't choose to remember our wedding day when I hear it."

"No Becky, it's not stupid. It's just what you need to help you remember that night. The fear, the sound of screeching tires, the smell of burning rubber, I need you to remember Becky. It's not about you and Ron, it's about the life you took."

Gen was losing ground. The strain of keeping up her shield to hide her presence from the demon while swaying Becky was starting to drain her. Gen wiped perspiration from her brow and stretched to relieve some of the achiness that was beginning to set in.

Once again, Schlosser pulled Becky back to where he wanted her to go: the memory of the car accident where her wedding song billowed out the open car windows. Gen now understood that Becky hadn't told anyone— not her husband, not even her therapist—that her wedding song was playing on the radio the very moment of the accident. Schlosser was using the song as some sort of mental trigger.

"Now we're getting somewhere. You know it's ridiculous, but you can't help it, can you? The trip over the edge starts with the wedding song! This is perfect, just when I thought the night was a bust." Schlosser let out a roaring sinister laugh.

Gen watched the nightmare come alive again: Becky was driving alone, smiling and happy when the wedding song came on. Gen could see Becky's past-self turn up the volume and start to sing. With the windows down, Gen could even feel the damp air rush over them as if Schlosser were somehow able to make Becky relive the night of the accident all over again. Gen could sense Becky was driving too fast that night. The road was wet, the tires weren't fully gripping. Gen watched in horror as she saw the memory of Becky losing control of the vehicle. The steering wheel spinning wildly out from underneath her small hands. Gen was surprised by how real the experience felt; she needed to influence Becky back to the present day.

Schlosser reveled. "Now, every time you hear that song you don't think of your wedding day, do you, Becky? You think of that horrific night, the one that nearly killed you and stole your unborn baby."

Gen focused her energy and pushed back hard against Schlosser's barrage; the force sent Becky barreling back to the present. Reaching for the dial Becky changed the station.

"No, no, no Becky." Schlosser's tone turned menacing. "You must remain in the memory of that night. I need you to continue reliving it. Why are you pulling away from it, from me?" Gen could see the demon's scowl through Becky's eyes as Schlosser came into focus in the rearview mirror. "How are you able to resist me, bitch?" He spit the words into her ear.

A mile up ahead Becky slowed for the toll booth. As she opened the window Ron stirred, but didn't wake.

"He's not waking up to help you, Becky. I have him knocked out. No one is coming to help you. Now let's not waste any more time." Schlosser sneered at her as she pulled away.

Having turned the radio down to pay the toll, she was shocked to hear the sound of music slowly increasing inside the car. Just as she was about to turn it down again, she heard the melody and froze, it was the beginning of their wedding song.

Becky instinctively pleaded, "Oh God, why does this keep playing? I need a little help here." Pushing the on / off button didn't shut the radio off. The song came in and out, riddled with static before clarifying and coming in normally.

"What is going on?" Becky whispered. "Why won't this shut off?"

Gen could see Schlosser smirk. "Darling, there is no divine help coming for you tonight." He let out a loud malevolent laugh. "Now, go ahead and sink back into despair."

Gen assumed Becky had uttered the plea under her breath to keep from waking her husband, but it was enough. Gen felt a sweeping surge of energy wash over her. Becky's plea to Heaven would temporarily strengthen Gen and weaken the demon's hold. That was part of the bond between human and Guardian.

Becky turned the dial and found some country music. "This station should be safe."

Schlosser was quick to disagree. "Oh Becky, how I wish you could understand, there is absolutely nothing safe about your situation."

This dance between good and evil continued for several more hours. Gen managed to keep herself quietly anchored to the roof of the car with her shield, but the effort was daunting. Her power allowed her to hear Becky's thoughts and feel the weight of her emotions, but her view of Schlosser was limited to random images. The demon wasn't giving up. Gen was thinking of getting off the car and facing him. Maybe he would back down if he knew it was pointless, that he wouldn't win this one.

The last hour ticked by and the sun broke through to warm the morning. Gen knew Schlosser would be able to feel Becky's confidence gaining by the mile. Her plea had carried them through most of the trip. It wouldn't be long now; they were close to the exit Becky needed to take. Gen took the opportunity to update Xavier on where she was and told him she would need her full shield for the remainder of the ride. She needed to reserve some energy in case there was a physical altercation with the demon.

Gen could hear Schlosser begin again. "Oh how I love playing with my food." The demon snarled. "Now that I have you primed and know what buttons to push, let's start again, shall we? It seems you are once again pregnant; that is fantastic news. I thrive off the energy new mommies have." Gen felt Becky's nausea and cravings, but knew Becky had no idea she was once again pregnant.

"That baby inside of you is but a speck, you don't even know it's there, but I ..." Schlosser paused to take a deep breath. "It's such a high for me when that life force leaves you, I'm just gonna eat it up." Gen was repulsed and it threw her off balance. The strain to regain control and remain unseen meant she had to temporarily let go of Becky, leaving her vulnerable.

Becky had pulled off to get gas and as she drove toward the onramp, she noticed a broken-down car, its yellow flashing lights beamed through her windshield. She couldn't tell what was wrong, but she rolled her window down to ask if they needed assistance. When the man behind the wheel rolled down his window, she could see the couple in the car were much older than her and Ron.

"Are you okay? Do you need help?" Becky asked.

Becky felt Ron stir and assumed she'd just woken him.

The man leaned out to speak to her. "No thank you, my wife is just a little car sick. I'm waiting to see if she's okay before I start driving again." He smiled and waved at Becky.

"Listen closely, Becky." Schlosser ordered malevolently.

The older couples side window began to ascend, but not before the song from their radio could be heard playing; it was Becky and Ron's wedding song.

Pulling out and onto the highway Gen felt the power inside the car grow darker and Gen knew things had taken a turn for the worse.

"How are you still asleep Ron?" Becky mumbled "What's happening to me? Am I losing my mind?" Tears ran hot and swift down her cheeks. Gen could feel Becky break a little inside and knew she was losing.

CHAPTER TWO

"There it is, the weeping! This is going so well, Becky. Now, I just need you to drive off the road and die!" Gen could hear Schlosser's jovial tone turn threatening. His prodding and memory placement had Becky vulnerable to his suggestion.

Gen had recovered from her momentary lapse. The image of Schlosser eating the soul of Becky's unborn child was more than a little unnerving. She needed to counter his attacks and fast.

Becky wiped her tears and turned the radio up, hoping it would wake up Ron. Schlosser had her confused, but she always felt better after talking with her husband, her partner. Gen experienced Becky's muddled racing thoughts over what the world was trying to tell her. Becky began reciting her mantra but couldn't seem to make it all the way through. She kept getting stuck in the middle and would start over. She thought about work, but that only confused her more. Becky was remembering the past several weeks when she'd been sick several mornings in a row, and how when she heard her favorite client was leaving to go to a competitor, she cried openly.

"They must have thought I was crazy," she said aloud, denouncing her own behavior.

Moving her arm over to Ron, she nudged him. "Honey, you okay?" Ron mumbled something incoherent in return and rolled over.

"Great, he chose tonight to sleep like the dead." Becky huffed. "No one to talk me down from the ledge, guess I'm on my own in crazy town."

"That's it, Becky, keep thinking you're crazy. You're no good to anyone. Work thinks you're crazy, Ron thinks you're weak. Maybe that's because you are!" Gen could see in the rearview mirror that Schlosser was on the edge of his seat, he was leaning over the driver's side, whispering the words into Becky's ear, a lullaby of lies.

Gen could hear Becky willing herself to concentrate on the road, but more disconcerting was feeling the sense of doom that Schlosser washed over her. When the GPS came on with instructions to exit the highway, she felt Becky jump, obviously startled.

"I'm so close, I can do this, I can do this."

The sun was shining brightly and on this stretch of road the pavement was nearly dry. As the GPS began to direct more frequently, Ron stirred again.

"No, you are not waking up to ruin it for me now." Schlosser's voice was low, but Gen heard the words clearly.

"What was I so worried about? And the crying, what's up with the crying?" Slowly Becky's fingers released their grip on the steering wheel as she worked to calm herself.

"It will all make sense soon, Becky." Gen heard Schlosser's taunt and knew he wasn't done.

"All you have to do is stay straight ahead and within a couple of miles your demise awaits." Schlosser ceremoniously threw himself against the backseat with exaggerated effect, his long arms stretched the width of the window, cocky, overconfident.

Gen closed her eyes and pulled Ron from his deep slumber. His voice raspy from sleep she heard him ask, "What time is it, honey?"

"No, no, no." Schlosser slammed the interior side wall with a closed fist. "What are you doing awake, Ron? I put you out, go back to sleep like the useless piece of crap you have been all night!" Schlosser's anger vibrated through the car.

Genevieve had alternated her position several times and was sitting cross legged once again, her shield forcing the wind to whip around her. Every move Schlosser made, Gen had countered. This was no small task as evidenced by her fatigue and his growing impatience. It had been a long night. If Gen could get them to the wedding in one piece, her strategy of staying out of sight will have been worth it.

Gen could feel Becky's hunger; it mirrored her own. Deciding at the last minute to stop at a nearby coffee shop, Becky pulled off the road and into the drive thru lane.

"Hey, what, where are we?" Ron was still throwing off the remnants of deep sleep. "Are we here already, honey? What are you doing? Are you getting food? What time is it?"

"I'm soooo hungry and I just have this mad craving for a donut. Do you want one?"

Ron's easy laugh rang through the car. "No thanks. I'll wait until we get to my parents' house. What's gotten into you? You drove all night. I feel so much better. That might have been one of the best night's sleep ever. I can't tell you how much I appreciate your help with this, Beck."

"What is going on? Why did you pull over? He should not be awake! I knocked him out, why is he awake?" Confused, Schlosser's anger grew. "This was not part of the plan, Becky! Stuff your fat face and get back on that road." Schlosser was yelling at them. Gen had hoped he'd give up, but it was clear that was not in the plan.

The car edged its way through the line and Gen listened to the playful banter between Becky and Ron, flirtatious and loving. It made Gen's entire chest ache with longing.

So much like we used to be, Gabe. Gen sat with her head against her knees trying to stay focused. With unspoken words, she told Xavier what was going on. *He's not going away, I'm going to have to show myself, Xav. If I do that, he'll know I've been countering every move all night. He'll be pissed, but that should put the focus on me and away from Becky.*

"What is going on here? Eat your stupid donut while you're driving. Why have you pulled over into a parking spot? And why are you so damn happy?" Schlosser was seething. "You didn't beat me tonight, did you Becky? You had help, which means something else is here with us. Come out, come out wherever you are."

Gen hopped off the car and turned to face the demon in the back seat.

Schlosser smirked. "If you think you can stop me, you're wrong. I am in the vehicle and unless you want a confrontation, I'm staying right here with her. You can't make me leave and I doubt you want to join me in the backseat." Becky's laughter redirected Schlosser's attention back to the scene playing out in front of him.

"Baby you'll have to wait for tonight because we have ourselves a wedding to get ready for." Becky was brushing off her husband's romantic advances with a smile.

Ron nodded in agreement. "And we aren't even going to smell." Gathering up the trash he put his hand on the door handle. "I got this, babe." He jumped out of the car and walked toward the trash barrel.

"Thank God we made it here in time to shower," Becky proclaimed softly.

"No! No! No! You will not bring God into this, not now, not ever. I have spent the entire night working you over. You are mine!" Schlosser waved his hand in the direction of the car next to them, raising the volume on the other vehicle's stereo.

As Ron got back inside, he crooned to Becky, "Do you want to dance, darling?"

"Dance? Yes, later I'm sure there will be lots of dancing at the reception."

"Our wedding song, can't you hear it? It's coming from the car next to us. You do remember, don't you? I mean I know it's been awhile but ..." His words trailed off as he surveyed his wife. Her brows furrowed and formed a crease above her nose. Her eyes, still damp from earlier, sprung new tears. "Becky don't worry. It's okay that you forgot our wedding song. there's no need to get upset about it."

"No, I didn't forget. Of course I remember our wedding song." Putting the car in reverse she pounded the gas pedal and backed out of the spot a little too quickly. Gen sprinted to get back to her position on the roof, there was no way she was abandoning Becky now. Gen could have used her power to teleport but saving energy wherever possible was the smarter play.

"Okay, do you want to tell me what's going on then?" As they pulled up to the light, Gen could feel Ron's touch as he reached for his wife. "Beck, what is it? What just happened? Why are you so upset?"

"You never told him the song was on during the accident, did you Becky? No, you're a liar and a conniving bitch, just like your little Angel friend back there," Schlosser bellowed.

Becky snapped at Ron. "I'm not upset, I'm just tired. Maybe a little cranky, you know, like you were earlier."

Ron reached out and covered her hand with one of us own. "Yeah, I totally get being overtired."

Schlosser continued to read Becky's thoughts and use them against her. "Oh no, Becky, you aren't getting out of this. You want to know what the world is trying to tell you, bitch? Die!!! That's what the world is trying to tell you."

Becky wrapped her hands around the top of the wheel, gripping it with the strength to turn her knuckles white and her fingers numb. Gen heard the wedding song replay, the melody rising in tandem with Becky's anxiety.

Becky turned and looked at Ron. "How is this possible? This is a country music station. Why are they playing this? They shouldn't be playing this!" She turned the radio up a pinch more just to be sure. "Earlier, I tried shutting it off, but I couldn't, it wouldn't turn off. Has that ever happened to you in this car, where you couldn't turn the radio off? It's strange right? Weird even." Becky's words were tumbling over on themselves as she sped forward.

"Beck, I think you should pull over. Honey, I want you to pull over. Do you hear me?"

"Oh, here we go." Schlosser banged triumphantly on the inside roof of the car, taunting Gen. "He thinks you're losing it, Becky. He's already starting to panic. I hope that bitch Angel is still around to see the two of you splattered in a ditch. She's no help to you now, to either of you! I've got you. She can't help you, no one can!"

Gen's fury was rising with each taunt, but damn him he was powerful.

In her mind Gen spoke to her brother. *I thought this was a good tactic Xav, but now I'm thinking I may have underestimated him.*

The car was picking up speed and Becky's driving became erratic, veering from lane to lane as drivers pulled out of the way and honked their horns.

Schlosser yelled at Ron, "I thought this would have been easier if you had just stayed asleep, but now you get to witness your crazy wife lose it. I know that Angel is responsible for waking you up, but it doesn't matter. She's not powerful enough to stop me. No Angel is, you're both mine now. I have your wife right on the edge and I'm going to watch her take the two of you right over it."

Becky began to rant. "This can't be, Ron, this just can't be. I can't do this, I don't think I can do this anymore. I mean I should have just told you. Then maybe things would've been different, but now I realize nothing makes a difference, when the world has it out for you, it wins, right?"

Schlosser continued the onslaught. "Look, Becky, Ron is looking at you the way you always feared he would one day. Can you feel it, Becky? It's all spinning away."

Becky was mumbling, blaming the music. "The song, it's the song, Ron. It's not me, I swear it's not me."

Schlosser's pace made it hard to counter his influence, it was wave after wave of negative energy and interference.

"Today the song is going to kill everyone you love, Becky, right in front of you. Or maybe I shouldn't do that, maybe you should live as your baby and husband die!"

Gen felt Ron's fingers colliding with Becky's, trying to grab the wheel from her.

"Becky please, stop, pull over, please!" Ron's voice squeaked under the strain of mounting dread.

"Here we are, Becky, a little patch of road picked out just for you and hubby to die on." Gen looked in horror as this part of the road had no guard rail. "Becky you need to let go now." Schlosser sang the words. "It's okay Becky, it will all be over quickly."

The demon shifted in the backseat, his eyes caught Gen's through the glass. "You can't stop me, you will never be able to stop me!"

Gen could feel a surge of power come through the roof, it was so strong it knocked her off balance and she somersaulted backward onto the trunk of the car. Gripping tightly to the edge where the trunk lid connected to the car, she managed to keep herself from tumbling onto the road. Schlosser smiled at her, his crooked yellow teeth and black gum line made her stomach clench. She had to use all dexterity just to hold on. His final commanding words echoed solemnly through her head. "Becky. Just. Let. Go."

Becky loosened her grip on the wheel. Ron's pulling jerked them hard to the right, tires unable to grip, rotated the vehicle several times before it spun off the road and sailed over the embankment, where there was more than a fifty-foot drop to the bottom. The fall would send them through tree branches and heavy brush, the area's rocky terrain created a pool of swampy wetland below.

Becky never hit the brake. People nearby could hear Ron screaming as they flew off the road plunging to their death. Schlosser was inside the car, reveling in every moment of terror the couple experienced. He was too busy to notice that Gen had recovered and made her way back to the center of the roof.

At first the car seemed to float, the outer branches of the trees scraped against the driver's side door panel. Becky had never rolled up her side window when she left the parking lot. The sharp edges of the tree limbs grazed her forehead, abrasive enough to tear the skin and send blood dribbling down her cheek.

Gravity tilted the car forward. Gen was running out of time, a few more seconds and the car would roll over on itself and plunge to the bottom. She closed her eyes and concentrated on pulling the car level, using her shield to break the fall and help steer them away from the largest of the boulders at the bottom. In mid-air Schlosser broke the back windshield and made his way onto the roof behind her, but Gen never turned around. As he attempted to grab hold of her, he bounced off her shield. The force sent him sailing through the air away from the car and toward the boggy wetland beneath them.

Becky and Ron's car landed just feet from the deepest part of the swamp. The violent thud rocked them back and forth in their seats. Water splashed up and inside the car, a tire burst, the windshield cracked, and the engine hissed, but they were upright and virtually unharmed.

To the casual observer above it might appear as if someone had picked the car up and placed it down below. The car was still running. When Ron finally caught his breath, he leaned over and turned the key shutting off the engine.

"Becky, are you okay?" Ron's voice was hoarse from yelling.

She looked at him and replied, "What just happened? Are we dead?"

"No sweetheart, we aren't dead, we're okay." Ron was out of the car. It took a minute for him to get his legs back underneath him. Gen knew all his training could not have prepared him for this situation. He walked around the vehicle twice sloshing through muddy liquid as he went.

Becky joined him. She stared between him and the car. "I did this?"

He looked at her. "Yes, you had some sort of episode and I couldn't get you to pull over or stop." He couldn't finish the sentence he was so choked up. "Oh my God, Beck, what happened to you?"

Becky went to him and maneuvered them to a dry patch of land. There, they held onto to their trembling bodies, collapsing to the ground in each other's arms. What they couldn't see, what they couldn't know, was who else was there with them.

Gen could hear Xavier in her head telling her he was on his way. She was quick to stop him. *No, Xavier, I got this. I am fine, they are fine. This demon keeps coming, he won't be fine.*

Gen watched Schlosser pick himself up out of the mucky water and make his way toward her. "That's interfering!" Schlosser pointed to the car sitting upright. "You can't do that. Now you're going to pay."

"So, you're a Roamer Demon, Schlosser is it?" She waited to see if the knowledge of his name would alarm him. He barely flinched. "You roam the earth with no specific purpose, no particular allegiance to anyone or anything, enjoying the moment when you can influence a human into destroying themselves or those they love with your incessant nudging. She never would have driven off that road if you hadn't been whispering in her ear all night."

Gen stood her ground as Schlosser stopped feet from her position. The stench he gave off made her stomach recoil. He was a good foot and half taller than Gen. His clothes were layered, mismatched, and stained.

"You had an equal amount of time to influence in the opposite direction, bitch. I assume you are the reason hubby woke up early. You just failed to beat me, so then you had to cheat. It changes nothing, you're going down for this."

Gen watched him labor the angrier he became. The yellow puss that oozed from a wound on the side of his head was probably partly to blame for the rancid odor. He'd been using too much energy to kill Becky and Ron. She was betting that he'd weakened himself.

"I saw you interfering first, demon." Gen launched the accusation to see if he would work himself up more, she wanted him to start the confrontation. If she was only defending herself, there would be less explaining to the higher ups on the back end.

"You Angels think you can decide who lives and who dies. What makes you so special? You aren't supposed to fight battles, isn't that what the rules say?"

Gen laughed a reply. "Oh, you want to debate the Accord. You think you're some sort of genius on all the bylaws Heaven and Hell setup for us to abide by down here?"

"You have been chasing me all night. Well you caught me. You want a fight bitch, then let's fight."

Gen watched Schlosser pull a knuckle knife out of his pocket and slip it on. His fiery eyes narrowed down on her; his sneering revealed a snake-like tongue, split and forked at the tip.

"You will perish here today for what you have done, Angel. I will make sure of it. You can't kill me, but I, I can kill you." He was fuming mad and ready for a fight.

"It's you who doesn't get to decide who lives and who dies, not today damn you, not today!" Gen leered at him and took a defensive posture, waiting for his next move.

Done arguing, Schlosser ran full speed and lunged straight for her. Gen never moved. As Schlosser reached her position, he simply bounced off her shield.

"Good to know you dumb asses make the same mistakes twice," Gen quipped.

Crashing to the ground Schlosser yelped when he landed hard against something sharp. Cursing her and everyone else, he pushed himself up and off the object while dark green blood escaped his shoulder. The thick liquid burned soil, branches, and shrubs as it left a destructive path between them.

"Your shield can't hold forever. I will break it, and then I will break you."

He started hurling vials of demonic fire at her head. He was right, the shield wouldn't hold forever, she just needed the right moment to let it down and engage.

Schlosser laughed. "I can feel your shield weakening, Angel. It's only a matter of time now."

When there was a small break in his offensive, Gen dropped her shield. "Good thing I'm not an Angel then." She pulled a dagger from the front pocket of her sweatshirt. "I'm a Guardian and you're done messing with my Charge." She hurled the weapon at him.

Schlosser had drawn his arm back in preparation to continue the onslaught when her dagger pierced his wounded shoulder and sent him once more to the ground.

This time she jumped on top of him and pulled the blade out. He swung at her, but she moved her arm adeptly to block him. In one swift motion she stabbed him several times in the chest and neck. He howled in pain.

They continued to swing and smash each other, their blood mixed and made the muddy grass beneath them slippery. Soaked in his blood she screamed at him, "You are not going to kill them or anyone else for that matter, not today." She pulled up to stab again, but he pushed her off and rolled on top of her. Seizing the moment, Schlosser folded his large hand around both of her wrists and used his weight to hold her in place. He removed a small vial from his pocket. it wasn't like the others, it was molten red, the color of magma. He broke the vial in his palm and sprinkled it all over her neck and body, narrowly missing her face.

The burn sent spasms of pain rolling through her; it was Hell Fighter venom. The venom was the weapon of choice against those in Heaven. She arched upward and managed to free enough of her leg to roll them over. He lost his grip when they spun; now she was on top of him again. She took the dagger and slammed it into his chest.

"Guardian" was the last word Schlosser uttered.

"Go back to Hell damn you and stay there!" Gen continued to stab until she felt the twitching body underneath her loosen and crumble. His remains hissed as the body began to decay and disappear. All that remained was the stench of death.

Standing, she wiped the fluid off her body as much as possible and felt the warmth of Xavier's arrival behind her.

"Genevieve, what the—?" Gen turned in time to see the look of horror wash over her brother's face. "Why didn't you call for backup? A Roamer Demon attacking? That's crazy. What happened?" Before she could answer he pointed at the car and the couple on the ground next to it. "Who are they? What's so special about them?"

Gen snapped. "Nothing! Does there need to be something special?"

He looked concerned. "I think we need to talk about this."

Gen had finally caught her breath. "Do I look like I want to talk about it?"

"You better get your head on straight before our siblings see you. Whatever this was, you better let it go, Gen."

"I took care of it, I'm fine." Gen made her way past Xavier and over toward Becky and Ron.

"You are not fine and it's not you I'm worried about, it's Michael killing me when he finds out I didn't back you up here."

"Just let me finish. We'll talk about it later, ok?" Gen's olive branch worked.

"Sure, but you better not run into anyone until after you've showered. The sight of you would scare the crap out of them. You wouldn't believe what you look like right now." Xavier left her alone with the couple.

She went over and touched them both on the shoulder. She gave them the one final act of kindness she had left to offer: the strength to get through another horrible car accident.

Becky turned to Ron. "I thought I was going to die today."

He nodded in agreement "I thought for sure we were both going to die, Beck."

"Not today, not on my watch." Gen spoke the words knowing they would never be heard.

CHAPTER THREE

Genevieve walked among the trees. Snaking her way in and around the rough and stumpy terrain she cautiously stepped toward the voices rising and falling above the mist. The branches had shed the last remnants of the fall season. A scattered blanket of dead leaves was covered by a thin layer of snow. Every step was a noisy mix of crusty terrain and breaking branches. The air was dry and cold; soon this fog would be swept away by blustery wind laced with snow.

"The Dakotas are no joke in November." She said the words aloud, no fear of being heard by anyone other than her siblings. Her shield was up, but she was staying open, they knew where she was and what was happening; that was the compromise after what Xavier considered to be a disastrous outcome with Schlosser six months ago.

Kelly's voice pierced her brief recollection, asking Gen why she was drawn there if her mark wasn't irritating her. Always the skeptical one, Kelly worried about the possibility of being lured into a trap.

"I've learned not to question my instincts, Kell. Besides, it's more like a pull; it's just this thing that won't stop until I follow it. I wish I could describe it better, but I can't right now. You're just going to have to trust me." Gen moved some branches out of the way and caught her first glimpse of the entities speaking to one another.

"Found the source, whatever they are, they're all male, and they're getting aggressive." Gen smiled as she heard her sister quip about the shocking nature of male aggressiveness.

Up ahead, the dense tree-lined area thinned and opened to a clearing. Even at this distance, Gen knew there were humans present, Hunters of the supernatural she imagined. The argument was getting louder, and she overheard one of them talking about children, human children.

"Ok, so apparently there are children here. I don't see them, but they could be cloaked. I'm not close enough to tell if any of these entities would have that power. I'm going to get a bit closer, but you know the non-humans will see me eventually. I see some Hollows, but I can't tell if they're friendlies or not. Just an FYI, it's raw and starting to freeze, if any of you are coming, dress for it. Kell, no shoes out here, you need boots my friend." Gen chuckled as she heard Kelly groan in protest.

Walking laterally now, Gen looked to see how far the clearing extended and whether there were any homes nearby. She was always evaluating how close these encounters were to human activity. Though most humans couldn't see, nor hear the supernatural, they could inadvertently become hurt or even die. That was the real cost of this fight, human collateral damage in the never-ending war between Heaven and Hell.

To the east it seemed to expand into a sprawling field. From where she stood, she could see the top of a large building. There were lights on, and smoke was billowing from the top, but nothing seemed out of the ordinary. Gen was looking for people but saw no movement. At this distance it was impossible to clearly see the ground level and surmise how many people were inside.

"One of the men in the field is replaying the story of what's going on in his head. I just picked up the back end of it and listened as he went through the story from the beginning. It's weird, it's like he's replaying it for me, or he's stuck in some sort of loop. There's something odd, yet familiar about his voice." Gen was making her way back to the group when she heard Deb ask if she had spotted the children.

"Not yet, but basically some unfriendly Hollows kidnapped children from the surrounding area and these human men, working with friendly Hollows, tracked them down. The friendly Hollows are trying to negotiate the children's release, but the kidnappers are saying no one has anything they want."

Gen was about to make her entrance when a shadowy gateway opened just behind the group and several more entities walked through it.

"Ok, so this is getting more bizarre. There are two demons, an unclean spirit, and a vampire in the mix now. One of them uncloaked the children. Deb, if you can see what I see, you have about five kids between six and eight years of age. I would suggest you get to them first, that way you can project your shield and keep them from getting hurt. They are tied up and crying, but otherwise appear unharmed. The humans are taking out weapons that are not going to work on any being on this field. I don't know that I would classify this as an all-hands on deck situation, but I'll need some help if anyone wants to join the party."

As Gen continued to survey the entities her eyes rested on the Hollows, she knew they were souls that refused to choose a side upon death. She felt sorry for them, their neutrality alienated them from both Heaven and Hell. They were doomed to walk the earth empty, with no purpose and no allies. When one gazed upon them, there was no emotion in their facial expressions; they were stiff and stoic. They moved liked ghosts: detached, cold, and aloof. The Watchers called them *lost souls*, but everyone else referred to them simply as Hollows.

Gen and her siblings had encountered many an unclean spirit; this was an old term for a demon that could attach itself to humans, even possess them if desired. This one was tall and lean, with sunken eyes that seem to disappear into his abnormally large head. Gen and her siblings investigated claims of the existence of unclean spirits on behalf of the Catholic Church. That was their cover while on earth. They had been paid advisors in this capacity for generations, never staying too long in any one location. These days, they called Boston home, but they rarely dealt with the clergy in person.

Gen despised vampires. They were blackened souls who preyed on the weak. They were inherently selfish because their very existence depended on it. Human blood was sacred, consuming it kept them satiated and immortal. This one was old—his bony frame was more of a skeleton with skin, no hair, barely any muscle, a bent-over posture from years of animalistic scavenging—certainly not the heartthrob Hollywood depicted. His lips were blue, indicating he was already suffocating from starvation; he was here for dinner.

Special humans, who could see the supernatural world, would often capture and tie down vampires; using rope dipped in Holy Water that was interlaced with rosary beads and blessed palms, they would leave them to starve, a slow painful death where they rotted away in some desolate wasteland. This practice was more than a thousand years old, but no one knew where it started or who shared this knowledge with the humans. This practice had dwindled the number of vampires roaming the earth. They were practically an endangered species, but Gen was most apprehensive about their presence because vampires were unpredictable, much like a serial killer. The only thing you could count on was their propensity for violence and their appetite for bloodlust.

Gen quickened her pace and walked out into the clearing approaching the group from an angle, one that had the best vantage point.

"You guys lost or something?" Gen watched the demons turn toward her, but then they turned their attention back to the group they were with.

"Get lost Guardian, you have no business here," a demon shouted.

Another demon pushed his counterpart out of the way and took a jab at the Hollow closest to him; stunned and unprepared the Hollow went crashing to the ground.

"So much for a conversation." Gen moved in front of the humans, her shield would protect them, but only while they remained physically close.

The demons threw hot, blistering balls of fire in her direction, Hell cannons. For now, they bounced off her shield. She couldn't leave the humans unprotected; one hit would be deadly. The blasts were wild and sent several shimmering sparks into the air above them. Behind her, she heard one of the men shout to get down and another gasp in awe as nothing made it past her and onto them. This wouldn't be making sense to them right now. She would probably need to show herself if she had any hope of getting them to leave the area.

Xavier arrived first, taking a swing at the largest demon, the battle erupted. Greg engaged the unfriendly Hollows while Frankie calmed the friendly ones and ordered them to leave; he didn't have to tell them twice. Deb was with the children. She untied them and told them to take hold of a long twisting rope that she slowly pulled bringing them away from the chaos. One child wouldn't move, presumably too traumatized to walk, so Deb swept him up into her arms while continuing toward the hillside that led away from the battle and toward the safety of the building below.

Gen felt Tom arrive beside her. "This is an odd collection of thugs. I can feel your anxiety, what are you so nervous about? Dan just arrived and took out the second demon, this will be over soon."

Gen shook her head "I don't know, that feeling, that tight gnawing sense in the pit of my stomach, it's still there. It normally subsides when I get to where I'm supposed to go."

The men were shooting at the demons, their bullets melting upon contact. The demons laughed and looked over at Gen pointing and gazing conspiratorially in her direction. There was a queasiness in her stomach. "They're looking at me like I'm lunch, Tom. Not exactly the reaction I expected."

"It could be the glee over being reunited with Satan. I mean that's what's about to happen." Tom put his hand on her shoulder attempting to reassure her, it wasn't working.

"There's something else going on here, I just don't know what it is." Before Tom could retort, multiple gateways opened and they were overrun by several more demons, weapons in hand they were prepared.

Three demons among them were more ominous than the rest, their hulking stature, leathery skin marred with scars half healed, and burns that still held heat, told her they were battle tested. Their sweat singed the ground and each one carried with them a chunk of the Chain of Chaos, a network of jagged wire braided together with shrapnel and dipped in Hell fire. This weapon was meant to tear and gouge the body on contact, like being flayed and burned alive.

"We need to move, get these humans out of here," Tom shouted his order as he ran toward the melee.

Gen turned around and allowed herself to be seen by the humans. "You need to go, none of your weapons are going to work on any of these entities. Me and my siblings have this, now go!" They gazed upon her confused.

"Who are you people?" one shouted.

"Where did you come from?" another added.

"I don't have time to explain what's happening, you need to listen." She paused as she noticed how many stood in front of her.

"Wait, where did the other guy go? There were five of you, now there're only four." She turned back trying to spot him among the ruckus with no such luck. He wasn't there. He was either dead or had already run away. It was hard to tell as the bodies began piling up. Though they were outnumbered, the O'Mara's were better fighters. Gen turned her attention back to where the Hunters had been standing but they were now running in the same direction as Deb, toward the safety of the building in the distance.

Gen pulled out a dagger and joined her brothers in the battle. Slicing one of the demons on the back side of both knees she drew him down while Frankie finished him off with a stab to the neck. Her boots splashed through the bloodied grass as she made her way deeper into the fight. Dan punched one demon knocking him back, but Gen used her shoulder to body check him back toward Dan who had drawn his sword. The demon fell onto the blade he never saw coming.

She threw her dagger into the heart of a demon preparing to stab Xavier. Her brother pulled the weapon out and tossed it back to her on her way past them. She hurled herself toward another demon holding Greg. She landed hard on his back and nearly decapitated him as she lifted his chin in the air and sliced his neck.

Everyone felt the sudden shift of power when Michael arrived. He held a harpe sword in one hand and parrying dagger in the other. He engaged the three larger demons that Gen had been nervous about. Though they were more than eight feet tall, their hulking nature burdened their movement. Michael was imposing but agile. He decapitated the first demon pushing his body down and stepping on top of him, this brought him level with the other two. One demon lunged, while the other prepared to swing the Chain of Chaos. Michael swung his sword backward, lodging the sickle part of the blade in the demon's eye and removing half his face. He threw his dagger at the other demon's forehead sending him to the ground along with a clanging of chains. Three dead in less than a minute, Michael tilted the battle in their favor.

Gen looked up as the sky shook with thunder and lightning pierced the darkness. A large reddish-brown glow formed around them, something was coming.

"Get back, go to the tree line, now!" Michael shouted as he ran motioning with his hands. Gen watched her brothers run toward the trees and followed them. As they got to the relative safety of the forest, they turned back just as a Hell Fighter and two Hellions arrived in the middle of the field noticeably pissed at the number of fallen comrades that lay at their feet.

Hell Fighters hadn't been seen on earth in decades. Gen couldn't remember the last time they encountered one.

At least it's not a newborn, Gen sighed in minor relief. Watching the demon's somewhat labored movements she thought, *He's older, he shouldn't be able to stick around too long.*

The demon was set ablaze in Hell fire. His large frame, long arms, and dragon-like head just a mere outline in a shadow of rolling flame. Once away from Hell, the flame dwindled, and its skin cooled to a leathery black veined with streaks of red. The Hell Fighter's blood was made of venom, cast from those tormented in Hell, it was Hell's deadliest weapon against Heaven. The upper level demon's venom was fatal, even its sweat was enough to cause serious damage. Newborn Hell Fighters carried the most lethal dose of the venom in their blood, because the essence of the tortured still lingered. Though the Hell Fighter's venom was poisonous, its physical strength faded over time, which meant they couldn't stay away from the source that manifested them for very long.

The arrival of a Hell Fighter would typically signal the end of the battle. In most cases a Guardian would be forced to vacate the scene, but the O'Mara's had a weapon of their own.

Before the Hell Fighter could make a move, Kelly arrived, taking a stance between the demons and her siblings. One of the Hellions lunged wildly at Kelly's head, but she ducked and the demon's momentum sent him tumbling across the field behind her. Michael stepped out from under the treelined covering and stabbed the beast through the ankle, quickly stepping back away from the animal in case its blood had been tainted by the Hell Fighter. The hideous beast howled like a rabid animal. Michael's blade had penetrated all the way through to the ground, effectively pinning the hound in place.

Kelly threw a knife at the second Hellion's ear landing a blow that sent the monster to the ground in a heap. It attempted to gain relief by clawing at the blade, trying to remove it as it rolled back and forth across the grass. Blood gushed from the dog-like creature's head and he squealed as his skin began to burn, puffs of steam wafted above its head.

She must have dipped the blade in Holy water, Gen presumed. *Nice touch*, Gen thought.

The odds were even now, it would be Kelly one-on-one against the Hell Fighter. The demon stomped forward taking an enormous swing toward Kelly. She blocked it and then used the demon's own momentum against him. Kelly pulled down as the demon's weight was propelled forward. The demon fell to one knee and Kelly grabbed onto his neck and swung up and onto his back, harnessing her legs around his shoulders and tucking her feet under his arms for stability. The Hell Fighter got back to his feet, grabbing at her twisting and bucking as he tried to pull her off, but she held on. She threw a katar at the second wounded Hellion's heart and its chaotic rolling movements instantly halted.

The pinned Hellion pulled at its leg until it ripped and tore away from the ankle still tethered to the ground by Michael's sword. The beast hobbled toward Kelly leaving a bloody trail behind it. By the time the wounded Hellion reached its master, Kelly had killed the Hell Fighter. As the Hell Fighter collapsed to the ground, Kelly jumped off the demon kicking the wounded Hellion lurching toward her. Jumping onto the Hellion's back, Kelly pulled out a long silver blade and plunged it into its head, killing it instantly.

Getting to her feet Kelly turned to her siblings. "Sorry, I couldn't find my stupid boots." Kelly's sweatshirt smoked as the remnants of demon blood soaked through. She swiped hard, but it would burn through to her skin if she left it on. Though she was immune to the poison, her clothes weren't.

"I'm surprised the Hell Fighter didn't put up more of a fight," Michael commented.

"What do you mean?" Dan asked.

"Did you notice anything odd when you were engaging it?" Michael asked Kelly but then didn't wait for an answer. "It should have been harder to kill. Even though he was obviously older, he should have put up more of a fight."

"He was pretty feisty," Kelly shot back.

Gen interrupted them. "Do you smell that?"

Kelly was quick with a retort. "Yeah, I know, Hell Fighters reek, it's all over me." Kelly attempted to clean the venom off, huffing loudly she finally gave up and pulled the sweatshirt off tossing it into the burning pile of debris.

"No, not that. It smells like a fire, a real one." Gen was looking in the direction of the building. She could no longer see nor feel Deb. "I can't feel Deb. They didn't want us walking toward the building, they wanted us up here. Whatever pulled me here, it's down there." Gen pointed toward the hillside. "This must have been a distraction from the real target!"

"We need to move. Go! Go! Go!" Xavier started running and everyone followed.

.

CHAPTER FOUR

"There is no way I'm running in these boots!" Kelly's protest went unanswered. "Seriously, why are we running, it's like ten miles away, why aren't we using our powers?" Relenting, she began a painstaking jog when she heard her brother Dan's reply.

"It's less than a mile from where we just were, and you know using our powers can be draining. You just got into an intense fight, and you might need to conserve your energy in case you get into another one." Dan was correct, but Kelly grimaced all the same.

"I don't see how running is conserving my energy. Anyone have a cheeseburger? Now that might restore me, especially since that little charade back there interrupted my plans to go get one from Jake's." Jake's was Kelly's favorite local hang out.

Kelly had arrived last, what was left of her burned T-shirt still warm to the touch. As she crested the hillside, she observed the full structure and grounds which unfolded before them. A fire alarm was going off somewhere deep inside the structure. The three-story building was made of brick which was worn to a faded red. Every few feet double-hung windows adorned the surface, each with a thin sill painted white, but it was the oversized steel doors that exposed its older age. The track and football field that lay just beyond it were pristinely manicured, but unoccupied. Tall stadium lighting partially lit up the area, revealing an additional car park, which was nearly full.

Dan spoke first "It's a high school and there is obviously some sort of event going on."

"Both parking lots are full, parent teacher night?" Frankie questioned.

Kelly spotted Deb at the far end of the lot maneuvering the children around parked cars gradually making her way toward the building. Before she could get to the front door another alarm went off. This one sounded closer, perhaps from the first floor. Surveying the exterior, Kelly noticed smoke hanging in the air above the building. She heard people inside yelling, along with the stampeding echo of shoes stomping tile. People inside were running. Shadows of light began to dance across the cream-colored walls on the second floor. *Oh no,* Kelly thought, *the fire's spreading quickly.*

"We need to get in there, now! These kids are in trouble," Gen yelled. Tom grabbed Gen's arm, keeping her from advancing.

"We need to wait, Gen. We don't know this is anything more than a natural fire, in fact, it feels like a human started this," Tom reasoned.

"Tom has a point. It wouldn't be the first time we were tricked into action." Michael's argument was valid but frustrating.

As if on cue, the sirens from a fire truck rang out in the distance. The piercing sound of its horn drifted through the trees that lay beyond the property line. No lights could be seen yet which meant they were still a few minutes out.

Smoke fogged the windows on the second floor, and the first shrieks of terror rang out as people realized the danger enveloping them. Kelly noted the size of the windows, they were large enough to exit through, if you could break them.

"We should break a window for them, no?" Kelly waited for a reply, but none came. They were caught in that terrible space between action and inaction, that pause in the chaos that she hated most. She countered the lull. "The silence is deafening, tell me something or I'm just going in."

Dan had walked off to the west hillside, perpendicular to where she stood. As he reached the top of the embankment, he answered her. "Just give us a minute to assess what's going on here."

Kelly couldn't sit still and began pacing back and forth. Watching her siblings separate and fan out trying to cover as much ground as possible was an excruciating exercise and all she could hear was the ticking away of precious time, like an invisible clock taunting her. She observed Michael making his way toward Deb's position. She was the only one of them that was visible to the humans. She had to be, or she wouldn't have had the children's cooperation without them being able to see and touch her. Deb had been able to project her shield onto them but being in human view during a potential supernatural event was risky.

Kelly was about to call out Dan on his one-minute timeline when an explosion erupted deep inside the first floor. Smoke rolled like a sandstorm through the corridor, while tile and pieces of sheetrock rumbled to a halt at the windows. The pressure cracked portions of the glass. The haze inside thinned, and she watched the outline of a being take shape.

"Good guy or bad guy? I'm going with bad since lately it seems like they're everywhere." Kelly let the statement hang in the air, not expecting a reply.

Out of the corner of her eye Kelly could see Deb coaxing the children to turn back needing to avoid the building now, she gathered them onto the grassy area that lined the tarmac. They were behind the relative safety of parked cars.

Kelly saw the Hunters from the field as they staggered into view, sweating and breathless they looked back and forth between the building and Deb.

Michael's voice distracted Kelly. "A watcher just arrived on the opposite hillside. Tom she's closest to you, go have a chat. In a minute this area is going to be overrun with people, it would be good to understand what they are really running from."

I'm dying here people, let's just go in already! Kelly thought.

A side door burst open and people began to pour out chased by the billowing smoke and fumes from inside. The scene was devolving, chaos was unfolding, people were yelling and crying for help, with no idea where to go when they left the building. They huddled together on the outskirts of the parking lot and watched in horror as the façade continued to falter under the tendrils of fire consuming it.

"We've dealt with that Watcher before," Gen told them. "Her name is Lacey. I saw her with Harry a few months back." Kelly didn't recognize Lacey.

"Speaking of our Angel, where is Harry? Shouldn't he be here? I feel like he's slacking lately." Kelly heard Dan sigh in reply.

Blue flashing lights splashed across the pavement, with police cruisers escorting the fire department, emergency vehicles spilled into the parking lot. Firemen were unloading equipment when they were interrupted by a second explosion that rocked the building. They took cover and Deb used the distraction to her advantage. She brought the children to one of the police officers, speaking only briefly with the female cop before leaving the children in her care. Walking around the cruiser Deb disappeared behind the firetruck coming out the other side no longer visible to the human eye.

"Where are the other firetrucks? One isn't going to do it, people!" Kelly was impatient, and she could feel Gen's anxiety increasing in tandem with her own.

Deb made her way back to the Hunters who were noticeably looking around for her. "They're probably wondering where you went Deb," Kelly snickered.

The men had their cell phones raised in the air trying to find a signal. One of them was pointing at the building as if trying to convince the others to accompany him inside.

Kelly saw Deb walk around behind them, touching each man on the shoulder, she sparked influence. Her sway could persuade them to charge toward the danger and not away from it.

"That's it, Deb. That's what we can do here, we can guide until we know what's happening." Gen's voice lilted upward. Kelly thought it expressed forced optimism.

Before anyone could agree, Tom's voice rang out with answers. "It's confirmed, what's inside is supernatural. Lacey says the two Hell Fighters Kelly just killed infected a student then went to distract us while the venom did its work. This fire will mask the birth of one of their own. What's inside is a newborn Hell Fighter."

Heat rushed through Kelly's body and flushed her cheeks. Her hands closed into tight fists at her side and her heart was hammering as she sensed the anger surging. This was the reaction she felt whenever anyone mentioned a Hell Fighter. She killed the one in the field handily, but newborns were different. Though she had never faced one, she had done plenty of research on them. They were said to be tenacious, unpredictable, and their venom was at maximum strength at the time of creation.

"What's your plan?" Dan had come up alongside her.

"Engage." Kelly turned toward her brother and smiled, but he didn't return the sentiment.

"That's not a plan, that's a suicide mission." Michael's piercing brown eyes caught hers from across the parking lot.

"Hey, it's not like there's a manual for this," Kelly retorted. "And it's not like you can join me inside."

She closed her eyes and attempted to quiet the inner swell that was building. "Maybe I can track it, give me a second." She wondered if it was the figure she saw earlier, the outline that had faded and disappeared when people rushed out. The screaming from the people inside was interfering with her concentration. It wasn't helping that Gen's concern was turning into sheer terror at the thought of Kelly having to enter the building alone.

"What choice do we have? It's a newborn, you guys shouldn't even be in the parking lot. The fumes, the flames, the smoke, it's all poisonous to you."

"We are not leaving you, Kell, don't even go there. Just tell us what you need us to do." Gen walked toward her.

"This place is getting overrun, soon it will be hard to manage through all these people and their emotions, especially their fear," Gen said. "If you go inside there is no guarantee you will even hear us out here." Gen spanned the crowd with concern.

"I need that window broken, and it's going to have to break outward, so we don't hit anyone inside with glass," Kelly told them. "Deb, you may have to project your shield onto those firefighters along the front." Kelly was pointing at the building, but looking at Deb.

Deb was about to influence the last Hunter in the line, but before she could touch him, he turned and faced her.

"Thank you, Deborah, but I don't need your divine intervention, I'm good. Please thank Gen for me. It took a few retellings, but she finally heard me recapping the story of what was going on in the field." The scruffy faced male turned and winked at Kelly before running for the building.

"Jared" was the only reply Deb could muster.

"Oh my God, Jared! Wait! Stop! Don't make me chase you. You know I hate running!" Kelly watched him run toward the building heading for the same spot she had just been speaking with Gen about.

"Quick, break the glass, he's going to jump through and I'm heading in after him." Kelly was running now too. She held her arm up in front of her spreading her fingers wide and concentrating her powers on the window. Out of the corner of her eye she saw Gen doing the same and assumed Deb was also.

The glass panes that remained exploded outward and Kelly watched the firemen jump back and take cover. They would not know it wasn't necessary. Deb had projected her shield over them sending the shards of broken glass cascading down to the ground in shimmering fashion just behind where they stood.

Having successfully made the leap, Jared was inside the building, where he quickly disappeared. Kelly was close behind; in a mid-air leap she removed a weapon from a holster attached to her back and readied herself for the newborn Hell Fighter inside. She landed on her feet but was forced to crouch down as she slid a few yards further into the school corridor. When she turned back, the thick smoke obliterated any view of her siblings in the parking lot.

Now that she was inside, the screams for help were piercing, human souls tormented by Hell share their pain with any nearby Guardian. Right now, all their fear was palpable. Given how many people were inside, the weight of their agony hung heavily around her, making it difficult to get to her feet quickly.

She could faintly hear Deb praying for her safety. She could feel Gen, racked with guilt over not being able to join her inside. She could sense Dan puzzling through how else they could help her from outside. The sound of steel cracking pulled her away from their concerns. Up ahead an exit door was thrust open and she felt the rushing relief of cool air as it swept down the hall toward her. She watched people run through the door to the safety of the outside. Just beyond the parade of people jockeying for position she saw Jared staring at her. The hood of his sweatshirt was down, his black hair shaggy and longer than last time she laid eyes on him. His brown eyes and rosy complexion mimicked her own, but the scarring on his forehead and along the side of his neck was evidence of serious battle.

He must have opened the door on his way by, she thought to herself.

He smiled as she took steps in his direction, but then she was forced to stop and turn back when she heard Dan's voice.

"Kelly, people are stuck on the second floor, we're going to break the windows upstairs too. The opening should allow rescue via a bucket truck for some, but there are too many, you need to try and kill this thing as fast as possible if we're to have any hope of getting them all."

"I don't know where it is. I think Jared opened the side entrance. You should see people fleeing through it now. I'm going to see if I can catch up to him. I don't know why Jared came inside, he shouldn't have risked it, but now that he's here maybe he can shed some light on what the heck is going on."

She cautiously moved forward. Jared left the doorway, disappearing once again. She stopped when she heard the distinctive sound of something banging against thin metal.

"It sounds like someone is throwing themselves against a set of lockers. Since that's ridiculous, it's probably what I'm looking for." Kelly turned left and followed the noise.

She came upon a scrawny teenage boy flailing himself around the hallway. Panting and breathless, his pores nearly burst open from the bubbling venom she saw running through his veins.

"Oh my God, how's he going to make the transition? He's too small, too weak. How can his narrow frame handle the strain of what's coming? I've never actually seen a Hell Fighter born. This is torturous." Kelly looked on in horror as this unsuspecting high school student buckled under the demonic force overtaking his body.

He yelled out, "Help me, please, someone help me!"

His shoulders flung back, arms extended, his skin slit open, and his eyes filled with blood. With each excruciating breath his body tried to hold on, but one at a time his bones began to crack and stretch, until his height nearly reached the ceiling, his fingers and nails grew like talons and his hair fell out when his head gorged with venom. Each moment of madness brought him one step closer to beast form. There was no way to stop it and he was burgeoning to explode into true demonic form. Kelly felt an arm around her waist pulling her away from the teenager.

"Get back, you can't stand that close to it," Jared yelled the words as he sent her flying backward. She landed with a thump about six feet away, her head ricocheted against the wall. Her vision temporarily blurred, but she heard the last of the teenager's air leave his lungs like the hiss of a balloon not properly tied.

The explosion rocked the building and Kelly covered her ears and tucked her head down against her knees. The force brought pieces of the ceiling down upon them. Peeking up, she saw Jared had turned away from the newborn and faced her with his arms extended outward as if he could shield her from the blast. Behind him a massive swath of flame licked the ceiling.

It worked. You were able to protect us! How did you do that? She really wanted to ask him, but the words would not form.

The heat from the blast melted lockers, while one massive step from the Hell Fighter dented the floor. Now he would be coming for them.

"He's enormous, of course he's frigging enormous!" Kelly's sarcasm did nothing to temper the panic she felt coming from her siblings.

"Run, we need to wear him down first, make him run!" Jared turned and distracted the newborn allowing Kelly to stumble to her feet and awkwardly escape down the opposite hallway. Once she was far enough away, she told her siblings about the plan.

Michael was quick to give additional guidance. "Newborns are weak in the joints. Go for the knees first chance you get."

Her vision returned, but throbbing pain remained in her head. She searched for another weapon as she had lost the spear when Jared tossed her backward.

"Ok, he's coming, I'm running toward the back." Kelly lurched forward and began running. She heard the hammering of his footsteps coming up fast behind her. Given his height it wouldn't be long before he caught her.

She abruptly changed course and the Hell Fighter was too big to make the tight turn. He slipped and smashed through a wall, taking part of a classroom with him, and Kelly momentarily got caught up in the destruction of his fall.

She could hear his breathing was uneven; he was expelling a lot of energy to keep up. The heat coming off him made her feel like she was nearing the sun.

"Why are all you guys so ridiculously hot?" Kelly wiped the sweat from her brow and pulled the T-shirt away from her body, it snapped back and clung to her skin. She was soaked in sweat and venom. Looking around she couldn't place where the closest window was.

She was slowly trying to make her way out when she felt cold air sweep in and wrap around her ankles. She looked back over her shoulder and spotted Dan and Xavier influencing firemen to spray their firehoses through an open window.

"Run through it, Kelly, you need to get your body temperature back down," Dan ordered.

She ran through the cooling spray, but the demon didn't follow. She watched him step back, spreading his arms along the wall to avoid it. The reddish glow of Hell fire that encircled him danced all around as he moved. Unlike the one in the field, the newborn's fire wasn't abating. It seemed to flicker and re-ignite sending spasms of movement though it's body. When his eyes fell upon Kelly, they betrayed confusion.

"He's not sure what the water will do to him and neither am I." Kelly watched the newborn attempt to slither away and yelled to her brothers. "See if you can hit him with it."

The water line came close, but the demon's temperature was so hot it turned the water to steam. The beast roared a reply, clearly irritated but unharmed by the attempts to cool him off.

Kelly went back to running, stopping to catch her breath only once she was certain that she was out of his sightline. "This really sucks, I want to be done running because panting and sweating are so not fabulous."

She returned to a jog and continued down a new hallway until she reached the next cross-section. Unsure of which way to turn, she stopped to listen for footsteps, but heard nothing.

"What if he's no longer following? Crap, I need to double back." Talking out loud she had no idea if she could still be heard, the connection to her siblings seemed to be cutting in and out like an old transistor radio, staticky and unreliable.

As she turned the next corner, the smell of rotting flesh and burnt hair washed over her as she nearly slammed into the newborn Hell Fighter.

"You adapted, learned to teleport, great." Kelly's sarcasm went unabated. The newborn shoved her. With no time to brace for the impact or slow herself down she crashed against the wall. Pain seared through her shoulder as it took the brunt of the force.

She pulled a small dagger out of her boot and watched the newborn gasp rapidly for air, the breaths congested like his lungs were filled with poison, which they were. He had an arm against the wall for support and he was no longer looking at her.

"He's laboring guys, this might be as good a time as any to engage." She heard her own labored breathing as she spoke and wondered where she was going to get the energy to fight.

She threw the dagger and the beast moved his hand to bat it away, but he missed. When it pierced his skin, he yelped in pain and pulled the weapon from the side of his neck. He awkwardly threw it back at her, but she caught it in mid-air, spinning it between her fingers she angled the blade down into a defensive position.

"Why are you here, why now? Why did you go after this kid?" Kelly watched as the Hell Fighter looked over but didn't respond. "Ok, so when do the powers of speech show up? I feel like it would have been helpful for that one to have come first."

He grumbled something incoherent then jabbed with his fist, she ducked and targeted her counter punches on the side he was favoring. He bellowed in pain like a howling wolf. He swung his arm hard landing a blow against her right side. Though she had braced herself and was still on her feet, the impact winded her.

The dance of contentious punches continued, each of them landing occasional blows. Kelly noticed sparkling flames would scatter through the air every time she landed a punch. Each glowing ember started a new fire wherever it landed. The space they were in was clogged with blackened clouds that were getting thicker by the minute.

Coughing hard, Kelly was bent over. The Hell Fighter pulled its leg back and kicked. Seeing the maneuver coming, Kelly leaned forward and grabbed his foot, yanking as his leg was in mid-air. Using his own momentum against him she pulled and brought the demon down to the ground. He landed on his back with a thunderous boom. She grabbed the dagger and stabbed several times in the side of the knee as he howled in pain and flipped over. He crawled away from her taking down pieces of wall as he went.

"Oh no pal, we aren't done, you are not getting out of this building." She said the words but doubted they conveyed the bravado needed to dissuade him from trying to escape.

"Alright, why don't we end this thing, what do you say? You go back to Hell, I go home to a cool bath and a hot meal, that's a win–win." She caught up to him just shy of the door, still on his stomach. He would need to smash his way out. Neither of them was getting out that door since the extreme heat of the fire caused part of the frame to fold inward, encasing the exit in a mangled knot of steel.

She jumped on his back and raised her arm preparing to stab him with her blade. But he pushed back, elbowing her in the chest she rolled onto the tile floor. He managed to get up and curled his claw-like hands around her neck. He pulled her up and off her feet. She hung, feet dangling, several feet off the ground at the mercy of a Hell Fighter who wanted her dead.

Gasping for air, she clutched his hands and used them for leverage. Swinging her legs upward she kicked with full force and landed a blow to the newborn's chin. Stung, he flailed backward releasing his grip. Kelly fell free, but instead of hitting the floor, she landed in Jared's lap.

"This is taking too long, you'll win, but not without paying a heavy price. Let me just take care of this for you, luv." Jared kicked the Hell Fighter's one working knee, nearly caving it in.

The newborn yelled out as he collapsed to the ground. Jared put both hands under the newborn's head and pulled up and to the left, breaking its neck and nearly decapitating him in the process. Dropping the limp body on the tile floor, they both watched the Hell fire that had been encircling it finally flame out. Its rotting decay smoldered until it was nothing more than a pile of ash.

"Where have you been? I have been fighting this thing for like an hour. I assumed you were dead." Kelly was leaning against the far wall for support.

Jared went to her and pulled her into his arms. "It was only fifteen minutes."

"Whatever, thankfully I weakened him for you." She paused trying to even her breaths. "What are you doing here? Where have you been all this time? Who are you with? How are you even in here with me? Since when are you immune to Hell Fire?" Kelly was fumbling the questions but at least she got them out.

Jared smiled at her. "I missed you too." He leaned in and kissed her passionately, her mind went blank and she fell into him.

Regaining her composure, she put a hand on his chest and pushed him back, but not before he had time to slip a ring over her knuckle and onto her finger.

"No Jared, wait, don't do this! You can't just walk back into my life after like a hundred years and give me a ring." She watched the twinkle leave his eyes.

Shaking his head back and forth he replied. "Good to know you haven't changed, you're still a mad exaggerator. It doesn't matter where I've been, what matters is that you and your siblings need to pay more attention to what's happening. We believe you're all in danger, something powerful from Hell is already here."

"Wait!" She watched him lock eyes with her. "Who's we? Who's with you Jared? You need to tell me, is it Gabriel?"

"Just remember, there's only ever been you, you and no other." She watched him vanish and felt like someone had dropped the building on top of her. She succumbed to her trembling knees and slid down the wall onto the floor.

Dan's voice reached her just as she was about to call out to them. "Kelly, there is no time left, we won't get to everyone, but there are still plenty of people who can be saved."

She shook her head as if she could scatter the trauma away. "What do you want me to do?"

Dan was direct. "Deb has gathered a small group at the back of the building near where you are. That part of the structure has been weakened by the fire. When you exit, make a whole in the exterior as large as you can. A small opening still makes it hard to escape from. Make it big. It will be the last thing we can do for them."

Looking around she saw the magnitude of the fire's destruction. "I see where you mean, tell Deb and Gen to break it outward again. I'm going to need all the help I can get."

She took several long strides away from the door then turned back. She needed as much run up time as possible to make a large impact. Breathing deeply, she quieted her stampeding heart. Facing the rear of the building she bent over into a runner's stance. Grunting she took off like a shot heading straight for the back wall.

Halfway down the hall she took a literal leap of faith, closed her eyes, and pushed her arms out in front of her. Spreading her fingers wide she focused all her power on breaking through the wall.

She heard the crumbling of bricks as they cascaded down the exterior, felt the spray of water from the fire hoses as it bled through the cracks helping to separate the brick, sand, and cement which sealed the structure. The debris blasted her skin, coating her in a heavy gray dust. As the wall began to fail, cool air pushed its way in thinning the poisonous gas that hung over her like nuclear fallout.

The destruction sent glass, shards of rock, and blackened debris several feet across the parking lot. She saw her sisters first and continued to run toward them. They engulfed her even though she was covered in venom that burned the saturated parts of their clothing.

"Nicely done. That exit you just made is big enough to drive a truck through." Kelly followed Dan's stare and saw firemen pulling people out of the building.

"Gen and I heard what Jared did to that thing, we all heard it. Are you all right?" Deb's brow was creased with worry.

"I will be, once one of you helps me get this stupid thing off." Kelly held up her hand, displaying the ring Jared gave her. The band of silver was wide and etched with flowers, each petal encrusted with varying shades of amethyst stone. Kelly watched Gen and Deb exchange a look.

"That's definitely a conversation for later." Gen nodded in the direction of the school. "We better get ready, not all of them made it out."

"Harry's not here. Do we wait? Or just take them?" Kelly watched as everyone looked to Michael.

"I think this is the first encounter like this we've ever faced without Harry," Gen stated.

"We have to trust there's a good reason for that," Tom replied.

"If Harry isn't here, it falls to us. We'll escort them to the line. Hell has caused enough damage for one day. We're not letting them pick off these souls on their journey to the afterlife." Michael looked over at Kelly. "I know we lost some today, but you all did good work. Especially you Kelly, you did great against that newborn in there."

Stunned, Kelly stood alongside her siblings at the top of the embankment awaiting the dead. They watched the last of the school's structure tumble in on itself as the fire finally petered out. One hundred and forty people survived that day, but it was the twenty-three dead, all under the age of eighteen, that put this battle in the loss column. Kelly knew that even though the Hell Fighter was dead, they would all feel the sting of failure and it would never leave them.

During Deb's prayers, Kelly felt Gen's heartache, it mirrored her own. The loss of any human life is said to make the Angels in Heaven weep, but the death of a child caused by those in Hell brings the wrath of Heaven's Guard to those responsible. The Guardians would get justice, but right now that didn't help the souls taken before their time.

Kelly felt the electricity in the air; a storm was coming. The first raindrops fell upon her exposed skin. Even though she was still feverishly hot, she didn't allow herself to feel relief from the burn. *This was a loss, it should hurt*, Kelly thought.

As they stood side by side, their heartache opened the skies, bringing thunder, lightning, and wind. In a place known for its snowy dry conditions, the humans who remained clung to each other, shocked and confused, as they were drenched in Kelly's family's storm of sorrow.

CHAPTER FIVE

"Good morning, how can I help you?" Deb noticed Margaret's name badge was nearly falling off. Her wavy brown hair was a bit tousled as her blue eyes stared into Deb's.

"Good morning, can I have a large Scottish breakfast tea and a blueberry scone please?" The woman efficiently punched the order into a small handheld device and then turned it toward Deb displaying the total.

"That will be $8.75. I'm sorry I can't remember if you have a tea pass. If you do, go ahead and enter your phone number, otherwise you can just swipe a card." Margaret then turned and busied herself pulling together the order.

I wish I was able to come here enough to warrant a tea pass, Deb thought.

She paid for the order and then perused the shop for anything new since the last time she visited. The Tea Pot was a small tea shop and bakery located just a few blocks from the house she shared with her sisters. Though Deb was up early most days, it was rare to be able to sneak away and indulge in the calm of the shop's setting.

The walls were painted a cream color that reminded her of sugar cookies. There were floral- and tea-themed works of art hanging on nearly every available wall space. There were five wooden tables and chairs with plush cushions embellished with a tiger lily pattern. The tables were decorated with what looked like a small tower of Jenga blocks that someone had written inspirational quotes on and then glued together in haphazard fashion.

Deb could see the one closest to the register: Why, sometimes I've believed as many as six impossible things before breakfast. *How very appropriate*, Deb thought, *quotes from* Alice in Wonderland *in a tea shop!*

The skylight in the center of the roof warmed her back, it was Spring, but in New England there would be a morning chill until you closed in on June. As she picked up her order, she spotted the antique bookcase in the corner by the back entrance.

"Your bookshelves, they're pretty full now, that's nice." Deb watched the woman glance at the shelves and then back to her.

"Yes, customers have slowly been filling them up. When it gets too full, we'll sell some for charity or drop them off at the library. It's nice, lets you unplug for a moment and get lost in a world of words while you drink your tea." Margaret gave a bright smile as she moved along to help a newly arriving customer.

Meandering toward the bookshelves, Deb noticed a handwritten notecard dangling above the first case: *Book exchange: bring a book, borrow a book.* She felt cool air drift in and realized one of the doors to the back patio was ajar. There were a few customers out enjoying the sun-filled morning, brisk as it was. At this time of year, you could drink your tea amid the budding flowers and plants that littered the veranda, the blossoming lilac spires fell over the railing in abundant fashion. The trees limbs were heavy with the light-purple flower, which filled the air with its sweet fragrance. The outdoor tables were decorative wrought iron, painted in light shades of yellow, blue, and purple. She chose an open table closest to the hedgerow of sprawling lilac and sat down.

Setting down the scone and removing the lid from her cup, she sat back and inhaled the bold flavors of the rich black tea. *This is a luxury,* she thought to herself.

Moments like this seemed few and far between since more and more encounters with Hell were occurring lately. Michael had noted that the uptick within the past six months was nearly double what they typically dealt with in that time span. Kelly told her and Gen that she felt not only was Hell's interference increasing, but the entities they were dealing with also were bolder—more inclined to skirt the rules, so to speak, nothing seemed normal.

We expect Hell to cheat, but not rewrite the rules altogether, Deb thought.

She herself had been sensing an increase in anger and impatience amongst the humans who were around these supernatural events.

People are being affected by these encounters, and not in a good way, she surmised.

It had been just a few weeks since the fire where they ran into Jared. Kelly hadn't seen him since, and she still wasn't talking. Deb and Gen were trying to give Kelly some space, some time to work through it all, but soon they may have to push the issue. Kelly needed to at least tell them more about the encounter with the Hell Fighter. She hoped Kelly would feel comfortable enough to tell them what happened between her and Jared too. Maybe talking about it would help. Deb was worried about her, about both her sisters.

It's horrible losing the person you love most in this complicated world, but now Jared walks back in after being gone nearly forty years. Should we be hopeful that Gabriel might be alive too? After all this time, where have they been? Not to mention giving Kelly a ring!

Deb couldn't help it, she believed they must have been together, *it can't be a coincidence that the two of them have been gone nearly the same amount of time.* Deb paused and took a sip of her tea.

Well, maybe not just two of them, what if it's all three of them? What if Dmitri is with them? Originally, we thought Jared and Dmitri must have been ordered to a different plane, and we just didn't know it. After all, Michael had seen Dmitri in person after Gabriel went missing, so we didn't suspect they were together back then. But what if our assumptions were wrong, what if they've been together all this time? I don't know why I haven't thought of that before now. Why I haven't thought of Dmitri before now.

Deb's shoulder felt hot and she instinctively reached behind her, tucking her hand down through the top of her blouse and rubbing the outline of the rose that tattooed her skin. Heat radiated through her mark's floral pattern and bore into her hand. She saw the reflection of light gleam against the glass in the patio door.

Well, so much for a little time to myself, she thought.

Using her powers, Deb spoke to her siblings telepathically. "Guys, I have a charge in need. It's a woman I've been drawn to over the past several months, she's fighting cancer, it's very sad. She's one of four children, the other three have all passed away and she's only in her late twenties; one sibling died from an illness, while the other two, twins I think, died at the hands of a drunk driver. I don't think it's demonic interference, but I'll put my shield up and cloak my entrance just in case. I'll update you when I get there." Deb pulled the collar of her jacket a little tighter attempting to keep the light from being seen by humans nearby.

The last thing she wanted was to be exposed. Guardians in human view, such as she was now, who encountered Hell or one of their human charges, can become exposed, and that causes a host of problems for her kind. Deb knew of Guardians who had lost their powers, or still others that had been seriously injured by demons who took advantage of them in that state. Worse, she knew of one family who was separated and sent to varying planes never to be reunited with their loved ones.

I need to get moving, nothing good comes from being exposed. Standing, she managed to get the lid back onto the cup with one hand, then she stuffed the scone in her pocket and made her way through the double doors back inside the shop. There was no exit from the outside, so she was forced to walk inside to exit. She nodded to Margaret who waved at her and thanked her for coming in.

Once outside she rounded the corner, used her powers to disappear from human view, and made her way to Sophia's house.

A demon stood in Sophia's living room glaring at the picture frames displayed along the mantle above her fireplace. Deb had manifested behind him in the kitchen, but with enough of a view to see the scowl on his face, he turned slightly upon her arrival but couldn't see her.

Deb updated her siblings. *Good call on the cloaking shield, there is a demon here, he's pretty big, and wreaks of burning ember, but he can't see me. I'm going to keep it like that for now, I'll let you know if I need help.* She smiled as she heard Frankie respond that he was available if she needed him, or just wanted the company.

This wasn't her first visit to Sophia's house, but it had been several months, anything could have changed. Sophia lived on the south side of the city, her townhouse was a corner unit with an open concept living and kitchen area which tricked you into thinking the space was bigger than it really was. There was no dining room, but the layout allowed for a small table with four chairs. Sophia lived alone so that was more than enough space for one person. The windows above the table overlooked a modest common area that was supposed to pass as a backyard. Overall the space was bright and clean, with charming touches that made it feel lived in and loved. Deb noticed toys on the floor and coloring book pages on the refrigerator. Those would be from Lucy, Sophia's cousin Stella's four-year old daughter. The pictures drawn by the child made Deb smile. They were renderings of two women and a child, with a park along the ocean in the background.

"You might as well show yourself. I know you're here." The demon's voice was low and raspy, more like a growl.

Goosebumps rode the length of Deb's arms, before she could respond she saw a figure come out of the doorway to the bedroom just opposite of where she was standing. The tall male turned right and made his way toward the demon still standing in front of the fireplace.

"I should have known it was you, the stench of betrayal precedes you, Sentinel." The demon turned and faced the approaching male.

"Schlosser, I heard a rumor you were killed and sent back to Hell."

The demon laughed. "Don't believe everything you hear."

"What are you doing in this woman's house? Little off from what you normally chase, isn't it? I mean she's in the bathroom puking, but it's not from pregnancy. She's ill, cancer, not exactly your type."

"Oh, I'm interested," Schlosser quipped.

Deb had to work hard to control her hammering heart, the Sentinel was Marcus, someone she knew. He was someone she had a lot of dealings with over the past several years, someone who had helped her on more than one occasion. In the time between encounters she's found herself thinking about him, his dark brown eyes, chiseled face, and muscular frame flustered her. She had to admit, she had unexplained and confusing feelings for him, but that was something she was still trying to figure out, after all, it couldn't be love. Sentinel or no Sentinel, he was rumored to be from Hell.

What is he doing here? And how does he know Sophia? Deb wondered.

"How would you know what my type is, Marcus? It's not like we're friends." Deb heard Schlosser's tone dripping with sarcasm and wondering how much longer Marcus was going to be patient with him. "It's not even like we're allies, in fact, I think we're more like enemies you and

I." Schlosser's tone betrayed the anger that Deb sensed was building in the room.

"None of this is helping," Marcus replied.

Deb watched the demon wave his arm in the air knocking one of the picture frames over in the process. "I don't care about helping you. Why would I help you?"

"No need to get worked up, I'm just wondering what your business is here. In my line of work, we ask questions, that's part of the job. Seems your name has been circulating recently and many are curious where you've been. Most heard you were sent back to Hell. Care to explain how you managed to get back out?" Marcus turned and faced the kitchen and Deb swore he looked straight at her. She held her breath until he turned back toward Schlosser.

Does he know I'm here? He couldn't know, could he? Her thoughts were scattered, she was startled, Marcus' presence was affecting her more than it should.

"I don't have to explain anything to you." Schlosser practically spit the words at Marcus before stalking off into the bedroom. Marcus followed, Deb behind them both, but at a safe distance.

"Fine, don't explain, I'll just make sure the powers that be know you're back and you can explain it to them." Marcus crossed his arms and leaned back against the bedpost while Schlosser picked through Sophia's drawers.

"Screw you, Marcus, tell whoever you like, but while you're at it, explain why your so chummy with that bitch from Heaven. I've heard rumors too. Heard you're getting it on with an Angel." Schlosser let out a howl of a laugh. "No accounting for taste, I guess."

Deb's heart sunk, was Marcus in love with an Angel? It was possible. She looked at Marcus trying to read his body language, he was shaking his head back and forth, but other than that, she couldn't tell anything more.

The swooshing of water spiraling down the toilet broke the silence, then the flow of water as it cascaded down the tile wall echoed from the bathroom, Sophia was about to get in the shower.

"Thanks for the dating advice, I'll be sure to ignore it. You'll need to start with a shower yourself if you're going to be walking around up here. The aroma of death you're carrying is more than a little noticeable. If you don't want to answer my questions that's fine, but the next thing you encounter from Heaven might not be asking." Deb watched as Marcus never took his eyes off Schlosser, monitoring him closely as the demon circled the bedroom, coming back around toward the doorway to exit. Deb backed up into the kitchen again.

"Oh, I'm counting on it! Stop fretting about your little girlfriend. I'm not looking for an Angel, I'm looking for a Guardian, one in particular, and I heard this woman might lead me to her." Schlosser was feet from Deb's position, she nearly stopped breathing when he began sniffing the air in her direction.

"What's the matter, Schlosser, finally get a whiff of your own stench?" Marcus turned his head toward the bathroom, he clearly seemed pre-occupied with Sophia's whereabouts.

"You'd be smart to stay out of my way, Marcus. You interfere with me, I won't be so talkative." Schlosser walked toward Deb but dematerialized right as he neared her position.

The air hung heavy with anticipation, *maybe I should talk to him now, while it's all still fresh, have him walk me through what's going on, what does this demon want with a Guardian? I've never seen him before, he must have the wrong charge, right? Not to mention that I think he's a Roamer, but with advanced powers that I don't think belong to him. How he got them wouldn't have been pretty, a deal with the Devil perhaps?* Deb shuddered at the mere thought of Lucifer. She was muddling through all the information when she heard a phone ring, then the shower shut off, and she saw Sophia run across the doorway, wrapped in a towel, her hair still dripping from the shower. Leaning across the bed Sophia scooped up the phone and answered it.

"Hello." There was a pause. "Hey, I was just thinking of you guys. How was today?" Deb watched Sophia walk back into the bathroom as she continued the conversation. "Sure, ice cream always sounds good to me. I'm not feeling great, but I'm always good enough for dessert."

Deb updated her family. *The demon's gone.* She paused and re-cloaked her inner thoughts.

How much more should I say? Should I tell them about Marcus? Should I tell them Schlosser might be hunting me?

She hesitated before uncloaking to finish updating her siblings. *Sophia is heading out to meet family, I'm going to wait until she leaves before I take off.*

When Deb focused on Sophia, she could hear the other end of the conversation and recognized the voice as Sophia's cousin, Stella. She was fascinated when she saw what looked like a smile spread across Marcus' face when Stella quipped about Sophia sustaining life on ice cream alone.

How can he hear the other end of the call? He shouldn't be able to. Deb made a mental note to ask Marcus about that ability later. She watched Marcus leave the bedroom, walk over and pick up the photo Schlosser had knocked over, he placed it gently back on the mantle.

Why would he care about that, why would he take the time? He almost seems protective of her, but why? Deb had so many questions, but was now the time for them?

This is ridiculous, she thought. *I'm just going to show myself and confront him, why wait?*

The fatigue of cloaking herself was kicking in; she was out of practice, lately there were so many confrontations that cloaking seemed useless, but now she wished she had continued flexing that muscle. She closed her eyes, took a deep breath and felt the warmth of Heaven wash over her. It was like sunshine on a cool morning, or the taste of soup when you aren't feeling well. It was warmth and comfort wrapped into one, there was no mistaking the presence of Heaven.

Deb opened her eyes and spotted two forms taking shape within the glow of light that had overwhelmed the room. Two male Angels, both with dark brown wavy hair walked to either side of Marcus, one stared at the Sentinel, while the other let his eyes roam the room. They were unassuming, each with a similar build wearing jeans, sneakers, and a hooded sweatshirt.

"Marcus, are you sure he's gone? I mean, really gone?"

"I'm sure, or I wouldn't have told you to come, Lucas." Marcus turned and looked at the Angel on his left.

"I don't trust this. We shouldn't be here. The scent, the power, the chances of us being found by the Guardian watching over her, it's all too risky." The second Angel didn't wait for a response, he walked off into the bathroom toward Sophia who was still chatting on the phone with Stella.

Deb watched Lucas half turn, helping to project his voice into the next room. "Leo, calm down. Marcus is right, he wouldn't have called us if it wasn't safe to do so."

"You two need to be careful, it's not safe around here now." Marcus had turned and was facing Deb again.

"How are we supposed to watch over her and make sure she gets better if we can't come to her home?" Leo continued to talk as he walked back to the doorway. "Marcus, we have to be here, we have to! We cannot let anything happen to her, not after everything—" Deb heard Leo stop in mid-sentence, but it was Lucas who had her attention, he held his hand up silencing all in the room as he walked precariously close to where she was standing.

"What is it Lucas?" Deb saw the look of concern form on Marcus' face and she almost faltered to reveal herself right then.

I'm not the enemy, and maybe you aren't either, she thought

"I think something else was here." Lucas paused as he pushed both hands out in front of him as if trying to touch her. "Or is here."

How do you know? Deb was shocked.

"What do you mean? Where, who, are they from Hell? What do we do? What do we do?" Deb nearly chuckled, Leo's voice had lilted upward to that of a pre-pubescent teen.

Clearly you are not prepared for encounters in this world, Angel. Deb paused examining both Leo and Lucas now that they were facing her direction. *Oh my, they're twins! I've never seen that, Angel twins.*

"Did you get any more information on who's watching over Sophia?" Marcus' question caused her to look in his direction once more.

Lucas answered him. "Yes, we know what's watching over her, but it's not an Angel." Deb influenced Lucas to turn back toward Marcus and Leo.

"It's not, then what is it?" Marcus was quick to inquire further.

Lucas answered. "It's a Guardian." The room fell silent with the weight of the news.

This isn't good, how the heck did they find that out? she wondered. We call their type *Gifters, Angels bringing messages of peace and hope to humans, they shouldn't have such connections; unless they saw me, that would not be good!*

Marcus continued. "Which one?"

"We don't know yet, but female, and powerful. Maybe that's what I'm feeling now, the after affects, but honestly I'm not sure." Lucas replied.

"Alright, I'll take it from here. You two, I brought you here to see what you could sense, but after this I don't think you should come back here for a while." Deb smiled as she saw Marcus point over at Leo, there was such care and concern in his tone. "I will take care of it, of Sophia, and we'll meet elsewhere from now on, changing meeting spots so we don't get caught. Now go, whatever it is or was, I'll deal with it."

Deb's curiosity became utter fascination when she watched Lucas put a hand on Marcus' shoulder. "Be careful, we need you to be safe too."

With that the Angels left and the light in the room dissipated, while the chill of ventilated air returned. Deb watched Marcus fade away.

This is getting messier by the day, she thought to herself.

CHAPTER SIX

Gen heard the last of Deb's update and knew she was safe and heading back home. Gen wanted to be there to greet her, debrief on what happened with Sophia, but that would have to wait. Right now, Gen needed to find Harry, she had hit all the usual spots and couldn't find him. Earlier she had gone to Harry's house, but he wasn't there. She was circling back one more time before escalating the situation and calling her siblings for a meeting.

Gen and her family hadn't seen Harry in months, with all the encounters they were facing that was extremely unusual.

How could he not have been at the fire? Gen thought.

Harry was their Angel, their confidant, their friend. He ministered to her family, watched out for them, and always gave the best advice; he was the reliable in an unreliable world.

Gen thought more about the fire. *He should have been there, would have been there, except he wasn't. He didn't even come for a debrief afterward, there would have to have been something more pressing to keep him away, but what? I scanned the news, there was no supernatural event bigger than the fire that night, at least none that I've found so far.*

Gen's mind sifted through the past several weeks. She was thinking about the work she had done going back through all the television footage she could find leading up to, and including, the night of the fire. Though none of her siblings could understand her gift of sight through photographic evidence, it rarely failed her. Gen was able to look at any camera footage, any photograph, and see the supernatural in it, if it existed. Television and video were the best because it was rolling live action, so the supernatural event would essentially replay itself. Pictures, well, those could be deceiving.

Pictures do tell a thousand words, but you can't always rely on them to be factual, Gen thought.

It was almost noon, and Harry was an early riser. The sun was working hard to burn away the morning chill, but it was still noticeably cooler in the shade. She wasn't in human view, but she was walking down the streets of Boston right alongside them. Walking helped her think and it saved her the energy she might need to rush off somewhere, which lately she was doing more and more.

Harry lived in what was currently considered a posh section of the city, a brief walk behind the State House and she'd be in his neighborhood. The Federal-style brick homes situated on these streets were worth millions, and Harry had a corner lot with a small yard he filled with a garden. The plants that grew there were large and abundant. It was one of her favorite places, a rare feature in an overcrowded cement backdrop.

I just need to see him, make certain he's alright. Not that Harry can't take care of himself, obviously he can, Gen thought.

The cobblestone streets and gas lanterns that adorned this section's narrow winding neighborhood added a charm that was distinct. The fact that the layout was unchanged from most of its original footprint, which was made for cows and not people, was amusing to Gen. Boston was unapologetic for its grip on the past and simply moved around the monuments and landmarks that founded it.

The history of this place is Harry's favorite part. He always calls himself a student of history more so than anything else, Gen mused.

Years ago, in the big boom of the eighties, developers had turned most of these homes into two and three family condo units. Now, more and more wealthy individuals were buying them up and spending millions to convert them back to single family homes wanting to get more space in the city.

Still no parking, Gen noted.

She examined the streets crammed with cars parked one on top of the other, barely a crack between them and knew they most likely hadn't moved in days.

They move, they lose, Gen quipped.

She rounded the last turn and spotted a car double parked at the next corner, there was a man sporting a windbreaker and baseball hat hauling large bags of potting soil and mulch out of the trunk.

Before she could see Harry, she could feel him, the presence of Heaven, right here in this little part of the world was like a beacon in the middle of a gale-force storm. Gen could see his angelic glow warm the sidewalk as he neared the man at the car and overheard part of their conversation.

"Thank you so much Rafi, you've been a tremendous help to me this morning. I truly appreciate it." The driver shook Harry's hand, and bowed his head slightly at the tip Harry passed him.

"Thank you, Harry." Rafi got in his vehicle and rolled down the window. "Don't forget to add lime to those hydrangeas this year. You want them nice and colorful come August."

"You know I will, Rafi, now get on home to your better half. Seems I've got company of my own to entertain now." Holding onto a bag of potting soil, Harry looked back at Gen and winked. He wore an old fishing hat over his bald head. His dark brown pants were the color of dirt, and his sweatshirt had seen better days.

How does he do it? He always knows I'm here even before he sees me. Gen smiled; she couldn't help it. She ducked behind a parked car and changed into human form. *Thank God he's alright,* she exhaled and released a heaviness that had been growing with every hour she couldn't find him.

She watched the driver wave to Harry as he drove off, then Harry made his way through the side gate to the backyard. Gen followed him, closing the door and hooking the latch behind her.

The slender walkway that led to the back was boarded by the house on one side and a tall fence on the other. From the entryway back to where it opened into the yard, the pale colored posts carried the weight of a trail of sprawling Boston ivy. This type of ivy was unique in that its leaves changed colors in fall, bursting into red and orange before they fell. The arrangement complimented the red oak and Japanese maple trees that Harry had planted decades ago.

The site of the ivy instinctively made Gen grab for the ring that hung around her neck.

This place is a sanctuary, I wish you were able to see it now, Gabe. Gen pushed the thought away and let go of her wedding band.

She reached the end of the walkway and paused to take in the sight of Harry dumping mulch into his wheel barrel.

She spoke first. "Where have you been Harry?"

Without turning he answered. "Well now that's a silly question. I've been here, where else would I be?" He turned toward her. Pointing just to her right at a small wooden gardening table, her eyes followed. Laying on top were a pair of small gardening gloves. "You might as well make yourself useful, Genevieve. It's a fine day for gardening. We garden and then we talk."

She thought about arguing, but what was the point? He was fine, she could see that, so she might as well relax and enjoy her time with him. At some point she'd bridge the topic again and ask him about the fire.

"How do you always manage to know I'm here before you see me, Harry?" Gen put the gloves on and walked to the hydrangea plant where Harry had already measured out the lime into a container. She reached down and sprinkled the soil around the hydrangea with fertilizer.

"I suppose it's the same way you know I'm nearby. Now, don't forget to rake that through and be sure the soil is moist, so it will take. Those hydrangeas will be purple and pink this year I think." Gen followed his instructions and then made her way to a large wrought-iron planter overflowing with petunia flowers and began to deadhead the plant.

Working quietly side by side for the next thirty minutes she tried to clear her mind. She watched Harry move from plant to plant with the care and nurturing she knew came naturally to him. His beady blue eyes inspected every plant, occasionally a whistle would escape his thin lips as he got lost in his work. Gen noticed the lilacs were already heavy with perfumed purple flowers, rose bushes were budding, and his pothos container plants had giant happy leaves turned toward the sun.

Gen watched him walk toward her, handing her a rag he said. "That's plenty for today, I'll get to the rest later. What do you say we stop for a bit to enjoy the fruits of our labor?"

"Sounds good to me" Gen replied with a smile.

She wiped her hands and followed Harry through the yard, under the pergola-canopied patio, and in through the double glass doors to his kitchen.

"Tea or something stronger young lady?" Harry was staring at her as he asked the question.

"It's a little early for whiskey, Harry. Tea will be fine, but I wouldn't turn down a piece of coffeecake to go with it." Gen sat at the table and watched Harry maneuver around the kitchen preparing the tea.

"I always have coffeecake and it's never too early for whiskey." Harry placed two mugs on the table and handed her a knife. "You're on cake cutting duty. You know where it is."

Gen walked to the corner of the marble countertop and removed the glass lid covering the cake. She opened an upper cabinet, retrieved plates, and cut two big slices to go on them. Cake in hand she rejoined Harry at the table.

"Now, you have your cake, what do you say we start over?" Harry's lips curved upward, his eyes expressed kindness as he looked at Gen. "I'm sorry to tell you that I have no new information to share on Gabriel. But I'm guessing based on your impromptu visit that perhaps you do?" Harry picked up his fork and took a bite of cake.

Gen smiled at him. "I didn't come here about that, but since you brought up Gabe, I have to tell you, it's strange. These last few months have been, well, different." Gen reached for her ring and held it momentarily. Then she let it fall and took a bite of cake.

"Well, maybe something is happening, softening perhaps," Harry said softly. "Have you given more thought to what we talked about last time you and I spoke?"

"I think about it all the time, there is a piece of me that wants to let go, move on, but then I think of him, of us, and I can't picture him gone, not for good." Gen paused trying to make sense of the conflicting emotions that have become her normal state.

"I don't know that moving on is exactly what you need to focus on, in some ways you have already moved on. You give yourself to your work, to your family, to humanity, that sounds a lot like you've already begun to move on. But, we both know, that's not all you need to do." Harry paused.

"You want me to forgive him." Gen's eyes watered as she looked over at Harry.

"Forgiveness, true forgiveness is not something you can force, it has to come naturally, from the same place love does. To do that, you need to open yourself again, the same way you did the day you opened your heart to Gabriel. It's not going to be easy, but you need to do that if you really want to be free. The weight you carry, it continues to pull you down. Anger, resentment, those are dangerous things. You let them fester, they can rot and manifest into something else. I think we both know the price of an anchor like that." Harry's words were cutting but Gen felt the love and care they carried.

"I know you're right, but …" Gen couldn't finish her thought.

"But what? Forgiving is not forgetting, Genevieve." Harry's sympathetic eyes fell upon hers.

"I don't want to be the one to give up, I feel like I already did that to him once." Gen had a hold of the wedding band again as she said the words.

"Have you ever tried putting that back on? It might feel less of a burden than wearing it like an albatross around your neck." Harry half smiled as he asked the question.

Have I ever thought of putting it back on? Are you kidding me, only about a million times since the day I woke up to find it not on my finger! I'm frightened of even attempting it. I don't know how it came off. Gen's mind reeled at the thought of what it would mean if she put it on and it didn't bind, or worse, it did bind, and she was the reason they were not together. She didn't think she could bear either scenario, so she stayed right where she was, in a torturous limbo.

"It's not a burden, it helps to remind me of what I'm fighting for, Harry." Gen forced a smile.

"Well, I'm glad you came by. Now, if you didn't come to discuss Gabriel, why don't you tell me what this visit was really about?" Harry reached over and gave the top of her hand a little squeeze.

Gen sighed. "Honestly Harry I'm here to talk about the fire."

"What fire?" He pulled back and sat a little taller in his chair.

"The fire at the school, the newborn Hell Fighter we chased down. Jared killed him. I wanted to know why you weren't there. Where were you?"

"What are you talking about?" Harry's forehead creased in concern. "You encountered a Hell Fighter, here, on Earth?"

Chills ran up Gen's arm. Something was wrong. Harry knew nothing about the fire. *How can that be?*

Gen was about to explain when Harry suddenly stood up.

"What is it Harry? What's wrong?"

Gen watched recognition cross Harry's face. "It's okay, it's just someone else is here."

"Who's here?" Gen asked as she began to look around.

"It's alright. It took me a moment to process why she would come to my home. We will have to finish our conversation as soon as she leaves." Harry got up from the table and walked toward the front door.

Gen watched him walk away. "Friend or foe, Harry?"

"You would have known before me if it were the latter," he retorted without turning around.

You have too much faith in me, Gen thought.

The doorbell rang just as Harry reached for the door handle, when he pulled the door open, Gen saw Lacey, the Watcher from the fire, standing in the doorway. Harry welcomed his guest and clicked the door closed behind them.

Gen walked the plates over to the sink and turned to face the doorway. Lacey stopped when she spotted Gen, her big brown eyes widened as she looked back at Harry.

"I'm sorry for interrupting, should I come back?" Lacey turned her attention back toward Gen. She noticed Lacey's hair was tousled, and her cheeks were flushed as if she had been running.

"No need to come back. You are welcome to speak freely in front of Genevieve. She's not Joan of Arc for goodness sake." Harry chuckled and walked toward the larger table in the open dining area. Lacey followed him as did Gen.

"I'm sorry, it's just, well, I've never spoken to one outside of work, you know?" Lacey was looking back at Gen as the two pulled chairs out to sit down at the table together.

"Aren't we always at work?" Gen quipped, but after an awkward moment of silence Gen continued, "It's no problem, I'm happy to help if I can." Gen was short in her response, she really wanted Lacey to be the one talking and answering questions. Always on alert, Gen was more than curious as to why a Watcher would come to Harry's house.

"I'm sure you can help, that's why I'm here. I need to understand what is going on and when there will be justice for Sebastian," Lacey stated.

"Justice." Harry let the word hang in the air like a question.

"Yes," Lacey answered simply. "It happened while I was working on this case where I encountered Hell."

"Well, a Historian encountering Hell during a case is not exactly unusual, Lacey." Harry was quick to point out the obvious.

Historian, I always forget to call them by their official title. My siblings and I aren't the only Guardians to refer to them as Watchers, beings that don't engage in battle but merely record the facts of the events and preserve that information. What good that does I'll never know. Above my pay grade, I guess, Gen thought.

"I know, Harry, but this was different. This resulted in an actual confrontation, surely that alone would warrant an investigation." Lacey was indignant in her response.

"I don't mean to upset you, Lacey. Please go on, tell us what happened in your own words." Harry's statement seemed to calm her.

"It's only been a couple of weeks, but I would have thought someone would have already been in touch to follow up. I really need to know this is being prioritized and taken with the seriousness that I believe it deserves." Lacey puffed out the words quickly.

Gen watched Lacey as she spoke. Gen had no idea what she was talking about, and judging by the look on Harry's face, neither did he.

Well this visit just got a whole lot more interesting, Gen thought.

Harry spoke first. "It's been a busy week, can you start from the beginning, perhaps share what you were expecting someone to follow up on exactly?"

Gen watched Lacey's body pull back as if she had been physically pushed.

Clearly, she thinks we already know what this is about. What if Harry should know what's going on, but doesn't? He didn't seem to know about the fire. What if signals aren't working the way they should? Gen pondered. *That could be bad. I better jump in and cover for Harry. That will give us time to figure this out after Lacey leaves.*

"If you don't mind Lacey, please do start from the beginning. After all, unlike Harry, who I'm sure knows the story already, I wouldn't know what you were referring to." Gen's words seemed to soften Lacey's demeanor.

"Of course." Lacey leaned forward slightly, relaxing her shoulders. "Why would you know, right? I mean if you aren't the Guardian to exact justice, why would you know anything about this?"

"Right, it doesn't mean I can't help and I'm willing to just listen. This must mean a great deal to you if you came all the way to Harry's home to speak about it. Please start from the beginning for my sake," Gen replied.

"Ok. Several weeks ago, I was finishing up a case when I was called to another location nearby. That's unusual, but then I thought, lately everything seems unusual." Lacey turned to look at Harry. "Do you mind getting me a glass of water?"

This woman is clearly on edge, she is all over the place and easily distracted. Gen was fascinated.

"I'll get it for you, please continue." Gen got up from her seat and made her way to the fridge to retrieve a bottle of water, which she then handed to Lacey.

"Thank you, I don't know why I'm so nervous." Lacey opened the bottle and took a long sip.

"Nonsense, there is nothing to be nervous about, you're safe here Lacey." Gen saw Harry reach out and reassuringly pat Lacey's arm.

"Thank you," Lacey replied. "Sorry, I'm just so easily rattled these days. Lately, everything throws me off. Sebastian was always so good at getting me refocused after a difficult encounter with Hell." Tears welled up in Lacey's eyes.

"What happened to Sebastian, Lacey?" Gen asked.

"A demon killed him, and I was there but could do nothing about it." Gen froze.

"Lacey, I'm so sorry for your loss, our loss really. Sebastian was a peaceful soul, with such a calming presence. He will be missed."

Gen let the pause in the room expand a bit before she commented on the obvious.

"Lacey, blaming Hell for the murder of an upper-level Historian is a serious accusation," Gen told her. "Are you sure?"

"Let me tell you what happened and then you tell me if it was murder or not." Lacey sat back preparing to launch into her story.

"Stop, not another word, my siblings will need to hear this too." Gen looked over at Harry. "I don't want Lacey to have to re-tell this story more than she has to and I know there will be questions.

If Lacey's story is true, and this Sebastian was murdered by something in Hell, then we may end up going to war over it. Gen's mind raced through the possibilities.

"We need Michael, and if I know my older brother, he'll be keeping a close eye on Kelly today. He's been watching over her since the fire, and I know exactly where Kelly is. We need to go and find them." Gen's voice betrayed a bit of urgency, using her powers she took the three of them from the house.

CHAPTER SEVEN

"Oh my God, I'm in love with these shoes!" Kelly exclaimed as she looked down at the bright red strappy sandals, turning to appreciate them in the shop's mirror. The small boutique didn't have a large selection of shoes, but all of them were high end and fashion forward.

"They look spectacular on you, Miss O'Mara, you must buy them." Violet, the owner of the shop called V's, was quick to agree with Kelly before turning away to continue pulling out the rest of the shoes Kelly had requested to try on.

Kelly sat down and pulled the shoes off her feet to take a closer look at them. She turned the shoes over and pulled at the straps a bit. Then her eye caught the price on the box.

Of course, they're like a million dollars. Danny will absolutely kill me if I buy these, but how could I not?

She dropped them back into the box and begrudgingly moved on to the next selection. The next pair of sandals were sleeker with more of a stiletto heel. She walked around in them, but they felt too dressy for what she was looking for. She removed them and pulled a pair of black wedge sandals that were cute and practical, but not as exciting.

"Here are the last two you wanted to try on. Should I take any to the register for you?" Violet asked.

"Not yet, I still don't know which way I'm going, but one of these is coming home with me today," Kelly replied.

"Not a problem, I'll be at the front if you need anything else." Violet made her way back to the front counter while Kelly slipped on a pair of navy blue open-toe sandals. She was staring down at her feet when she felt Harry, his aura was like a wave of tranquility rushing over her.

Really, I'm therapy shopping for goodness sake. This couldn't wait? Not that I don't miss you, Harry, but you could have had better timing, Kelly silently griped about the intrusion just as she heard the bell on the shop door ding. Turning to greet him she widened her smile and attempted to look thrilled to see him.

"Harry, where have you been, we've missed you!" Kelly declared.

"Really, is that why you had to build yourself up for that greeting, because you were so happy to see me?" Harry was smiling, but the empathy in his eyes spoke volumes.

"Oh Harry, it's not that I don't love you, and I have missed you, but today, really? Of all days you come and find me today? I was out for the day trying to forget about these last few months, it's been an absolute drain. I'm exhausted and just wanted a day to myself." Kelly sighed as she sat back down on the long-cushioned bench and removed the sandals she was about to parade around in.

"I can't wait to hear all about these past few months, but we have other things to get to today. It's not like I get to decide when things escalate and when they don't. Believe me, I wish I could." Harry sat down next to her.

"I know, I was just hoping a little shopping would clear my head and help me deal with things, work through it all, you know, prepare me for what might be coming." Kelly looked at Harry, he seemed concerned, but she sensed he wasn't there about the past.

"You're going to be alright, you always are. These things ebb and flow just like an old river, sometimes it's calm, but every so often, it's wild and overwhelmingly powerful. In the end, you O'Mara's make it, not because of what you are, but who you are; you're a family. That's all you'll ever need when things are tough, not this silly shopping thing." Harry waved his hands out in front of him with his reply.

"You always know just what to say Harry." Kelly smiled genuinely and reached over to hug him briefly.

"Yes, well I'm awesome like that. Now why don't you meet us outside, but not before you buy the red sandals. Those looked the best, it's the color of your soul after all." Harry put his arm around Kelly's shoulders and gently lifted her to her feet.

"How do you know about the red shoes, that was many pairs ago?" Kelly was staring at him in shocked surprise.

Harry turned and walked toward the exit, he laughed as he neared the door. "I know you, now get moving, I'll see you out there."

Kelly picked up the boxes of shoes and made her way to the counter. She separated two away from the rest and handed the black wedges and red sandals to Violet who was patiently waiting at the register for her.

"I'm so excited you're going with these, they really did look gorgeous on you. Let me just move these others out of the way first," Violet said.

The store owner made her way over to the back wall to leave the shoes by the stock room entrance while Kelly dug through her oversized purse for her wallet. The sound of a credit card slapping down against the countertop next to her made her stiffen in surprise.

"You felt Harry come in, but not me? You're slipping, I need you re-focused, we all do. You need to put this behind you Kelly, you're going to be fine, we all are." Michael said the words but never looked in her direction.

Stop telling me I'm going to be fine! I hate that word, FINE. What does that even mean? I'm definitely not fine with you stalking me, that's for sure. I must be losing my mind. What if I am, and no one is noticing? Kelly's frustration bellowed internally.

"Oh hello, I didn't even hear the bell above the door this time," Violet said as she looked over at Michael.

So out of practice with the human world Michael simply nodded in reply.

"Violet, this is my oldest brother Michael," Kelly remarked. "He's pretty stealthy, but I am assuming he came in as my uncle was leaving."

"Yes, I can see the resemblance to one another. It's quiet striking actually." Violet appeared to be studying them as they stood side by side. "You have a big family, right?" she asked Kelly.

"Yes," Kelly answered as she looked at Michael. "Some days it feels too big."

Violet laughed. "Well, my brother has never bought me a pair of high-end shoes, so enjoy it." Violet took the credit card and swiped it.

With the sale complete Michael walked to the door and held it open for Kelly to exit through.

"Have a wonderful day and enjoy the shoes, thank you for coming in." Violet moved toward the stock room, eventually disappearing into the back. Kelly walked through the open doorway to the street and stopped short when she saw Tom standing with Harry.

"You have got to be kidding me!" Kelly said.

"Hi Kell, sorry to bother you during your shopping spree, but something serious has come up," Tom stated.

I haven't taken a break in months, Kelly thought, *and the one day I go out to clear my head, the cavalry tracks me down. It must be bad.*

"Based on how many of you have suddenly shown up, I can surmise it must be serious," she replied dryly.

Kelly could feel her agitation boiling. She felt the weight of their eyes fall on her, based on their body language she suspected her face betrayed the sentiment.

"How about if we lessen the blow by taking you into Jake's? Come on." Tom turned first and walked toward her favorite pub a few doors down from where they were standing.

"Well now you're just bribing me, smart play, Thomas." Kelly picked up the pace and walked off toward the pub. Tom opened the door and she walked through ahead of him.

She scanned the room, abruptly coming to a halt when she saw who was inside.

Seriously, Kelly internally agonized, *even Gen is here, this must be worse than I thought. I just wanted to enjoy the simplicity of a shopping day, forget about the demonic, pretend life was normal, even if it was for just one day. I needed to recharge. I don't think I have the energy for this right now.*

Giving up, Kelly mumbled in disgruntlement and made her way toward the bar to sit down.

Gen saw Kelly's excitement disappear the moment recognition set in. Gen watched her sister sulk as she made her way toward the far end of the bar. She took a seat next to Father Donovan, who had come in for his afternoon pint while Harry was next door retrieving Kelly.

She's so mad at us right now, Gen thought. *I wish I didn't have to be the one to ruin the time she was taking for herself.*

"She'll understand, once she hears what's going on, she'll know we had no choice." Tom's voice was low, obviously meant for only Gen to hear.

"It's like you're reading my mind, Tom. I hope you're right, it's been a rough few months," Gen answered.

"Well," Harry said coming up behind them, "maybe it's time to get it all out in the open then. Silence is poison, a festering wound that never heals." Harry walked past them and motioned for them to follow him toward the bar.

Gen sat on the long side of the L shaped bar, diagonal to Father Donovan who was joyfully sharing a joke with Lacey and Kelly. The priest was an Irishman, with a shiny bald head, a twinkle in his hazel eyes and stout body that shimmied when he laughed. Despite being in

Boston for more than two decades his brogue escaped when he drank beer and told jokes, which was often.

Jake, the tavern owner and cheeseburger maker extraordinaire, turned and came toward her.

"What can I get you, Genevieve?" Jake was wiping the glistening bar top. His short sleeve T-shirt strained to cover his muscular body and Gen caught sight of two young women ogling him as he worked. Gen smiled. Despite his professional manner, clean-cut hairstyle, and boy-next-door charm, it was his near perfect five o'clock shadow that drew many a young woman to flirt with him openly.

"Just a club soda with lemon please. I'm afraid this will be a short visit today." Gen smiled as Jake nodded in reply.

Turning toward her sister she asked, "How was shopping? I see you got some loot."

"It was fine, could have been quieter," Kelly quipped.

Jake walked into the kitchen and grabbed a basket. Coming back around he dropped the heaping portion of fresh potato chips in front of Kelly. "Maybe that will cheer you up."

"I'm so hungry, thank you Jake, you're the best." Kelly dumped a handful on a side plate.

Jake threw the bar towel over his shoulder and made his way back down to flirt with the two women.

"I didn't know you guys ate." Lacey was staring at Kelly's plate as she said it, clearly not thinking of how that sounded.

"Junk food you mean, you didn't think we ate junk food," Kelly responded quickly to try and mask Lacey's odd comment. Fortunately, Father Donovan was onto another joke with Harry and Jake was chatting up the two women at the center of the bar. Gen looked around and assessed no real harm had been done.

Judging by the easy banter between Lacey and Kelly it was clear the Watcher was letting her guard down and feeling more at ease. Gen was concerned about how on edge and distracted Lacey was at Harry's place. She hoped bringing Lacey here first would allow her to get to know and feel comfortable around Gen and her siblings. The story she needed to tell them was important. She needed Lacey to be forthcoming and trust them with it. She already knew she was going to have to hold Michael back from turning this story into an interrogation. It didn't hurt that they were starting at Jake's. It was Kelly's favorite place. Maybe it lessened the intrusion just a bit.

Gen looked around and sighed, she wished Deb was with them to see how well everyone was enjoying themselves. Well, everyone except Michael, who always seemed to look like the sky was about to fall. Gen knew that was why it was important for Deb to find reasons for them to be together in a setting where they were forced to talk about something other than work. The business of the past several months had kept them from going out, getting away, or even having a family breakfast together, something Gen was now realizing had been sorely missed.

The restaurant was surprisingly busy for the time of day. Gen was grateful the few groups sitting at the bar had spaced themselves out enough to allow for relative privacy. The bar was made of real wood, stained chocolate brown and smooth as glass to the touch. The rectangular shape ran the length of the building with flat screen TV's the bar area's decoration. Gen was musing that in just a few more hours people will have a hard time finding a seat at all, never mind leaving empty chairs between them.

Unless you're Kelly, she always gets a seat.

A few pints down and Father Donovan needed to excuse himself to go to the rest room. Jake was at the far end of the bar chatting up a group of local fishermen who, judging from their clay stained boots, sunburned faces, and scruffy appearances, had just returned from work on the fish pier.

"Who's going first, we don't have a lot of time before he returns?" Michael was the first to get down to business.

"Why are we here at all? I haven't been seen by humans in nearly a century! I got to tell you, it feels weird." Lacey was now eating the chips off Kelly's plate.

"Who is this?" Michael asked, his eyes narrowing at Lacey.

"What do you mean? I just worked with you at the fire, it wasn't that long ago. How could you have forgotten the fire?" Lacey demanded.

"We didn't forget the fire, Lacey. I believe it was me you dealt with that night, not Michael." Tom was quick to try and calm the tension.

"A Watcher, you brought a Watcher to a bar to meet up with us? What is going on here Gen?" Michael was done being patient.

Gen knew this was all about to go sideways, but Lacey, draining the light brown liquid from a whiskey glass Gen hadn't noticed she ordered, distracted her.

"I'm not a Watcher, that's a vulgar term. I'm surprised at your lack of professionalism Guardian. I'm a

Historian, and proud of it." Lacey was standing now and was about to either walk out or fall over, Gen wasn't sure which.

"We need to stay on point. I was at Harry's house today when Lacey showed up to inquire as to the status of her mentor's ..." Gen hesitated.

How do I describe Sebastian's murder in terms a human could potentially overhear and not get suspicious?

"I want justice for his murder, he didn't deserve what that vile thing did to him," Lacey chimed in before Gen could put her thoughts in order, but Kelly steered Lacey back to her seat and shushed her.

"Lacey, sit back down, just give us a second and try and remember where you are and who can see and hear you," Kelly reminded, then turning back to Gen. "Is this related to the fire, to Jared?"

"I don't know."

"What is this fire you keep referring to?" Harry was standing now.

"The one in North Dakota, twenty-three dead, all high school kids, ringing any bells? You couldn't make it I guess." Michael answered, and Gen could feel the chill of his words as though a cool breeze has just wandered in.

"I had no idea. This is the first I've heard of it. I mean I know the fire, I read about it in the paper, saw it on the news, absolute tragedy, but I didn't know it was, well for you to handle," Harry replied. Harry's eyes grew with concern as the conversation moved along.

"We have only seconds before he returns now. What does Lacey's mentor have to do with the fire?" Tom's follow up was directed at Gen.

"I don't know if it does or not, but Lacey is claiming that Sebastian's untimely departure was caused by our enemy, and that it was a deliberate act." Gen stood now.

"We should get the check and move along." Michael was brooding. "Obviously, we all need the chance to speak more freely on this matter."

"Lacey was nervous when I first met her at Harry's house." Gen looked at Michael. "I was hoping to give her a little time to process everything, prepare her for what will be a difficult conversation. I wanted her to feel more comfortable with us and I didn't want her to have to repeat the story a hundred times."

"That was not the best strategy, Genevieve," Michael scolded. "We need to get out of here. Let's just head out now."

"Here comes Father Donovan, let's get our game faces back on." Kelly spoke quickly and then smiled at the priest as he made his way back.

"I'm sorry Father, I need to drag Kelly away," Gen said as he neared her. "We need to get going. This was just a quick stop on our way home to meet up with the rest of the family for dinner." Gen's tone was friendly and apologetic.

"That sounds lovely. I'm glad you all make time for one another, even with your busy lives. Family is the most important thing." The priest smiled at Gen, then picked up his beer and pointed toward the fishermen. "There's a group over on the other side that never tires of my old jokes."

Father Donovan waved his goodbyes as he made his way to the large crowd forming around the fishermen at the other end of the bar. Gen looked over at Lacey and noticed she looked a little green.

"Are you feeling alright?" Gen asked her.

"I'm not sure, but I don't think so. Maybe I should have some more of that brown liquid," Lacey replied.

"What did you give her Kelly?" Gen asked

"It was nothing" Kelly said indignantly. "She shared a little bit out of the drinks I ordered. The poor thing looked like she was going to choke from all the chips she shoved in her mouth."

"And what is it that you're drinking?" Gen knew better than to ask. She saw the empty glasses in front of Kelly and knew the answer before it came.

"It was just a little Jameson." Kelly's voice trailed off as Lacey's head fell forward slightly. Gen watched in horror as Lacey's whole body slowly slid down on top of the bar.

"Did you just get a Watcher drunk?" Michael asked from having returned from paying the bill. "We can't leave her here." Michael was clearly unhappy.

"No, it wasn't like that, I swear," Kelly offered.

"She's fine, it may not be the booze. She hasn't been, you know, in this state shall we say for a long, long, time. I think the drink and being out of practice she's just tired." Harry chuckled as he said it and then Gen couldn't help but laugh.

Lacey hiccupped waking herself up temporarily, that caused the rest of them to join in the laughter, even Michael smirked.

"As amusing as this is, and it is," Tom said. "We don't want to get Jake in trouble. To a cop, this would look like a drunk person in a bar, in the middle of the afternoon. No need for us to put Jake's liquor license in jeopardy."

Tom was right of course. He walked over and partially blocked people's view of their drunk friend. He pulled Lacey back to a somewhat sitting position, albeit resting sideways against him.

"What are we going to do?" Kelly asked.

"We need Deb, I assume you were going to call her anyway, right?" Tom asked Gen.

"Yes, I was going to call her to meet us as soon as we got outside." Gen answered.

"I'll go outside and call her," Michael stated.

Gen watched him walk off toward the door and frowned. *Too bad you can never just enjoy the moment, Michael.*

A few minutes later Deb appeared in the bar behind Kelly but wasn't visible to the human eye. She quickly projected her shield onto Tom and Lacey. Tom proceeded to pick Lacey's limp body off the chair. Kelly reached over and placed her shoes on top of Lacey's stomach.

"What? I assume you're going back to the house, no reason I should have to walk around with them all afternoon," Kelly told Tom.

Gen saw a soft glow of light and then Tom was gone.

"I'm heading outside, Harry, see you out there." Michael walked off toward the door and Kelly made her way over to Gen and Harry.

"I'm going to head outside too; I'll give Deb a heads up. I'll see you out there, Gen. Always good to see you Harry, maybe next time you and I can get drunk." Kelly smiled slyly before giving Harry a quick hug. She turned and made her way out.

"I'm devastated about Sebastian, he was an old soul, like me." Harry's voice rang somber. "I can't believe I missed such a major event with the fire, whatever is causing that level of interference must be pretty powerful."

"Well at least now we know the signals are being interfered with," Gen told him.

"Yes, it will be good to try and get ahead of whatever is doing it. Lacey will be out for hours, you can catch up with Kelly and Deb, let them know what happened. I'll go talk to Tom and Michael, then we can go find the rest of your brothers and get them up to speed as well. I know Michael is going to want to get right to work, you have maybe two hours before he starts making waves or worse, goes and wakes up Lacey before she's slept it off." Gen knew what Harry meant by waves: Michael would be demon hunting tonight.

"Thanks Harry, I'll catch up with you soon. I appreciate the time today. Wish we could have ended our afternoon on a happier note. I'm sorry for your loss, for Lacey's, I know you had a lot of respect for Sebastian, but don't worry, we'll get to the bottom of this," Gen assured him.

"I know you will, but from now on, let's not assume I know what's going on. No more guessing I'm unavailable. Something is causing serious Angel interference down here, so we need to be sure to stay in touch about everything. Oh, and the *Jared* Kelly was referring to earlier, was it *the* Jared?" Harry asked.

"Yeah, she hasn't seen nor heard from him since," Gen answered.

"He's the reason for the shoe shopping then," Harry noted. "He's also your current lead on Gabriel."

"He is the only lead I have on Gabriel right now," Gen said. "There were several reasons for her to be shopping today. We had some intense battles with Hell Fighters, a newborn even, plus Jared. Oh, I almost forgot, he put a ring on her finger." Gen felt her eyebrow arch as she said the last words.

"Oh my," Harry said in surprise. "I'm going to assume it stayed on and I just missed noticing it?" Harry asked.

"Yup, much to her dismay," Gen said. "I think she's focusing on his absence, not that I blame her of course, but if she listens to her heart, I know she'll be happy. The two of them are a match made in Heaven, pun intended."

"You run along. Go get Kelly some actual lunch. Take care of your sisters." Harry walked toward the exit with her.

I'm trying Harry, but I'm barely sane enough to take care of myself some days

Genevieve nodded a goodbye to Jake and walked out of the bar.

CHAPTER EIGHT

Gen felt the warmth of the shifting sun on her face as she walked toward her sisters. They had stopped at the next corner waiting for her.

Deb smiled at her. "Where to?" Deb asked. "We have to meet back up in two hours."

"That's up to Kelly, but I was thinking the Tequila Bar on the waterfront, the water taxi is just a few blocks from here, we can be there in ten minutes or so." Gen knew food was the key to getting Kelly past her disappointment. Gen smiled as she saw the shocked surprise light up Kelly's face.

"Um yes! Hello, I love that place!" Kelly gleefully remarked. "I don't know that it fully makes up for interrupting my afternoon, but it's really, really, close."

"Yes. We're aware of your passion for all-you-can-eat tacos," Gen said as Deb snickered.

"And let's not forget tequila," Deb added

"There is a lot to like about that place. So much food, so little time." Kelly sighed with her response.

"Ok, let's go, I'll catch you up on the way over," Gen told them, then added, "We won't have a ton of time, but we probably have at least an hour and a half before Lacey wakes up. I wouldn't let her tell me the details of the story until we were all together. I know it's shocking, but I wasn't anticipating her getting drunk."

"That was shocking!" Kelly mocked melodramatically "But, I'm not feeling sorry since it's allowing us to go for an amazing late lunch together."

"Let's walk faster, we don't have a lot of time to waste and there are too many people around for us just to teleport over there. Michael will be too impatient to wait any longer than he has to. Not that I blame him, if what little Lacey did share with me turns out to be true, our normal is about to be a thing of the past. Our brothers are always near combat mode, but soon we may need to join them," Gen noted.

"I know, but that's not how the three of us work best. We need to talk it out, catch our breath, strategize, form a plan before we go looking for answers," Deb said.

"Agreed, but I have a hunch we're going to find trouble when we go looking for answers," Gen added.

Kelly agreed. "Lately, I feel trouble is everywhere. We don't need to go knocking on doors to find it. More encounters with Hell, increases in demon possession, not to mention whatever this thing is you're about to dump on us. Something is definitely going on, and it doesn't feel natural."

As they boarded the water taxi, Gen was happy to find they were the only passengers. The Captain was an older man, with a round weathered face that was partially shielded by the brim of a sea-battered baseball hat. He made quick work untying the boat from the dock, oblivious to the noticeable swaying from the choppy water. The briskness of the ocean breeze ruffling Gen's hair stung her cheeks and reminded her that summer was still many weeks away.

The engine roared as they pulled away heading straight across the harbor to the Seaport district. As the sun-bleached planks of the wharf disappeared, Gen took a deep breath of salt air; danger was coming. *Kelly was right*, Gen thought, *the trouble Hell was causing did seem to be everywhere. Evil felt like it was encroaching.* She could sense it, and so could her sisters.

Kelly knew something was wrong. Gen's eyes closed as her hair billowed in the rawness of the April wind. Her sister appeared outwardly calm and confident, but Kelly knew different.

Gen not only intruded on my day off, but brought everyone else with her, obviously this is bad, but what could be worse than a Hell Fighter on Earth? Or their marks going off at an alarmingly high rate for months on end? Kelly wondered.

She wasn't looking forward to the conversation that was going to accompany what otherwise should be a happy lunch together, but knew they had no choice.

It took mere minutes for the driver to maneuver across the bay. He cut the engine and the sloshing of the ocean swayed the boat back and forth. The potbellied captain expertly pulled alongside the pier, as the rocking of the buoys clanged between the boat and the posts of the dock. The captain hopped over the side and tied off the boat, then he opened the small gate allowing their exit off the pier.

Deb paid the man in cash and then the three of them made their way up the short, but steep incline to the busy waterfront district above. Though lunch was over and dinner was still several hours away, the restaurants were busy. This part of the city bustled with both tourists and employees from nearby businesses. Kelly requested a table outside in the sun and was pleasantly surprised at how much warmer it was from the other side of the bay. Fortunately, there was distance between them and the other occupied tables. Kelly felt they would be able to speak more freely to one another about the problem at hand. Spotting a young waitress heading their way, Kelly pondered her drink order.

"What can I get you ladies to drink today?" the waitress asked.

"We'll have three of your top-shelf margaritas with chips and salsa," Kelly answered.

"I'll put that right in and be back to get your order," the waitress replied.

"That was efficient," Gen remarked.

"Well, you said we didn't have a lot of time and I'm still hungry, a few house chips from Jake's does not a lunch make," Kelly retorted.

"I'm fine with whatever," Deb added.

"Great, I know Kelly already knows what she wants so she can order the same for us when the waitress returns. I'm going to get started with what's going on." Gen paused to double check the proximity to the nearby customers then began. "I went to Harry's this morning, went there twice actually, the first time he was out buying fertilizer and potting soil which is why he wasn't home. It was bothering me that we hadn't heard from him, especially after the fire."

"Yeah, I would have bet he would have been with us at the fire, and if not, I expected him to connect with one of us later," Kelly responded.

"It is unusual that it's been this long since we've seen him and so much has happened without his guidance," Deb added.

"I agree, that's why I finally went looking for him today. I found him and after I helped him in the garden for a bit we went inside. I asked him where he's been, but he said he's been right where he always is, home," Gen told them.

"Wait," Kelly said leaning in toward Gen. "So, he didn't acknowledge missing a major battle?"

Kelly pulled herself back as the friendly waitress returned with their drinks and dropped off the chips and salsa.

"Are you ready to order?" The waitress asked. "Or do you need more time?"

"I think we're good for now, we may order something else in a little bit," Kelly answered.

"No problem, take your time. My name's Melanie, just flag me when you're ready," she replied.

Once Melanie had made her way back inside the restaurant Kelly continued. "How could our Angel not know about a pretty serious infraction by Hell?"

"I don't know. There wasn't enough time to get into it, because while I was at his house, Lacey showed up. She was definitely surprised to see me there and actually asked Harry if it was alright to speak with me," Gen recounted.

"What, why wouldn't it be?" Kelly chuckled.

"I don't know all the rules for Historians," Deb replied. "But I think it's frowned upon for a Historian to fraternize with, well non-Historians."

"Well she didn't seem to have a problem going to Harry's house, would that not be considered fraternization?" Kelly argued.

"We're getting off track. We can debate the merits of who should be friends with whom later," Gen scolded. "She came there because she claimed a demon killed Sebastian, her mentor. He was a Historian of the highest order according to Harry." Kelly could scarcely believe what Gen was telling them.

"Hold on a minute, Lacey is saying she has proof that Sebastian has been murdered?" Kelly asked. She could feel her head start to ache as her eyes darted back and forth between her two sisters.

This is bad, I mean I knew it would be bad, but this is really, really, bad, Kelly thought. *This is yet another battle brought right to our doorstep. What the heck is going on around here?*

"That can't be right," Deb interjected. "We would have heard about it. Harry or someone would have come to us. They would have to, right?"

"Lacey says she witnessed it herself," Gen answered.

"Oh no," Deb murmured.

"Before either of you pepper me with more questions," Gen said with hands raised in an attempt to stop the onslaught, "that's all I know. That's as far as it went. I made her stop talking and brought her and Harry to the shoe shop. Lacey came across as fearful at Harry's house. She was worked up believing Sebastian's murder wouldn't be avenged. I think the possible injustice of it all was what gave her the courage to go to Harry. I didn't want her to have to re-tell it and I was worried that in that state she would miss something, something important."

"You are so patient. I would have grilled her a hundred times before I ever even considered calling for you guys," Kelly retorted.

"Well, this is going to be a real test of our family's patience as we wait for Lacey to wake up from her drunken stupor so she can tell us the rest of what she knows," Gen said.

"I think we need to get going," Kelly told them. "As much as I would love to order fish tacos, I think we need to get home and start piecing things together. Everything that has been happening cannot be a coincidence. All these things have to be connected somehow."

Kelly's stomach roared and she felt it rumble. She had eaten most of the chips and salsa, but still the hunger panged.

"We have more time," Gen said to her. "Let's order something to eat and you can tell us all about Jared while we wait for it to come out. Lacey isn't waking up for at least another forty-five minutes."

Kelly motioned for the waitress. When Melanie arrived at the table, Kelly ordered several appetizers and another round of drinks for all of them.

They want to know about Jared, where the heck do I begin? Kelly crossed her arms and pushed back into her chair preparing to be interrogated.

"Great," Gen said, "food is in and more tables have cleared out, now spill it. What exactly happened in the school with Jared?"

Kelly felt a tightening in her stomach, just the thought of the Hell Fighter made her blood boil. She could sense the anger building and had to push the memory down.

"Well, honestly it was brief, but ..." Kelly paused, trying to pull the right words together. "It was intense, that's how I would describe it."

"Intense how?" Gen inquired.

"You seem to have no problem grilling me, Genevieve!" Kelly blurted.

"We have been patient, Kell and believe me I wish I could give you an eternity of time to get through this, but unfortunately, I don't think we have it," Gen answered. Kelly saw the compassion in her sister's eyes but still felt as if she was on the hot seat.

Kelly sighed and let her arms fall into her lap as she slumped back against the chair. "I know, I know, it's just that I haven't fully wrapped my mind around it all. He's been gone for so long and I worked hard to accept that. I didn't mourn, I held on to the happiness, but now that he's here, I'm feeling exposed and unsure. Where has he been and why is he back?"

"You love him," Deb said. "He obviously loves you. This doesn't have to be a bad thing." Deb reached over and covered Kelly's hand with her own.

The warmth strengthened her. "It's just a lot to process. He was in the fire and I am assuming he used a shield to protect us when the demon exploded into true form. I have no idea how he did that. He should have been burned alive from that blast. Early on, he helped me escape so that I had a fighting chance to beat the demon, but then he showed back up and killed the newborn, like it was nothing. He shouldn't have been able to do any of those things. Then, he kissed me." Kelly felt herself drift back to that moment.

He kissed me, and in that moment all his other kisses flooded my memory as if unleashed from a hidden box. How could I have left them locked up for so long? she chided herself.

"He gave you a ring, he won't be gone for long. He'll want the promise that goes with it." Gen's statement broke Kelly's train of thought.

"Well, I hope it's soon, he needs to answer a few things," Kelly said.

"We can talk more about Jared later. What are we going to do about Lacey?" Kelly asked Gen.

"First, we need to hear her story, all of it. Not the bits and pieces I got at Harry's," Gen said.

"We also need to talk to Harry again. We need to understand what would cause Angel interference. I am unaware of anything earthly that would have that kind of power," Kelly insisted.

"I know, but he was unaware of both Sebastian and the fire," Gen stated.

"That means something is blocking signals, which I assume we give off when we are in danger. It's also blocking communication to and from Heaven?" Deb questioned.

"I agree with the blocking and interfering, but what if whatever it is, is already doing damage?" Kelly asked. "I mean, you feel the anger in the air, don't you?"

"Yes, something is causing people to inflict more damage on one another than normal," Deb said. "I've seen an increase in anger, intolerance, and cruelty. Something is brewing, but what?"

"I don't know, but brewing is a good word," Gen commented. "It's like something is stirring things up. People who would normally walk away from a fight, are engaging. People who would normally yell, are getting in physical altercations. People who normally punch, are killing. There is a definite escalation that has accompanied this heaviness in the air."

Heaviness, more like Hellishness, a precursor of things to come, Kelly suspected.

"You're right, except, it's not a consistent heaviness," Kelly said. "Today for instance, the sense of evil nearby has been strong, it started at the shoe shop and it's still here." Kelly paused as she heard police sirens approaching.

Deb pointed toward the bar. "They're coming for the drunk guy at the bar. The bartender shut him off, I've been watching them, waiting to see what would happen. He's become more belligerent and they gave up and called the police."

"The anxiety," Kelly added, "the adrenaline or sixth sense, whatever you want to call it, we feel when this heaviness occurs is real. But it doesn't last; it will suddenly dissipate, and for no apparent reason." Kelly was sure that came out wrong and that her sisters wouldn't understand, but then she saw recognition cross Gen's face.

"You're right, it does seem to come and go, and it's not attributed to us encountering something," Gen commented

"What does that mean?" Deb asked

"It means something's either combating it, or—" Gen stopped short as the police entered the restaurant heading for the bar.

"What's the matter, Gen?" Kelly asked

Gen looked around, away from the chaos of the police scene inside. "I think it's dissipating right now," Gen replied, then added "Do you feel it fading away?"

"Oh it is, I feel calm, warmth even," Deb commented.

"It's getting stronger now. I feel like something from Heaven just walked—" Kelly jolted to her feet. "Antonio, I can't believe it!" She dropped her napkin, hopped over the red velvet rope dividing the seating area from the pier, and ran. Just as she neared Antonio, he opened his arms and scooped her up.

"I can't believe it, where have you been? I've missed you. Who are you with? Is Maxine here with you? Of all places I run into you, a tequila bar, seriously?" Kelly could feel her cheeks were flush. Antonio wore loose fitting cargo shorts, boat shoes, and a white cotton shirt that looked like he just stepped off an exotic island. His bronze skin, bulging muscles, and chiseled chin commanded the adoration of every woman nearby.

"Ciao Bella," Antonio replied as he returned the warm hug Kelly had greeted him with.

Stepping back Kelly watched him lean down and lower his voice. "I wish this were a social visit, my old friend, but it's not. I've been tracking something between realms, and it's led me here, to you, to all of you." Antonio pointed past her to the table she was sharing with her sisters.

"Oh my goodness, I was so caught off guard seeing you here I lost my manners. Please, come and meet my sisters." Kelly grabbed his hand and pulled him toward their table.

As they passed the few remaining occupied tables Kelly smirked as she noticed the number of women admiring Antonio on their way by.

He is delicious, ladies. I don't blame you one bit. I get lost in his presence myself, Kelly gushed to herself.

"Gen, Deb, this is Antonio."

Gen's eyebrows arched upward. "*The* Antonio?" Gen asked with a mix of confusion and awe.

"The Arch Angel Antonio?" Deb followed.

"Yes, one in the same! Kelly sang her reply and sat down, urging Antonio to do the same.

Kelly snickered as she saw Melanie make a b-line toward their table. She had no doubt Antonio's Heavenly attributes were the reason for the waitress' renewed attention.

"Can I get you something to drink, sir?" The waitress practically cooed the request.

"Oh, no thank you. I won't be staying long, just stopping to catch up with an old friend," Antonio replied.

"Oh, just a friend," Melanie flirted while twirling her hair.

"Yes, a dear friend, but thank you for checking," Antonio answered curtly.

The dejected waitress disappeared back inside, and Kelly smiled at her friend.

"So, you are tracking something evil between realms and it brought you to us?" she asked him.

"Well, yes and no. I was tracking this energy source through realms and it brought me to this pier. I look over and there you are, in human view no less." Antonio's voice had the hint of concern and scorn at the same time.

"Well, now that you've lost it, I think you should spend the rest of the afternoon with us," Kelly insisted.

"I haven't lost it, perhaps you have?" Antonio's bright brown eyes betrayed confusion as he looked at Kelly.

"We never had it, we've just been hanging here, drinking margaritas and contemplating love, life, and happiness," Kelly replied.

Concern replaced the look of bewilderment on Antonio's face. Kelly felt her sister's anxiety levels increase, and saw it wash over him as well.

"What's going on, is the something you were following here?" Gen asked. "If it is, we can't feel it Antonio."

"Yes, if you can't sense him, then he must be cloaking, but I can see him. I don't know what he is, but he is powerful, more powerful than what should be here," Antonio relayed.

"What do we do?" Deb asked.

"We aren't exactly in a position to *do* anything right now," Gen declared.

"I have the power to drop the demon's cloak," Antonio told her. "He will probably leave as soon as he knows you can see him, but at least you'll have an idea of it. Maybe it helps you figure out why he's following you."

"Drop it," Kelly demanded.

Gen was about to protest the decision when suddenly the form of a large demon took shape at the end of the pier, leering at them. Deb shuddered at the size of him, then she projected her shield over them, a defensive reflex.

"This was a bad idea, we are vulnerable in this state, Kell," Gen scolded.

The demon was large, easily seven feet tall by Kelly's estimation. He wore a long white trench coat that covered what she guessed were multiple weapons. His green eyes pierced the dullness that clung to him. He wore his bleach blonde hair slicked back; his whole appearance made him seem translucent.

"He's not going to do anything. If he were, he would have done it already." Kelly stood and stared in his direction.

The demon rolled his eyes and shook his head back and forth, obviously agitated by the intrusion. Before she could take a step toward him, he vanished and then the remaining heaviness in the air lifted with it.

Gen stood. "We need to go home, now!" Gen walked off toward the water taxi.

Deb stood up and reached her hand out to Antonio. "It was nice finally meeting you, Antonio. Kelly has told us so much about you and your brethren. I'm sorry our visit was short-lived." He shook Deb's hand and then she turned to pay the bill.

"I'm afraid we have agitated your sisters. Not the way I was envisioning our first meeting," Antonio smiled at Kelly.

"I know, it's my risk taking that's upset them and there's a lot going on. I told you to drop the cloak because I knew you had my back," Kelly said. "Unlike us, your powers are not weakened in human form."

"I will always have your back. You are a part of our family now too. We will never forget how you risked your life to save Novo during the surge of Harac's Hellions. You were a warrior on that battlefield," Antonio recalled.

"Thank you, but you guys are the real warriors. I just wanted to help. I need to go now, but please come visit me soon. I've missed you all so much," Kelly said before giving him a brief hug.

"I will, but please, watch your back. I doubt that was the first time that demon was following you guys. A demon that powerful stalking a Guardian, it can't end well," Antonio remarked.

"My family and I will handle him, that's what we do."

CHAPTER NINE

Gen teleported to the house first, she felt her sisters arrive seconds later. She had insisted they all teleport once they were away from the water taxi and no longer in human view. Kelly had no problem with it, while Deb wanted to argue the point, but didn't.

The house was quiet. No one was in the front parlor, which is where Gen assumed Tom had brought Lacey to sleep off her drunkenness.

"Ok, where is everyone?" Kelly called out.

"Someone's in the kitchen," Deb replied.

Gen entered the kitchen to find Lacey slumped at the table next to Tom. Her shiny black hair was matted on one side of her face. Her beautiful brown eyes were glassy and bloodshot as she held an ice pack to her head. Greg sat reclined at one end of the table with his arms behind his head and his feet up on a chair.

"You don't look so hot my friend," Kelly said to Lacey.

Lacey looked like she was about to vomit. "I don't feel well. I don't think I'm made to drink alcohol."

"Well, perhaps it was the quantity," Greg offered with a smirk.

Kelly added, "Next time go with the 'less is more' approach until you build up your tolerance."

"We don't have time for this," Tom said dryly. "She can get the Drinking 101 lesson next time." Tom waved his hand back and forth between them. "Where have the three of you been? We were worried."

Lacey seemed to perk up, she lifted her head in surprise. "*Next time I come by* ... you mean I can come here after today?" she asked.

"Well it's not like we're moving anytime soon," Kelly quipped.

Tom scolded them. "You guys need to focus. You know we can't communicate with you when you're in human form. Why would you risk being in human form with all that's going on?"

"Wait," Lacey blurted out. "I didn't know you had telepathy, that is so cool. I wish I had that with my peers, but then I don't think I want anyone else in my head. Unless you can block it, can you block it out?"

Gen tried to refocus the conversation. "We really should get everyone together to hear her story, then someone can take her home to sleep off the rest of her hangover."

Gen communicated out loud with the rest of her family. "We need all you guys back at the house, we're in the kitchen. We have more information and Lacey's awake."

"Gen does that count as telepathy if you're speaking out loud?" Lacey asked, no one answered.

One by one, the rest of her brothers teleported into the room. Michael arrived last bringing Harry with him.

"Oh Lacey, you look a little pale, have you had any water?" Harry asked.

"No," Lacey replied. Harry dug a bottle of spring water out of the fridge and handed it to her.

Gen felt the heaviness in the room. *It's like storm clouds hovering,* she thought.

"Lacey, please tell us your story," Michael said.

"Wait," Gen jumped in. "We have something that just happened that we need to tell you first."

Tom's eyebrows arched upward. "Something that just happened, while you were in human form?"

"Yes, after we left the bar, we took Kelly to a restaurant on the waterfront. We were obviously in human view at that point." Gen paused, as Michael sighed heavily and Kelly rolled her eyes at him.

Deb jumped in before Gen could continue. "It was a good thing we did go there, given who we ran into."

"Who did you run into?" Frankie asked.

"I'm getting there," Gen said impatiently. "When we got to the restaurant, we were able to sit outside away from the dwindling crowd. Once we had our order, we started rehashing everything we knew so far and discussed what our next steps were going to be. We noted how the air feels heavy lately, laced with anger and hostility. Kelly was talking about the increase in demonic interference, while Deb was caught up in the sensation of evil being nearby." Gen's thoughts were interrupted as Lacey grumbled something that sounded like agreement.

"Sorry," Lacey said to Gen. "The heaviness mixed with anger, it's true. Lately, the sense of danger is so much more pronounced. And evil clings to the area, sometimes lingering long after the encounter is over. It's like the air is poisoned by the presence of something." What little color there was left in Lacey's face drained.

"What is it Lacey?" Harry asked.

"I feel it now, but—"

Gen finished her thought. "You didn't feel it earlier, before we got home. That's because something's following us and bringing it with him."

"What?" Michael bellowed. "Who's following you?" He moved toward the windows and looked outside.

Kelly offered, "Don't bother, you won't see him, he's cloaked."

Now Tom stood up and moved away from the table heading to a different window. After a moment of peering outside, he asked, "Are you sure it's cloaked? From us? What could be that powerful?"

Gen answered, "Let me finish the story and then Lacey needs to tell us about Sebastian."

Forget storm clouds, it's like a powder keg in here, Gen thought.

"Fair enough, please continue," Harry told her.

Gen began again, "As we were discussing the sensation of evil hanging in the air and how sometimes it comes and goes, we heard sirens. The police were enroute to our bar to deal with some guy who had too much to drink."

"A drunk guy at a bar is hardly cause for alarm, Genevieve," Michael said gruffly.

Gen shook her head in agreement before replying. "Then Antonio showed up and told us some demon was watching us, one we couldn't see."

"Wait, what?" Frankie asked.

"*The* Antonio?" Dan added.

Greg took his feet off the chair, his typical casual demeanor changing to vigilance.

Defensively Kelly asked, "Why does everyone keep asking me that? I only know one Antonio."

"Apparently," Gen added, "Antonio was tracking this demon from a different realm, and it led him right to the dock we were eating lunch on."

Tom was suspicious. "Antonio transitioned into human form and approached you?"

Deb answered before Kelly could. "He was in human form, but he barely made it to the entrance of the restaurant before Kelly jumped in his lap."

"I don't think it was quite like that," Kelly defended.

Gen quickly agreed with Deb. "It was a little over the top, even for you."

"Come on," Kelly remarked dryly "He's just a friend and I haven't seen him in forever."

Gen finished the story before Kelly could argue further. "Anyway, he came to the table and asked us who the demon was, and why we were in human form when such a powerful entity was nearby. Then we had to tell him we had no idea what he was talking about."

Deb added, "He offered to expose the demon, using his powers to break the cloaking and Kelly told him to do it."

Michael's sharp tone reverberated through the room. "Are you serious? Why would you do something like that? That was reckless, Kelly!"

Kelly rebuffed Michael's remarks. "If that demon wanted us dead, he would have attacked us before Antonio arrived while we were vulnerable, and unaware of his presence. I was betting something that powerful, suddenly finding itself visible, would realize what Antonio was and not want that fight."

"You gambled and got lucky today," Michael replied. "There is no guarantee that streak continues with decisions like that."

Kelly yelled back at him, "We saw the damn demon! Are you interested in that? I doubt your 'bull in a china shop' routine got you anything close to what we got today, Michael."

"Let's calm down," Deb said trying to de-escalate the rising argument. "We have more to share and I think we're traumatizing Lacey."

"I didn't know Guardians fought amongst themselves," Lacey said timidly.

"Well, not all Guardians are a ginormous Irish family," Kelly said as she plopped down at the table next to Lacey.

Breaking the momentary quiet Xavier asked Gen, "What did the demon look like?"

"And what did he do when he realized the cloak was down?" Dan added.

"Male," Gen told them. "He appeared to be more than seven feet tall, a large hulking presence. He wore a long white trench coat and his skin was whiter than an albino's. He had bleached out blonde hair that was of medium length and he wore it slicked back. He was nearly translucent, except ..." Gen paused as she recalled his face.

Lacey filled the silence. "His eyes, were they intensely green?" Her voice trembled as tears trickled down her face.

Kelly reached out and covered Lacey's hand with her own.

Gen agreed. "Yes, his eyes were a brilliant green color. Lacey, you're saying the demon we just encountered is the same one that killed Sebastian?"

Lacey nodded. "It was awful, what that demon did to Sebastian, I can't imagine the pain he must have felt."

Lacey did her best to pull herself together. She closed her eyes for a moment before launching into her story. "We had just finished recording an encounter and were making our way to meet some other Historians. Sometimes, I walk a bit to clear my head before I go home, but Sebastian didn't want any of us to walk alone anymore. Historians believe we're being targeted, even though no one else apparently believes that."

Greg interrupted her. "Why do you say that?"

Lacey was emphatic in her response. "Because if they did, they would have done something about it! We are not part of this fight, we're neutral. This should never have happened."

"She's right, Sebastian should be alive," Harry replied.

Lacey continued. "I felt something arrive and knew right away it was evil. I assumed we had happened upon another encounter. It wouldn't have been the first time that happened. We split up and I raced to a nearby hiding spot and waited. Sebastian walked just beyond the tree line out into a field. He was so brave; he didn't fear it or at least he didn't appear to."

Gen felt the onslaught of questions forming in all her brothers' minds. *Just hang in there, guys, give her the space to tell her story, her way,* Gen told them telepathically.

Lacey went on. "The entity wouldn't show himself. I felt the air tightening around me like a noose. I got so scared I called Sebastian for help, but he never moved from where he was in the field."

Lacey fought the urge to stop, the memories obviously painful, but she pushed through and kept going. "I called out to Sebastian again, but he never looked in my direction. Instead, I heard him calling my name. He was looking around as if he could no longer see me. I tried to move, but I couldn't. My legs were frozen, my arms felt pinned to my sides. My heart started to race. I yelled out again 'Sebastian, I'm here, I'm right here!' but he never turned toward me."

Lacey's face tilted away, her eyes glazed over, and her body stilled.

She's reliving it, Gen thought.

Lacey's voice quivered. "That's when I saw him, the demon, his white coat a stark contrast against the backdrop of the tree trunks. He seemed to float toward me, even though leaves rustled under his feet, I don't think they ever touched the ground. Then he smiled and my whole body shook in revulsion. A horrific shriek broke the peacefulness of that suburban wooded area. It was Sebastian, he was being attacked. I could hear his bones cracking, the sound of his lungs choking on his own blood, and the shattering sensation of being beaten. At that distance I nearly experienced his death and I could do nothing to help him, I could do nothing to help myself."

Lacey's head fell into her hands as she began to sob, and the entire room fell silent. Deb moved into the seat Tom had vacated and did her best to comfort Lacey as Kelly did the same from her other side.

Letting her grieve is the best thing we can do for her now, Gen thought.

After several minutes, Deb spoke first. "How about some tea? Gen can you put the kettle on please?"

Gen went to the stove and placed the kettle over the open flame. Pulling down a mug she dropped in a tea bag.

Now she can begin to heal, Gen thought. *We could all use a little of that.*

Deb cleared the last of the cups from the table. Once Lacey left, everyone else cleared out. Michael had warned against doing anything unsafe, but by the look on Kelly's face she knew her sister would continue bucking his advice.

As Deb passed the living room, she saw the flashy headline of breaking news come across the TV screen. Gen sat cross legged in a chair with a tablet in her lap that was streaming more news and Deb knew she would be immersed for several hours. She did not envy her sister's gift for seeing the demonic amongst those stories.

Kelly maneuvered around the study frantically sifting through piles of books, and Deb peered in to check up on her. "How's it going?" she asked.

"Fine. I'm still trying to find those books I *borrowed* from the Vatican." Kelly held up air quotes as she said the word 'borrowed' and Deb smiled.

"The Vatican has books on demons?" Deb asked.

"You wouldn't believe what the Vatican has books on," Kelly retorted.

"Alright, well I'm heading up to lie down for a bit," Deb told her. "I have a little headache. Gen's watching the news, so she'll be busy for a while."

"Do you need us to try and heal it?" Kelly offered.

"No, I'll be fine, nothing a pinch of rest can't fix." Deb smiled and left the doorway. Making her way up to the second floor she thought, *thirty minutes and I'll be good as new.*

She entered the room and felt a wave of nausea wash over her. The light gray walls were blurry, and she fumbled for the small desk chair that sat closest to her and felt a hand steady her instead.

Startled, she turned to find Marcus standing in her room, confusion took over and her thoughts were scattered.

"What are you doing here? How did you get in?" Deb asked.

His smooth voice tried to calm her. "Breathe Deb, you're fighting the sensation instead of letting it settle over you. The seasickness and brain fog will pass in a minute."

"Stop, stop doing whatever you're doing Marcus." She felt like she could barely stand and suddenly found herself sitting on the bed. Looking up at Marcus she saw the curtains from her windows billowing around him as they swayed in the air of the open window. As he loomed over her, he appeared to be wearing a cape. She shook her head to clear the jumbled thoughts away.

Just as she was about to yell out for help, the confusion receded, and she regained her vision, bringing her surroundings into focus.

"I need to speak with you in private, Deb. I have been waiting for hours outside your house for everyone to leave, I couldn't wait any longer."

"How did you know where we live?" she asked.

"I need your help, please, we need to leave here, now." Marcus held out his hand to her, but she didn't reach for it.

"I'm not going anywhere with you. Who do you think you are coming in here like this? What did you just do to me Marcus?"

He hesitated, looking back at the door almost as if he felt someone coming.

"What are you doing?" Deb asked.

She saw then that he was breathing heavy, whatever he was doing was taking a toll on him.

"Marcus, are you cloaking, is that why I felt the way I did? It won't work for long, I can see you're out of practice, you're already exhausted. It's only a matter of time before it falls and then my sisters will know you're in the house."

She watched him shake his head in agreement. "I haven't slept in days, that's why I'm exhausted. I didn't want to do it like this, I wanted you to just come with me. I'm sorry." Reaching out with both hands he grabbed hold of her upper arms and pulled her from the house.

For a moment Deb thought she was dreaming; maybe she had fallen asleep and all of this was just a mirage. The air around her was still, there was no sound, and the image of the tree-lined riverbank stood frozen as if she were looking at a picture and not standing in the actual location. Then time caught up and instantly the environment thundered to life. The wind whistled swaying the trees as the shrubs that lined the foot path rustled. The river's small waves lapped against the side of the embankment drenching the soft grass. The sun began its descent cascading yellow streaks of sunshine through the trees and over the calm water. She wasn't dreaming, she was at her favorite spot in the city, and she felt Marcus behind her.

"I don't have a lot of time. I need to know which one of you is watching over Sophia Kane?" Marcus asked.

"I see, so you thought you would come to my house, my bedroom, how did you even know that was my room by the way?"

Marcus interrupted her. "I didn't know, not until I saw the décor."

Deb stood silent for a moment debating what to say to him.

He continued, "Light gray walls with lilac laced curtains, it had to be yours, so I waited and then you came in."

"How long were you there for?" Deb asked him.

"Not long. Look, none of that matters right now. I need to know who's watching over Sophia, is it you Deb?"

"You don't get to show up, kidnap me, and then decide what matters. You said you needed my help. I didn't say I would give it to you."

"No, you didn't, and I shouldn't have barged in, but it's urgent. Please, is Sophia your charge?" he pleaded.

"It's none of your business who our charges are. You are way out of bounds here Marcus. Why don't you start answering some questions? Let's start with how you knew where I lived and since when are you able to cloak?"

"I will answer all of that and more, but Sophia is in real danger. Whichever one of you is watching over her needs to know she's being followed by a Roamer Demon.

Schlosser is bent on revenge and he thinks he can get it through Sophia."

"Revenge for what?" Deb asked.

"He claims one of you killed him unprovoked. He's back from Hell for revenge." Marcus' quiet confidence did nothing to calm the storm brewing inside her.

"What? No, we don't do that. We don't murder demons unless they attack us, which by the way, they do often. We abide by the Accord, that's how earth has been able to remain relatively demon free for thousands of years. Hell doesn't want the compact to remain in place, they want to invade earth, that's why they do everything they can to cheat and draw us in. How did he even get out of Hell in the first place? Why aren't you and the rest of your buddies investigating that?" Deb lost her patience and brushed past him. She was heading toward the brick wall that housed the steps to the bridge overhead.

She felt his hand on her wrist and turned to push him off her, but he was able to pull her into his arms.

"This isn't some joke. I need help. I came to you, and you're treating me like the enemy. I'm not the enemy here Deb," he chided.

Marcus released his grip slightly, but she could still feel the warmth of his body against hers. His dark brown eyes held her gaze with passion and she felt her heart speed up, as her hands were balled into fists against her own body. She felt a rush of adrenaline come over her, tingling the hair along the back of her neck. Her body and mind were not aligned, one wanted him, the other wanted to get away from him.

Why does everything about being in his arms seem scary, yet familiar? she wondered.

She reached up and knocked his arms away, using his body weight against him she spun him around and threw him hard against the wall. The blow sent small pieces of rocky ledge down around their feet. As he regained his composure, she pushed him back with one hand and left it open against his hardened chest.

"You've made the mistake of underestimating me, you've taken my kindness as weakness. Don't put your hands on me again, Sentinel." Deb watched the fervor in his eyes fade and turn to defeat.

A soft glow lit up the area and warmed her back, Frankie had just arrived.

Marcus had the last word. "Conversations over, I hope you pass along my message. Sophia shouldn't pay the price for whatever happened between Schlosser and you guys."

She watched Marcus teleport away as she felt Frankie approach from the side.

"You want to talk about it?" her brother asked.

"No, but I'll tell you all about it, at breakfast tomorrow." Deb walked away certain Frankie would allow her the space to work through it on her own.

CHAPTER TEN

en pushed through the door to the kitchen, despite the brewing coffee, sizzling bacon, and warmth from the hot stove, she shivered. The underbelly of tension was fermenting and the palpable nature of it chilled her. All six of her brothers and both her sisters were in the kitchen. Gen couldn't remember the last time they came together to share a meal, this was a rarity, then again so was Deb's encounter with Marcus.

"Good morning Gen, tea or coffee this morning?" Deb asked cheerfully.

"Tea would be great, thanks," Gen answered. "I didn't realize we would have a full house this morning."

Kelly's eyebrows rose. "I didn't either."

Deb moved along without missing a beat. "Friday breakfast is a standing invitation; we shouldn't need to be pushed into attendance."

Tom moved artfully around Deb in the kitchen. As she prepared eggs, Tom flipped bacon and stirred batter.

Without turning around, Tom spoke to them. "Breakfast will be ready in ten guys. Might as well make yourselves useful and set the table."

Gen noticed the extension leaves had been added to the table to accommodate the nine of them. Deb's favorite gray and white pinstriped placemats and matching napkins were already displayed. In the center of the table someone had filled two short vases with fresh lilacs from the small garden behind their house. Kelly carried two glass pitchers from the counter to the table, one with orange juice, the other with ice water.

Gen walked to the antique hutch in the corner of their kitchen and removed plates and glasses for everyone. The white plates with small gray, purple, and yellow flowers matched perfectly to the rest of the table décor. Dan carried a large handful of silverware and they walked around each other readying the table for breakfast.

For the next sixty minutes the song and dance of normalcy swirled around them. They ate breakfast together speaking little of anything remotely supernatural. Dan and Tom argued the merits of the role of technology in today's world. To Gen, Dan was a technical marvel compared to the rest of them. He was the one that kept their papers in order, changing identification when needed and paying all the bills. Though Dan was the IT genius, Tom was the legal mastermind. He handled dealing with lawyers and accountants for the many trusts they had created over the years. Gen thought of all the properties across the country that their trusts had acquired, she knew it made it easier for them to move from one side of the country to the other when they needed to. This house was by far Gen's favorite, but she knew they wouldn't be here long.

We can never stay in one place too long, Michael would never allow it, Gen thought. Memories of life with Gabriel stirred, this was their first house. Her eyes caught sight of a few of the lilac blooms drifting down upon the table, their delicate structure not meant to be jostled around. *You planted that lilac tree for me Gabe. It's still here, you should be here.* Gen shook her head slightly as if she could scatter the pain of his loss away.

Xavier, Frankie, and Greg rehashed a controversial soccer game. Gen never understood why they cared so much for a sport they rarely saw on TV in the states. Though she knew on more than one occasion the three of them had used their powers to watch a game or two live, most of the time they had to get up early to catch the playoff games on TV.

Deb and Kelly took a deep dive into who had the best pizza in town. Deb was rating the actual pizza, while Kelly was rating the pizza's accompanying appetizers and dessert. To Kelly the entire meal was part of the calculation, not just the pizza itself. Gen and Michael mostly listened, chiming in only when prompted.

Stopping to take in the scene playing out in front of her, Gen pictured that to the outside world this was nothing more than a family gathering. Conversation lingered for a while after the food was gone, and with her brothers present, the food truly was gone, there wasn't a scrap of leftovers to be had. Greg and Frankie began clearing plates. Xavier loaded up the dishwasher. Gen took a calming breath and felt the swell of foreboding wash over her.

Storm's coming, she thought. Her mind raced with an overwhelming sense something bad was coming.

Once the dishwasher was running and the voices quieted, Frankie asked. "This was great Deb, but when are we going to hear about what happened with Marcus last night by the river?"

The river was a meaningful place for Deb, a place she used to visit often with Dmitri. Gen and her sisters each had sacred places, somewhere they could go to escape the craziness of their world. Deb tended to visit scenic water ways, the riverbank, the beach, a quiet lake. Deb had often told her sisters that the serenity of the water and its natural surroundings calmed her.

Gen knew that to share that space with someone else would have been a big deal. Years ago, when Deb spent a great deal of time roaming her favorite spots with Dmitri, she and Kelly were convinced Deb had found her soul mate, everything about her and Dmitri fit. In Gen's eyes, nothing about her and Marcus fit, so hearing that she was at the river with Marcus was somewhat disappointing. Gen felt Marcus was no replacement for Dmitri. Then again, Dmitri was gone, and Marcus was here.

Strange you would agree to meet him there, Gen thought as she waited for Deb to answer Frankie's question.

Deb went to the counter and refilled her cup with tea. As she walked around the island she stopped and stood facing the table. Quietly, they awaited her response.

Gen held her breath and had to force herself to release it.

Clearing her throat Deb's first words lit the powder keg inside the room. "Last night, I opened my bedroom door to find Marcus standing in my room. He pulled me right out of the house and down to the river."

The idea that Marcus had invaded their home and dragged Deb out scared Gen. Her head swam with emotion, the clanging sound of panic disoriented her. Gen struggled to process what Deb was telling them and knew her siblings were doing the same.

How is Marcus that powerful? Gen grappled with the revelation.

Gen caught site of Michael who was the only person in the room that appeared unfazed by the revelation of Marcus' ability. In his typical business-like manner, he asked questions that Gen knew would lead the group down a rabbit hole.

"How did he know where you lived? Has he ever been here before?" Michael asked.

Deb's face fell. She was clearly disappointed that Michael would think she would ever tell anyone that kind of information. "I don't know how he knew where we lived. As far as I know he's never been here. At least, I never brought him here."

Frankie was next. "You know we have to ask the questions, Deb. Without them we can't unravel how this happened or what he actually is."

"What do you mean, *what* he is?" Deb uttered. "He's a Sentinel, everyone knows that. Are you suggesting he somehow isn't?"

"That's exactly what Frankie's suggesting," Kelly said. "That power is not an attribute a Sentinel would have, so the natural assumption is that perhaps he isn't who he says he is."

"That's ridiculous!" Deb shot back. "Guardians aren't typically immune to Hell Fighter venom either, but you are." Deb paused before making her point. "Doesn't make you something else, Kell."

"Everything is on the table when we don't know all the facts." Tom's soft tone attempted to calm Deb's defensive stance. "Deb, what happened when you got to the river? Frankie says he came to assist you when he felt your fear. Why were you afraid?"

Deb reached behind her and pulled a bar stool out to sit on. "I was confused, whatever power he used to mask his arrival at the house fogged my mind and threw me off balance. I had a literal physical reaction to it. It was an unnerving situation, I think at the river I was still trying to clear my head."

"I can only imagine," Gen told her. "Why didn't you call out to us when Marcus was in your room? Kell and I were just feet away."

Deb shook her head before responding. "It all happened so fast and at first, as crazy as it sounds, I wasn't worried. I figured he'd tell me why he was there and then leave. It wasn't until my feet hit the grass that I became anxious."

"You need to be more vigilant, all three of you actually." Michael barked his response. "You should have called out, it should have been the first thing you did, it should have been instinctive."

"I think that's a bit much, Michael," Kelly replied dryly.

A flash of impatience crossed Michael's face. "No, it's not. You know what's a bit much? The three of you running around without a care in the world as if something isn't out there trying to harm you." Michael's temper bled through his words. "Finish the damn story, what did he want?"

Gen was distracted by Michael's eyes as he held fast to Deb's position, she watched them darken with anger.

"Fine," Deb responded. "He wanted to know which one of us was watching over a charge by the name of

Sophia Kane. He said a demon was following her, which I already knew, because I was in her house when said demon showed up. The demon didn't attempt to harm her, he just rummaged through her things and then Marcus showed up and chased him away."

The weight of silence returned as Gen and her brothers tried to calculate what this all meant. Deb had just told them a Sentinel powerful enough to drag a Guardian from one location to another, chased off a demon.

What the heck is going on? Gen asked herself.

Deb continued, "It gets better. Marcus told me that the demon had just fought his way out of Hell, back for revenge."

"Revenge against who?" Tom asked.

"What did the demon look like?" Gen's own voice, barely a whisper, cracked.

Frankie asked a series of questions delaying Deb's response to Gen. "Forget about looks, did Marcus know who he was, did you hear a name? You said you witnessed him chasing the demon away, how was Marcus able to do that? And you Deb, you were able to cloak and not be seen or felt by Marcus?"

Deb answered Tom's question first. "Apparently, he's seeking revenge against me, since I'm watching over Sophia. The demon was large, ugly, bald, and stunk like death. I'm able to cloak myself with my shield in small spaces and not for very long."

Kelly interjected. "I'm sure you'll get better at it over time. But Deb, this demon is after you, yet you didn't recognize him?"

The siblings' voices faded, and Gen could feel her powers pulsating. Her head was filled with a thunderous, hammering ache. Her hands trembled as she struggled to steady herself.

It couldn't be, could it? Gen lamented internally. *It can't be him, that's impossible, he wasn't that strong, was he?* Trying to remember back to that day Gen's racing thoughts swirled for clues, was Deb talking about Schlosser? Was Deb in danger because she killed a Roamer Demon? The thought rushed through her mind nearly debilitating her.

Gen temporarily lost track of the conversation until Deb's voiced reeled her back to the present. "I overheard a whole conversation between them. It wasn't friendly. Marcus accused one of us of killing the demon." Deb paused. "Oh, his name was—"

"Schlosser," Gen interrupted. "His name was Schlosser. He's a Roamer Demon."

"That's right, how did you know, Gen?" Deb asked.

"Because I killed him, the night I saved Becky," Gen confessed.

Xavier tried to clarify. "It was self-defense though, he attacked you and you defended yourself."

Gen didn't respond.

"Genevieve O'Mara." Michael was glaring at her from across the table. "You answer that question truthfully right now. Did you kill that demon unprovoked?"

Gen shot up nearly knocking her chair to the floor. "Schlosser taunted Becky all night, literally all night. I did everything we were trained to do, and nothing worked. He wanted her blood on his hands, he wanted her unborn baby's soul!" Gen could feel her face flush with anger while her hands turned to blocks of ice. The unfairness of it enraged her all over again. Gen's power escaped her hands causing a tremor. The table shook as she clasped firmly onto the edge.

Michael stood up. "Did the demon put his hands on your charge or throw a weapon in your direction?"

Gen paused knowing the crushing weight her answer held. "No."

"What?" Xavier exploded out of his seat. "How could you have done that? You know what that means. We're all in jeopardy now."

Michael was quick to respond. "We need to move, we need to get ahead of this. I'm going to find Harry, he needs to know what she's done." He doled out marching orders, but Gen didn't hear them.

One by one Gen felt her brothers leave the kitchen, none of them saying anything to her. The absence of words carried its own judgement. She had broken trust and though they may forgive her, right now they were angry and presumably disappointed. Their reaction crushed her; she felt like a child scorned and punished.

Michael looked at her. "From now on there are no secrets, and no one goes out alone." His voice commanded cooperation. "Do the three of you understand?"

Kelly answered, "That's fine, but I personally don't understand why everyone's so worked up over this. I have no issue with what Gen did. I'm sure he deserved it, let him come, let him find out what we'll do for an encore." Kelly had slid out of her chair and was standing beside Gen facing off against Michael.

Michael was in combat mode, he had reeled in the brief escape of emotion. "We need to remain calm, the last thing we need is for you to run around starting a war. I'm heading out. Kelly, see if you can reach Antonio, find out if he knows anything more about the demon trailing you guys. We need information: are the demons following you working with Schlosser or not?"

Kelly rolled her eyes. "It's not like I can just ring up an Arch Angel." After a moment she sighed. "I'll try and get him a message." Before leaving she squeezed Gen's arm in a show of support.

With Kelly dispatched, Michael turned his attention to Deb. "You should—"

Deb shook her head. "No, I'm coming with you. We aren't going anywhere alone, remember?"

"No!" Gen cried out. "It should be me, Deb. I'm the one that should be cleaning this up."

Michael's stern voice stopped Gen cold. "No, you need to remove yourself from this, you've done enough damage as it is, Genevieve." Michael's response stung. "If you're coming Deb, I'm leaving now in human form." Michael walked out of the kitchen toward the front door.

Deb turned to Gen. "I can't believe you didn't tell us. How could you not have told Kelly and me? I defended you to Marcus, I told him he was wrong, that we wouldn't risk breaking the Accord by murdering beings unprovoked." Deb walked to the kitchen doorway and turned back. "You need to think this through, you aren't in a good place, Gen."

Deb turned away from Gen, walking briskly toward Michael. Silently Gen screamed at them, *I haven't been in a good place for forty years!*

CHAPTER ELEVEN

Deb kept pace with Michael, but she was curious to know why they were walking. They were no longer in human view, yet they were meandering through the small cramped streets as if they were.

"Why are we walking, Michael?" Deb asked. "Better yet, where are we walking to?"

"I need to collect my thoughts, I need to be prepared to make a valid argument on her behalf and I have no idea if it's going to work," he answered.

"We've been to several places," Deb thought out loud. "It's Friday, why don't we head to St. Ann's Church. Father Donovan may already be setting up for quiet hour, more times than not Harry attends."

Deb stopped walking when Michael didn't answer. She was frustrated with his lack of cooperation. "Hello, I'm not one of our brothers, you need to communicate with me before we keep going."

Ten paces in front of her, she watched him stop and slowly turn around to face her. His voice laced with impatience he asked, "What? We don't have time for this, we need to keep moving."

"Stop talking to me like I'm a child, I'm not, none of us are," Deb told him.

"Well, if one of you hadn't just acted like a petulant child then maybe I wouldn't need to speak this way."

Before Deb could respond, Michael held up his hands in surrender and walked back toward her. "Look, I know you're not a child, I just can't believe she did this. It's not like her, it's reckless, against her better judgement. I can't make sense of that."

Deb paused before answering. "Maybe we've been wrong, maybe she's not the rock we all like to pretend she is."

"What do you mean?" he asked.

"Maybe the loss of Gabriel has been slowly eating away at her this whole time, eroding something, perhaps she's nowhere near over it."

Michael let out a deep breath. "I know how hard she took losing Gabriel. I know the lengths to which she went to find him. She literally walked the earth looking for him. I'm the one who brought her collapsed body back from that desert, remember? That doesn't justify what she's done, Deb."

"I'm not arguing it does. I'm just saying, maybe we thought she was alright because that's what we wanted, for her to be fine." A look of guilt washed over him as she continued. "Never talking about it or volunteering to help when she would go out on every wild goose chase to follow leads, maybe it kept her from healing."

"I don't know, Deb. I don't. Right now, what I do know is that we need to find Harry. I'm out of ideas, we've been to his house, to Jake's, to all his local hangouts and there's been no sign of him. Let's go with your gut and head to the church." Michael turned and walked away, the conversation was over.

Well that was unexpected, Deb thought. Rarely does Michael speak of such things, emotions were an impairment in his view. Catching up to him again, she fell back in lock step as they made their way through a well trafficked area and over to the neighborhood where St. Ann's was located.

The treelined street with wide pristine sidewalks calmed her, she didn't know if Harry would be at the church yet, but any opportunity to visit was welcome. As they neared the entrance she couldn't tell if it was open. Getting closer she spotted the dark wood grain of the doors tucked in the bedrock of the building's surface and knew the doors were shut and most likely locked.

Michael walked past the front steps. The polished gray cement ran the length of the structure with its majestic decorated stone face and tall steeple reaching for Heaven. He entered through the large wrought iron gate that would lead them to the gardens that ran along the side and back of the property. The Archdiocese owned several acres of land adjacent to the church. For years residents pitched in to clear the land of large boulders, overgrown shrubs, and dead bushes. Deb remembered that it had been one of the first things Gen had volunteered to help with when they first relocated back to this area after a long absence.

We thought we lost you Gen, but somehow this garden brought you back to us, maybe it gave you a purpose, Deb thought.

The community had left intact a labyrinth of worn out paths that wound their way up and down the sloping landscape. Each path guaranteed a magical journey around some of the city's oldest trees: oak, sycamores, white pines, and sugar maples. The jagged placement of the trees and the sloping inclines made the property feel more secluded than it was. The ground was littered with sap-laden needles and seeds of flowers just opening. The red oak burst into orange and red in fall while the sycamore's soft yellow leaves cascaded light in the spring. The large floral heavy garden just outside the side entrance flourished under the watchful eye of the administrators who helped Father Donovan with maintenance and new plantings.

The scent of jasmine lightly swam through the air while the early blooms of blue crocus and yellow daffodils dotted the stone walkway to the back. The sound of water gently lapping in the ornate stone birdbath up ahead echoed quietly toward them.

Such a remarkable place, one of many if you know where to look, Deb mused.

Michael walked to the side door and turned the knob, it didn't open. "Is it unusual for all the doors to be closed and locked at this hour?" he asked.

"Honestly, I don't think I've ever been here this early," Deb told him. "Father Donovan could be running late this morning. What's the plan, are we going in human view? If not, what do we need the doors to be open for?"

"Use your powers and go inside to look around." Michael peered up toward the treelined hillside. "I'm going to look around out here, there's a lot of ground to cover, so stay open so we can hear each other."

Michael made his way around the bird bath water feature and disappeared up the first path. Deb knew he would go to the highest peak to get the best vantage point. The yard was shaped like a round, top-heavy tree with sprawling bushes and dwarfed red maples dotting the area closest to the church. To the right, just past the back entrance, there was another small gate attached to a stout stone wall that separated the yard from a historic burial ground. Before heading inside the church Deb looked through the trees one more time for Michael and couldn't see him. He was in a militant frame of mind, the advantage would be his should any unexpected visitor show up.

Deb used her powers to teleport inside the church. With the main lights off, emergency lighting dimly lit the alter and front of the church. The only other light came from sunshine seeping through stained glass. She saw no one. Going on instinct she walked toward the alter because it felt like the correct direction. If a human were here, they would most likely be working to get ready for service later, so they should be in the sacristy, the room behind the alter.

She crossed over into the middle aisle and proceeded straight ahead. The church was old, maybe one of only a handful of originals left in the city. There weren't many left like this one. Most of the ornate churches had been sold off and replaced with luxury apartments.

Deb took in the intricately carved marble statues that adorned the back wall of the elevated alter. Out of the corner of her eye she noticed shadows dancing along the bronze railing, slivers of candlelight were coming from the devotional stand. Through the air she could smell the remnants of incense mixed with candle wax. As she gazed upward, she caught site of the large crucifix that hung from heavy chains bolted to the ceiling. The eyes of the statue penetrated through her and she took in a deep breath.

You must save her, please God don't let anything bad happen to Gen, Deb silently pleaded.

The darkness behind her brought a chill and she circled around half expecting to find someone standing behind her, but there was no one.

Turning back toward the alter she spoke to Michael. His silence was unnerving. "Michael, what's happening out there? Someone was here at some point, there are candles lit already, but no one is here now. There is nothing else to report from inside."

Except for me scaring myself that is, she silently quipped.

She started to walk on but stopped when no response came.

"Michael, can you hear me?" Every fiber of her being stilled. "Answer me, please."

No response.

Her body shot into action, she darted between the breaks in the pews back toward the side entrance by the yard where she had left him. It would be faster to teleport, but she wouldn't know what she was teleporting into if she didn't look outside first. Hastily heading for the exit her eyes nearly missed the cascading darkness that pursued her.

Something is here with me Michael, it hasn't manifested yet, Deb telepathically told him.

As she went to look out the window nestled in the top of the door she had to turn away. Her eyes burned from the bright light outside.

What on earth is that? she wondered.

Pushing hard against the locked wooden door did nothing, it wouldn't budge. She turned around preparing to run to another exit. The being standing behind her nearly crushed her. She gasped. The demon towered over her, he was at least eight feet tall, the veins on his face were raised, bulging lines as if his body were filled with tar instead of blood. He wore a black cloak over black clothing, he was the embodiment of darkness. He said nothing, he just stared at her with his head tilting slowly from side to side as if trying to gage her level.

"Who are you and what do you want?" Deb knew her words lacked the confidence needed to intimidate a being this ominous.

His wide shoulders were partly covered by his black hair. His long cloak billowed in the windless space between them as if it were a living creature. Perhaps it is, thought Deb. She was within inches of him, yet she couldn't hear him breathing, everything about him was quiet and dark, except his eyes; he had the same eyes as the demon Antonio exposed. The demon floated just above the red carpet and slowly bent forward narrowing the small distance between them.

Leering into her eyes he asked in a deep and raspy voice, "Where's my brother?"

Deb shook her head. "Who's your brother? Better yet, what have you done to mine?"

The being raised an eyebrow in her direction, his green eyes peering into hers. "Clever, but I don't have time for this. I just want to know what you know. Now give me your thoughts." The being raised his hand to her forehead as if to touch her. Deb pushed back against the door frame. He left his hand in the air palm down hovering just above her head. Feeling him trying to penetrate her mind sent a shockwave of panic through her body. She instinctively put up her arms and sent her shield toward him. Even if it didn't knock him down, she hoped it would be enough to escape.

The figure slid back away from her, stunned. Then he swatted in the air as if annoyed by a small insect. "Enough you foolish thing. You want to go outside and join your friend, so be it."

Deb watched him raise his arm as if to strike her, she threw her forearms around her head to lessen the blow that never came. He lifted her body off the ground and threw her across the room, where she landed hard against a pew. Before she could catch her breath, she was hoisted up and sent flying through the air once again. She felt her back and shoulders crash through the door first. As she grappled with nausea, she felt the darkness lift and the brightness of outside envelop her.

The fresh air blew onto her face and she saw the green grass coming up to meet her much too fast. As she hit the ground she attempted to curl up and roll with the impact, but she wasn't fast enough. Pain surged through her and she felt close to passing out. The ringing in her ears muffled the sounds outside. Every image was streaked with red as blood dripped down her face from an open wound. There was a lot of movement and the thumping vibration of something running toward her scared her into lucidity.

She wrapped her shield around herself and hoped it would be enough to stop whatever was heading her way. As her eyes adjusted to the brilliance of the sunny day, she caught site of a demon rushing at her. When he bounced off her shield and rolled down toward the church, she realized just how far she had been thrown.

Stumbling to a standing position she heard the faint roughness of Michael's voice yelling to her. "Deb, run to

Harry, to Harry. He's behind you, project your shield Deb, now!"

In one sharp breath she took in the scene, Michael was much further up ahead battling multiple demons at once. Deb could sense their Hellish nature. The demons were moving quickly, but she caught glimpses of ragged clothing, pale hairless skin, and black combat boots. Michael's shirt had been torn off, his mark, the Shield of Trinity, was ablaze across his back. She turned behind her and saw the back of Harry's head, he was just beyond the gate's entrance. With him, were the two angels that Deb had previously seen with Marcus. Harry was urging the angels to run through the gate and out onto the street. The angels didn't move. They looked shell shocked, both faces were crumpled in horror as they witnessed the carnage of the demons' attack. Harry must have felt her looking at him and turned toward her.

"Go help your brother, Deborah, I've got this, go." Harry pointed past her toward Michael.

Turning back to Michael, Deb saw the demon that Antonio had revealed to her and her sisters lurking in the far-right corner near the cemetery gate. He stood looming over the scene, yelling at the demon she had just encountered inside the church.

Demons seemed to be everywhere.

Deb ran toward Michael, as a demon leaped toward her, he too bounced off her shield and rolled away from her. This time she took the opportunity to grab the weapon he had dropped. It was a short makeshift knife with a crude serrated blade, but it would have to do.

Deb, stop, go back. Use your powers to get to Harry. Michael's voice was steady, but she heard it lack the gusto it normally held.

I can barely stand, Michael. My head, it's jumbled from the fall. I think I have a concussion, she told him. *I can barely keep my shield in place, there is no way I can teleport, can you?*

No, the demons are too close, if I try, they'll just come with me and drain my strength. Go to Harry, he can't defend himself against this many Gutter Demons. The area is being cloaked, Deb. You need to get to Harry. Michael was firm.

Gutter Demons, of course, that's why they're moving so fast, they only know one fighting technique: the swarm. Her mind was clearing but the lifting haze clarified and sharpened the pain coursing through her. Her left shoulder burned from her mark, its glow shining through her top, just as Michael's was.

The demons chased her down and as she attempted to turn back, they encircled her. Two of them were young, she could tell by the brightness of their skin and the small tint of color still left in their eyes. The third one was old, his gray skin and translucent eyes the stuff of legend. Deb knew Gutter Demons lived in the wasteland outside the gates of Hell, swarming and pillaging for survival, but they were fast and resourceful. She couldn't remember encountering them before, but her memory would be unreliable right now anyway.

She swung up and through the first demons jaw, knocking him off balance he bumped into one of the others allowing her to kick the third one to the ground. Before he could rebound off his knees, she used the jagged blade to slice his neck. It would be a slow death as the dark blue essence sprang from his injury.

She turned back to the other two and plunged the blade several times into each of them. She hit their arms, chest, and face sending thin fluid splashing over them. She pulled the blade back and wiped it on her pants, but it didn't burn. She was half expecting it to be like Hell Fighter venom, but it was the opposite. The cold liquid was runny, and it made her attempted quick movements sloppy and haphazard.

She heard Michael in her head. *Don't waste movement, Deb. Strike them in the neck and the high thigh area pulling vertically, not horizontal, like humans those two spots carry the majority of what's keeping them alive.*

Michael's voice calmed her, and she struck the demons exactly where he instructed, successfully taking them down. She moved on toward Michael thinking that the two of them touching would be strong enough to break the cloaking but, encountered two more demons. With each kill she managed to pick up a new weapon, in her hand now was a piece of the Chain of Chaos. She swung the chain in the air and managed to land it across three demons at once. One demon lost his head, while another grabbed his throat falling to the ground, and the third tried to hold in his stomach, but it was too late; the chain had gouged a hole nearly straight through him.

She moved on picking up a dagger, this was more her type of weapon; lightweight and small she wouldn't need a large distance to wield it. The fight was daunting as she swiped, stabbed, and clawed away at them. One by one they fell to her, but not without extraordinary effort. Falling to her knees several times she was able to peer in between the twisting and turning of battle to catch glimpses of Michael in a turmoil of his own.

How are we going to get out of this Michael? Deb implored.

She heard her brother's reply echo in her head. *Steady yourself, Deb. I don't think the two of us reaching each other is going to be enough to break the cloaking. I think one of us needs to touch Harry, we need a piece of divinity. I'm heading your way as fast as I can.* Deb heard the slight tremor in his voice and it scared her.

She furiously slashed at one of the demon's legs bringing the Gutter Demon down. She took the opportunity to move past the female demon to head downhill, but the demon was fast. She caught up to Deb and pulled her back by the hair. Violently, the female demon tossed Deb toward the church. Rolling wildly, Deb hit the far end of the bird bath slowing her momentum but not stopping her. She tumbled to a halt just near the side door. It wasn't with the same force the first demon struck her with, but she was now farther away from both Harry and Michael and struggling to catch her breath.

Deb crawled to the church wall and used her hands to walk herself back up to a standing position. She saw Michael stumbling awkwardly toward Harry with several demons on his back. Each demon was stabbing, clawing, and biting their way into his skin. Fear propelled Deb off the building and sent her staggering toward Michael, but she stopped short when she heard Harry's agonizing scream.

Her boots covered in Gutter Demon blood she slid to a stop and turned left toward Harry, his head ablaze in demonic fire. Someone had doused him with Hell Fighter venom. His body swayed back and forth teetering on collapse, his hands trying to tamp down the flames, only to catch fire themselves.

Deb screamed, her world folded in on itself. *This is it, we're not going to make it.* Her own fear cascaded down upon her, a wave of self-defeat, was a crushing blow.

She heard Michael's voice just as he tore off the last of the demons on top of him and slid down the hill toward Harry's collapsed body. *Once I touch him project your shield Deb.*

No! Michael, don't touch him, you're sure to catch fire! she pleaded.

Michael was able to get within a few feet of Harry. At this distance, free of the demons he had been carrying, Deb was able to see the entirety of Michael's wounds. He was covered in blood, dirt blanketed his clothing, and she could see gouges up and down his spine. Several short-bladed weapons protruded from his leg and waist. On the side of his head, there were sections where his hair had been ripped out, bloody bald spots now covered his scalp. She could hear his thrashing heartbeat, the pain coursing through his body reverberated as her own.

As a demon lunged toward Michael, he spoke to Deb. *Don't be afraid, you are much stronger than you know, Deb. They will come, family always does, remember that.*

Michael dove forward covering Harry's body with his own and was consumed by the fire. Deb projected her shield and held her breath. Seconds passed as the demon flying made impact. He was aiming to come down on top of Michael, his crooked sword bent out in front. As the demon bounced off the shield she had projected, she noticed that a weight had lifted from the scene. Looking toward the street she heard cars and people talking, the cloak that had enveloped the church and surrounding gardens was broken.

It worked Michael, it worked! she yelled to him but there was no reply.

Marcus arrived behind the two angels. Deb knew he never saw her, and she watched him take Leo and Lucas and leave the scene immediately. Deb's breaths were growing shorter and the pain was causing small black spots to dance throughout her vision.

She shook her head to scatter them away and called out to her siblings, "Help! Michael and Harry are dying! Hurry!"

Deb stumbled toward the burning heap in the center of the yard, not sure what she would find when she reached her brother and Harry.

As she neared them, demons sprinted toward her, continuing to attack. She lifted her blade to fight one but didn't have to, his throat was sliced from behind. She watched his decapitated head fall to the ground and roll away from her. When she looked up, she saw Frankie's forehead creased with concern staring down at her. All her siblings had arrived and were now engaged with the demons.

"Deb, where's Michael?!" Frankie demanded.

She shook her head, tears stung her eyes, she couldn't speak so she pointed instead. The fire had all but burned out now, the shield starving it of its power. She continued toward the bodies growing more and more afraid with each step.

Kelly was yelling, "Don't touch that, Deb, it's Hell Fighter venom, you'll burn."

Deb knew her siblings had yet to grasp what was happening. Deb felt her stomach roll. Just as she neared the grisly heap two beings arrived above her brother and Harry. Their faces were obscured under oversized hooded sweatshirts. Reaching down, the two entities pierced Deb's shield with ease and pulled the bodies up into their arms. They took a step or two back, half-dragging, half-carrying Michael and Harry. Before she could process what was happening, the two beings took her brother and Angel and disappeared as quickly as they had arrived.

Deb's mind reeled in confused terror and she collapsed to her knees.

Looking up, Deb yelled after them, "No! Don't you take them! No! No! No!" Her lungs burned, and her body quaked.

"Michael!" Deb's scream brought her siblings to a standstill.

CHAPTER TWELVE

Gen watched in horror as Deb collapsed to the ground screaming Michael's name. She was yelling at two beings who had just hauled away bodies from the hillside.

"Deb get up, there are too many demons, you need to keep fighting!" Gen yelled to her sister.

Gen saw no movement, it was as if Deb was frozen in that spot.

This was Gen's worst nightmare, every terrible moment she had ever felt before could not compare to the utter agony coursing through her. She knew by Deb's body language, the wounded burning bodies that had just been taken were Michael and Harry.

What have I done? Gen thought in horror.

Gen watched Kelly wrap her arms around Deb and help her to her feet. She needed to get to them, but her trembling legs were slow to move.

How can I make this right? I need to find them, I need to bring them back. Oh God let them be alright, Gen agonized.

Gen snapped out of her anguish when two Gutter Demons pounced on her. She viciously slashed at their throats, missing one but killing the other. The first Gutter

Demon swung a crooked piece of metal toward her shoulder. Her skin slit open, blood burst out of the gaping wound and splashed onto the ground. When he pulled back and lunged again, she used his body weight against him grabbing hold of his torn-up shirt and pulling him down, tossing his body to the ground and away from her. Once below her, she quickly made her way on top of him, jabbing her blade through the back of his neck and taking him out. Looking up, she noticed the path between she and her sisters had been temporarily cleared by her brothers. Gen leapt up to her feet and began to run toward Kelly and Deb. As she neared them, she glanced to her right and spotted the demon that Antonio had revealed to them and stopped to stare in his direction. Her heart sped up, while her head spun with the throbbing pain of confusion and loss. Looking over at these giant larger-than-life demons flooded her with anger. Every step she took sent vibrations through the ground; she could feel the swell of hatred bubbling up.

Gen's head was a minefield. *Did you do this to my family? Are you with Schlosser? What do you want?*

A second demon, wearing all black stood next to the first, each pair of luminescent eyes tried to intimidate her. She met their gaze and held it, but before she could yell toward them the first demon, the one with the white coat looked away.

"Enough, you have failed us!" the first demon bellowed to the Gutter Demons still streaming from a portal one of them must have opened.

Gen saw the second demon, the one enraptured in black, wave his arm swiftly out in front of him and then felt the ground shift underneath her. A strong wind whipped through her and the accompanying dust seemed to disintegrate every demon on the field. One by one the Gutter Demons decayed and turned to ash. The frantic screeching of the demons was distorted by the whistling wind that came crashing down upon them. The force of the green-eyed demon's power knocked all her siblings to the ground, only Gen remained on her feet.

Gen heard the one in black say to the other, "They don't know anything. I already checked the female Guardian inside the church."

The white coat demon responded, "Something powerful enough to pierce a Guardian's shield just took the strongest one off the field. We aren't the only things here hunting them down, perhaps whatever that was shouldn't be here either."

Gen pushed through her fear and walked toward them as she heard Tom's warning in her head, *Gen be smart, keep your distance, wait for us. They're more powerful than anything we've ever encountered.*

Gen yelled to the demons, "Who was that? Who took our brother?"

The first demon vanished, using his powers he faded into a cloud of dust and disappeared. The one in black looked over at Gen. "Return our brother and we'll go. Do not, and your world will end."

The second demon turned his back to Gen and melted into a wall of shadows that seemed to drift up and out of sight.

"What the Hell is going on? What happened?" Kelly asked.

Tom answered, "I don't know, I don't know what they are."

Dan asked, "How are we going to figure out who has their brother if we don't know who they are?"

"We should get out of here." Xavier looked around the yard. "We don't know what might arrive next and we're all a little roughed up."

"No Watcher, there's not even a hint that one was ever here," Greg told them.

"I know, that is strange. I think Xavier's right, we should make a quick exit," Tom told them. "Let's get Deb home and healed up so we can talk through this."

Gen and Kelly used their powers to bring Deb back to the house. They arrived in the kitchen. Kelly pulled out a chair and gently sat Deb on it. Gen felt useless, she could barely move herself she was so stunned.

Kelly quickly made her way toward the cabinet.

"What are you doing Kell? Let's just heal her," Gen stated.

Kelly continued to rummage. "We will. Her hands and body are unstable. We need to calm her nerves as much as we can, otherwise she won't be able to handle the strain of the healing. That could cause things to heal incorrectly and cause more damage." She moved on to the bottom cabinets and then returned with a bottle of Irish whiskey. Removing the cap Kelly took a quick sip, then handed the half-filled bottle to Deb. Their sister paused, but then shakily grabbed the bottle and took a swig. Deb's face contorted and scrunched up. She let out a half-breath, half-cough accompanied by a trickle of blood.

"Good, now take a few deep breaths and try to calm your racing heart, Deb," Kelly instructed.

A slight change come over Deb; the whiskey had helped, her convulsing slowed to a shake. Though she was panting, her breathing got steadier.

"That was a good idea, Kell," Gen told her.

"Sometimes I have them," Kelly quipped.

A small smile flashed across Deb's face before an assault of pain crumbled it away. The moaning nearly made Gen cry, her sister was obviously severely injured internally from that battle.

Gen and Kelly stood over Deb attempting to heal her. They were drained from the fight, and Deb was weak from the trauma, so the healing was taking too long to be effective.

Gen's patience ran out. "This is taking too long. Why aren't they back here yet? We need Frankie to boost our powers."

"Frankie get your butt over here already," Kelly barked.

Frankie arrived behind them moments later sporting a black eye of his own. He looked a little pale, but he put a hand on each one of their shoulders. Gen could feel his power enter her body, the healing strength she sent Deb magnified and she watched her sister's wounds begin to heal and fade. It took more time to get all the internal injuries sorted, but Gen felt relief when she realized Deb would be alright.

Stepping back Gen stared at Deb. On the surface she looked good as new, but she knew Deb was anything but.

Gen had been so focused on healing Deb that she missed the rest of her brothers setting up a command post in the kitchen. There was a large white board placed in front of the double French doors out to the yard. Greg and

Dan were standing in front of it creating some sort of timeline. Xavier and Tom were comparing notes they had scribbled in a notebook.

"What's going on?" Kelly asked them.

"We're going to try and work backward to piece this together, maybe we can unlock something we've overlooked," Dan answered.

"Can you tell us what happened, Deb?" Tom asked her. Everyone turned their attention to Deb. She sat quietly in the seat Kelly had placed her in. *She looks so frail and lost,* Gen thought.

"I can try, it's still so foggy and everything happened so fast," Deb replied.

"Do the best you can, it's all we have right now," Frankie told her.

Gen fell into silence with the rest of her siblings during Deb's horrifying retelling of what happened. Deb spent the next hour answering the barrage of questions her brothers threw at her.

You are so much stronger than me, Deb, thought Gen. *There is no way I could have sat through this near interrogation like you just did.* Deb was emotional yet amazingly resilient under the pressure.

Gen's brothers periodically added to the board with notations of who, what, when, and where. It felt like an excruciatingly long exercise that Gen knew no one wanted to be a part of.

I can't believe this. I can't believe they're gone. Gen's mind drifted, she came back to the conversation when she felt Kelly healing her shoulder. Up until that moment she forgot all about her own injuries.

"I'm sorry, were you talking to me? I drifted off," Gen said.

"What else do you know about Schlosser?" Tom asked.

"Nothing really. He gave off the aura of a Roamer Demon. He was after Becky, he seemed to be able to read her mind, use her worst memories against her. I tried countering, but I wasn't in the car. I don't know if that made a difference or not."

"You stayed on the roof of a car all night?" Greg asked.

"Yes, I didn't want to lose her, I couldn't lose her, she'd been through enough."

"That must have taken a tremendous amount of your energy to stay up there and concealed from the demon," Greg commented.

"Yes, I think we've concluded I made the wrong call already. And now this, I know it's my fault. None of this would have happened if it hadn't been ..." Tears rushed to Gen's eyes as she choked on the end of her words and stopped talking.

"Don't do that to yourself, Gen," Kelly told her. "We don't know that these demons have anything to do with Schlosser."

"I just can't get it out of my mind. I should have gone with Michael, that should have been me on that field, not Deb, not Michael, not Harry!" Gen's voice cracked.

"You would have been dead and so would they," Deb told her. "I projected my shield, and it worked, the demons were bouncing off, but then ..."

"But then what, Deb?" Kelly asked her.

"But then, they were taken. How did someone pierce my shield, how did they get through?" Deb was shaking her head, there would be no answers tonight.

"We should stay in pairs as Michael suggested and split up into teams." Tom was doing his best to fill Michael's shoes, but it was a lot to ask. "We need to get out there and see what people know."

Gen never realized how lost they would be without Michael. His leadership had carried them through every battle. How were they supposed to just carry on without him now?

"I'll take Dan and meet up with the closest Guardians to see if they can lend a hand," Xavier told him.

Greg added, "I'll head out with Frankie to find Lacey, perhaps she can help. Maybe she can find out why no Watcher was at the scene today."

Tom looked at Gen. "What are you three doing?"

Kelly answered first. "I'm getting food and taking them with me."

"No, I need to lie down, I don't feel well. I haven't slept in days and I'm too drained to do anyone any good out there," Gen told him.

"Fine," Tom said. "Deb you should go with Kelly. Food will help your energy for continued healing. I'll stay here with Gen."

"Maybe we can find Marcus and get some information," Deb said.

"Are you sure, Deb?" Gen asked. "Are you up for going out tonight?"

Deb paused before answering. "I couldn't sleep even if I wanted to right now. A distraction would be welcome while I process all this."

Tom shook his head in understanding. "I will stay and work here in the library. There's a lot of research to be done. Make it a quick cheeseburger, Kell. I could use the help back here."

Gen was the first to leave the kitchen and make her way upstairs. She closed the bathroom door and took a deep breath. The quiet of the house felt like a hammer of regret. She slipped into a hot shower and quickly found herself on the tile floor quietly sobbing into her hands.

Please, please, please, don't let anything happen to Michael and Harry. I just can't take it. I can't take another loss, I can't. I won't make it, I'm not strong enough. Gen's muddled brain snapped free when the hot water cooled. She had remained in the shower so long her fingers pruned.

She turned the shower off, made her way into her bedroom to the warmth and comfort of pajamas, and collapsed into bed. She wasn't expecting to be able to sleep—she told her siblings she needed to stay behind so she could be alone—but sleep enveloped her swiftly.

Deb could see Jake's Bar up ahead and felt Kelly pick up her pace. "You are practically vibrating with excitement."

"I'm just really famished," Kelly told her. "I'm always a little hungry, but then after an intense battle like that one, I'm almost ravenous."

"There's a line already?" Deb commented.

"No worries, we always get in," Kelly told her.

"No, I know you always get in, but why is there a line this early?" Deb asked aloud.

"What do you mean this early, it's Friday night," Kelly answered.

Deb stopped and looked up at the sky, it was dark. "What time is it?"

Kelly dug a cell phone out of her bag. "It's like dinner time."

"You always think it's dinner time. I see you didn't have your cell phone on again huh?" Deb remarked.

"I always forget" Kelly pressed the button on the phone and lights flashed indicating it still had some battery life. "The stupid thing shuts off when it's running low."

"I'm pretty sure it's supposed to do that," Deb commented.

"There." Kelly held the phone out to display the time for Deb. "Seven o'clock on the dot."

"What? That can't be right," Deb told her. "I left the house with Michael at eleven this morning."

"Yeah, that's about right," Kelly nodded.

"That fight did not even last an hour," Deb told her.

"Do you know what time you got to the church?" Kelly asked.

"Maybe 1:30, the sun was out, it was really bright on that field. Inside the church the sun was beaming through the stained-glass windows."

"Okay, let's stay calm and walk this through, Deb."

"I know we were not there for hours on end." Deb's mind was racing

"Let's say you're correct, that the encounter started around 2:00 pm and you think it took how long?" Kelly inquired.

"Maybe twenty or thirty minutes. It all felt like it was happening really fast, and I was getting my ass kicked left and right, but I would say no more than thirty minutes."

"We brought you back to the house just before 6:00 pm," Kelly said. "So, you were at the church for four hours."

"No, no way. That is not true!" Deb shook her head back and forth and put her hand over her mouth.

"Well, let's assume you're right, that you were only there an hour." Kelly started to pace in front of her. "That would mean, either you were unconscious for three hours or, you lost time."

"But it couldn't just be me that lost time. There is no way Michael, as strong as he is, would be able to fight Gutter Demons for four hours straight," Deb told her.

"This is a clue, Deb. They didn't just cloak that scene, they altered time. That means time inside the cloaking field is different from time outside the perimeter."

"Why would they alter time? Better yet, how did they do it?" Deb asked.

"I'm not sure, but the Gutter Demons, you said they were fast and were able to swarm." Kelly didn't wait for an answer. "Maybe the altered time was to accommodate them."

Deb felt her forehead crease, either her head was still concussed, or she was lost in this conversation. "I'm not following."

"Think about it." Kelly paused. "We don't see Gutter Demons on earth for a reason, the essence their bodies thrive on is in the wasteland. If I remember right, they are not an earth-bound species."

"So, the green-eyed demons altered or slowed time to ensure the Gutter Demon's essence didn't dissolve or die off?" Deb was catching on.

"Yes, that's what I think," Kelly said, "but, I won't know until I get back to the house with Tom and research it some more." Come on, dinner is waiting. Deb felt Kelly pull her by the arm across the street.

"Shouldn't we go home?" Deb asked. "This seems an important revelation."

"I think better on a full stomach. Besides, who's to say you didn't have this realization because you were free of the witness stand our brothers just had you on," Kelly retorted.

As they walked up to the front of the restaurant, the door opened and standing before them was Marcus.

"Brilliant and scary that you are here, Marcus." Kelly's sarcastic greeting didn't seem to affect him.

"We need to talk," Marcus said to Deb.

Deb heard Kelly in her head. *You want to be alone with him or no?*

Deb turned to Kelly and purposely spoke out loud so Marcus could hear her. "It's all good Kell, go on inside. The couple at the bar closest to this window are about to leave."

"I totally need that power," Kelly quipped then added. "You two stand right here and don't go anywhere." As Kelly passed Marcus to enter the restaurant, she made eye contact with him. "Show up uninvited again to our house and attempt to drag my sister away and I'll have an Arch Angel rip you in half and feed you to the Hellions in the wasteland." Kelly flashed a quick smile before turning to speak to the bouncer and enter the bar.

"She's delightful," Marcus said to Deb.

"She's probably not kidding," Deb shot back.

"I'm sure they're upset, as are you, but I've been out looking for you. I didn't want to go back to your house, for obvious reasons." Marcus nodded his head in Kelly's direction. "How is your brother?"

Deb saw Kelly hop up on the bar stool just inside. Deb stepped diagonally backward to give Kelly a better view without having to turn in her chair.

"You saw Michael in that field?" Deb asked him.

"Yes, I have been looking for you, I wanted to make sure he was safe. I know he can handle himself and all, but the place was overrun—"

Deb interrupted him. "With Gutter Demons, I know." Deb paused. "I was there. I saw you come and take those two Gifter Angels out of the yard, but you left Harry and Michael and me behind." A tear streamed down her face.

A terrified look of realization came over him. "Deb, I didn't know you were there, I swear."

"Doesn't matter, you saw my brother there, you left him to die." She felt anger stir inside her but lashing out at him made her feel worse somehow.

"You can't think that. Not after everything we've been through this past year." Marcus pleaded.

"Why did you take those Angels out of there, who are they to you?" she asked.

"Deb, what happened to Michael?" As Marcus took a step closer to her, Deb took one full step back. She could tell this was his attempt to change the subject.

"Answer me, who are they?" Deb felt a well of emotion bubbling up. "Why were they there today? Why are they watching over Sophia? Why would you save them?"

"You are watching over Sophia, aren't you?" he asked. "How could you not tell me it's you!"

Deb launched forward and hit him square in the chest. "You don't get to dictate to me. Why were they there today? What were they doing there? Did they see the green-eyed demons or not?" She could feel herself seething, all patience lost to the stress of the day.

"They only saw the Gutter Demons, Michael, and Harry," he answered. "They didn't see any green-eyed demons and they didn't see you. They would have told me if they did."

She went to pull back, but he grabbed both her arms and pulled her in to his chest. "If I had seen you there, I would have come back for you."

"Why?" she yelled at him.

Deb was so close to him that she felt the whisper of his response on her neck. "Because I care about you, because you've come to mean a great deal to me."

I want to believe that, why can't I just let go? she asked herself.

She pulled back slightly. "I don't have time for this. Someone has taken Michael and Harry and we're hunting them down," she declared. "If those Angels have information, they need to send it up the chain of command now."

"I'm sorry Deb, I truly am. I will find out what I can and get back to you." Marcus turned to leave just as Kelly exited the bar with a steaming takeout container.

"Wait!" Deb yelled. "You still haven't told me who the Angels are!"

"They're Sophia's brothers. I do what I can to watch over them and her. They're family. In case you couldn't tell they aren't exactly equipped for this world." His cynical remark landed a blow.

Kelly walked between them. "Ok, enough for today, Deb and I need to go and so should you, Marcus."

Kelly hooked her arm around Deb's starting to pull them back the way they had come, but something inside Deb broke loose.

Why is it always so difficult with you Marcus? Why can't being with you just be easy? she lamented.

CHAPTER THIRTEEN

Genevieve stood in a grassy meadow, staring at a large gate, one door open, the other held firmly in place with a spike in the ground. The tall ornate doors held the vines of heavy perfumed roses cascading down its spindles. On either side of the gate was a large stone post connected to a wrought iron fence. Behind her, she could see nothing but thickly settled woods leading down into a valley of farmland miles below her position.

Guess I'm going through the gate, she said to herself.

Walking through the entrance she saw only one path; it disappeared around a large willow tree encompassing the center of the courtyard. The tree's limbs were lush with light green leaves that hung down from its bushy top. The gentle breeze swayed the branches just enough to hear the hum of rustling leaves against the grass below. The tree was old, the stump betrayed its age with protruding roots having heaved their way free from the ground below in multiple places. The tree's long limbs a peaceful, but perfect camouflage for whatever might be waiting for her on the other side.

She followed the worn dirt path and circled behind the tree. The only way forward was over a narrow rocky footpath, made more claustrophobic by the treelined canopy overhead. As she marched on, a chill brushed over her, the trees above obliterating the warmth of the sun. Fifty yards on, the property opened into a large garden. The thick grass below her feet seemed unaccustomed to being trampled on, so she walked to her left where there was a stone tiled path.

Strange that the dirt path didn't lead me to the pavers, she thought.

As she walked further into the garden the vibrant colors, perfect blooms, and luxurious aroma took her breath away.

"Amazing," she whispered.

There were lilies, lilacs, roses, and hydrangeas. Looking up ahead the garden had a large pond featuring a romantic bridge that could take you from one side to the other. The expansive stairs to the bridge were made of polished white stone, the railing and ends of which were covered in rambling wild ivy.

Right after Gabriel disappeared Gen would dream of him often. In each dream there was ivy, the same variety that they had etched inside their wedding bands. She was convinced the ivy was a sign that he was trying to reach her.

What a fool I was, thinking you were talking to me in my dreams, Gen thought.

Gazing further upon the top of the bridge wall, she recognized crocus, hyacinth, and daffodils all in abundance. Shrubs of azalea and mountain laurel sat at both ends as if inviting you to enter and exit.

"What is this place?" Gen mumbled.

As she continued down the pathway toward the bridge, she felt more cold air wrap around her ankles and cover her bare feet. When she made her way to the last tree on her left, she sensed the land was more extensive then she could see. She stepped off the last paving stone and took in her full surroundings. Looking to the right, beyond the bridge were acres of sprawling garden grounds. The dense trees, heavy shrubs, and copious amounts of flowers were luscious and opulent, unlike anything she'd ever seen. At each glance, the eye fell upon a more intriguing plant, flower, or tree. The extravagant nature of the garden coupled with the heavy fragrance of perfumed flowers added to the dream-like quality of the setting. Each planting was perfect in its imperfection; nothing looked manipulated, yet it had to have been tended with the utmost care to be in such immaculate shape. The sun's rays cascaded throughout, each drop of light shimmering against the pristine beauty of the landscape.

I must be dreaming, this is just too perfect, Gen thought. *Except it doesn't feel like a dream, it feels real.*

Before moving toward the bridge, she looked left and froze.

Through a trellised opening, Gen could see darkness envelope the other half of this oasis. The obsidian sky spread like fog blanketing a serene wonder of its own. She walked closer to the wall of shadow taking several minutes for her vision to adjust. The trellis was attached to a worn-out fence that hugged a tree line on either side. Just beyond the entrance was a pergola-covered dirt path that was adorned with short stumpy evergreen shrubs, most of which were gouged with dead spots. The path was sprinkled with the shrubs' pine needles still fresh enough to be sweet smelling.

Through the opening she could see an eerily similar setting to the one she was standing in. There were plenty of trees and shrubs, but most were bare. As if in a state of suspended animation, each empty branch seemed to stretch toward a sun that it could no longer reach. In the center of the darkness she could see a large fountain with several carved statues but could not see the detail from this distance. No water flowed from the fountain, but the sheer size of it was magnificent.

The air was cooler on this side and the wind seemed to crawl across her skin as if trying to figure out who she was and what she was doing here.

I don't belong here, it doesn't want me here. Gen could feel a sense of foreboding wash over her.

Her body reacted instinctively to her feelings and she took a big step backward. Gen tried taking a calming breath but felt the cool air sting her lungs and she paused to listen.

No sounds, there are no sounds on either side. She struggled to make sense of the scene. *I'm standing on a line between night and day.*

"Well, since I'm convinced this isn't a dream, that means something's brought me here." She pushed the frightening thoughts away, found the courage to walk under the dark wooden trellis, and entered the darkness.

"You might as well come out and deal with me. You took all this time to put this together, now let's get this over with, shall we?" Gen said the words, not knowing if there would be a response. Her voice rang along the expanse of the park and softly echoed back to her, but there was no reply. As she took a few more steps inward a strong wind whipped around her.

Something's trying to stop me from moving forward, she sensed.

When the wind died down, she heard the soft footfalls of someone coming up behind her. Turning quickly, she saw the shadow of a large figure coming up the stone path on the light side of the park where she had just come from. She patted down her body, feeling for a weapon.

Of course I don't have a weapon, why would I have a weapon? I'm not supposed to be here. Gen's rambling thoughts came to a crashing halt when she saw the being turn toward her and approach the trellis. Male, wide shoulders, square jaw, with an uneven gait and a mop of unruly hair. He carried no weapon, but his looming physical presence was a weapon unto itself.

Gen's hands rushed to cover her mouth, but it was too late. A small gasp escaped her lips. The figure stopped and stared down the path at her still frame just beyond the pergola-covered trail.

"Genevieve! Why did you enter the dark half?" The familiar voice rang through her head and rocked her body as if someone had physically shaken her. Every emotion she held inside rushed to the surface: relief, anger, fear, disbelief, love. Her body's physical response to the intensity caused tears to well up in her eyes. Before she could pull herself together, he was upon her, standing just feet from where she stood.

"It's me Gen, it's Gabe." He paused. "But I assume you know that already."

"How? Why now?" Gen could barely form the words.

"I'm sorry, there is so much I want to tell you. I didn't—" He was interrupted when she flung herself forward with such force it knocked them to the ground.

Lying on top of him she felt his hands slip beneath her top and touch her bare skin. His roughness against her softness brought back memories of the morning she last saw him. Images of them making love in almost this exact position swirled around her head. Every ounce of restraint evaporated as his hands clung to the sides of her body. In a moment of surprise, Gen surrendered to the will of her heart, leaned in and kissed him. Her passion unfurled, and she felt his body respond immediately to the assault of her kiss. He wrapped his arms around her and pulled her tightly down upon him. Everything warm and familiar, yet surreal at the same time.

As they struggled for breath, her mind began to clear and with it the pain of his loss crashed down upon her. She slammed her hands into his chest and pushed away, managing to get herself to her feet. Before he could stand, she turned away from him and closed her eyes attempting to pull herself together.

Oh my God, it's really him. She felt the crushing weight of her own heartache.

She could hear him behind her getting to his feet, his racing heart matching the thumps of her own.

"Gen, please I'm not even supposed to be here, but we need to talk. Please don't turn away."

"Where have you been?!" She demanded. "Where are we right now?!"

"I will tell you everything, I promise, but I can't get through it all right now, there isn't enough time."

The idea that he could wait forty years to come to her and then only give her a few minutes both stung and infuriated her.

"You have some nerve telling me there's no time!" She could hear the anger in her voice. "I've looked for you for forty years! Do you have any idea what I've been through, any idea?!"

"Please, calm down, if you don't, we can't stay here, Gen."

"Can't stay where?!" She yelled the words and sent nearby tree limbs swaying. Feeling like she was going to be physically ill she maneuvered around him and stormed off under the trellis back over toward the sunbathed footpath.

As she neared the first pavers, she felt his hand on her arm swinging her back around to face him. Now she saw him, clear as day under the light of the shining sun. His beautiful blue eyes pleading with her to stay, she fought every fiber of her being not to fall back into him again. His wavy brown hair was longer than when she last saw him. He had some new scars running along his jaw and across his forehead. He wore dark blue jeans and a short sleeve T-shirt with a worn-out sports logo on it. She wondered how she looked to him.

"You look as beautiful as the day I married you," he told her.

She shut her eyes and squeezed them tight, when she opened them, she half expected him to be gone, the remnants of a dream she had yet to wake from.

"What's happening?" she asked.

"The demon that fought his way out of Hell to come for you, Jared and I think he stole a powerful demon's essence to escape. He's coming for you, and anyone else who gets in his way. You're in danger Gen, not just from him, but from the allies of the demon he stole the powers from to get back to earth."

"What? That's what you want to tell me right now? I already know Schlosser is after me. He tried to kill Michael and then someone took him and Harry." She paused "Oh my God Gabe, so much has happened."

Gen felt her body start to shake, her heart felt like it was breaking right there in front of him. "Why did you wait so long?" she asked.

He sighed before answering. "I had no choice, you have to believe me. You know I would never leave—"

"Except you did!" she yelled. "You walked out the door that morning and I haven't seen you in forty years. Do you understand? I've been looking for you for forty years, Gabriel!"

"I didn't know it had been that long until Jared and I got back here. None of us understood the price," he paused. "To me, it's only been four months, Genevieve."

"What are you talking about? Price for what? What's only been four months? Is Michael being kidnapped the price for my selfishness, Gabe?"

"Listen, I have Michael and Harry. Jared and I took them from that church garden before the Hell Fighter venom could completely consume them."

She couldn't comprehend what he was telling her. "Where are they? You bring them back here right now Gabriel, this is not a game!" Her words were stern, but she could feel tears streaking her face one again.

"You don't understand, they were near death, Gen."

"No, no, no." Gen shook her head back and forth. She stumbled backing away from him. He reached out to steady her, but she slapped his arm away. "You know Kelly, Deb, and I can heal. You bring them back, we will heal them! You hear me, bring them back!"

"I know you can heal, but this was much more severe than what your powers were meant for, they were near death. I can't bring them back yet, they aren't strong enough. It's taking a lot longer than we hoped. Gen, the rest of you need to carry on this fight without them."

"No, we can't, we can't do that, not without Michael. We need Michael," she told him.

"I promise we are doing everything we can, but you have to act, you can't wait."

"So now I can't wait, like I waited for you, for forty years." Gen watched the words sting him.

"It hasn't exactly been easy for me either, but at least I didn't give up on my connection to you." He held up his left hand, the shiny silver wedding band assaulted her like a slap in the face.

"You don't get to do that; you don't get to walk in here after all this time and make me feel guilty. I wear it, it's here, it's just around my neck." She looked down as the ground shook beneath her feet. She went to pull the necklace out and realized she was standing in front of him in pajamas. She was wearing red pants and a white tank top with pink and red hearts all over it, a gift from Kelly last Valentine's Day.

"Your powers have grown substantially since last I saw you, Gen." He paused. "If you can't control your emotions, I won't be able to keep us here."

Her body recoiled at the sharpness in his tone. "Well, I'm sorry my heartache is an inconvenience for you! Since you don't really have anything of value to tell me, you might as well send me back right now!"

"That's not what I meant, and you know it," he snapped. "Why are you punishing me? Do you think I haven't been punished enough?" His voice dropped, and anger seeped through his tone.

Gen knew she had hurt him. *Make this right Gen, stop fighting, is this really what you want right now?* Her heart was begging her to back off, but the pain egged her on.

"What do you want, Gabriel?" she asked coldly.

"How can you ask me that?" he answered.

She watched his furrowed brows crease together, then he shook his head back and forth and looked down at the ground. When he looked back up at her she could feel him, just as if she were wearing her wedding ring around her finger. She felt the swell of love he held for her, the heartache over their separation, and an agonizing physical pain from an onslaught of demon encounters.

"Gabe, what happened to you? How are you able to share this with me?" He didn't answer. "Answer me? What's happened?"

"We're out of time, I need to send you back," he told her.

"Why? No one is here, why are you giving up on us?" she yelled.

"I've never given up on us."

"No, Gabe, I have the ring, look it's here!" She held the chain out away from her pajama top as if it proved her point.

"I know you keep it close but won't put it on ..." he paused. "It's not the same, is it?"

"I can't believe this, I have been to the end of the earth and back looking for you and this is what you say to me after all this time." She stepped further away from him feeling the anger bursting to take over. "You want to hurt me Gabriel, well congratulations, you did, you leaving that day nearly killed me!"

"Damn it, Genevieve, I didn't leave!" he yelled.

The wind picked up and Gen felt the first drops of rain fall from the sky, looking up she saw storm clouds fast approaching.

He stepped quickly toward her. "You need to see this." He put his hand against her forehead, and she saw flashes of light encircle them. "I need to send you back, all I can do now is share what I know. Schlosser is coming, but something else is already on to you. You need to be prepared to fight back, Gen."

Gen felt dizzy with the sensation of falling and then felt Gabriel's arms around her as he carried her toward the bridge. Her mind was foggy as if she were falling into unconsciousness. She tried to fight it off.

"No, Gabe please stay, we can work this out, please don't leave," she pleaded.

"I love you, Genevieve." He leaned down and kissed her forehead.

"Stop! Don't go, don't go!" She yelled the words and threw her arms up to grab hold of him, but he was gone. The image of him was fading into the recesses of her mind. It was like a distant memory being swallowed by the ocean of time between them.

Gen was thrashing in her bed, the sheets tangled and caught between the movement of her feet as she attempted to get free. Her bedroom door flew open and slammed against the wall. A cascading light washed over the room, Gen's eyes adjusted to the brightness and she saw Deb and Kelly peering all around her bedroom.

"Crap, you scared the Hell out of me!" Kelly said breathlessly. "I thought you were being attacked."

"Thankfully, it was just a nightmare," Deb added. "Although it looks like it was a rough one, given how flush and sweaty you are, Gen."

"It wasn't a dream, it was Gabriel," Gen told them.

Watching her sisters stunned silence Gen tossed the covers off as she swung her legs off the bed. Standing, she looked between them. "It wasn't a dream, it was him, it was Gabricl. He's alive and he has Michael."

CHAPTER FOURTEEN

Gen caught the look exchanged between her two sisters before Kelly spoke to her. "I don't mean to sound like a negative Nelly here, I mean nothing would make me happier than to believe that Gabriel is—"

"I think," Deb interrupted, "Kelly's asking if you're sure it wasn't a dream?"

Gen held her hands up as if trying to calm the rising tide against her. "I know how crazy it sounds, but it wasn't a dream. I was in that park with him, just as sure as I'm standing in my bedroom right now with the two of you."

The stillness in the room made Gen tense, she broke it by walking between her sisters. When she reached the doorway, she turned back to them. "I need a few minutes to gather my thoughts, we need to work through this. Let me just go splash water on my face and pull myself together. It's obviously going to be another all-nighter."

"What do you mean?" Deb asked. "Is it going to take you all day to explain what just happened?"

Gen looked over at the wall clock, it read 8:45. "Wow, I slept solid for almost two hours!"

Watching Kelly's eyebrows rise and fall, Gen braced herself for what was coming next. "You've been asleep since Deb and I got back from chasing down Marcus, who we found by the way."

Deb then added "It's 8:45 am. Assuming you fell asleep shortly after we left, you've been asleep for nearly fourteen hours."

"What?" Gen's mind reeled. "Are you serious?" Kelly nodded to confirm the truth. "How is that possible? I couldn't have been with Gabriel for more than fifteen, twenty minutes."

"Oh no," Deb whispered. "Gen's lost time too."

"What do you mean?" Gen asked, "When did you lose time?"

"We have a lot to go over, I need coffee." Kelly announced, "Can we go grab breakfast?"

"Kelly!" Deb exclaimed.

"What, it's not like it's inappropriate to want breakfast in the morning," Kelly answered.

"Breakfast is fine, let's get dressed and head downstairs before our brothers show up," Gen said.

"Well, that may be difficult," Kelly told her.

"What, no way! Why would you call them?!" Gen squealed.

"I didn't, Xavier was already here. He sent Tom home last night and stayed in the house with you. When we got home, he was asleep on the sofa."

"We didn't have the heart to wake him," Deb said.

Gen sighed, she knew she was being overly sensitive, but she couldn't help it, she was more than rattled.

"I'm sorry Gen, but you just yelled out that Gabriel's alive and has Michael and Harry. If you really believe it wasn't a dream, shouldn't we be calling everyone back here anyway?" Kelly asked.

"Let's just pull ourselves together and start over downstairs. Xavier just used his powers to get coffee and muffins, he's in the kitchen now. Let's talk it out together and go from there," Deb suggested.

Gen made her way to the bathroom. *This is just great, I haven't even processed what happened and now I'm going to be thrust into an inquisition.*

Walking toward the kitchen Gen could smell cinnamon. She entered the sun splashed room and spotted Xavier at the table with his feet up reading a newspaper. The plate in front of him held half a cinnamon apple muffin from the bakery down the street.

"Morning," he said to her without putting down the paper. "Anything in that dream of yours you feel like sharing?"

"Morning, Xav," Gen replied. "Not sure I'm in the mood to share."

Kelly breezed into the room next. Xavier moved his right hand pushing the remaining paper off a large box with bright blue lettering on it. He flipped the box lid up and spun it toward Kelly so she could see its contents.

"Breakfast muffins! All is right with the world," Kelly proclaimed as she reached over to take one from the box. "Thank you for getting extra," she whispered conspiratorially as she sat across from him to enjoy the unexpected breakfast treat.

Xavier smiled as he folded the newspaper in half and put his feet back on the floor. Deb came in just as the tea kettle whistled, and she instinctively walked to the gas stove to retrieve it. Gen and Kelly loaded up plates while Deb made tea, then the three of them sat down at the table with Xavier.

"Tom told me Gen was conked out last night," Xavier told them. "I sent him home to try and get some sleep. He's taking the responsibility of older brother in Michael's absence seriously. Now that you've had something to eat, do our bothers need to come by to hear about the nightmare you just woke up from?"

"It wasn't a nightmare!" Gen emphatically told him.

"They can come if they bring more food." Kelly's remark slightly quelled Gen's annoyance.

"I think they know better than to arrive here in the morning without food," Xavier chuckled. "At least I know better."

Gen stared between the three of them and knew they still didn't believe her. "Fine, they should come," she sighed. "I don't believe it was a dream, I believe it was real."

It took several minutes, but her remaining siblings arrived. Despite the amount of time that had elapsed since Gen spoke with them last, most of them looked exhausted and worn down.

No one is sleeping, Gen thought.

Tom sat down next to Xavier. Gen recognized the T-shirt Tom was wearing as the same one he had on the day before, but with a beat-up baseball cap to hide his unkempt hair. Greg hadn't shaved in a few days and his five o'clock shadow had thickened to a low-cut beard. Dan and Frankie brought separate bags from different bakeries gaining Kelly's approval.

As everyone settled into the familiar stance around the kitchen table Gen began.

"Gabriel pulled me into another realm last night." Knowing she was about to be assaulted with a million questions, she held up her hands halting any follow up. "I already know you're going to ask me, but no, it wasn't a dream. I know it was real and I know it was him."

Taking a deep breath Gen launched into the details of the park's unique and beautiful setting. At some point, Kelly had gotten up from the table and retrieved a notebook that she was now writing and drawing in as Gen relived her encounter with Gabriel.

When it was over Tom was the first to ask, "How do you know it wasn't a dream?"

"I have dreamt of Gabriel more times in these last forty years than I care to count. Nothing has ever come close to the vividness of last night. Everything from the clarity of his face, his smell, his touch. It was him, no doubt."

Dan asked Gen his questions from the white board he was now standing in front of. "You mentioned feeling like something didn't want you there, what do you think that was? Was there something else there with the two of you?"

"I don't know, if something else was there, I never saw it," Gen answered.

Tom asked the obvious, "Where has he been for forty years, Gen?"

Gen's breath caught in her throat, her eyes welled up. Hearing it said aloud made the amount of time he'd been gone real, but the truth was, she still didn't know the answer.

She shook her head back and forth. "I don't know the answer. I think he told me, but I don't remember."

"So, he got there and you two just talked?" Kelly's tone implied disbelief.

Gen leered back, peeved Kelly would attempt to insinuate a romantic encounter in front of their brothers. "Look, I've told you what I can remember, but there are still fuzzy images that I cannot see clearly."

"I think I can speak for all of us and say we all believe you Gen, but I don't think we can be relieved," Tom told her.

"It would be comforting to think Michael and Harry are in Gabriel and Jared's care," Deb added.

"It would be, Deb," Greg agreed, "but if we stopped looking for them based on that and then later found out it was some sort of trick …"

"That would be disastrous," Xavier finished.

"Was there anything else besides this park between day and night?" Tom asked. "Kelly seems obsessed with drawing this place, anything else you can tell us?"

Gen thought about the end of the reunion with Gabriel. "Gabriel said we couldn't stay there, but that he needed to share something with me." She paused trying to recall exactly what it was. "I can't remember. I think he tried to give me information telepathically, but it's all jumbled now and fading as we sit here and talk about it."

Gen's thoughts were interrupted by Kelly swinging a pencil back and forth across her fingers as she stared down at the drawing she made. Gen found it to be a remarkable rendering from a second-hand account. The pencil swung faster, the rhythm of the drumbeat on the table echoed around the room like the ticking of a bomb.

Everyone looked in Kelly's direction just as she slammed the pencil down and stood up to exclaim. "I know what this is! Oh my, I think I know exactly what this place is!"

Kelly looked at Gen. "I'll be right back, I need to go get a book out of the Vatican library." Kelly's orange-streaked aura filled the room as her sister teleported from the house still wearing a bathrobe and giant pink slippers.

"Wait!" Tom yelled after her. "You have to stop stealing books from the Vatican!"

It was useless. Kelly was gone, probably already walking on the marble tiled floor of the library in Vatican City.

"Tom, it's pointless to stress about the books, you know she's going to continue to go," Gen told him.

"I just worry about her being discovered," Tom said. "One day the librarians at the Vatican are going to see books flying off shelves without a person in sight, it will be like some wild clip from Harry Potter."

For several minutes they waited quietly for Kelly to return. Contemplating during the silence, an idea came to Gen. "What if Greg pulls the memories of last night forward for me?"

Gen watched her brother's faces fill with concern one by one.

"That's risky, Gen," Greg told her. "You know what can go wrong. Memories are not something to trifle with, they don't like being manipulated."

"I know the risks, but I think we need to do this," Gen told him. "Gabriel was trying to tell me something, we need to know what it is."

A debate about the pros and cons of Gen's idea was interrupted when Kelly finally returned to the kitchen. She held a package in one hand and a steaming cup of cappuccino in the other.

"Ok, I've got it," Kelly told them.

"Did you actually go into a café in Italy with a bathrobe and slippers on?" Deb asked.

Kelly held the cup out toward Gen. "I plead the fifth. Now, hold this for me so I don't spill it on the book." Gen took the cup and moved it out of the way. Carefully, Kelly placed a large bound package in the center of the table, then walked to the kitchen sink to wash her hands. Once dry, Gen moved left to allow Kelly space to get back to the book. Unwrapping the linen cover gingerly, Kelly turned to a specific page in the book.

Tom groaned. "You took the sheathing the book was in?"

"Well of course I did," Kelly huffed. "You want me to get dirt and dust all over it?" It was a rhetorical question left appropriately unanswered.

Kelly pointed to the book while turning to Gen. "Here, this is where I think you were." Her sister stepped to the side retrieving her cup from the counter. Gen stepped forward and leaned down to examine the pages more carefully. Displayed in full color across both pages of the open book was a watercolor drawing of a garden. The scene a near replica to what Gen had walked through, right down to the gated entrance, willow tree courtyard, and ivy-covered stone steps of the bridge.

"That's it. That's exactly where I found Gabriel last night," Gen told them.

Tom was sitting across from where Gen was standing, reading the Aramaic text that surrounded the painting. Gen looked up as he sighed. "This cannot be where you were. And even if it were, how could it look exactly like this? You must have seen this before."

"I have never seen this book, I promise you. My Aramaic is more than rusty, what does it say?" Gen asked.

"The translation of the text is debatable, especially between Tom and me," Kelly said. "It's much too long a philosophical conversation for us to get into right now." Kelly paused before continuing. "In a nutshell, the depiction is supposed to be the entrance to the afterlife, the place where your soul is reaped based on the weight of its nature. If you are infinitely wise and good, you are sent to the light half. If you are troubled, selfish, sinful, etc., the dark half tugs at you, welcoming you to enter."

Gen stood up from the table and began to pace between the white board and the table. "What is your understanding of the depiction and surrounding text Tom?"

Tom rolled his eyes at Kelly before turning his attention to Gen. "Kelly and I agree in part. I believe it is a place where you are judged, but who makes that judgement is what we argue over. It could be, that in the end, we are the best judge of what we have done during our lives. That each human is the one that knows all. That each person is their harshest critic, and therefore the best arbiters of where they truly belong. It is a choice, not a reaping."

Kelly groaned. "Let's agree to disagree." Before Tom could argue further, she asked, "How can Gen have described, to a T mind you, a park she's never been in and never read about?"

"She would have to have experienced it to know that kind of detail," Dan remarked from the whiteboard.

As Gen stared at the notations on the whiteboard all she saw were the gaps. "We need more. We need the information Gabriel put inside my head, the rest of what he told me."

Gen faced Greg. "I'm apparently well rested, my bruises from the fight are healed, and we're all together. One cannot ask for a more opportune time to do this."

Greg sighed, his shoulders were tense, he didn't want to say yes, but Gen knew she had made a sound argument. "Ok, let's do this then," Greg said. "God help us if this goes horribly wrong."

"Before we do this," Dan chimed in, "I think we need to agree on some assumptions, so we can move forward. Since neither me, nor our brothers, has seen these giant demons without one of you present, can we agree, through process of elimination, that these two eight-foot, green-eyed demons, are following the girls and not the rest of us?"

Gen watched all in the room nod in affirmation. "Good, so the three of you," Dan pointed to his sisters, "let's list your charges on the board. We might need to increase security on them if they are being stalked. Maybe we'll get lucky and be able to catch Schlosser or at least start following him instead of the other way around."

"You want all our charges? It would take another board," Gen told him.

"Not all your charges, as you said it would be too long a list," Dan agreed. "The three of you tell me which one you feel a particular connection with? There has to be something about those three connections you are leaving behind, a strong essence perhaps, something Schlosser is able to trace long after you've gone."

Gen watched Dan write Becky's name on the board. "I think it's obvious this one would be yours Gen."

"I bet mine is Sophia," Deb told him. Dan wrote the name underneath Becky, along with some additional notes about the two Angels from Deb's meeting with Marcus the night before.

Gen looked over at Kelly who was writing a list of names in the notebook. "I don't know who mine would be," Kelly told them.

"How about the last one you saved, just before the fire?" Tom asked. "I think it's safe to say our world started to tilt sideways that night."

"That was more than six months ago," Kelly argued. "There have been dozens since then."

"I know," Tom said. "But think about it? Everything, out of the ordinary for our world, traces back to the night of that fire."

Kelly reviewed her list and then looked at Gen. "Gerry Wilson, from South Boston. He's a firefighter nearing retirement, likes to work on his boat in the shipyard on his days off. He's a widow, his wife died of cancer two years ago, his two grown children recently moved out of state."

Tom followed up. "Did all three of your marks light up? Was that what sent you to these particular charges? Or was there something different about them?"

"My mark lit up for Becky." Gen remembered. "I told you guys that night, the night I went to save her. Tom you brought a pizza over for Kelly." Gen looked at Kelly. "It was the night you had dinner with the priests who didn't want to accept your opinion on the possession case."

"That's the night my mark went off for Gerry," Kelly said. "Remember, you asked me why I was eating again? I told you I had to leave dinner early because my mark went off."

Deb then added, "I couldn't go to dinner that night with Kelly because my mark had already gone off, for Sophia. She collapsed at her cousin Stella's house and she was brought to the hospital. It was the night her doctor told her the cancer was back."

Dan marked on the board. "Ok, well there's the link," Dan told them. "All three charges were saved the night of Schlosser's vanquishing."

Gen was struggling to follow. "What does that mean?"

"It depends on what you believe happens to a demon the night he's thrust back to Hell," Xavier answered.

Gen asked the obvious question, "How in the world would we know what happens to a demon thrust back to Hell?"

Tom stood and walked to the front of the room. "What Dan and Xavier are referring to is undocumented. There have been some verbal accounts of Hell sanctioning the return of demons killed during battle with Heaven." He paused and then looked at Gen. "The demons in question are able to trace their executioner with the power of reprisal being near ten-fold."

Xavier clarified. "Meaning, it's not an eye for eye. It's more like five bodies for an eye."

"Oh my God!" Kelly exclaimed "You guys are not seriously talking about avenging spirits as real. It's fiction, it's lore, the stuff of Hollywood!"

"What is?" Gen asked.

"Long ago, when Heaven and Hell finalized the Compact, the one that keeps this delicate dance of ours from blowing up into chaos," Kelly said animating with her hands for effect. "Supposedly both sides agreed that if any being was killed unjustly, breaking the Accord, that an avenging punishment would hunt down the rule breaker. The knowledge of who the killer was, the brethren they associated with, and the charges they watched over, were eligible as retribution for the disobedient act."

Gen felt the room fill with tension, she had never heard of such a thing. "Is it true? Did my killing Schlosser bring revenge down upon all of us? Did Hell send Schlosser back to take us all out?"

"Hold on," Tom said calmly while holding up his hands "We can't know anything for sure, but we can't deny the connection between your three charges."

"I think it's pure fiction," Kelly told Gen. "How many times has Hell killed outside the quote–unquote rules?"

"Many," Gen answered.

"Exactly!" Kelly said theatrically. "Yet, we've never seen Angels, Watchers, or Guardians return from Heaven with an edict of wrath against their killers."

"It doesn't matter whether it's true or not," Tom announced. "Actions do have consequences, we'll deal with them, together, as we always do."

Gen could not find relief in Tom's words. What if punishment isn't just coming for her, what if it's coming for them all?

CHAPTER FIFTEEN

Gen sat quietly at the large table while several of her brothers moved furniture around the room. Greg motioned for Gen to sit in a chair in front of the patio doors, her back would be to the view of the garden that lay just beyond. Greg pulled a chair in front of her and sat down while Dan moved the large whiteboard into a corner of the room.

When the rest of her siblings settled around the large dining table, someone shut the light off, so they were now awash in shadow. Greg pulled his seat closer to Gen, nothing sat between them, their knees were nearly touching. He took Gen through several breathing exercises before he started.

"I don't know if I'm going to need Frankie's help," Greg told her. "It will depend on how deep the memory has fallen. I'm going to start, if you need to stop, just say so. The most helpful thing to try and do is relax, do not resist."

"I will try," Gen told him.

"Good, because resisting hurts us both," Greg reiterated. "Close your eyes and think back to last night. What did you see, smell, and hear? Don't speak, just bring those thoughts forward and re-live the moment you first saw Gabriel."

Gen shut her eyes and focused on the magnificence of the park. The aroma of coffee and muffins from the kitchen was soon replaced by the lilacs and roses. The sweeping warmth of sunshine accompanied by the sounds of rustling willow branches swirled in her mind. She felt the soft grass slip between her toes and then the rough terrain of dirt and pebbles as she walked under the curving trees that lead to the bridge.

The images were as vivid as they were the night before, but they were faster than when she experienced it last night. She felt something move inside her head and moaned. Greg placed his hand on her knee reassuring her that it was alright, so she moved forward. Suddenly, Gabriel was standing before her, they were arguing. She had turned away from him, he was pleading with her to stay calm. Gen felt cold air around her, as if trying to separate her from Gabriel. She reached out and felt Greg take her hand and place it back upon her lap.

Her face was cold from the chilly air, something didn't seem right, she didn't remember being this cold the night before. Despite wearing a tank top and not having socks or shoes on she didn't remember being uncomfortable. She heard Greg's voice in her head. "Stop resisting, Gen. Focus on Gabriel, what is he telling you?"

I'm hurting him, I don't want to relive this, Gen thought.

"Keep going Gen, we're nearly there." Greg's voice revealed a tremor of exhaustion, the toll this exercise was beginning to take on him.

"Gabriel don't go!" Gen yelled. She felt a wave of pain but kept attempting to reach out to the image of Gabriel before her. Then she heard Gabriel's voice and paraphrased what he was saying out loud. "He's telling me that I'm in danger, but not just from Schlosser, from the allies of the demon he stole powers from. Gabriel is pleading for me to remain calm, but I'm struggling, I can't seem to control my emotions. He tells me about demons taunting him about me, but I don't understand. Gabriel says he and Jared think what's coming is serious and that we should be prepared. I tell him we need Michael, he says he has Michael and Harry. I get angry. He's carrying me now, he says he doesn't have time to explain and touches my forehead."

Gen felt a rush of emotion as the scene dissolved in front of her. Somehow it was like losing Gabriel all over again. *No, please stay, I want to hold on to this, to you*, she pleaded.

She thought she was coming back to her siblings, but instead she heard the screams of war. Looking beyond the bridge she saw a fiery red sky. Off in the distance Gabriel had crested a hillside and disappeared to the other side. Gen raced forward, each step brought her closer to the thunderous roar of battle. When she reached the summit and peered over, she fell to her knees and screamed.

In the valley below were thousands of Heavenly soldiers, Gabriel among them, fighting an onslaught of Hell's worst. The ground was caked in blood and venom, the clanging sounds of weapons smashing against each other rang like bells through the air. On each end of the hillside were camps of wounded entities accompanied by thousands more preparing to enter the fray. It was chaos as far as the eye could see, a battle to end all battles. There were no distinguishing lines, each clash seemed to push and pull the enemies across the uneven landscape of the dead.

"Is this where you've been the whole time, Gabriel?" she asked.

She watched her husband savagely slice in half the demon he faced off against, then he turned and looked up at her. "You're the only thing keeping me alive," he told her.

Gen shut her eyes tight trying to purge the scene from her mind. When she opened her eyes, she saw perspiration on Greg's furrowed brow and felt the memory retreating once more to the far corners of her mind. "Did you see that?" Gen asked Greg "Did you hear me? I was telling you what he said." She looked over at her siblings who were just getting up from the table.

"No, sorry Gen, you didn't say anything," Deb told her "You cried, and moaned a lot, but no words we could make sense of."

Gen stood up as Dan pulled the white board back out from the corner. Someone took away the chair she was just sitting on. Everyone was moving around, but Gen stood still watching Greg walk to the board and pick up a marker. He wrote on the board.

The demon that fought his way out of Hell to come for you. Jared and I think he stole a powerful demon's essence to escape. He's coming for you, and anyone else who gets in his way. You're in Danger Gen, not just from him, but from the allies of the demon he stole the powers from to get back to earth.

Gen read the words and knew that was exactly what Gabriel had told her last night. She launched herself forward and hugged her brother. "Thank you."

"It's all good Gen, now I need some sleep," Greg whispered. Turning to the others he told them, "I'm heading home, I need to recover before I can go out. That memory was extremely intense." He looked over at her. "You may continue to get images, even when you're awake, as your mind works through the trauma and intrusion."

Gen watched Greg use his powers to leave the kitchen. The rest of them focused on Gen.

"I saw flashes of where Gabriel's been," Gen told them. "I think Greg did too. If he didn't see, at a minimum he felt the horror of it."

Kelly grabbed Gen's hand and held it tight. "Tell me Gen, where have they been all this time?"

Gen's eyes welled up before she could stop them, tears streaked down her face. "I didn't see Jared, I just saw Gabriel. He was in the Pit."

"Oh no," Deb whispered in anguished disbelief and hugged her.

Gen heard the legs of a chair scratch across the floor as Kelly's legs gave out and she slumped down into a chair. Dan laid a hand of reassurance on Kelly's shoulder, but didn't say anything.

What can they say right now? Gen thought, *there are no reassurances to keep us from worrying about the Pit.*

The Pit wasn't a place you freed yourself from, it was a penance of sorts. Gen knew it was the front lines of the infinite war against Hell. She had never seen it before, it looked so much more gruesome and violent than any painting had ever depicted. The sights and sounds of intense battle were more horrific than any text had ever described. If Gabriel and Jared were there, it wasn't of their own volition, and there was no telling when they'd be released.

"That bastard isn't back with a proclamation from anyone," Kelly announced. "Schlosser stole some upper demon's powers to get here. We can't do anything to help Gabriel, but we can do something about that."

"That makes sense," Tom added. "Gen said he was a Roamer Demon, they not only have the ability to absorb powers, but they have no allegiance. He wouldn't care who or what he stole from."

Gen's eyes fell on Tom. "Now what? This is when Michael would normally dole out marching orders."

"Look," Tom pronounced. "I know there's a lot to process right now, and I'm not Michael, but he'd be pissed if we wallowed. The whole point of his training sessions was so that we would be independent, prepared, and not reliant on him. We know what we need to do now. We know how to go out there and hunt down leads, send a message, and make our presence felt. Now let's get out there and do what we've been trained to do," he told them.

Dan asked him, "Are you sure Tom? You want us hunting the green-eyed demons or at least someone who can get a message to them?"

"That's right," Tom replied. "Let's throw a noose around Schlosser's neck. The green-eyed demons want their brother, let's tell them who stole his powers and probably left him for dead somewhere."

An hour after her brothers left the house to chase down leads and look for new ones, Gen was back in the kitchen with Deb and Kelly. They had reverted to their corners of the house trying to make sense of everything that had happened. Now they were dressed and ready to head out to tackle some of their own demon hunting.

Kelly rummaged through one of the bakery boxes left on the table. "We never took you for breakfast," Gen said apologetically.

"No, I didn't feel like eating after the news of the Pit," Kelly answered.

Gen had to ask her, "Why have you never talked about Jared in all this time?" Gen paused before continuing, wanting to be gentle. "Here you are wearing the ring he put on your hand, despite telling him you'd find a way to remove it."

"Once it was apparent he was gone," Kelly answered. "I mean really gone. I guess I assumed he went looking for Gabriel. That somehow, he was okay because they were together. Believe me I know how stupid that sounds."

"It's not stupid and it may have been correct," Gen told her. "If Gabriel, Jared, and Dmitri are together, even in the Pit, they are better off for it."

"I remember," Kelly said as tears filled her eyes. "I remember feeling like there was no room for grief, that I wasn't entitled to it." Gen heard the quiver in her sister's voice and was crushed by it.

Gen swiped at her own eyes as Kelly continued. "We hadn't been serious for that long, my time with Jared was special but short, so I held on to the happy memories and hoped he'd come back one day."

"Of course you were entitled to grieve," Gen told her, emphatically trying to reassure her sister. "I'm sorry if my grief made you feel differently."

"No, it didn't." Kelly answered. "I guess I just needed to hold on to the happy memories, that's what allowed me to move forward. What about you Deb? How did you make it through losing Dmitri?"

Deb appeared dumbfounded. "What do you mean? I was obviously upset to lose a friend, but that was nothing compared to what you and Gen were going through."

"A friend, you're referring to Dmitri as a friend?" Kelly asked.

"Well yes, a friend, a colleague, fellow brethren in arms, what would you call him?" Deb asked.

"Um, I don't kiss my brothers-in-arms," Kelly told her. "Not that the thought of kissing Antonio disturbs me on any level."

Gen smiled using the moment to push her guilt away. "I'm sure it doesn't."

"What are you talking about? I never kissed Dmitri," Deb told them.

Gen and Kelly exchanged a look between them before Gen spoke. "Deb, not only did you tell both of us you kissed Dmitri, but I saw you, down by the river."

Deb shook her head back and forth. "I don't remember what you're referring to, but I'm certain you must have misunderstood whatever you saw."

Gen saw the distressed look on Deb's face and chose not to push the subject further. Instead she blurted out, "I kissed Gabriel last night."

"I knew it!" Kelly yelled as she slammed her hand on the kitchen counter. "Spill it, I want to know every sordid detail.

"Kelly!" Deb exclaimed "Not appropriate."

"Why not?" Kelly answered. "It's not like sleeping with her husband after forty years would be an unforgiveable act!"

Gen and Deb couldn't help but laugh. Despite the grueling day, it was nice, Gen thought, to relieve the tension with some humor.

"I kissed him. The minute he got close enough, I launched myself right into his arms, knocking us both to the ground."

"Nice!" Kelly shouted as she held her hand up to Gen for a high five.

"Next time I see Jared, I'm doing the exact same thing!" Kelly told them.

As if on cue, a soft blue light swirled around the room and Jared appeared in the kitchen no more than five feet away from them.

Gen watched Kelly push her seat back and run right into his arms. Jared wasn't thrown off by her actions, he caught her with ease, whisking her up into his arms for a passionate kiss. Just as Gen was about to motion for her and Deb to leave the kitchen, Jared pulled back and placed Kelly down on her feet. Despite it being Kelly's idea, Gen thought her sister was the one who looked shell shocked, not Jared.

"Hi," Jared said as he looked down into Kelly's eyes.

"You should take me somewhere, like right now," she told him.

He laughed. "I would like nothing more, but that's not why I'm here, luv and unfortunately, I'm unable to stay more than a few minutes."

"Why are you here?" Deb asked.

"Why are you only able to stay for a few minutes?" Gen asked

Jared ignored their questions and looked at Gen. "I'm so sorry about everything that's happened. We had no idea how much time had passed since we've been gone."

Gen nodded. "Thank you. I'm sorry too."

"Who's we?" Deb asked.

Jared looked over at Deb. "Me, Gabe, and Dmitri," he answered.

"Is Dmitri here?" Deb followed.

Jared looked down before answering. "No Deb, I'm sorry he isn't. He had to stay behind and cover for us. We'll have to tell him when we get back how long it's been."

Jared cleared his throat and looked at Kelly. "Schlosser is after all three of your charges."

"Yes, we know," Kelly told him "We've been able to piece that much together as we walked through Gen's remembrance of her encounter with Gabriel last night."

Jared shook his head. "I was tailing Schlosser in front of Sophia's house, but he never went inside and then I lost him. I'm sorry, I have to get back."

Kelly leaned in and hugged Jared. "If you must go, please be safe."

He wrapped his arms around her just when a burning light escaped a small space between them. Jared pulled back immediately and gazed at Kelly's left arm.

Her mark, an anchor, turned white hot and Gen asked her, "Which charge is that, Kell?"

"It's Gerry," she answered without taking her eyes off Jared.

"You need to go," Jared told Kelly. "That's Schlosser. Be careful, he's not just powerful, he's unstable. The essence he absorbed is not intended for the vessel of an earthbound demon, he's not meant to wield it."

Before Gen or her sisters could follow up with further questions Jared used his powers to leave the kitchen much the same way he arrived, in a swath of blue light.

Kelly turned back and looked at her sisters. "Are you ready?"

"What are we walking into?" Gen asked.

"Gerry is back in the hospital, triple bypass surgery," Kelly answered.

Deb added, "We need to be prepared for anything and stay open to one another."

"I'll have Xavier stay connected to me," Gen told them. "That way he can inform the others while we're there."

Retrieving weapons, the three of them orbed from the kitchen to the hospital in unison.

"Let's go kick some demon ass!" Kelly hollered.

CHAPTER SIXTEEN

Kelly heard the beeping of machines as she entered Gerry's dimly lit hospital room. He looked tired, in and out of sleep as he struggled to get comfortable. There were multiple lights on his machine that were blinking, but no alarms were going off. A nurse was busy typing information about his vitals into a portable laptop strapped to a tall adjustable table on wheels.

There is no sign of a demon here, at least not in Gerry's room, Kelly informed her sisters knowing they were checking the intersecting hallways to be certain.

Deb entered the room as the nurse made her way out. "So, he's okay then?"

"From what I can tell," Kelly told her. "He seems to be resting as comfortably as one can in a hospital bed."

Gen arrived last. "I don't sense a demon anywhere near here, Kell."

"Yeah, well that's what happened the first time my mark went off for Gerry. He wasn't in danger from demons then either, he just needed help finding aspirin and a phone to call an ambulance."

"Hmm, strange," Deb commented. "We obviously don't always encounter demons when our marks go off, but ..."

"But what Deb?" Gen asked.

"Well, Jared seemed to almost send us here. I guess it could have been coincidence, but he seemed certain this would be Schlosser."

"True," Kelly agreed. "Since Jared has once again disappeared, I'm at a loss as to what we are supposed to do here."

"Are you guys sure Gerry's okay?" Gen was looking at Kelly when she asked the question. "His eyes are open and he's staring right at you?"

Kelly looked over at the bed, Gerry was in fact staring up at her. She stepped a few feet to her right and his eyes followed. "Oh crap" Kelly said out loud. "Can he see us?"

Before anyone could respond Gerry slowly shook his head up and down in the affirmative.

"Oh boy," Deb said before taking a step away from the bed.

Kelly could see Gen step forward. "Gerry can you hear me?" she asked, but Gerry didn't acknowledge Gen, he kept his eyes firmly on Kelly.

"Ok, well he can only see you apparently," Gen said.

"That's not making me feel better," Kelly uttered quietly.

Deb asked, "What do we do? Are we on the verge of being exposed?"

"I don't think so," Gen said.

"I don't see how we can be exposed when we aren't in human form," Kelly replied.

"Does he have psychic abilities?" Deb asked. "Sometimes people open to the supernatural can pick up on us."

"I doubt it, this guy is as straight and narrow as they get," Kelly answered.

"Here comes another nurse," Gen told them.

The door pushed open and in sauntered a large framed female nurse with purple scrubs and a cup full of pills.

"Afternoon Gerry how are we today sweetheart?" she asks him.

"Who is that?" Gerry pointed past the nurse and over to Kelly.

"I think you're still a little groggy hun. There's no one here right now, except me. Your daughter just left to get something to eat for lunch, she'll be back soon. She's been so worried about you, that child is a Godsend, spending the time to rub that soothing lotion all over your hands and arms."

"Gerry, trust me, only you can see me," Kelly said to him. "If you tell her you're seeing someone that she can't see, you're bound to end up on anti-psychotic meds."

"I don't know that we should be telling him we're real," Deb offered.

"Why not?" Kelly shot back.

"I don't think this is helping, he thinks you're talking to yourself," Gen interjected. "Remember, he can only see you, not us."

"True," Kelly agreed. "Gerry, I have to leave now, but just know I'll be watching over you. You're in good hands here, you should be good to go home soon."

Kelly watched the nurse hand Gerry the cup of pills, which he took with several sips of water.

"Ok Gerry, I know these make you sleepy, so you rest now." The nurse soothingly told him. "Sleep is good for the soul," she emphasized before turning and making her way through the three of them and back out to the nurse's station.

"Let's step out into the hall for a few," Gen suggested.

"Good idea," Deb agreed before heading for the door.

Kelly took one last look at Gerry. His normally healthy black skin was ashen from the fatigue of the procedure. His hands and arms were peeling from either too much sun or a side effect of all the medication they had him on. She looked at the chair next to the bed. Draped along the back was a bag and a lightweight raincoat. On the table were some magazines and a bottle of medicated lotion.

Kelly approached the bed. "Close your eyes for me Gerry." She watched him hesitate but eventually comply. Once he did, she placed both her hands, palm side down, above him and healed his skin. When she was done, she smiled. "That should help a little Gerry, now get some sleep."

Outside the room, the bustle of nurses and visitors filled the hallway. Kelly walked far enough away where Gerry wouldn't be able to see her out the small glass cutout in his patient room door.

"Ok, even if he strains, he shouldn't be able to see me," Kelly told her sisters. "Now what? Do we just head back to the house?"

"I think we wait for him to fall asleep and call Tom and Frankie," Gen told her.

"Why?" Deb asked. "There's nothing happening here."

"Gen wants to snoop in Gerry's dreams," Kelly pronounced.

"It's not snooping if we need the information," Gen said defensively.

"Hey, I'm with you Gen," Kelly said lightheartedly. "It's just unusual for you to suggest such a thing."

Deb wandered back over to Gerry's room. "He's asleep already, and he looks much better. Not only is his skin healed but his coloring is less peaked."

"Great, let's get started," Kelly said.

"Not yet, he needs to get in REM." Gen was quick to add, "Let's walk some more of the hospital while we wait, we could have missed something."

Kelly was quick to agree. "Works for me. Stay open, you know our brothers would be pissed if they found out we separated from one another here, but obviously we'll be more efficient if we separate. It'll allow us more time here in the room with Gerry. I'll take this floor, you two take the one above and below."

Deb and Gen nodded in agreement before walking off in different directions. For the next fifteen minutes or so Kelly meandered throughout the ninth floor looking for any sign of the supernatural and found none. There was a steady conversation between the three of them as they went about their search. Kelly was feeling confident there was nothing supernatural happening.

Returning past the nurse's station Kelly stopped when she heard the television beep. Looking up she read the beginning of a weather advisory crawl across the bottom.

"Hey, bad weather heading our way," she said to Deb and Gen. "I'm reading a weather advisory on the TV and it says severe thunderstorm warning for this immediate area for the next thirty minutes."

Her sisters remarked they were on their way back to her. She continued past the station toward Gerry's room to meet up with them. A few nurses were already complaining about the possibility of sporadic power outages in the non-patient areas. Some of them were groaning about the age of the building and how temperamental the electrical system gets in a storm.

As Kelly rounded the last corner, she stopped short. Gen was standing in front of Gerry's hospital room. A big bruising demon was standing between them.

"Deb, can you still hear me?" Kelly asked.

"Yeah, I'm almost there," Deb answered.

"Hurry, Schlosser's here, outside Gerry's room."

Kelly cautiously approached from his right. She thought about shoving him down but then stopped when Gen held her hand out to halt her.

They know me too well sometimes, Kelly thought grumpily.

As she neared them, she heard the demon's labored breathing and caught a whiff of his foul odor.

Rot, he smells like he's rotting right here in front of us, Kelly thought.

She approached slowly from his right, catching sight of his head she could see splits in his sallow sagging skin. The green puss that oozed from wounds that weren't healing were most likely the cause of his stench. He turned right to look Kelly over, his eyes were black as coal, his pupils fully dilated, the surrounding white iris sprinkled with red-orange venom.

Good God something vile is coursing through his body, Kelly thought.

"What are you doing here, Sunshine? Back for round two?" Kelly mocked. "I gotta say, this look," Kelly waved her hand up and down the length of his body, "you're really not pulling it off."

Schlosser chuckled and smiled in Kelly's direction. His teeth were crooked and yellow, *par for the course,* Kelly thought, but the forked tongue was unique. He was much taller than Kelly and her two sisters. Obviously, he was heavier too, but in looking him over she saw weak points.

If he attacks go for the left side, he's favoring it. Kelly told her sisters telepathically but heard no response.

Great, he's cloaking, Kelly begrudgingly thought.

Deb approached from the far side and her eyes grew wide as the demon turned left to face her.

Suddenly Deb's voice swirled in Kelly's mind bringing relief. "He's getting worse," Deb explained. "His wounds were not gaping this severely when I saw him last. And the wreaking smell of death is much stronger."

"Deb, I think you just broke his cloaking. I couldn't hear either of you until you arrived," Gen added.

"She did," Kelly relayed. "I was trying to tell you guys to go for his left side if he attacks, he's favoring it."

"Good to know," Gen replied as Kelly saw Deb nod in the affirmative.

"Well, looks like I hit the trifecta tonight," Schlosser said. "I've been looking for one of you and now I've found all three."

The lights flickered just as a bolt of lightning streaked across the sky.

"Storms coming!" he told them, then Kelly saw the corners of his mouth curl up as he smiled at Gen. "I've waited a long time to find you, Genevieve O'Mara."

"Yes, crawled your way out of Hell," Gen said to him. "That's no small feat, must have begged, borrowed, and stole from a lot of entities to do it. I mean, you're a bottom feeder, Schlosser, so there's no way you were strong enough to get back here on your own. From what we hear, you've pissed off a lot of demons along your journey."

"No one's more pissed off than me," he spit the words toward Gen and splatter escaped his thin lips. "An unclaimed soul in Hell is worse than death. The torture I endured will be paid back to you ten-fold. You will suffer, as will all those you love." He laughed, but it was cutoff when a large war hammer whirled into view. The demon was smashed across his right side and sent tumbling several feet in the air toward the other end of the hallway. The impact opened skin and cracked bone, leaving a bloody venomous trail along the way. His body crashed to a stop in the far corner and he labored to recover.

Kelly looked to her left and saw Tom standing directly across from Gen. She couldn't remember ever seeing her brother this mad, he seemed larger than life at that moment. The rest of her brothers stood in the hallway behind Tom; there was no question who was leading the charge.

"You're not doing anything here demon. You come after her," Tom thrust his finger toward Gen, "it's an act of war against all of us."

Schlosser got back on his feet and bellowed a laugh, with each peak of his voice the electricity sparked. "You think I'm afraid of you? You think you can stop me? I'll have my revenge," He told them. "She'll just never know when it's coming."

"You think you can steal something that powerful and slither out of Hell unnoticed?" Gen said to Schlosser. "Something's here for you Roamer, something a lot more powerful than you."

"There's nothing more powerful than me now!" Schlosser howled. His piercing shriek burst the light bulbs above their heads.

Kelly felt the floor shake, most of the humans walking through the hallway had to grab the wall to steady themselves. Screams erupted as the lights switched to emergency power, and thunder and lightning roared across the sky outside.

Kelly's eyes strained against the breaking bulbs and dimly lit hallway. Just like a scary movie Schlosser was somehow standing directly in front of Gen. The demon had used his newly acquired powers to push the O'Mara family several feet away from the two of them. His arm extended toward Gen, and grabbed hold of Gen's throat, picking her entire body several feet off the ground. Gen's screams were muffled as her feet dangled wildly below her.

Kelly struggled, but couldn't move, she was unable to lift her arms from her side or take even one step forward. *Physically frozen, but able to see and hear everything,* Kelly's mind reeled. *Just like Lacey described the night of Sebastian's murder,* Kelly remembered in horror.

"You're gonna die for what you put me through bitch." His tongue slithered out to lick Gen's face, as it rolled along her cheek his venom burned and split her skin open. Her muffled screams echoed all around them. "You have no idea what it was like for me down there. No allies! No allegiance! No relief!" He leaned in closer to Gen, their faces nearly obliterated by the smoke coming from the burning wound he had inflicted on her face. "They tortured me for months! You will die when, and where, I say you're gonna die, but first I'm gonna destroy your life. Then I'm gonna eat your soul when you fall."

Kelly anguished watching Gen trying to fight him off, her thrashing and kicking seemed to have no effect. Somehow Gen was able to retrieve a weapon from her waist band and stab him, but he barely flinched.

How is Gen able to move, but not us? Kelly silently screamed in frustration. The power he used to keep them frozen was too strong. It was agonizing watching his attack unfold, knowing there was nothing she could do to help herself or her siblings. *It's just as torturous as Lacey described,* Kelly thought.

Kelly caught a glimpse of Deb, who seemed closer than the rest of them. She saw Deb's body shaking, her pale face contorted in horror at what she was witnessing.

Oh no, Deb is reliving what happened to Michael all over again, Kelly realized. Deb's hands flew to her face to stifle a scream. In that moment Kelly understood it was the previous trauma that had Deb paralyzed and not Schlosser.

"Fight Deb, fight!" Kelly managed to yell. "You can do this Deb, you're stronger than you give yourself credit for!"

The words reached Deb, and Kelly felt her sister snap out of it. Launching herself forward Deb crashed into Schlosser's left side causing him to lose balance and fall to one knee. Schlosser shrieked in pain and he lost his grip on Gen in the collision. The violent thud broke the demon's concentration, enabling Kelly and her brothers to slowly regain their movement.

Gen tumbled to the floor but managed to scramble back up and pull away. Kelly felt Deb's shield wrap around them. Deb's defensive mechanism seemed to knock Schlosser even farther away from her and Gen. Deb had managed to send the Roamer Demon within feet from Kelly and her brother's position. Tom leapt forward, but it was too late, Schlosser used his powers to teleport away before he could be reached.

Kelly and her family heard the echoes of Schlosser's threat as he escaped. "I'm coming for you bitch, and there's nothing you or your kind can do to stop me."

"Gen, are you alright?" Kelly asked as she ran to her sister's side.

The lights blared to life as electricity was fully restored.

Deb was searching in her pockets. "We need to stop the venom from burning any further into her skin."

Kelly saw the fear in Gen's eyes, she was stunned at Schlosser's ability to hold them all at bay. "Gen, Deb's got Holy water, hold on. It's going to hurt, but we can't start healing you until we put out the fire in the venom."

Deb opened a small vial and doused Gen's face with it. The scream Gen let out as the liquid made contact put Kelly further on edge. Slowly Gen descended to the floor, her legs giving out underneath her.

"It's okay, it's out now, Gen" Deb told her.

Kelly looked at Gen's partially slumped body against Deb's kneeling frame and her heart ached. "Let's go

Deb, come on!" Kelly implored. "We need to start healing her!"

Kelly and Deb held their hands just above Gen's face and slowly began to heal her skin. When they were done there was a small red scar across her cheek.

"We couldn't get it all here, we'll need Holy oil and more time," Deb told her.

"It's fine, it's better," Gen huffed. "Thank you." She slowly got up and faced Kelly.

"I sent the guys out to see if they can pick up a scent," Tom said over Kelly's shoulder.

"I doubt they'll be able to track him," Kelly said.

"We have to try," Tom replied.

Hospital personnel were continuing to show up, cleaning carts were scattered throughout as staff swept up broken glass and picked up furniture knocked over during the battle.

"I think that's a waste of our energy. Since you're here, wait" Gen said to Tom "How are you here?"

"Deb called us, but she was cut off before she could relay your exact position in the hospital, so it took us a few to find you. When we arrived, we felt nothing supernatural. Whatever he's using to cloak, it's the best I've ever witnessed."

"It's exactly like the one used at the church.," Deb said. "It even leaves the same ragged electrical signature I remember feeling from that day. I was unsure before, but now I'm convinced. He must have stolen those powers from the green-eyed demon that's missing."

"How did you get through it, Deb?" Kelly asked. "You saved Gen."

"I think it was Gen, not me," Deb replied. "When he put up that forcefield and knocked you and our brothers back, Gen and I should have been knocked back too, but we weren't."

"Well, he already had a hold ot me Deb," Gen said.

"Yes, but I think you wouldn't have moved. Just like at the church, when the green-eyed demon knocked everyone off the field, you remained on your feet." Deb added, "I think because I was closest to you, somehow your blocking covered me too."

"The building swayed, people were knocked into the walls," Kelly said. "You're saying that was Gen, not Schlosser?"

"Yes, that's exactly how it felt in the church yard too," Deb answered.

"If only Michael were here," Kelly said to Gen. "He would know how to help you harness that power, so you could use it."

"I know, but we'll figure it out," Tom told Kelly. "For now, we should get Gen home."

As they turned to leave Kelly stopped. "Wait! What about Gerry? He saw me, Tom. He can actually see me."

"Are you sure?" Tom asked.

"Yes, we all saw," Gen answered.

"We want you to walk through his dreams," Kelly told Tom. "The medication should have sedated him, not sure if he's still asleep now, but we should try."

Tom looked at Kelly but then nodded. "Frankie, we need you back here, if we're going to do this, we need you to boost my power, so we can be fast about it." Tom called.

Frankie arrived in the hallway next to Deb. "Where to?" he asked her.

Kelly turned and walked into Gerry's room, his daughter was on her cell phone relaying the shaking floor incident to someone on the other end. She wandered out of the room and into the hallway. Deb projected her shield to keep her there.

"He still looks out to me. The medication must be pretty strong," Kelly commented.

"Let's get to it then." Tom positioned himself on the other side of Gerry's bed.

Fascinated, Kelly followed Tom as he sat in a chair. He reached his arm out and placed his hand on Gerry's forehead. "Let me enter first and call you in when I need you Frankie."

Frankie nodded his reply.

It took a few minutes before Tom started to relay what he was seeing. At first there was nothing of interest, but then Tom stopped talking.

After a few moments of silence Tom ordered, "Frankie grab my shoulder and project this image."

Frankie grabbed Tom's shoulder with his left hand, then Kelly saw him swing his right hand out in front of him as if propelling something into the air. Within a few moments a 3D image started to form around them. Like a circular movie screen in full color, the dream was projected. They were now seeing what Tom was seeing.

There was a woman in a car. Kelly saw the driver's side window was down and her long brown hair was billowing around her face.

"That's Becky, but not recent," Gen said.

Kelly could see the car was speeding along a wet road. In scattered images the vehicle skids across multiple lanes of traffic and comes to a thunderous halt. Becky was slumped against the wheel, blood dripping from her forehead. The image jumped again, now Becky, still bandaged from the accident, was crying into the arms of a tall man as they stood over a headstone.

"That's her husband," Gen explained. "This is the first accident from three years ago when she lost the baby she was carrying."

The scene changed, gray and white snowy streaks scattered the image. As a new picture formed Kelly could see herself standing next to Gerry's bed the night he was brought into the ER. "That's me, from six months ago. The night I saved him."

The scene was quick to jump once again, but Kelly could still make out her own image. "Oh crap, that's me from tonight."

"Yes, but look Kell, it's not just you," Deb added. "He's dreaming of me and Gen now too."

"I see that," Kelly agreed. "That's from today before we ran into Schlosser."

"There's more," Tom said. "He's somehow seeing us right now!"

Kelly peered through the washed-out picture awaiting the next visual to come to life. Finally, it became clear, and there the five of them stood. Tom's hand laying on Gerry's forehead, Frankie gripping his shoulder. Kelly, Deb, and Gen watching the images of themselves dance in the air in front of them.

"What the heck?!" Kelly exclaimed. "How can he see what we are doing right now, while he's asleep?"

"How can he see all of us, when before he could only see Kelly?" Deb added.

The image blurred a final time and went nearly black.

"He's resisting," Tom told them. "I'm nearly losing my grip."

"Hold on," Frankie said. "Let me adjust my focus, I can sense the next image in the dream Tom's trying to wrangle."

Kelly heard beeping on one of Gerry's machines. Reading his blood pressure gage she could see it was rising. "I think we might need to stop, he's having a physical response, Tom."

"One more minute, I have it, I just need to push it to Frankie," Tom answered.

Kelly looked through the glass cutout in Gerry's door. The two nurses were headed their way. "We're out of time guys."

"Look!" Deb yelled "It's Gen with Schlosser."

Kelly's heart skipped a beat as she saw Gen kicked to the ground by Schlosser. All around her were demons, Gen's hands were bound behind her back, by what appeared to be a piece ripped from the Chain of Chaos. Blood had soaked her hands, her face was bruised and burning, tears streaked down her cheeks. The view followed Schlosser as he hauled Gen to her feet, a smile spread like wildfire across his hideous face.

Kelly wanted to turn away, afraid of what she was about to witness, but she couldn't. Instead, she focused on the image playing out before them. A large Hell Fighter placed his hand on Gen's shoulder pushing her to her knees, the demon dripped sweat and venom as it moved around above her. Gen howled in pain as the drops of burning fluid scattered across her skin. Schlosser lifted his sword aiming to strike Gen down with it.

Kelly heard Deb gasp, just as the image collapsed into a blinding white light that they had to shield their eyes from. When the last of the outlines evaporated Kelly looked at Gen. Her sister looked like she was going to throw up. Deb got to Gen first and wrapped an arm around her.

"I'm taking her home." Without waiting Deb teleported the two of them out leaving Kelly alone with Tom and Frankie.

The nurses burst into the room to check on Gerry, his daughter right on their heels. Thankfully, Gerry's vitals were already returning to normal. "It's alright Gerry, it's just a bad dream hun, nothing to worry about," the flamboyant nurse called out.

Kelly watched Gerry's daughter hang up the phone and race to her father's side, grabbing hold of his hand.

"Tom," Kelly whispered. "What did we just …" She couldn't finish the question.

"Not here, all of us need to get back to the house," he told her. "Now Kelly, let's move!"

Kelly was stunned, she stood frozen for a moment trying to process what they just saw.

Did we just witness Gen's death? Kelly thought the question her body refused to verbalize.

CHAPTER SEVENTEEN

Gen sat in the kitchen while Deb busied herself making tea. She heard the whistling sounds of the kettle as it started to boil, but nothing seemed real.

How many times have we sat in this kitchen recovering from demonic interference? Gen wondered.

"What the Hell did we just see in Gerry's dream?" Kelly burst into the room with Frankie and Tom close behind her. "Where's the booze? I could use a drink!" she declared, "and from the looks of it, so could Gen and Frankie."

Gen felt the rest of her brothers arrive, the room was once again thrust into organized chaos. Dan pulled the whiteboard forward, Xavier poured drinks, Greg rummaged through cabinets looking for food, while the rest of them clamored to find a chair or place to rest.

Deb approached quietly, handing Gen a piping hot cup of tea. It smelled of citrus and cardamom. Gen wrapped both hands around it. As she pulled the drink close to her mouth, she caught the strong odor of alcohol and knew Deb had spiked it with whiskey. Gen sipped slowly, letting the drink warm her from the inside out.

"Ok, I know Frankie was projecting to all of you," Tom said to the room. "Did anyone not see Gerry's dreams?"

The room fell silent, Gen watched her siblings looking around at each other.

Great, everyone saw how I'm going to die, Gen thought as she closed her eyes and took another sip to calm the rising tide inside her. *Maybe once he kills me, they'll send me to the Pit as penance. At least I'll get to see Gabriel one last time.*

"Alright, so we don't need to relive it then." Tom's words pulled Gen back to the present.

"I didn't know Frankie was projecting beyond the room," Deb offered.

"Yes, it took a lot of effort, but it seemed the most efficient thing to do," Tom answered. "We didn't want to have to keep wasting time retelling information if we could share it in real time."

"I didn't know Frankie *could* project beyond the room," Kelly commented.

"It's new," Frankie told her. "Michael and I have been working on pushing the boundaries. We've been testing my ability to project both Greg's memory retrieval and Tom's dream walking out beyond those present in the space."

Kelly's eyebrows furrowed as she looked at Frankie. "I guess we should have volunteered for more training," Kelly lamented.

"There will be plenty of time for that when Michael returns," Tom told her.

Plenty of time, how does he know we'll all have plenty of time? Gen thought. *Who's to say how much time any of us has?*

"Do we know what Gerry is?" Dan asked.

"I had no idea Gerry was anything more than a charge until tonight," Kelly answered.

"Through Gerry we heard Gen talk about Becky from three years ago, how could he know about that?" Xavier asked.

"How could he know about any of it—the past, us in the present ..." Kelly paused.

"You forgot the future, Kell," Gen said. "Me with Schlosser was obviously the future."

"The future isn't set yet," Greg told her.

"That's true, anything can happen between now and then that could change that," Tom agreed.

"How do we know that wasn't planted there by Schlosser? We don't know the extent of the powers he's acquired," Frankie added.

"The truth is we don't know anything," Kelly answered.

"We know he's coming for me. For us." Gen heard the resigned tone of her own voice and squirmed. "We know enough."

Tom reassured her. "We can't get stuck here, Gen. We need to stay positive and work on the things we can control."

Gen's hands shook, splashing tea over the rim, down the outside of her hands, and into her lap, as she nearly dropped the mug.

"Enough!" Gen slammed the mug on the table with such force it broke into several pieces. Shards of ceramic scattered across the table as hot liquid spilled onto the floor.

"We don't know Michael's coming back! We don't know that we're ever going to see Gabriel, Jared, Harry, or Michael ever again!" Choking back tears she tried to reel back the anger exploding to the surface.

Tom held up his hands as if he could stop her tirade.

"I'm tired," Gen told them. "You're tired." She paused to take in their faces, their gaze firmly fixed on her.

"What do you want to do about it?" Kelly asked her.

"I want to get out in front of Schlosser," Gen replied. "I'm sick of us running around chasing our own tails and getting our asses handed to us in the process."

"How do you suggest we do that Genevieve?" Xavier asked.

"I'm not waiting around for Gabriel and Jared to come back and give us another subtle hint," she bitterly remarked. "They both seem more powerful than before they left. We need that and whatever other information they are hiding. Tom is doing an incredible job holding us together, but we are suffering without Michael and Harry."

"You have some way we are unaware of on how to find Gabriel and Jared?" Deb asked.

"Yes!" she said emphatically. "I'm going back to that park Gabriel brought me to."

The room tensed as her brothers silently debated which of them was going to shoot down her idea.

"I'm in," Kelly chimed in.

"Good," Gen answered. "Deb, we're going to need your help."

"How?" Deb asked. "It's not like I know some magic spell to get you there.

Gen replied, "It takes trust to let go of this plane and project elsewhere. Only you can calm our nerves so we can do that."

"Plus," Kelly added with a smile "You make one hell of a hot toddy. Gen and I are going to need one for the road.

"I am not in favor of this plan." Deb looked between Gen and Kelly.

"I know, neither are they," Gen said as she pointed at their brothers, "but it's the only real lead we have to follow up on."

The mood in the room grew glib. Gen knew it wasn't the best plan, but at least it was something. *Anything to keep moving,* Gen thought. *I can't sit around here another day waiting for that bastard to hurt me or someone else I love.*

"What do you need?" Xavier asked.

Gen felt a bit of relief, she wasn't sure they were in agreement with her idea, but at least they weren't stopping her. *Could have been worse,* she thought.

"Should we get something to bind them together?" Dan asked.

"That might not be a bad idea," Tom said. "We don't always know where we end up when we leave this plane, so I think tethering them together might work."

"Well just in case, we should make sure they have weapons," Frankie added.

"We have about thirty minutes before whatever Deb puts in the tea takes full effect," Tom said. "Everyone go retrieve what we need and be back as soon as you can."

Gen saw streaks of light flicker across the kitchen as her brothers vanished from the room. Deb threw out the shards of broken glass and walked to the stove to make more tea.

"I'm heading up to change clothes," Kelly told Gen. "I think we should wear layers and I need to find those stupid boots I wore the night of the fire."

Kelly left the kitchen heading for her bedroom. Gen walked over and got a warm cloth from the sink to clean up the mess she had made on the table.

"I appreciate you not putting me on the spot about coming along," Deb said to her.

"I can't imagine what you've been through. I still feel that should have been me in that church courtyard."

"No, everything that's happened, it's the way it was supposed to happen." Deb pulled the kettle off the stove and poured boiling water into new mugs. "You just make sure you come back, both of you."

Gen placed a hand on Deb's shoulder. "I'm going to do everything I can to make this right, I promise."

Gen left the kitchen. Pulling shirts and sweatshirts out of her closest she realized she needed to change her pants too, everything was wet with remnants of whiskey and tea. Once she was dressed, she pulled her black combat boots out of the closet and sat down on the corner of the bed.

Tucking her ring below the multiple layers of clothing she spoke to Gabriel. *I don't know if you can hear me, I'm not ready to put this ring back on, so we're still disconnected, but I need your help. Please meet me there, Gabe.*

Gen was lacing her boots when she heard Kelly leave her room down the hall. She moved quickly to join her; once back in the kitchen, they drank the hot toddies

Deb made for them. Together the three sisters moved down the hall to the front living room.

Gen looked around at the furnished yet rarely used room. The wood floor was stained a dark chocolate brown. There was a sofa on one wall and two overstuffed matching chairs on the other. Each seat had a small end table next to it. Gen looked at the large fireplace in the middle of the room and struggled to remember the last time it was lit. The floor-to-ceiling built-ins on either side of the fireplace were dotted with pictures of the entire family, including one from many decades ago when she and Gabe lived here as husband and wife. On top of the wide mantle were the most recent photos.

"I put them up several weeks ago," Deb told her. "It was going to be a surprise, but then everything happened."

"It's great Deb, it is a surprise and it's beautiful. For my second time around in this house, it's nice that I get to share it with my sisters. It makes the loss of him less painful," Gen told her.

"You two better come back safe and sound," Deb warned, "or, I'll figure out how to go there and drag you back myself."

"I have no doubt you would," Kelly told her.

Deb gave hugs to each of her sisters and then sat on the sofa.

"So how are we doing this?" Kelly asked Gen.

"I say we pull out the sleeping bags from the hall closet, lay them on the floor. Deb can take us through relaxation breathing techniques. Once I can clear my mind, I'm going to focus on my memory of the park, pushing all other images away. Then, I should be able to project us there."

After getting the room setup, Gen felt her brothers arrive in the kitchen.

"We're in the front living room!" Deb yelled to them.

One by one they filed into the formal room.

"What've you got?" Gen asked them.

Xavier and Frankie handed her and Kelly a weapon each.

"Good idea, I remember wishing I had a weapon last time. Before I realized it was Gabriel that pulled me there, I was feeling pretty vulnerable," Gen said.

"I'm sure he's thankful you didn't," quipped Kelly.

Those in the room chuckled nervously while Gen smirked at Kelly's sarcastic remark.

Gen noticed the Holy palms in Dan's hand and asked, "What are those for?"

"We figured if you are going off on a magic carpet ride, we might as well pack it with as many Sacred or Blessed things as we could get our hands on."

Gen laid down to Kelly's left. Dan tied a loose fitted knot around Gen's right wrist and attached the other end to Kelly's left wrist. He intertwined pieces of the palm between the threads of the rope. Both Gen and Kelly held the weapons in their free hands, then Gen closed her eyes.

Deb, wanting a few moments alone with her sisters, ushered their brothers out of the room. She lit a few candles around the living room. It took a moment for the scent to reach her, but Gen realized they were Deb's favorite aroma therapy candles. Deb placed a Bible on the floor between Gen and Kelly and, as her final send off, she wiped what Gen assumed was Holy oil underneath the rope on their wrists.

"We'll be fine Deb," Kelly stated. "Don't worry."

"You better be okay, I can't do any of this without the two of you. Don't linger, get in and get back, you hear me?"

"We will," Gen told her. "Remember, when I went before, I was asleep for fourteen hours, so we'll be back, but I think we should assume the same skewed time difference."

Gen heard Deb's footfalls on the floor and then the light dimmed. As Gen focused on her breathing, she felt Kelly fall asleep almost instantly. She continued to focus on the images of the park and felt the memories coming back to her. In and out she breathed, as she saw the outline of the big willow tree, she felt a tug on her right hand. It was light, but somewhere in the recesses of her mind she knew Kelly was resisting. Gen was falling, spiraling down into unconsciousness. It was too late to turn back, and somehow, Gen sensed things weren't right.

Gen woke in the grass, cold enveloped her. She sat up, the rolling fields spread across the valley below, just as they had the first time. She felt relief, but only temporarily. As she moved her right hand to wipe her hair away from her face, the rope tying she and Kelly together dangled in front of her. It had been cut, the end frayed as if it had been torn free.

She rolled to her right and stood, a glint in the grass caught her eye and she spotted the weapon, a long sharp spear, somehow it had made the journey. *Thank goodness for small miracles*, Gen thought.

Kelly! Are you here? Gen looked up at the large wrought iron gate and felt her first wave of uncertainty, both doors were closed. A giant lock hung from a thick chain wrapped around both doors.

"That doesn't seem inviting," Gen huffed as she made her way toward the gate.

She took the spear Xavier had given her and stabbed it into the lock. Jostling it back and forth she managed to get the pin inside to pop. The lock opened and she unwrapped the heavy chain and pushed the door open to enter the courtyard.

The big willow swayed as she approached, the branches swung up nearly hitting her in the process. The sun was out, but it was cloudier than when she was here last. It made the old tree appear ominous, adding to the overwhelming sense of unwelcome she was already feeling.

Gen hastily walked around the willow and made her way onto the canopied dirt path toward the park. Halfway down the rocky terrain she heard an owl and stopped. *There were no sounds from the night with Gabriel, were there?* Gen was starting to question herself but kept walking.

Coming out the other end of the footpath she found only grass, no stone tiles to walk upon. *Am I not remembering everything or is this all different now?* Gen questioned. The trees to her left were taller with more blooms than she recalled but she spotted the floral covered bridge and marched on.

"Kelly! Are you here?" Gen yelled again "Kelly!"

Looking at the bridge she spotted the first of many blue jays and shook her head.

Kell, I don't know if you can hear me, but I see and hear birds. I swear there was nothing alive when I was here with Gabriel.

As she passed the last of the trees, she looked to her left expecting to see nightfall. The wall of darkness did not disappoint. It lay across the park like a lion waiting to pounce.

Gen heard the rustling of leaves and the feathers of birds as they scattered up and out of trees flying away from her. She was an intruder, she felt the sensation of trepidation and recognized it as she had the first time she was here with Gabriel.

"Gabriel!" Gen bellowed. "I need to talk to you, if you can hear me, please meet me!"

The wind picked up and she swore she heard the whisper of a response. Goosebumps rode her arms as her brain translated the word. "Go" the trees sang.

She walked toward the trellised opening to the dark half, but stopped, she felt she could walk no further, something was coming, but she had no idea what.

She backed up several steps and felt the warmth of the light side on her back. The extremes of the two halves of the park seemed palpable, whereas before she remembered it being subtle.

Gen tried speaking to her husband telepathically. *Gabriel, I don't know if you can hear me, we need your help. I need you.*

If you only knew how much I needed you Gabe, she thought.

Stopping, she peered under the wooden trellis and saw shadows dancing near the fountain. *What is that?* she thought.

Every gut instinct was telling her to retreat, run back toward the bridge, to the safety of the light half of the park.

As she stood staring at the dark half, she heard claws scraping against something hard. Her eyes squinted to make out the movement in the darkness, and she saw the outline of something swoop down from the top of the fountain and land hard against the lip of the pool below. Water splashed up and over the creature. The bird-like animal shook off the wetness that covered it and flew back up toward the top.

"What the Hell is that?" Gen whispered. "There was definitely no water in the fountain last time I was here."

Just as she was about to turn away a flash of lightning momentarily lit up the dark half of the park, as the sizzling bolt faded the flying creature turned and looked in Gen's direction. The gray skin, pointy ears, and grotesque distorted face were crystal clear. The animals red eyes blinked in her direction as it shrieked an announcement of her presence.

Gargoyles. They're guarding the fountain, Gen thought. *Oh God, please don't let Kelly be on that side of the park*. The thought ripped through her and at that moment she was certain that's exactly where Kelly was.

Gen shook her head back and forth. *I need to cross, she's over there, I just know it*. She ran toward the trellis and spotted the gargoyle sweeping down from above. It landed on top of the pergola with its long talons stretched out in front of it. She slid like a baseball player stopping inches from the entrance.

I'm only getting one shot to make it to the safety of the nearest tree, she thought.

Patting down her pants she hoped the vial of Holy water Deb had given her made the trip. As she pulled the small tube out, the animal shrieked and flew up into the night sky. The wind picked up, a tornado-like storm erupted in the middle of the dark half, just beyond the fountain. *Something's coming*, Gen's mind shrieked.

"No," Gen whispered in reply. "Something's already here."

Taking a deep breath for courage, she got to her feet and stepped underneath the trellis. The sight in front of her nearly stopped her heart, the image obscured in twilight had now become clear.

"Kelly!" Gen screamed as she raged into the darkness.

CHAPTER EIGHTEEN

Kelly was bent forward sitting on her knees. A wave of unrelenting pain woke her. The chill in the air was frigid and her hands were nearly numb. Able to pull her arms across her body, she understood immediately that she was no longer connected to Gen.

Using her right hand, she felt the ground below and scraped her palm along sharp gravel until it bumped into a rocky wall. Kelly's right side was leaning against a cold slab.

"Gen," Kelly grunted. "Are you alright?"

Hearing no response, she moved her left hand toward her stomach, and felt the edges of the small trident weapon Frankie had given her before drifting off to sleep. Somehow, Gen had managed to bring her to the park, but they were separated and now she found herself alone on the dark half. Face down, the weapon had punctured her stomach, nearly killing her in the process. Picking her head up to survey the area she was surprised at how pitch dark her surroundings were.

"Damn it," she grumbled. "I can't believe I'm on the dark half."

Taking a deep breath and holding it, she used her right hand to pull the weapon out, warm liquid burst from the wound. She coughed and slid down to sit on the hard ground. Removing several layers of clothing, she used a couple of the T-shirts to make a bandage. Fortunately, a long piece of the rope Dan had used to bind she and Gen together was still connected to her wrist. Untying it, she wrapped it around her waist to help keep the T-shirts in place and then pulled her sweatshirt back on over her head. Every stretch of her body pulled at the gaping wound and made her wince.

Once her eyes had adjusted a little more to the lack of light, she hauled herself up to her feet. Pain coursed through her body and she felt a wave of nausea wash over her. Putting her arm out to defensively navigate, she pushed off the rocky ledge and limped away a few feet.

This is just great, where the Hell do I go from here? she complained.

She trailed her right hand along the rocky wall as a guide as best she could. When she reached the end of the wall, a strong wind picked up and nearly knocked her off her feet.

"Gen!" she yelled. "Where are you?!"

She coughed and tasted the saltiness of blood and knew yelling would stress her body too much if she continued.

Shuffling forward, she stumbled several times over large boulders that seemed to be dropped haphazardly along the path in front of her. Her eyes continued to adjust, she was finally able to pick up the outline of shapes in front of her. Kelly was now able to avoid the remaining rocky formations. Nearing the last one, she sensed she was at a precipice, the top of a small hillside perhaps. She took a moment to stop and rest. Stilling her body as much as possible, she listened.

In the distance she heard water, she couldn't tell how far away it was, but she remembered Gen talking about a fountain.

If I was a betting girl, and I am, Kelly thought. *Then Gen's on the light half of the park. If the water I hear is coming from the fountain Gen described seeing from the light half, then that's the direction I need to head in.*

Shuffling in darkness she made her way to the edge and as she stepped down, her foot slipped out in front of her and she fell several feet down an embankment. She screamed out in pain.

How am I going to get down from here? her mind reeled.

"Don't panic Kelly, don't panic," she reassured herself.

Rolling to her side, she struggled to get back on her feet. Once there she had to re-adjust the bandages. Slowly she proceeded forward trying not to let gravity propel her downward until she could sense a less steep part of the hill to continue on toward the bottom. Finally, she found a path down that appeared less arduous. Descending slowly, and at an angle, she didn't like how much time it was taking her, but knew the pain was dictating her stride.

Crap, this path is taking me away from the water, she thought as the rhythmic pounding of rushing water faded behind her.

As she peered through the darkness the trees ahead seemed to be more visible than the ones behind her. Taking that as a sign she was moving toward light and in the correct direction, she gripped her stomach tightly and picked up the pace as best she could.

When she heard what sounded like flapping wings, she halted and waited for the sound to repeat. In the quiet that followed she thought she heard the hoot of an owl, maybe more than one.

I don't think Gen heard anything when she was here, Kelly told herself. *Is that good or bad?*

Kelly descended further, several times along the way, she swore she heard the wind whispering to her. The voice wasn't clear, and because of the rustling tree branches that rattled every time the air swooshed, she couldn't be sure. If she had to guess what was being said, it would have been the word 'go'.

Go where? she thought impatiently.

Arriving at what she believed to be the bottom of the hillside, Kelly felt no relief. With minimal light to guide her, she realized that her blood had pooled into one of her boots. Still gripping the weapon in her left hand, she carried on. Limping down a path with tall evergreen shrubs lining both sides, she felt air encircle her ankles and legs. The wind felt like it was wrapping itself around her, trying to bind her in place.

Pushing through the sensation, Kelly reached the end of the path, it opened to a courtyard with what she thought was a large oak tree in the center. The trees outer limbs rambled away from its wide stump as if trying to escape.

I want to escape this nightmare as much as you my friend, Kelly thought as she stared at the tree.

Looking at the size of the tree and how high the trunk's offshoots were protruding up out of the ground, it would be better if she could just teleport to the other side. Closing her eyes, she tried to picture where she wanted to go, but it didn't work. She was unable to bring herself beyond the tree.

Great, she thought. *Either my powers don't work here or I'm too weak.*

If she could manage to climb over or under the limbs, she saw a path pickup on the other side of the tree. Realizing it would take too long to find another path around, she lumbered forward. Approaching one of the wider branches, she gingerly sat down. Bracing herself for the pain, she used her arms to push off and swung her legs over to the other side, then hopped down. She had to repeat this exercise several times; the entire process was slow and painful.

When she made it past the tree, the pebbled dirt road in front of her wound past several smaller trees, bringing her out to a larger park. Looking up and to the right, she saw the hillside she had just labored down from. Looking left she saw light shimmering off water in the distance.

Well look at me stumbling my way in the right freaking direction, she thought.

Feeling a moment of confidence, she stood a pinch taller and staggered toward the water feature. The large back wall holding the water in place was too far away to make out any details. She remembered Gen telling her about a fountain on the dark half of the park, one she had drawn a pretty good rendition of based on her verbal description. Hoping that was what lay ahead she kept moving.

As she got closer, the light beyond the water grew brighter and began to illuminate more of the line separating night and day.

This must be it, she thought. *But I still don't see any sign of Gen.* Kelly reached the edge of the pool, she felt the lip of the fountain wall and realized it was made of stone. Now that more light was coming from the light half of the park, she could see more details of its ornate decoration. The carvings appeared intricate and three dimensional. It was a depiction of an Angel being chased by demons. The Angel held something close to its chest with its left hand, while the right hand reached to the sky. The Angel's wings were being clawed at by beasts, the hideous act seemingly kept the Angel from ascending. Kelly turned away and sat on the edge of the fountain's pool, her labored breathing getting worse.

Don't stop! her body screamed. As she willed herself to stand, she heard a noise and froze. *What the Hell was that?*

Her body trembled as she realized she wasn't the only thing breathing.

Briskly, Kelly moved away from the water's edge and behind a wide jumble of barren hedges. The shrubs had lost their leaves, but the skinny branches had wrapped themselves around each other and grown into a masterful piece of camouflage. Like a giant wall of wicker, she hid behind its thick woven pattern. From behind the thorny wall Kelly peered in every direction looking for whatever else was with her, but she saw nothing.

Great, now I'm hallucinating, she thought to herself.

Stepping to her right she had to catch her breath to keep from screaming as a large gargoyle, facing away from her, flew up from a nearby boulder and landed at the top of the fountain.

It's not a fountain, Kelly's brain screeched, *It's a purity pool!*

She scrambled back to the start of the barrier she was hiding behind and judged how many steps it would take to reach the pool. If the water was what she thought it was, it may help heal her wounds faster. The only reason it would be on the dark half of the park would be if the stories are true that Hell stole the Holy water, which wouldn't be a stretch. Purity pools were from Heaven.

Kelly struggled to remember the full origin, but the legendary stories were only coming in bits and pieces. She knew that long ago, Harac, the leader of the Hellion beasts, led a rebellion against the Accord. It wasn't his first nor his last such battle.

Harac murdered the Angels watching over the Garden of Eden. Stealing the sacred water from the garden, he hid it in an unknown plane. The demon leader created several pools which helped demonic beings maintain their strength and was even thought to give some of them immortality. Kelly remembered the lore of how the first Hell Fighter was born from a Hellion drowned in the pool. The beast had been beaten, mutilated and then lit aflame with Hell Fire. With its body twitching in pain it ran to the pool for relief, but instead found itself being held under to the point of death. What came out of the pool was not what went in. The demon that burst to life out of the pool was taller, stronger, and its venom was so potent it had the power to kill Heaven's Guard. Legend says the pools are ferociously defended by gargoyles who drink and bathe in its waters.

The gargoyle Kelly was watching had begun to dive back and forth from the top of the fountain to the bottom, partially submerging himself along the way. As it shook off the remnants of water, it turned toward the light half and flew away.

"Here goes nothing." Kelly grunted and then ran for the pool.

When she reached the edge, she leaned in, and with a leap of faith splashed as much of the water up and onto herself as possible. When the frigid drops of fluid reached her skin they sizzled, her entire body shook. The force of the shock to her system knocked her back and off her feet. When she landed, a streak of lighting shot across the sky. She looked for the gargoyle who had flown off to her right. When the lightning bolt lit up the sky, she saw its red beady eyes find her in the distance. Shrieking, it darted down from a wooden perch aiming straight for her with its large jagged talons ready to attack. Feeling for her weapon, Kelly sloshed on the wet ground, never taking her eyes off the gargoyle's position.

She took a deep breath and when it got within a few feet she felt the cold metal of the trident. Grabbing the handle, she swung the weapon across the gargoyle's ankles. The beast howled in pain and retreated to the trees. She got to her feet and knew the fountain was working as she felt a surge of energy. Before there was time to be relieved, she heard footsteps running up behind her. She turned to face whatever was coming, but it was too late. Kelly was punched in the chest, the force thrust her to the ground. She slammed her head against the marble decking that lay in front of the fountain.

A large demon loomed above her. She guessed it was female by the shape of her curvy figure. She must have been eight feet tall, skinny, with long braided hair that swung across her back. When Kelly locked eyes with the demon, the luminescent green glow was like a flashlight in a storm. Kelly saw the trident down by her bloodstained boot. She kicked the weapon up toward her hand. Kelly felt minimal pain; the water from the purity pool was working. Wrapping her fingers around the handle, she jumped back to her feet.

"What do you want demon?" Kelly spoke first.

"Feeling better, Guardian? I have to say, I didn't think you'd be smart enough to bathe in the fountain," the demon mocked. "I followed your trail of blood. Seems you've lost quite a bit since you arrived."

"Who are you?" Kelly asked.

"Who am I?" The demon responded. "I think you mean what am I?"

"Fair enough," Kelly retorted. "What are you then?"

"I belong here, and you don't," the demon taunted.

"I'm just passing through, not a whole heck of a lot going on here," Kelly feigned bravado. "I'm happy to make my way out now."

"I don't think so, Guardian." The demon crept closer. "You're not going anywhere."

Kelly knew she was in trouble. "What could I possibly have that you want?"

The demon slithered closer which revealed more details about its features. The demon's protruding breasts were barely covered by the billowing drape-like top that hung loosely off her shoulders. Her pants were the same tone as her skin, in the darkened setting she appeared nude.

Her hair was the color of sand, her skin like dust. Everything about her was washed out and pale, made more ghoulish by the glow of her green eyes.

"Tell me what I want, and I'll kill you quickly," she hissed at Kelly.

"That is quite the offer," Kelly retorted.

Kelly circled around and with her back to what she believed to be the light half of the park she began slowly retreating. The demon smiled and seemed content to walk straight toward her.

"Not in the mood for a fight, Guardian?" the demon taunted. "That's too bad."

Kelly watched the demon come at her. Sticking her right arm out in front of her to defend, Kelly swung the weapon in her left hand, taking off a slice of the demon's flesh as the blades of the trident made contact. The screech from the demon echoed throughout the park, the gargoyle shot into the air mimicking the sound.

As loud as it was, Kelly could still hear the seething breaths of the female demon. Kelly swung again but missed. This time the demon counter punched hard and landed a blow right in the center of Kelly's stomach. On impact, Kelly was thrust through the air and rolled several feet before crashing to a halt against a large boulder.

Gasping for breath, Kelly felt the pain in her abdomen return. Whatever stamina the fountain had provided was now fading. The demon rolled her over and sat on top of her, gripping her face in one hand, she used the other to lean down on the open wound of her stomach.

"Now, tell me what I want to know," the demon demanded. "Where is my brother?"

Kelly felt the demon's hand slide from her stomach, up across her chest and stop on her forehead.

"You're bleeding badly inside, Guardian," the demon crooned. "Tell me, why do you smell of Hell Fighter?"

Leaning down closer to Kelly's face the demon sniffed, her crushing weight against Kelly's chest nearly made her pass out. As Kelly felt her body wanting to give up, she could feel the demon enter her mind and panicked. Yanking one arm free from beneath the demons knee she swung straight up and landed a blow just below the chin. The demon howled, and Kelly used the opportunity to thrust up and roll the demon off.

Once on her feet, Kelly used the adrenaline coursing through her and took off running for the light half of the park. She had no energy left to teleport, all she could do was hope to get close enough to be able to talk to Gen. Kelly assumed the area was being cloaked, that's why she couldn't see or hear Gen. Maybe, if she got to the other side and connected with Gen, the cloaking would falter or break. As her feet brought her closer to a wooden pergola overhang, she heard the demon laughing behind her. The wind carried the sound of the demon's high-pitched cackle and Kelly focused in on the target, panting hard as she made her getaway.

The sun's cascading rays warmed Kelly's body, with each step she gained confidence and sensed her strides were getting longer. She never slowed, and she never looked behind her. The memory of her brother Michael's words rang through her head: *Don't turn around. Turning around slows you down and wastes time, time that an enemy can use to narrow the distance.*

As Kelly neared the trellised opening, she saw the outline of a figure on the other side of the entrance and knew it was Gen. She had no strength to call out, she was struggling just to catch her breath.

Just a few more feet, damn it! Kelly's mind screamed.

She heard the flapping wings, but never saw the gargoyle until he was hovering in front of her. Its feet tucked in, the beast thrust them out toward her as she reached it. The gargoyle appeared in front of her so quickly that she had no ability to change course or stop her forward momentum. As his feet connected, she was knocked several feet back through the air, rolling to a stop at the foot of the female demon. Kelly could feel her back split open with a new gaping wound.

The demon lifted her foot and stomped it on top of Kelly's chest, then she leaned down to peer into Kelly's eyes.

"You are brave, Guardian," the demon hissed, "but oh so stupid."

Kelly coughed up more blood, gasping for air, she couldn't respond.

"Did you think I was going to let you cross to that side?" The demon chuckled. "Now what fun would that be? We're just getting to know one another. My name is Sonoran."

The demon stepped off her chest, reached down and grabbed Kelly by the hair, dragging her away from the light half.

"My family will come for me." Kelly choked out the words as tears of pain wet her bruised and ripped face.

"Let them come," the demon bellowed.

"They're already here," Kelly let the words roll out not knowing if they were loud enough to be heard.

The demon dropped her and turned around to face the light half of the park.

"So, that's your family over there, is it?" The demon loomed above her peering over to the other side. "She is not as brave as you."

For a moment the demon paced back and forth as if contemplating her next move.

The demon smiled down at Kelly. "Let's go say hi, shall we?"

"Wait, what do you want to know?!" Kelly yelled trying to stall. "I'll tell you, just ask!"

"You already told me, when I was in your head," the demon spit at her. "You don't know where my brother is but maybe your family does?"

The demon grabbed Kelly by the back of the sweatshirt and dragged her back toward the light half of the park. As the sun washed down upon her, Kelly saw the bloodied trail the new wound on her back was leaving behind them. Her jeans were soaked in blood, one of her boots had been ripped off, and Kelly could feel unconsciousness tugging at her like an old friend.

When the demon released her grip, Kelly rolled over and knelt in the grass below the pergola. "No!" Kelly screamed at the back of the demon. "Leave her alone!"

She watched the demon ascend the walkway, each step shed more and more light toward the figure standing at the entrance. There in the bright light of day, Kelly saw Gen standing under the trellis unaware of what was coming.

Kelly labored to her feet, but she saw two of everything. She knew the dizzying effects of blood loss meant she could be of no real help to Gen and she was too weak to make it back to the purity pool. Kelly looked down at her left leg, somewhere in the engagement she got caught up with her own weapon. The trident was wrapped in the tattered T-shirts that lay dragging behind her. She retrieved the weapon, pulled it back and prepared to throw it. As she slowed her breaths, she heard Gen scream, "Kelly!"

Fear focused Kelly's vision, she used the last of her strength to throw the weapon at the demon. As the trident left her hand, Kelly collapsed to the ground, unaware if it reached her intended target.

Lying faceup, Kelly viewed the sky, one side pale blue with puffy clouds, the other a scarcely lit starry night. *Well isn't that something*, Kelly mused.

The cold had seeped into her bones, she felt numb. *Thank God for small miracles*, she thought. She heard yelling and screaming, but nothing was making sense. She heard the sound of stomping feet, something was running toward her, then Gen's face blocked out the sky.

"Kelly!" Gen cried, but the clarity of Gen's voice soon drowned in the darkness that enveloped Kelly.

Attempting a reply Kelly's lips moved but only muffled moans escaped. Kelly felt transported, the aroma of flowers and fresh cut grass filled her lungs. Somehow Gen must have taken her to the light side of the park.

Kelly vaguely heard the female demon taunting after them. "It doesn't matter, she's as good as dead. You're never getting out of here." The demon's voice was like an echo far away and sing song.

Kelly felt Gen cradling her body. The beginning words of prayer whispered all around her, but Kelly could not form the words to join in. Sleep was beckoning, Kelly desperately wanted to drift off into slumber.

As she felt Gen's tears reach her cheeks a calming sensation came over her. The end was near, her mind beckoned her to say good-bye. Inhaling sharply Kelly whispered, "I love you. Tell them I love them."

Kelly felt Gen tremble. "No!" she mumbled in the mash of Kelly's hair. "You tell them yourself, when we get home."

Kelly coughed and more blood trickled from her trembling lips.

"Tell Jared …," Kelly heard the weakness in her own voice. "I would have married him. Tell him he was worth waiting for."

Gen was speaking, but Kelly could no longer decipher the words through the siren of silence that wrapped itself around her. The ground beneath her shook and the wind picked up. Kelly's vision went completely dark, her beaten and broken body gave out. Her hands fell into the lush grass below. Feeling at peace, Kelly closed her eyes and felt the last breath of air seep from her lungs.

CHAPTER NINETEEN

Kelly woke to the sound of her name being called. The voice was masculine with a gravelly tone that sounded worn with age. Though the voice was unfamiliar, she felt no apprehension nor concern. Swinging her hands up over her face she shielded her eyes as they struggled to open against the glare of a blinding white light that seemed to press against her body. She was lying down, but the surface beneath her back was rock hard. Fortunately, she felt no pain nor discomfort.

Hello!" she yelled out. "Who's there?"

"You know who I am," the voice answered.

"I don't actually," she said as she sluggishly pulled herself up to a sitting position. "Why would I ask who you were, if I knew who you were?"

"You're just disoriented, it's perfectly normal," the voice told her. "Things will clear and begin to make sense shortly."

Kelly looked around, the floor was polished white tile, but the rest of the space was clouded in fog as far as the eye could see. There was no furniture, no walls, no ceiling, just endless fog. Even more distressing than the appearance of endless emptiness, was that she was alone, no one was visible. So who was speaking?

"Great, I'm not on earth and I'm hearing voices." Kelly huffed. "I've clearly lost my mind."

"You're not lost, nor are you crazy," the voice retorted.

"So, are you the invisible man?" Kelly asked as she managed to get to her feet and shuffle a few steps forward.

"You'll see me when you're ready," the voice answered. "That's how this works. You're in control, not me."

"Fantastic!" Kelly bellowed. "I would like to go home then. Can you make that happen please?"

"I'm afraid I can't do that," the voice told Kelly.

"What a shock! I was sure simply asking would work." Kelly could hear the sarcasm dripping from her voice but had no idea how the voice would respond.

"I'm quite certain you're rarely, if ever, shocked, Ms. O'Mara," the voice quipped.

Sense of humor, points for the invisible man! Kelly thought.

As she stared at the wall of vapor, she noticed it was shifting. The movement was subtle, like billowing clouds that moved up and away from her as she walked. Once her eyes had fully adjusted to the brightness, she saw black and white lines forming something in the distance. It was as if she were watching an artist sketch a giant mural, each line connecting to another to form a shape. In time, the park she and Gen had visited, the place where night and day met, unfolded before her.

Kelly stopped moving, rooted in place she was captivated, content to simply watch the images arrange themselves into a near perfect rendering. She turned her head to the side, the image stretched out around, behind, and above her. As if she were in some sort of bubble, the depiction remained away from her with the ground beneath her feet still solid tile. As she looked down, she realized she was wearing a long sleeveless white dress with no shoes. Her purple painted toe nails a stark contrast to the colorless surroundings. Kelly's dress had a delicate lace on the top, with ruffled straps and a lightweight material at the bottom that swung freely when she moved.

"Not my dress," Kelly remarked. "Perfect fit though."

"I can't say if the dress is yours or not, but it would be odd if it weren't," the voice told her.

"Hmm, well I probably can't account for every item of clothing I've ever purchased, but I don't generally wear white," she commented.

"You've never purchased a white dress?" the voice asked.

Actually, I did buy one. Kelly thought, *A long time ago for something I can't quite remember.*

"So where are we exactly?" Kelly asked.

"We'll get to that," the voice told her. "First, you need to take us to your selected space."

"Is that some sort of riddle?" Kelly questioned.

"I can help you," the voice told her.

"Excellent, please do. What is a selected space?" Kelly asked.

"Close your eyes," the voice instructed. "The image in front of you is where you were last, where the trauma took place. It's typical to bring that with you when you arrive. But staring at it will only muddle your concentration and keep us from where we are meant to meet. You need to focus on the place that brings real joy, that speaks to your soul like nothing else does."

"Ok, so you want me to find my happy place?" Kelly asked.

"No. I want you to find your connected place," the voice told her. "The place where you are not just happy, but where you're grounded. The place you can go to hear your own thoughts, especially when things are stressful or confusing."

"That's where my family is," Kelly said.

"Yes, but when you need your alone time, where do you go?" the voice prodded. "Take us there."

Kelly followed the voice's instructions and closed her eyes. She saw various images running through her mind. There were parks, beaches, her favorite house on the coast in California. She saw a winding path through redwood trees she used to get lost on with Jared, just for the fun of it. There were sunsets and sunrises, scenic vistas, and beautiful memories of vacations long ago past.

Why am I thinking of all these things? Kelly chided herself, *I should be thinking of how to get out of here.*

Unable to stop her rambling thoughts, Kelly saw each house she and her sisters stayed in, along with the pieces of furniture that always made the trek from place to place bearable. The kitchen table and chairs expertly carved by hand purchased in the early eighteen-hundreds. The wrought iron headboard from her bedroom that Jared designed personally based on a painting she once fell in love with. Various side tables, wooden chests, and antique lamps scattered throughout their house whisked through her mind.

Finally, she settled on the image of the dark wooden desk and accompanying chair in her home office. She had brought the custom desk from house to house for many decades. Thinking of it now, Kelly was reminded of the endless hours of research, reading, and analyzing she had done behind that desk.

As she focused on the makeshift library and all the hours spent behind her favorite desk, Kelly saw the stacks of books littered throughout the room and thought about how many didn't belong to her.

I really should have been better about returning those, Kelly thought, *now those books will be lost to time.*

Feeling warmth from the sun Kelly opened her eyes and looked up. Through a stained-glass window she saw a perfect cloudless sky above. Beneath her feet she felt cold marble floors and as she looked left then right, she saw pillars adorned with gold trimmed frescos. Comfort washed over her, a sense of calm soon followed. Hearing no sounds Kelly felt the familiar closeness of narrow bookshelves and smelled the aroma of antiquity with hints of vanilla and almond.

"We're here," Kelly said out loud.

"You know where you are?" the voice asked.

"Yes, we're at the library."

"Not just any library."

"No," Kelly agreed, "The Vatican library is something special, a treasure trove of humanity."

Kelly took in more of her surroundings, she saw the familiar black-and-white diagonal tile floor running up to meet several walls covered in tapestry and gold. She saw glass cases that held letters and historical artifacts, while others displayed coins and pieces of jewelry. From this vantage point she could see the marble statue from the side entrance. Up ahead the ceiling was arched with a colorful reproduction of the Sistine Chapel. The seemingly endless row of books, letters, archives, music, and manuscripts lined the outer edges of the room that lay sprawled out before her.

Kelly felt there was a peacefulness in the quiet of the empty space, but that was broken when she felt a presence. About halfway down the long row of maple-colored desks she spotted a figure sitting alone, facing away from her. The desk was awash in sunlight as it was one of many aligned with floor-to-ceiling windows that had a perfect view of the Palace courtyard.

"You found me," the voice said. "Please, come and sit."

Kelly approached from behind making note of the male's slightly overweight form, he was dressed in a crisp white shirt and brown pants. His hair was short in length and neatly combed. She passed him on his right, came around the opposite side of the desk, and abruptly halted when her mind registered recognition.

"Gerry?" Kelly asked perplexed.

"No," he answered "This is how you chose to see me. I assume this man meant something to you or something about him stuck with you."

Kelly nodded her head as if she understood, but she didn't, nothing about what was happening seemed normal. She pulled out a chair and sat across from the figure who looked exactly like her charge, Gerry.

"I hope you're not God," Kelly said.

The statement garnered a jovial response as the Gerry look-a-like belly laughed.

"Not even close I'm afraid."

"Good, so there's still a chance God's a woman," Kelly smirked at him.

"I suppose there is," he responded with a smile of his own.

"So, you're not Gerry. Who are you then?" Kelly asked. "Why not show your true form?"

"As I've already told you, you know who I am," he said. "You'll see me, when you're meant to. Until then, you'll see what your psyche is willing to accept."

"This is going to be a really long night if the conversation keeps at this pace," Kelly retorted.

"I normally send others to do this work," he began "But, I have to admit, in your case I made an exception. For you, I came personally."

"I'm honored," Kelly said "I'm remembering things the longer I'm around you. I'm assuming that's by design?"

"It's an unfortunate side effect for those that are restless," he said. "I'm here to support you while you decide what choice to make."

"I'm generally distrusting of strangers, especially ones that don't show their true selves," Kelly said sarcastically.

"I understand, that's not an unusual response." He held his hands out, palms up, one to each side of the room. "Which book will you choose first?"

Kelly looked at the stacks lining both sides of the room, each shelf crammed full of books. Without thinking she stood, walked to her left, and pulled down a book without reading the title listed on the spine. She carried it back to the table and placed it between them.

"Excellent choice," he told her. "Family is almost always the first choice. I must admit the bond you share with yours is deeply rooted and the envy of many. There is lots of history for you to ponder."

Kelly looked down and flipped the book open. The papyrus paper crinkled with each turn, its shiny pages blurred and then cleared with each new image of her and her siblings. There were pictures from the current year as well as black and white photos from decades ago. Each image made her smile, some were of long-ago forgotten moments and some from the house they just re-located back to in Boston. She recognized one as being the same photo Deb framed and placed on the mantle above the fireplace in the living room. Gen commented on it before she and Kelly left for their investigation in the park.

"Something bad happened at the park didn't it?" Kelly asked without looking up.

"All of it will come in time," he answered.

"Look, I appreciate the kindness and I feel at peace here. Strangely, I'm not anxious about you, or about my circumstance, which is definitely weird. But what is this about?"

"I have been truthful with you, Ms. O'Mara. You have a choice to make, I'm simply here to assist, should you need or want my help."

"Except, you're not really assisting and you're definitely not answering questions," Kelly told him.

"I cannot answer what you already know," he told her.

"How many books will I need to review?" Kelly asked.

"Clever," he said to her smiling. "Three. You are compelled to look at three books."

Kelly looked around, getting up again she moved to the opposite side of the room and took her time perusing the aisles. Walking up and down each row, she picked up and returned several books before she came to one that seemed familiar, as if she had once held it. Bringing it back to the table she flipped it open and was startled at the depiction staring back at her.

The oil on canvas painting was of Jared, he was running, a Hellion chasing after him. The beast loomed large at his back, nearly two feet taller with paws for hands and claws that stretched to nearly reach his neck. She didn't remember anything about an encounter between Jared and a Hellion, it should have been hard to forget.

She flipped to the next scene, across both pages was a pencil drawing of herself, she was tied to a stone slab, demons hovering all around her. The artist didn't detail her face, but she saw the reflection of her anchor as her mark glowed brightly on her back. The only color on the page was of wounds across her body. Liquid cascading down from the table and onto the floor formed large pools. The bright red color was effectively used to portray blood and put the viewer studying the artwork on edge. It worked, Kelly was disturbed by the imagery.

As she continued to flip through the book, depictions of caves and prison cells came to life. Demons and Hellions dotted the pages with fervor, all in gory and horrific detail. Kelly had never seen anything like it, she'd never been anywhere that resembled that setting, but something inside gnawed at her.

I couldn't have been there, she told herself. *I would have remembered a place like that.*

Turning the last page, the left side was fire, the red orange glow of flame danced up the page. The artist even managed to make the paper itself appear singed at the outer edges, as if it too had once been on fire. The page to the right was darkness, not black, but eerily charcoal, with images of demons and beasts looming in the background. Everything inside of her was screaming to shut it all out, to get away.

Close the book, she told herself. *This isn't real, he's just trying to get in your head, just close the damn book.*

The images were frightening, but she couldn't stop staring at them. The idea that Jared was in trouble, on top of the pictures of demons and Hellions attacking, was all too much.

She slammed the book shut and pushed it toward the figure sitting across from her. She hadn't realized that she was crying. She swiped at her face and inhaled deeply trying to pull herself together. Locking eyes with the Gerry look-a-like Kelly heard him sniffle and cough to clear his throat as if he were emotionally distraught at what he saw.

"One left?" Kelly asked.

"Yes," he said to her.

"Then what?" she asked.

"Then you decide."

Kelly got up from the table and wandered around the first floor of the library. No matter how many turns she made, she came back to the same section they were sitting in. She tried walking upstairs, around corners, then downstairs, all to no avail. She made her way through the restoration entrance and even the restroom, but it was all the same. In the end, no matter which aisle, door, or staircase she took, all of them returned her to the section of tables with the Gerry look-a-like.

I can't get out! Kelly screamed. *Oh God, I can't get out of here. What am I going to do? I need to get home, I need to get back to my family, to Jared.*

Something inside her told her this was an ending of sorts. There was still confusion, but bits and pieces of her time in the park with Genevieve had been coming back to her as she circled the library halls.

She remembered running into a demon on the dark side of the park. They fought. Kelly had the overwhelming sense she lost more than just a fight. Returning to the table without a book, she sat down across from the chaperone she seemed unable to shake.

"Alright, I can't pick, and I apparently can't leave," Kelly said.

"Would you like me to assist?" he asked.

Without saying anything Kelly nodded her head up and down.

"Close your eyes and picture someone or something that means more than anything else does!" He said emphatically, "Don't think about it, just do it!"

Almost without wanting to she closed her eyes and saw Jared and her siblings. Images of Jared flashed before her without any sort of order. She pictured him laughing, heard his voice, felt his lips touch hers. Something inside of her shifted and broke. Kelly felt anxious and irritated for the first time since arriving, but more than that, she felt longing. She yearned for more of everything.

I need more time, she thought. *I need to see my family, I need a chance with Jared. There's too much left and said that's undone.*

"Ah. I see you've made a decision," he said to Kelly.

Opening her eyes, she saw a singular book on the desk, the other two she had brought over to the table were now gone. The one that lay before her was beautiful, with a calligraphy pattern across the cover, a thick black backside, and silver trim running along the outer edge.

She moved her arm but stopped when she saw the ring on her left hand. The one Jared had slipped on her finger the night of the fire. The diamond cut silver band caught her eye when it sparkled in the sunlight. The design etched into the ring looked remarkably like the calligraphy pattern on the book laid out before her.

"I open the book, I go back," she said in almost a whisper.

"Yes," he answered.

"There's no pain here, no loss. One should be at peace here," she told him.

"Yes. They should be, if they are meant to stay."

"I know who you are," she told him.

"You've known the entire time," he replied.

"Will I remember this?" she asked.

"Most don't, and if they do it's fragmented images. But, you O'Mara's, you're different."

"I don't know if I want to remember." Kelly pointed at the shelf she had picked the second book up from. "That book, I don't remember anything about it, something yet to happen? Or is it something from my past I can't remember?"

"Your story is not for me to tell, it's yours and yours alone, Ms. O'Mara."

"You're politer than we give you credit for," Kelly said to him. "Not to mention this form makes a lot more sense than the typical Halloween costume."

"Thank you, Ms. O'Mara. It was a real pleasure meeting you," he said with a wink. "I can't imagine carrying a scythe around for all eternity anyway, it's just plain silly."

"Yesterday, I would have told you a conversation with Death, inside the Vatican library, was just plain silly," Kelly flippantly retorted.

Death's laugh reverberated through the halls. Kelly realized for the first time it might have been Gerry's form, but it was not his voice. She wondered if she'd remember it.

"For the few I come to meet directly, those that I respect, I allow them to call me by my real name." Death paused. "My name is Abaddon."

"I wish I could say it was a pleasure meeting you, Abaddon." Kelly locked eyes with Death. "Perhaps next time it will be."

Looking back to the table Kelly took a deep breath, reached out, and flipped open the book. A thunderclap of pain vibrated through her body, while images flashed before her in rapid succession. Family, friends, Heavenly colleagues, and of course Jared, all swirled in front of her. Her mind reeled as it caught up to the present and with each passing depiction, she lost a little bit of her conversation with Abaddon.

Kelly gasped for air as her eyes burst open. Her heart roared to life beneath her chest as pain muted her hearing. The cold water felt like a slap in the face, as she was raised up out of the frigid waters of the purity pool, she saw a familiar face staring down at her.

"Hold on Kelly, just hold on," Marcus kept repeating the command nearly breathless himself.

Kelly heard wings flapping and somewhere in her mind she knew it was the Gargoyle though she never saw him. She felt faint as Marcus used his powers to teleport them out of the park. Her eyes were heavy, begging her to disappear into the fog of oblivion. She felt compelled to give in and fell into unconsciousness.

CHAPTER TWENTY

Heading to the kitchen for yet another cup of tea, Deb stopped to stare at the ornate handrail that ran the length of the hallway from the library to the kitchen. She remembered Gen had spent months restoring it, now in the glow of antique lamps the protective coating her sister had shellacked it with made it sparkle. Bending down she peered at the detailed carving that bulged from its surface.

"Ivy," Deb said out loud. *I should have known,* she thought. *I wonder if Gen and Gabriel installed it all those years ago when they lived here?*

Her sisters had been gone for more than fourteen hours, though she tried several times she was unsuccessful at hearing or sensing them. The quiet was unnerving, the sensation of waiting around for something to happen was like the calm before a storm. The rattled nerves and restlessness were eerily like what she experienced after Michael was kidnapped from the churchyard. Pushing through the door she found Dan sitting at the island typing something into a laptop. Xavier and Frankie were standing reviewing paperwork from several case files Tom left strewn about. The table was dotted with crumb-filled plates and coffee-stained mugs.

"Where are Tom and Greg?" Deb asked.

Dan answered without looking up from his computer. "They went to get food. You realize you guys have literally nothing in this house to eat?"

"I'm not surprised, we mostly eat out," Deb told him. "Even if we had snacks, they wouldn't last. Kelly can devour a quart of ice cream in less than ten minutes."

Normally, her brothers would have laughed at her comment, but Deb knew no joke would break the tension that had been building since Gen and Kelly projected out of the house. A steady dose of anxiety now accompanied Deb's impatience.

There is nothing worse than waiting, Deb thought.

As she watched for the water to boil, she thought about Marcus. She needed to find him, she needed his help. *I wonder if he can find Gen and Kelly?* The question hit her like a flash, before she could dismiss it, she flipped the gas stove off and turned back to her brothers.

"I need to do something. I need to find Marcus," she blurted out.

"Why?" Dan asked. Deb saw the concerned looks on all their faces.

"Maybe he can help. Maybe he knows this place they've run off to," she said.

"Fine. Who's going with you?" Xavier asked.

"No one," Deb replied.

"I'll go," Frankie answered.

The soft glow of Tom and Greg returning to the house momentarily distracted Deb. Tom walked grocery bags over to the fridge and began to unload them. Greg handed out fast food bags from the local bakery while sliding a pastry box onto the counter next to Dan.

"You think leaving the house right now is a good idea, Deb?" Frankie asked her.

"Where are you going?" Tom asked.

"I'm going alone, to find Marcus," Deb told him.

She sensed everyone stop and stare over at her. She spoke before objections could be raised. "He won't talk to me as freely if one of you is hovering around us."

"I won't hover then," Frankie told her. "Promise."

"Fine, I'm going to the river, stay out of sight," Deb told Frankie.

"How do you know he'll be there or that he'll come?" Greg asked.

"He'll come," Deb answered, then used her powers to take off before any more debate could take place.

The early morning sun cascaded ribbons of light across the river. The embankment's rocky barrier remained shrouded in darkness. Deb closed her eyes and thought about Marcus, about their last conversation the night he took her from the house. She focused on the sound of his voice, his smell, his touch. She opened her eyes sensing something was coming, confident it was him when she heard footsteps rustling the leaves behind her. Turning she caught sight of Marcus walking toward her.

"What is it?" he asked as his eyes roamed the immediate area for others.

"Frankie is here with me," she told him as he neared her. "We aren't going anywhere alone these days, but I made him keep his distance because I wanted a private conversation with you."

"Ok." His eyes softened as he processed her words. "What's wrong?"

"A lot actually. But, first, I'm sorry."

Deb watched his head tilt, clearly, he wasn't expecting an apology.

"You're sorry, for what?"

"I was wrong, I didn't know, but it doesn't matter. I was wrong, and you were right. Genevieve killed Schlosser, he is back for revenge, quite possibly against all of us."

Deb could see his head nod slightly in her direction, a gesture of understanding.

"Is that all?" he asked, once again looking behind him.

"Why are you looking around so much? I already told you Frankie is here."

"I'm not looking for friendly faces," he answered cryptically.

"Oh, I didn't think of that." Deb found her eyes wandering across the landscape now too but, she couldn't see or hear anything. Only her brother could be felt, who, much to her chagrin, was not nearly as far away as she would have liked.

"I was referring to Sophia when I asked if that was all," he told her. "It's you watching over her, isn't it?"

Deb's eyes fell on his and she felt an immediate pull, an urge to be with him. *Why does this keep happening?* she thought.

"Yes, it is me," she confessed. "I was in the room when you chased off Schlosser, though to be fair I didn't know anything at that moment. Just what I saw, you seemingly running a demon out of my charge's house."

"I felt you there," Marcus told her. "I kept looking around but never caught sight of you. I think Schlosser felt something too, but he probably didn't know what or who it was." He paused and shook his head in surprise. "That was a huge risk. To stay that close to us, not to mention the power it must have taken to stay cloaked from both a demon and a Sentinel."

"I was cloaking myself from him, not you."

"I see, well either way I appreciate you watching over Sophia. I just don't understand why you would. I don't know how the whole Guardian thing works, but she has two brothers who are Angels, one would think that's enough."

"We don't question why we're called to the people we are." She felt her heart race a bit as he stepped closer to her. "It's not for us to question, they need us, we go. Besides, who decides when you have enough Heavenly protection?"

Deb instinctively crossed her arms and wrapped them tightly around herself.

"What is it?" Marcus asked as he leaned in. "What are you afraid of?"

"You," she told him. Watching him pull back slightly at the sting of her words, she clarified. "I'm afraid of how I feel when I'm around you."

The corners of his mouth ticked slightly upward and he moved his arm around behind her and pulled her in against him. "I feel it too Deb."

"I need your help," she whispered. "Please, I can't lose another sibling."

Deb felt his hand on her chin angling her face up toward him. "What do you mean?"

"My sisters." Deb didn't know if it was the proximity to Marcus, fatigue, or anxiety, but she felt her eyes fill with tears and pulled herself back away from him. "They projected to another plane looking for answers, they've been gone too long. I'm worried. Can you help us?"

When Deb's eyes fell back to his, she saw that pulling away from him again had hurt him. She wanted to take that away. Before she could squash down her desire, she took two steps forward, leaned in, and kissed him. She felt his lips respond first, then his arms wrapped around her. His hands clutched her sweater and he pulled against the small of her back sending her body crashing into his. After a brief moment and nearly gasping at her own foolish actions, she stepped back from him and attempted to pull herself together.

What am I doing? Gen and Kelly are off putting their lives in danger, and I'm here kissing Marcus! What is wrong with me? she scolded herself.

As she tried to regain composure, her mind reeled from a flurry of scattered images racing through her thoughts, almost all of them of Dmitri. None of them made any sense. *What the heck was that?* she wondered.

More disorienting than the burst of incomplete pictures was what her gut was telling her. The kiss she just shared with Marcus, though their first, felt more like their thousandth. *How can that be?* She struggled to make sense of her jumbled thoughts.

"I'm sorry," he apologized. "It's just I've wanted that to happen for a long time."

"No," she said shaking her head back and forth. "Don't apologize, I obviously wanted that too, it's just, it's not the right time, Marcus."

"Of course," he answered. "You asked for help. You said your sisters went somewhere, where did they go?"

"I don't know exactly, otherwise I would go get them myself." She huffed the answer and then began pacing back and forth in front of him. "Gen described it as some sort of park between night and day. She talked about lots of flowers, trees, and a fountain I think."

Marcus reached out to stop her pacing "That can't be right?"

"Why?" Deb asked him.

"She wouldn't be able to just go there." Marcus' tone was dismissive.

"How do you know? Are you saying we can't go there, but you can?" Deb heard the flippant nature of her tone and cringed.

"Deb, I'm allowed almost anywhere, I'm a Sentinel, remember? I'm supposed to investigate both sides, so yes, I can go there, although ..." he paused.

"Although what? Come on, I don't have time for games, either you're helping or you're not."

"I will help you. I never said I wouldn't. Although I'm not sure how she could even get there."

"She was brought there by Gabriel," Deb answered.

"Gabriel, her husband missing for forty years, that Gabriel? He's back?" He looked shocked.

"Why does that matter?" Deb snapped.

"Deb, if you are asking for my help, I need all the information."

"I don't know if he's really back, Gen said he pulled her there." Deb waved her hands in exasperation. "I don't know a lot."

"How long have Gen and Kelly been gone?" he asked.

"More than fourteen hours." Deb sighed and used her hand to massage her neck, the fatigue was beginning to ache.

"Listen, go home. Tell your brothers I'm going to go there and see if I can find them." She felt him staring at her. "But, if they are where you say, it's a huge place. It's not exactly a needle in a haystack, but there's no guarantee I can find them. Now, go home, get some rest."

"Rest, as if I could," she retorted.

"Try, you're no good to anyone if you're rundown," he advised.

Deb nodded her head as Marcus walked over, leaned down, and kissed her forehead. "When this is over, we need to talk, alone next time." Deb saw the image of him blur and then fade away as he used his powers to vanish from sight.

Oh crap, Frankie saw me kiss him, she agonized.

When Deb returned to the house, she went to her room without a word to any of her brothers. Deb never gave Frankie a chance to comment on what he had witnessed. She knew while she was upstairs, they were probably in the kitchen recapping the events between her and Marcus.

Judging, Deb thought, *not recapping, but judging*.

She laid down on her bed and fell into fitful slumber for the next forty-five minutes. When she woke, she lay in bed tossing and turning for another half hour before forcing herself to get up. She had given up on any real possibility of sleep.

Returning to the kitchen she busied herself with making hot cocoa. Her brothers were in much the same position they were a few hours prior. Plates now filled the sink in addition to the random ones dotting the table.

As she poured hot water in her mug, she felt something of a tug, a physical sensation of distress. Deb's hand jerked, the kettle sprayed a steaming mist through the air as water splashed down the side of the counter. She yelped as the hot liquid burned her hand. The pain startled her, and she dropped the kettle turning back to her brothers.

Dan was on his feet and Deb felt all her brothers' attention fall on her.

"What is it Deb?" Frankie asked.

Deb couldn't respond, she felt anxiety and sorrow but wasn't sure where it was coming from.

She heard Frankie tell Tom something was wrong, but her brothers seemed to be far away, as if Deb were seeing them through a telescope. Nausea rolled through her and sweat began to bead along her forehead. Deb watched the kitchen floor fade in and out replaced periodically by lush green grass.

Quiet lines of prayer whispered on the wind in between crying. Then she saw her sisters. Gen was backed up against a tree, Kelly lay lifeless in her arms. The two were surrounded by a field of sprawling gardens.

"NO!" Deb screamed.

As Deb's mind cleared, she saw the shocked look on her brothers' faces back in the kitchen. She took off running down the hall, their stampeding footsteps close behind her.

The echo of their repeated calls for Deb to tell them what was happening chased her through the house.

Deb reached out grasping the doorway to help her maneuver the turn into the living room. She skidded to a halt upon entry nearly falling with the sharp angled turn. There was thick red fluid oozing out from underneath one of the sleeping bags, before Deb could speak, she heard Gen screaming, but her sister wasn't physically in the room with them.

The wailing sounds of Gen's sobbing resonated throughout the house. Deb looked behind her and saw her brother's grave faces. *They hear it too, it's not just me,* Deb's scattered mind told her.

"Where is she?" Xavier asked.

"She's coming," Deb answered. "I feel her now."

The room grew dark, wind rushed through the house and blew out the few candles Deb had ignited before heading upstairs to rest. The floor shook and there was a thunderous roar in Deb's ears. She clasped a hand over each ear, but it did nothing to muffle the hideous sound. Gen's yellow aura floated around one of the sleeping bags on the floor.

As the light faded, Deb could make out the silhouette of Gen's body taking shape as she came barreling back to the house. There was a second of relief until Deb saw her sister's flailing arms as if she were trying to fight something off. Her blonde hair swung messily in a loose ponytail. Her blue eyes wide with shock and fear. Her clothes stained red across her legs, arms, and chest.

Gen was screaming, tears rolled down her cheeks "No! No, don't you take her! No, send us together!"

Deb rushed forward, bending down she grabbed Gen's thrashing arms.

"Gen! It's us!" Deb yelled "You're alright! You're home now!"

Gen stopped yelling and looked at Deb. "Kelly, where's Kelly?"

"Gen, you're alone. Kelly's not here," Deb told her.

"No!" Gen trembled in Deb's grasp. "No, it can't be, he said he would bring her back. Right after sending me back, he said he would bring her home."

"Who told you that Gen, Gabriel?" Tom asked the question from the doorway.

Gen's head shook frantically. "No," she whispered. "Marcus, it was Marcus."

"What?" Deb shook Gen slightly forcing her sister to look at her. "Whose blood is this? Is it yours Gen, are you hurt?"

Deb watched Gen's face crumble and knew the answer before her sister gave it.

"No," Gen closed her eyes, tears continued to stream down her face. Deb felt Gen pull away, her sister curled her knees up, wrapping both arms around them defensively.

"Gen, tell us what happened?" Tom urgently pleaded "Whose blood is it?"

Deb placed both hands on top of Gen's. "You need to talk to us, please!"

"This female demon, I don't know who she was ..." Gen paused. "She..." Gen looked up at Deb. "She killed her, she killed Kelly. Kelly's dead!"

Deb couldn't understand, she had to have misunderstood. Her sister couldn't be dead, she couldn't.

Gen's voice cracked, hoarse from yelling, she shuddered. "I never should have taken her there, we shouldn't have gone! It's my fault, it's all my fault!" Gen cried, Deb pulled her into an embrace.

Deb's mind couldn't process the information. *It can't be true,* she pleaded, *please God no*, Deb prayed.

The somber silence in the room was broken when they heard a crash in the kitchen.

"Deb! Deb, come quick!" a male voice called out.

Deb immediately recognized the voice as Marcus and teleported into the kitchen first. Her siblings were fast on her heels.

Marcus stood in the open area just beyond the table. He was soaking wet, his hair and clothing stuck to his body. The water created large puddles on the floor. He held Kelly's limp body in his arms, her layers of T-shirts torn, and stained, all of it muted from being drenched in some sort of water. Deb saw she was missing a boot, the other one severely damaged exposed her blueish toes.

"I submerged her body in the dark side's purity pool, but we only have minutes!" Marcus said breathlessly as if he had just run a great distance.

"What are you talking about?" Gen asked. "The fountain?"

"Yes, but it won't work for long, she has a pulse but it's weak and fading," he told them.

Dan cleared the kitchen table by violently shoving everything off the surface and onto the floor. Marcus placed Kelly's body on the table and stepped back. Deb grabbed Gen's hand and propelled her sister into action.

Standing on either side of Kelly, Gen and Deb held their hands out, palms facing down, and attempted to heal Kelly.

"This can't be? She died in my arms. How can this be?" Gen sobbed as her hands trembled in the air over Kelly's bruised and battered body. "I felt her go."

Deb reached across and grabbed hold of Gen's hands to ease her shaking. She then yelled to Frankie. "Help her, she's unsteady!"

Frankie grasped Gen's shoulder to help stabilize her, then he used his power to enhance their healing.

The room rustled with quiet movement as Deb saw her brothers using some of the Holy water and oils on Kelly's open wounds. Dan removed what was left of her boot and Greg grabbed several blankets from the living room and wrapped them around Kelly. Tom's soft voice uttered prayers in Latin.

Somewhere in the flurry of movement Marcus quietly left the house. But Deb knew enough, he had somehow saved both her sisters. In another realm no less, he sent them back to her, but how? She struggled to make sense of everything but, she was too tired to concentrate on more than one thing and it was her family that needed her now.

After twenty minutes or so, Deb and Gen had to stop, their powers were draining. Deb felt Kelly's neck for a pulse, though her sister was alive, she wasn't out of the woods yet. Gen and Deb would need to take a short break before starting again and Gen needed some minor therapy of her own.

Once Deb healed the abrasions on Gen's face, she sent her upstairs to shower and put on new clothes. She told Gen to bring a change of clothes down for Kelly when she was done. When Gen returned, Deb sent her brothers out of the room for privacy. Without talking Deb and Gen removed Kelly's wet clothing and saw the severity of the wound in her stomach. Though it was closed over and no longer bleeding, Deb could tell they needed to focus more energy there before they would be able to safely move their sister's body. When they were done using their powers, Kelly would need to sleep to complete the healing process, at this point they all would.

"I don't know why he would take her back to the dark side?" Gen commented. "That's where Kelly encountered the female green-eyed demon. Why would he put her in the fountain?" Gen tossed the soaked garments to the floor.

"I don't know, maybe it's some sort of healing pool," Deb said.

"On the dark side though." Gen paused "I'm worried what that did to her. She was bleeding, a lot. I felt her last breath leave her body. I know she died in my arms, I felt it all over, inside and out."

"I can't imagine what you've both been through. But, Kelly's here and she's alive. We'll figure out the rest later. Right now, we need to concentrate on her stomach."

On and off for the next several hours they worked on healing different parts of Kelly's body. Finally, it appeared they turned a corner. The surface wounds were healed, including a pretty big gash on the back of her head and Deb noticed Kelly's color seemed to rebound as well.

"I think that's it," Deb said. "We should get her to bed. She's going to be out for quite a while."

"I can't believe how close we came to losing her," Gen said tearfully.

"But we didn't," Deb reassured. "She's here and she's going to be fine, the two of us will make sure of it."

Deb and Gen got Kelly settled comfortably in bed.

"Thank you," Gen said to Deb. "You were amazing today, and sending Marcus, that was brilliant. You have been such a rock for me, for both of us."

"You're welcome, that's what family does. Now, get some sleep, you need it and so do I."

Deb climbed into bed and waited for her mind to settle, the image of Dmitri's face as he lovingly looked in her eyes while caressing her face flashed before her.

What is my mind trying to explain? Deb thought as she felt herself give into the exhaustion of the last several days. *Why am I picturing Dmitri and not Marcus, shouldn't it be Marcus?* Darkness closed in and chased away the confusing thoughts as sleep finally enveloped her.

CHAPTER TWENTY-ONE

Gen left Kelly at the kitchen table, books sprawled out before her, like an endless sea of research her sister was anchoring herself to. It had been weeks since they returned from the park between night and day, Gen hadn't been able to let Kelly out of her sight since. Not that it had been difficult, Kelly had barely left the house since she woke from the deep coma-like state that healed her. Kelly had slept for days like only those on Death's doorstep can, heavy with fever and according to Kelly, dreamless.

She's still not using the office, Gen thought. *She made Tom return all the books she had previously taken from the Vatican library, why?*

Kelly was in a cycle where she appeared to be wrapping herself up in work. She was chasing every lead they brought her, doing additional research instead of facing the outside world. Her memory of their time in the park was jumbled, but the nightmares her sister was having indicated that the trauma lingered.

Gen's tea had grown cold, but she was too focused on the television to get up and re-heat it. This was her third time through the news cycle this morning, each time she spotted new demonic interference.

Why did I wake on the light side and Kelly the dark? Gen asked herself this question countless times, she assumed Kelly must have asked it a thousand times too. There was no apparent answer.

Deb entered through the front door and Kelly yelled a greeting to their sister from the kitchen. The news was wrapping up, so Gen grabbed her cold mug and made her way down the hall toward the kitchen.

As she walked into the room, Gen heard Kelly reassuring Deb. "Don't worry, I'll clean up my mess before dinner."

"I'm not worried about you cleaning up after yourself."

Everyone was trying to hunt down leads on Schlosser, but they had nothing. Since Marcus saved them from the park no one had seen, nor heard, anything about him or the eight-foot green-eyed demons.

"Tea?" Deb asked Gen.

"Actually, I have some already, I just need to re-heat it. Do you have any cookies to go with it?"

"Staying home all day with Kelly must be wearing off on you," Deb joked.

"That's a good thing," Kelly was quick to reply.

"I don't know if my waistline agrees with you," Gen groaned.

Deb and Gen went about their business as Kelly continued to hammer away on the keys of her laptop.

"What are you working on?" Deb's question paused Kelly's mad typing.

"A case file from the church, a new one," Kelly answered.

"Anything interesting?" Gen asked.

"Not particularly," Kelly paused, "except it's the third new one this week."

"There is an uptick in demonic activity," Deb commented. "I feel like my mark is going to short-out, the signals are coming so frequently."

"There is a lot going on, and it's all over," Gen added. "I've just finished watching the news for the third time today and I've seen new demonic activity in each broadcast, both here and abroad. That's extremely unusual."

Kelly flinched, then reached up and rubbed her eyes.

She just saw something, Gen thought. *Probably another flashback.*

"You okay?" Deb asked Kelly. "Need a break?"

"Probably," Kelly replied.

"You want to go grab something to eat?" Gen asked.

"Or maybe some shopping?" Deb enthusiastically suggested.

"No, thanks," Kelly answered.

There was a stillness in the air that hung between them, something wasn't right, and Gen knew Deb could feel it also.

"I don't know what to say, you haven't turned down a meal in decades and I don't think you've ever turned down shopping," Gen replied.

"I know." Kelly gave Gen a forced smile.

"Is there a reason you haven't left the house much?" Deb asked. "Something we can help you work through?"

"I don't remember a lot, just images that flash but don't connect or make sense," Kelly told them.

"What about the office?" Gen asked.

"I wanted to bring the books back," Kelly told her. "Tom was right. I should have been more careful. I just couldn't seem to find the energy to do it myself."

"Sending back the books with Tom is fine, but why are you avoiding your very clean and organized office now?" Gen asked.

"I don't know," Kelly answered. "I'm sure whatever it is will reveal itself eventually."

"Okay ..." Gen was shaking her head, she wanted more of an explanation.

She's holding on tight to whatever's going on inside, Gen thought.

Deb got up from the table. "Sorry, my mark is going off again, I need to head out. Frankie is going to meet me. I'll let you know what it is when I get back."

Gen watched Deb's aura surround her in a soft glow and take her out of the kitchen.

"I'm actually going to shower and change," Kelly told Gen. "Maybe I should get out of the house. An apple cinnamon muffin sounds good."

"It does sound good," Gen answered. "I'll go with you."

In the bathroom Kelly looked at her reflection in the mirror, something was missing. Her coloring was normal, her face looked flawless, not even a pimple tarnished her skin. "Benefits of eating less junk food I guess," Kelly mumbled to herself before turning on the hot shower.

As the water cascaded down, she heard flapping and knew it was a memory echo from that night in the park.

Damn Gargoyle is going to drive me insane, Kelly grumpily thought.

She couldn't remember exactly what the creature looked like, but the sound of its thick wings as it flew resonated clearly. The splashing of the water coming up and over the side of the pool was something that plagued her every time she took a shower.

She barely finished rinsing the shampoo out of her hair when she had to shut the water off and get out. At least she was able to finish this time. The first week her shaking hands shut the water off in mid-wash, she ended up wiping soapy residue off her body with a towel. She was still unable to handle the sound of running water for more than a few minutes.

What the heck is wrong with me? Kelly frustratingly asked herself.

Dried off, she jumped on the scale, not something she typically did but it confirmed her suspicion. She had lost nearly six pounds, though she was hungry, there was something else underneath it. She felt like there was a lump in her stomach, not a physical presence but a gnawing churning thing that was just sitting there taking up space. She never felt anything like it before.

Maybe it's stress. I need to get rid of it and get back to normal.

Kelly came through the kitchen door, her hair still damp from her quick shower. Dan had stopped by and was standing by the counter talking with Gen.

"Hi Dan," Kelly said.

"Hey, how you feeling?"

"I'm okay. Gen and I are venturing off to the bakery to get apple cinnamon muffins."

"Nice," Dan said with noticeable relief.

"Dan just dropped off a few more new case files from the church," Gen told her.

Dan pointed over at the table already cluttered with files. "Whenever you get a chance, let me know what you think."

"No worries, I'll get to them later," Kelly answered.

Dan left the house while Gen and Kelly walked out the front door in human form. The bakery was about a fifteen-minute walk from their house. The late May weather was warming the air, but the shaded parts of the sidewalk were noticeably cooler. As they approached the bakery there were a few empty tables outside in the sun. Gen made her way inside while Kelly snagged a corner spot looking out over the busy intersection. The outdoor ATM at the bank across the street had a short line of customers, but the diner next door was bustling, even the library's small parking lot appeared nearly full.

Everyone out enjoying the nice weather, Kelly mused.

A few minutes later Gen arrived juggling two large cups of tea with a white paper bag bulging with goodies.

"What in the world did you get?" Kelly asked.

"Donut holes were on sale," Gen answered through a wide smile, "Plus I got some muffins. Whatever we don't eat we'll just take home."

"Yeah, someone will eat them," Kelly answered.

"Someone?" Gen chuckled.

"Yes, that's all I'm going to say." Kelly grabbed the bag and pillaged through it pulling out baked goods and tossing small dough bites into her mouth.

"I'm glad you wanted to go out after all," Gen told her. "It's nicer out in the sun than I realized."

"Well, I had to leave the house eventually," Kelly retorted.

"It's not like there's a manual for how to recover from an event like ours."

"True," Kelly said pausing to lift the lid from her tea sending wafts of steam into the air.

"We all keep asking how you're doing," Gen said. "You still haven't really answered."

"I know, it's just kind of hard to explain," Kelly told her. "Some images are returning, but only in fragments. Nothing that makes any real sense. It's like seeing pieces of a giant jigsaw puzzle but not being able to sort through them or fit them together."

"I remember most of that night. I mostly recall how I stopped walking and just stared over at the dark half, almost frozen in place."

"I remember waking up in the dark half, I was hurt, my stomach was bleeding and I couldn't see anything..." Kelly seemed to drift off in mid thought.

"I'm sorry I didn't walk over the line sooner." Gen's voice revealed the guilt Kelly knew she must have felt. "I should have, I don't know why I didn't."

"Gen, it's not your fault," Kelly said emphatically. "I know you blame yourself."

"How can I not, it was my idea to go in the first place," Gen replied.

"I don't blame you and I wanted to go with you, remember?" Kelly said.

"I know but still, I nearly lost you." Gen choked up.

"This is what we do Gen, this is who we are. I always rush in, you're more strategic. Both of those things are okay, we're okay."

I am, aren't I? Kelly questioned herself silently.

Kelly reached across the small table and patted Gen's hand. "I love you, truly I do, but you, babysitting me, isn't going to change what happened or how you feel about it, only you can do that."

Gen laughed a little. "I'm sorry, I can't help it. I'm sure I'm driving you crazy, but holding onto you that night, feeling your body give out. I can't get that feeling out of my head."

"I know, there's plenty of things I can't get out of my head either, but we learn and move on, right?" Kelly asked.

"Yeah, we do," Gen agreed.

Kelly demolished the bag of baked goods while they sat and talked about everything from case files to the weather. Kelly was talkative about all the leads she was chasing down but didn't want to talk more about that night in the park.

Her tea nearly empty Kelly was just starting to feel like a small weight had been lifted from them, a bit of normalcy returning, when the energy around them shifted. There was an uptick in noise as people started honking at one another in the intersection.

"You feel that?" Kelly asked.

"Yes, but I have no sense of what direction it's coming from."

"It's moving, like a wave of something just passing through."

"We should get moving ourselves," Gen told Kelly.

"Agreed," Kelly stood up and started clearing the wreckage from the table.

Raised voices rose above the traffic, Kelly heard the stampeding sound of feet hitting pavement as both she and Gen stopped and stared across the street toward the library. Before Kelly could speak, she saw a stream of people running from the two-story brick building. Women were screaming for help as several others were pulling out cell phones and ducking behind parked cars.

"It doesn't feel demonic, either way we can't go in there in this state," Kelly told Gen without turning around.

"There's another entrance on the far side. We can duck behind the evergreen bushes on our way around the building and switch out before heading in," Gen told her.

They made their way across the street, Kelly felt tiny surges of power coursing through her. Whatever was happening inside must have been frightening because several people were praying. The result of those pleas to God sent her and her sister sparks of energy, those would grow stronger the closer they got to the source. Kelly and Gen scurried over the back lawn toward the side entrance, just off a small courtyard where they disappeared from human view and entered the library.

Moldy dry air wafted up to slap them in the face upon entry. Kelly stopped to take in the entire area, everything about the setting was familiar in a way that it shouldn't be. Though she had been inside more than once, it wasn't a place she frequented. The building was old and drafty with several floor-to-ceiling windows running along the side. The warm air whistled around their ankles as it sang through the large crevices that bulged between the wooden frame and its brick casing.

Inside the library Kelly could hear a man yelling, it appeared to be coming from the front.

"Someone's upset" Kelly remarked.

"Yeah, it's near the front entrance, makes sense, that's the direction everyone was just running from."

"Let's split up but stay within view of each other," Kelly told her and then took off maneuvering right. She walked through the first aisle of bookracks and a cold shiver of recognition came over her. She watched Gen move left and walk up through the long line of wooden desks that dotted that half of the library.

When they reached the end, Kelly motioned for them to turn right toward the front entrance. Kelly moved around a few copy machines and headed for the front desk but stopped short when she heard Gen gasp. Turning back, she saw her sister standing behind a woman bent over something on the floor and doubled back for a better look.

Kelly looked down, a petite blonde woman dressed in jeans and a pink sweater was quietly crying over the body of an elderly man lying in a pool of his own blood. The name tag on the man's blue sweater vest read Hal.

Kelly locked eyes with her sister then watched Gen grasp the woman on the shoulder. The woman would feel only warmth and reassurance from Gen's touch. Reaching out, the woman clasped Hal's hand whispering as tears streamed down her cheeks.

"Her name is Jenna," Gen told Kelly without looking up. "She was in the back writing on her laptop when gunshots rang out."

Kelly felt a stronger jolt of power as Jenna recited prayers pleading for God's help. Anytime a human prayed for Heavenly help the Guardians nearby were temporarily endowed with additional strength to help them.

Kelly walked to the front desk and called back to Gen "This must be personal, not many financial reasons to rob a library." Kelly surveyed the chaos of toppled books and broken glass. "There's a man with a gun blocking the entrance. He has an open box of bullets half hanging from the front pocket of his sweatshirt."

"Well, he's already shot and killed at least one, poor Hal here just passed," Gen told her sister. "We have to help these people."

Gen approached the man with the gun.

"I can't seem to get through to him, I'm not able to influence him to stand down," Kelly told her. "You try."

Kelly observed the gunman as Gen walked closer to him. He was in his early thirties, muscular, with a large scar on his chin. He was pacing back and forth as a woman close to his age hid behind the front counter. The woman was boxed in, the gunman stood between her and the front door. If she attempted an escape she would be exposed. There was nowhere for her to go.

"I can't influence him either," Gen told her.

"Did it feel like he was insulated somehow?" Kelly asked.

"Could be, but that would be strange since I feel no interference," Gen answered.

In the distance Kelly heard sirens, but knew they were still too far away to bring relief to anyone inside.

"How do you want to play this?" Kelly asked. "If we can't influence him, maybe we try influencing the women to escape."

The sound of creaking caused Kelly to look up; someone was upstairs quietly walking around.

The man aimed the gun at the ceiling and pulled the trigger.

This is crazy, what is going on here? Kelly grappled for answers as she felt the familiar prickle of anxiety wash over her.

"You have friends in here trying to help you out, bitch?" the gunman screamed. "You think they can get the drop on me?"

"Oh, he's completely lost it Gen."

"Yeah, I'm getting that vibe too, but it's weird that we can't reach him. I've never had that happen before, especially standing this close."

"We need to be quick Gen, he's going to shoot her if we don't do something."

Kelly watched Gen reach down and touch the woman. "Her name is Melissa. This guy, Bobby, is her ex-boyfriend. She's been running from place to place trying to get away from him, but he keeps finding her."

Kelly focused on Bobby as he walked around the front desk. He lifted the gun and aimed it at Melissa who was curled up behind the counter. Kelly could only see Melissa's dark long hair as it fell over the top of her curled up small frame.

Kelly felt another surge of power run through her and knew her sister would as well. Verses from the Hail Mary quietly drifted up from the floor.

"No," Gen whispered.

Gunshots rang out as Bobby pulled the trigger several times. Gen was momentarily stunned by his action, even Kelly shivered at the violence. The blast catapulted

Kelly's mind back to the night of her fight with Sonoran. Images of the park flashed in front of her. In that moment it was as if Sonoran were standing in front of her pummeling her all over again.

Fear quickly snapped her back to the present. Kelly shakily moved forward and hopped up onto the shattered glass countertop to peer over to the other side. She was shocked to see Melissa was still alive. The woman had slumped to her right, her face peered up toward Kelly. Melissa's breathing was labored. Blood covered her left shoulder and lower legs. The splattered liquid dotted her pretty face, as her big brown eyes widened in fear.

How in the world did he miss the kill shot from that distance? Kelly silently questioned.

Before Kelly could ask Gen if she knew what happened she heard someone stomp down the stairs behind them and run across the foyer. A young woman slammed her body against the front door exiting with the force only adrenaline can provide. Once in the parking lot the girl never turned, she ran full on toward the relative safety of the street. Her ponytail swayed briskly behind her as she disappeared from their view.

"I'll be back sweetheart," Bobby taunted Melissa as she lay wounded on the floor in front of him. "Don't go anywhere."

Bobby turned back and pursued the young woman into the parking lot, where more shots rang out as he blindly fired his weapon into the air. Clearly, he was angered by the girl's narrow escape.

"It doesn't feel natural, whatever his rage issues are this is something else," Gen told Kelly.

"We have to get these people out," Kelly told her as she walked over and influenced Jenna to leave Hal's dead body by the reference desk in order to help Melissa.

"I was able to reach her, so it's just him we can't reach," Kelly said rhetorically.

You have to push through this, Kelly thought. *Can't let this guy hurt anyone else.*

Jenna tried to help Melissa toward the back exit, but they only managed to get to the librarian's office before Bobby returned. Kelly heard glass rattle as Bobby fumbled with some sort of chain around the front entrance.

"He's trying to lock out the police," Kelly said. "It's a hostage situation now. The two women made it inside the office and locked the door behind them."

"That office door is no match for his gun," Gen observed.

"No, but he's about to be busy fighting off police," Kelly answered as blue lights splashed across the front hallway.

"Let's take a look around, see if we can find anything that explains why we can't influence him."

"Starting upstairs or down?" Kelly asked, feeling a bit more confident as if helping these women had somehow helped her.

"Down, there's never anything good in the basement," Gen remarked.

"That is so true," Kelly retorted.

Gen paused at the top of the stairs just as the police yelled to Bobby through a bullhorn.

The basement below was dimly lit and with their descent Kelly could smell the unpleasant scent of musty unfiltered air as it crept up to meet them. As Gen pulled open the door at the bottom of the staircase Kelly was stunned to hear voices arguing inside.

Gen turned back and arched her eyebrows in surprise at Kelly. Gently the door clicked softly behind them and they tiptoed closer to the source. Knowing whatever was ahead wasn't human, they used the aisles of archived books as cover.

Kelly heard a male voice. "You said this plan would work Leucous. We are running out of time, all of us! If we don't find him soon—"

"I know what I said!" Kelly assumed that was Leucous replying. "Something has to have him and it's most likely from Heaven. Why else can't we find him? Why else is his signal so delayed?"

Kelly locked eyes with Gen and realized she couldn't communicate with her sister telepathically.

Oh no, I can't hear Gen. Kelly's mind began to race. *This isn't good.*

Kelly reached back and braced her body against the bookshelf for support. Gen patted her body down then motioned to Kelly impersonating someone on the phone, Kelly nodded in understanding and fished out her cell phone.

In the distance Kelly heard a phone ringing, it was most likely the police trying to reach Bobby. The gunman was yelling obscenities while rampaging through the library. At various times you could hear furniture being dragged across the floor and the sound of books falling off shelving. The violence vibrated through the ceiling above them.

Kelly looked down and read the no signal line on her cell phone and felt herself frown.

No signal, of course we're in a basement, Kelly sighed.

"We need to leave, Raven," a female voice ordered.

Kelly felt her knees buckle as the recognition of Sonoran's voice rang through her muddled thoughts. Her heart raced as her mouth went dry.

"Someone is bound to take notice," Sonoran continued. "This idiot upstairs is being influenced by our presence. Don't call me again until you have a location, Leucous. I don't care how many Guardians I have to kill to get Vermillion back, I'm not going to stop until we find him."

Kelly's body went limp and she slumped to the ground. Gen reached Kelly just in time to catch a few falling books on their way to the floor. Gen searched Kelly's face for understanding.

I know who they are. Kelly's trembling hands gripped Gen's arms tightly, digging into Gen's flesh.

The police breached the library, Kelly could hear the stampeding sound of boots running, a cacophony of gunfire was exchanged, and flash bangs exploded upon deployment.

Kelly shook Gen. "We need to get out, now!"

CHAPTER TWENTY-TWO

Their powers took them into the kitchen hard and fast, the frantic nature of the journey sent chairs crashing to the floor.

"What the heck is going on?" Gen pleaded to Kelly. "Who are they? Why are you so scared?"

Kelly's eyes bulged with fear. "Everyone back here now!" Kelly yelled breathlessly.

Gen watched the aura of her sibling's Heavenly power light up the room like a Christmas tree. Soft colors of brilliant light splashed across the ceiling, reflecting in all directions as they arrived.

Tom was first to speak. "What is it?" he asked Kelly. "What's happened?"

Kelly's eyes were wild, Gen thought she looked almost as if she didn't believe what she was about to tell them. "I know who they are," Kelly said, her breathing sounding a bit calmer. "I know what they are."

"Did you just run into them?" Deb asked. "Why didn't you call us? We were going to confront them together."

"We were at the café," Gen answered. "All these people started running from the library across the street. We entered because it seemed urgent and there was nothing demonic about the scene."

Gen bent over and retrieved a fallen chair from the floor, putting it upright she sat down before continuing. "It was a madman with a gun, an ex-boyfriend of a woman who worked the front counter. He brandished a weapon and was shooting people. He killed an older gentleman."

"We felt nothing demonic," Kelly added. "But we couldn't reach the gunman, we were unable to sway him, calm him, neither of us could."

"How far away were you from the gunman?" Dan asked.

"We were practically on top of him," Kelly answered.

Gen continued relaying the events. "That led us to look around, we started with the basement. When we got to the door and opened it, we felt them, heard them, the demons. We could no longer hear each other, and we couldn't reach the rest of you."

Gen watched the wave of understanding wash over their faces before she continued. "Their voices were deep and menacing. They were arguing, with each other. We crept along the racks as quietly as possible to try and get a glimpse of who it was. As we approached, Kelly tried using her cell phone to text you guys, but she had no signal."

Gen paused to look at Kelly whose chest had stopped heaving, her sister was now slumped against the kitchen island that ran between the kitchen and eating area. Her sister seemed far away, lost in her thoughts.

"Okay, so I assume you got a look at them," Xavier stated.

Gen thought the heaviness in the room matched the fatigue running through them. How could she not feel exhausted after weeks of running around trying to track these things down?

Now, we finally stumble upon them and Kelly has us running scared from the scene, Gen thought. *This must be very bad if Kelly's afraid.*

"I only saw glimpses of them from the angle I was crouched in," Kelly said.

"Then how are you so sure you know who they are?" Greg asked.

"Or what they are?" Frankie echoed.

"It was the names, I heard all their names," Kelly answered. "Then when the female demon spoke, I remembered her from that night in the park. The night she nearly killed me."

Deb whispered, "Oh no."

Kelly swallowed with a small sigh escaping her rigid body.

"Kelly, tell us, who are they?" Tom asked.

"The first demon, the one Antonio exposed, his name is Leucous." Kelly looked up and into Tom's eyes. "The second demon, the one in black that Deb described during her encounter with Michael, is Raven. The third demon, the female that attacked me, is Sonoran."

How does she know who is who? Gen wondered.

"Their brother who is missing, the one we suspect Schlosser attacked and stole powers from, his name is Vermillion," Kelly finished.

There was quiet in the room, Gen felt like the others were struggling to understand, much as she was. She still couldn't comprehend why Kelly was so frantic, but slowly Gen saw recognition come into Tom's eyes.

"Leucous," Kelly said.

"White," Tom replied.

"Raven," Kelly lobbed out to him.

"Black," Tom answered.

"Sonoran," Kelly added.

"Pale," Tom said.

"Vermillion," Kelly finished.

"Red," Tom completed. Gen had never seen a look of such dread on Tom's face. "It can't be, it just can't be." Tom shook his head in disbelief.

"It can't actually be upon us," Tom said to Kelly. "It can't be their time to be here."

"You think there's a right time for them to be here?" Kelly retorted.

"Who's here?" Gen asked impatiently.

"*I watched as the Lamb opened the first of the seven seals,*" Kelly recited, looking toward Gen. "*Then I heard one of the four living creatures say in a voice like thunder, 'Come!' I looked, and there before me was a white horse! Its rider held a bow, and he was given a crown, and he rode out as a conqueror bent on conquest.*"

Kelly cited the reference with ease, as if she had read it a thousand times, perhaps she had. Gen felt a wave of dizziness as the realization set in.

"The Four Horsemen. You're saying these eight-foot green eyed demons are the Four Horsemen?" Gen was asking Kelly the question, but she felt the weight of truth before it was confirmed. Her siblings were spread out before her grappling with it themselves.

Kelly continued to make her case. *"When the Lamb opened the second seal, I heard the second living creature say, 'Come!' Then another horse came out, a fiery red one. Its rider was given power to take peace from the earth and to make men slay each other. To him was given a large sword."*

"That kind of makes sense," Deb said. "If that's the power Schlosser stole and is wielding down here, it explains why there's been such an uptick in violence, more road rage, more anger, and almost no tolerance in the last six months."

"We know the story, but remind us about the last two riders," Dan said.

"When the Lamb opened the third seal, I heard the third living creature say, 'Come!' I looked, and there before me was a black horse! Its rider was holding a pair of scales in his hand." Kelly paused. "This rider is most often thought to represent famine resulting from the war the second horsemen manifests."

"So that means the last one is destruction," Greg said.

"Yes and no," Kelly replied. *"I heard the voice of the fourth living creature say, 'Come!' I looked, and there before me was a pale horse! Its rider was named Death, and Hades was following close behind him. They were given power over a fourth of the earth to kill by sword, famine, and plague, and by the wild beasts of the earth."*

"The problem with this last one is it implies that the fourth horseman is Death," Tom said. "That has long been thought to be an inaccurate assumption by Humans."

"They also thought all Four Horsemen were male and clearly that was wrong," Kelly told them. "Sonoran may bring death and decay upon this world, but she is not Death itself."

"How do you know?" Dan asked.

"I don't," Kelly paused. "It's just my instinct tells me that she isn't."

"Now what?" Deb asked. "Let's assume this is all true, that the three demons are here looking for the Red Horseman. That obviously means they aren't here to bring on the apocalypse."

Gen looked at Deb. "What are you suggesting, that it's okay that they are here because it's not the end of days?"

"Not at all," Deb answered. "This is obviously bad, but, if all they want is their brother, then shouldn't we stick with the plan of helping them see it was Schlosser and not us? Shouldn't we give them what they want?"

"Should we?" Xavier asked. "If we don't help them, does that mean the apocalypse doesn't happen because one of them was unexpectedly killed?"

"I hadn't thought about that," Deb replied.

"Think it through with me," Greg said, "if a human had the chance to stop Hitler before he could annihilate more than six million people, would they? Should they?"

"I don't think this is up to us." Gen put her hands up to quell the rising tension. "These demons think someone in Heaven kidnapped Vermillion, that's why they're stalking and attacking us. We can't just do nothing and hope for the best."

"What do you suggest we do?" Xavier asked.

"I'm not sure but doing nothing isn't an option," Gen answered. "There are too many lives at stake. We can't just find them and tell them we don't have their brother."

"The weird thing is they already know that we don't have Vermillion, that we don't know where he is," Kelly interjected. "Deb said Raven looked inside her mind and then told Leucous she knew nothing. Sonoran breached my mind and would have seen the same thing."

"We need to show them," Deb suggested. "We need to prove we don't have their brother. They need to see Schlosser wielding Vermillion's power."

"Actually, that might work," Tom said as he walked to the corner of the room and pulled out the white board. It was covered in Dan's writing from the last several weeks. "We know Schlosser has been following you. What if all this time the Horsemen were following Schlosser?"

"Tracking his powers?" Kelly asked Tom.

"Perhaps," Tom answered. "Either way, we need to flush Schlosser out and keep him in our presence long enough for the Horsemen to show up."

"That is super risky!" Kelly squealed.

"Yes, but this needs to end," Gen said. "We want them gone and we need Michael and Harry back."

"How would you go about doing this?" Dan asked.

"We've been looking for weeks and couldn't find him, what makes you think we can do it now?" Xavier added.

"We give Schlosser what he really wants," Gen told them.

"No!" Kelly said sternly. "Absolutely not."

"We lay a trap," Deb said.

"Yes," Tom agreed. "We choose the setting, do things on our terms. When Schlosser arrives, we fight him long enough to bring the Horsemen."

"I don't like any part of this plan, but..." Kelly said with a sigh, "I don't have a better one."

"Anyone have an idea of how we can pull this off?" Gen asked.

"We use the church, a place familiar but not just to us, to the Horsemen also." Tom stepped forward his natural leadership skills commanding the room. "Imprints from their power probably still linger there."

"How do you suppose we get Schlosser there?" Frankie asked.

"I'm assuming he's been stalking us already," Tom answered. "He's probably been following us this entire time, waiting for an opportunity too good to pass up."

"What would that be?" Frankie asked.

"Oh my God!" Kelly exclaimed "Don't you say it, Thomas."

"It's me in human form," Gen replied. "Alone."

"This is the worst plan ever!" Kelly said emphatically.

"It actually might work," Deb told Gen.

"I think it would too," Gen agreed.

"Have you people lost your minds?" Kelly bellowed. "Michael and Harry are gone, I died, and now you want to go off alone in human form as bait for a psycho demon hopped up on powers that he knows nothing about?"

Kelly practically fell apart in terror. *She's still traumatized*, Gen thought. *It's not fair, but I need to end this.*

"When do we do this, Tom?" Gen asked.

"Now," Tom answered. "Anyone know where your charges are right now?"

"I know Sophia is working the craft fair at the church today," Deb told them. "But, if you go there in human form and make contact with her, you'll be exposed."

"That's even better," Tom replied.

"Am I the only reasonable person left in this room?" Kelly asked, no one answered.

"What do the rest of us do, Tom?" Frankie asked.

"Some of us go there ahead of time, a couple of us should walk with Gen while she's in human form," Tom directed. "The rest of us will stay close by the church until our marks go off. We'll know exactly when Gen's exposed because all of our marks will go off."

"Why put Gen more at risk by exposing her?" Dan asked Tom.

"Finally, someone else is coming to their senses," Kelly grumbled.

"When Gen is exposed, all our marks will go off, and we're going to need everyone," Tom replied.

The room was quiet, Gen looked at Tom not understanding what he was inferring with all their marks going off.

"What do you mean we're going to need everyone, Tom?" Gen finally asked.

"If you're exposed, all our marks go off," Tom answered. "All your siblings."

"Michael," Xavier said. "You mean Michael's will go off too, letting Gabriel and Jared know one of us is in trouble."

"I think Gabriel will know exactly which one of us is in trouble," Deb added.

"It won't matter that they aren't on earth," Tom added. "One of our marks goes off due to exposure, all our marks light up, no matter what plane we're on."

Kelly added, "Why is no one talking about all the people that could potentially be in harm's way with this plan?"

"We can draw the demons away from the building," Tom replied. "Into the surrounding field should keep them safe, Kell."

"It might be the best plan we have," Gen told them. "I'll head upstairs to get ready, what time is the craft fair?"

"It's running now until around five or six tonight," Deb answered.

"Let's get moving," Gen told them. "You guys work out the details of who's going where. We'll need weapons. I'll be back down and ready in twenty minutes." Gen walked out the door heading to the second floor.

Either way this ends tonight, Gen thought.

Gen did a few things in the bathroom and walked down the hall toward her bedroom, turning the nob she pushed the door open to find Kelly standing there waiting for her.

"Why are you doing this?" Kelly demanded. "This is a crazy plan that Michael would not approve of."

"I think he actually may be proud of Tom for this one," Gen answered.

"Whatever." Kelly waved off the reply and began pacing back and forth "There has to be a better way."

"Well if there is, it hasn't occurred to any of us in several months," Gen replied.

"Gen, this entire thing is nutty, you are running off on a whim, Deb is agreeing with Tom's risky plan, and I want to wait around for a better option." Kelly huffed a pause. "This is like upside-down world."

"Kelly if you don't feel ready to go back out there then you can always—"

"No way!" Kelly yelled. "I'm not staying home. I just wish we were all staying home."

"I know," Gen responded. "I wish a lot of things too, but we need to end this. I like the idea of trying something on our terms, not waiting around for him to attack."

Kelly plopped down on the bed and hung her head in her hands.

"Whatever happens, at least we did this together." Gen sat on the bed and wrapped an arm around her sister. "That's our real power, remember?"

"Yeah, I know, it's what Michael always told us, stronger together. You just make sure you're prepared for him this time; you be ready for anything. The minute that mark goes off, you cover it up. You get clear and change out of human form, quickly, you hear me?"

"Yes, I'm ready, I can do this," Gen told her. "I promise."

Genevieve now in human form walked briskly to the church. Xavier and Greg were following her, even though she could no longer speak to them she felt the warmth of their presence. Tom and Dan were already at the church. Frankie, Deb, and Kelly waited one block down from the church. Deb assumed if all of them waited at the church together they might give off too strong a signal when their marks went off. Deb smartly spread everyone out to negate that, but they were still close.

The church hummed with activity, there were balloons and banners advertising the craft fair, several people came and went through the garden entrance. Gen walked through the gate and entered the open door to the basement of the church, where tables had been setup all along the back and side wall. There were at least a hundred people milling about, shopping at the tables and gathering to catch up over coffee and fresh pastry.

The smell of sugared dough and fresh brewed coffee wafted through the air, Father Donovan spotted Genevieve and moved in her direction wearing a warm wide smile.

"Miss O'Mara what a wonderful surprise." Gen noticed the priest peer behind her and knew he was looking for her sisters. "Are you alone this afternoon?"

"I am Father, but my sisters will be along shortly," Gen said with a smile "They are running a bit late today."

"Oh, well please send them over when they arrive. I'll be running around trying to convince everyone Mrs. Spencer has the best banana bread in town."

Gen laughed. "Of course, Father, we'll be sure to come find you," Gen replied as she watched the priest move off to greet other guests.

It didn't take long for Gen to spot Sophia, who was working a busy table at the front of the room. As Gen approached, she noticed Deb's charge holding a large wheel of raffle tickets. Her cousin Stella was sitting next to her assisting with collecting money and making change for people.

Gen pulled out a ten-dollar bill, waited in line, and then held the payment out with her right hand.

Sophia greeted her with a warm welcome "Hello, tickets are 3 for $10.00 or 1 for $5.00"

"Three tickets please," Gen replied.

Sophia ripped the tickets in half as Gen filled in her name on the stubs. Once complete Gen handed the ticket stubs back to Sophia clumsily ensuring the two women touched.

"Sorry about that," Gen said to Sophia wincing at the burning sensation washing over her left wrist. The heat from her mark was stronger than anything she had ever encountered before. She wasn't sure if it was because she was in human form, or because she had been exposed, but it was more amplified than when a charge is in need.

Gen stuck her left hand deep inside the pocket of her dark red sweatshirt doing her best to hide the mark. She felt her face become flush as nausea rolled through her. She turned and walked away from the busy table aiming for the steps that would lead her out and into the courtyard.

As she felt the air bristle through the open doorway she exited to the yard and turned right to avoid the influx of new fairgoers. She stepped inside the church and disappeared from human view. Once she did, she saw Frankie and Greg about fifteen feet in front of her. Gen could see the beams of light hovering around them, they were experiencing the same strong sensation of their marks going off as she was.

"What now?" Gen said to them.

"Now, you come with me." The deep gravelly voice came from her left. As she turned Schlosser reached out and grabbed her shoulder.

She saw her brothers run toward her yelling, Xavier threw a weapon at Schlosser, but she couldn't make out any words. It was as if she were falling into unconsciousness, a dark dizzying sensation blurring her vision. When her eyes refocused her brothers were gone and Genevieve stood in the place where she first battled Schlosser.

"You brought me back here?" Gen asked lost in a fog of confusion.

She could smell the demon before she saw him, he came around from behind her with a broad smile. "Well, not exactly the same place, but close enough for your death."

"We aren't on earth." Gen, hiding her fear as best she could, goaded Schlosser. "Of course not, you don't have the nerve to confront me on earth."

"You can't say I didn't warn you," he said to her. "I told you that you would never see me coming and you would lose."

All that talk about doing this on my own terms, Gen thought. *Feels more like I'm fulfilling a prophecy.* Gen couldn't help but flashback to the images she saw in Gerry's nightmare. *I'm afraid I'm about to live out what I saw in Gerry's dream.*

CHAPTER TWENTY-THREE

Gen inhaled deeply, she smelled only Schlosser, who reeked of decomposition and death. She was tied to a tree with a long piece of jagged metal ripped from the Chain of Chaos. The sharp edges dug into her stomach and wrists. One barbed-wire strand was scraping against her mark, like a living thing trying to burrow into her skin. The weapon was wrapped tightly around her body, she could barely move, and the demonic nature of the chain made her teleporting powers useless; there would be no escaping.

Surveying the area, Gen took in as much as she could from her vantage point. It looked like the place she had saved Becky, but something was off about it. Despite the landscape of long-leafed trees and flowering shrubs, the breeze carried nothing but stale dry air. It was more like being in a desert than its facade portrayed. The muddy pond that Becky's car had narrowly escaped six months ago lay half a football field away, but it was still. The entire scene seemed like something out of a painting and not an actual place.

He's replicating, Gen surmised. *I wonder how much energy that's zapping? He had to bring me here and keep the surrounding images in place. I'm betting that's more draining than he thinks it is.*

Gen was doing her best to remain calm. Her situation was precarious, but she loathed to show Schlosser any weakness. The demon was standing about ten feet away, watching glimpses of her squirm and enjoying it.

"Now what?" Gen asked.

"Oh, you know, just the usual: torture, enslavement, maybe a little play time with the Hellions, and then death." He couldn't contain his glee. "I've already decided who I'm going to sell your soul to. He's a liar and a cheat; he'll do wrong by you for sure." The demon chuckled, but it was riddled with phlegm and mucus.

I can't sense anything nearby, Gen realized. *Either he's cloaking, or he's brought me to a realm where my powers are naturally weaker.*

Gen walked through the various scenarios in her mind. Given how much power Schlosser was already using to bring and keep her here, it was doubtful he'd be able to cloak at the same time.

"So, I kick your ass on earth, send you back to Hell, and six months later you return with all these upper level demonic powers. You know I have to ask, what happened? Do you even know who the demon was you stole powers from?"

"You did not kick my ass, you cheated!" Schlosser screamed. "You have no idea what they did to me for months down in the bowels of Hell!"

Gen watched Schlosser step toward her in anger but then he pulled back. "I narrowly escaped. I had to make a few deals to give myself a chance to make it out, when one such moment finally reared itself, I didn't hesitate. The entire time those torturers were ripping me to shreds, then healing me so they could do it all over again, I thought about you."

"I'm flattered, but you're not my type," Gen quipped.

"Your bravery would mean something if I didn't hear your heart hammering so fast. Your chest is heaving, your forehead sweating, even your mark is still burning. The chain is sniffing, because it knows weakness. It will find its way inside, just in case you were wondering. Don't try and pretend, it's useless on me. You're afraid, and you should be."

"What you do to innocent women, like Becky, isn't right." Gen tried to throw him off by bringing him back to the memory of that night.

"She's not innocent, none of them are." Schlosser spit the last part of the comment revealing his disdain for all things Human.

He has more contempt than the average Roamer Demon, Gen concluded.

"So, your plan." Gen paused for effect. "I have to say for months of strategizing, it's not that great."

"Ha," Schlosser responded before continuing. "You're stalling, but it doesn't matter. I'm waiting for, let's call them colleagues, to arrive. Then we'll get started. You can expect to be beaten, broken, battered, and burned, just like I was."

"Whatever, maybe I'm not the one stalling." Gen feigned indifference at Schlosser's threats.

"I'm not afraid of you, bitch." Schlosser's voice lowered to a sinister tone. "But you should be very afraid of me. You should be terrified of what I've been dreaming of doing to you these last several months."

The hair on her entire body stood on end. Gen was afraid. Not just of the unknown Hell that Schlosser was about to unleash on her, but of dying in some far-off realm never allowed to see her family or Gabriel again.

It can't end this way, she thought with sorrow and regret.

"Oh," Schlosser mocked her. "Are you upset? Are you going to cry now?"

"In your dreams, demon," Gen snorted. "I know where I'm going when this is over, but it's where you'll be going that will carry me through."

"I'm not going anywhere." He smiled, exposing his yellow teeth and brown gum line. Schlosser's horrendous breath wafted over to her.

"I'm sorry but you're an idiot, you really are. Did you miss the family I have back home looking for me?" Gen smirked back at him. "Do you think they're just gonna let you do what you want and not come after you?"

"I don't care what they do. They have no power over me, not anymore. They have no way of reaching us, which is all that matters right now. The rest I'll deal with later, and who knows, maybe you'll see them sooner than you think."

"Is right now all that matters?" Gen huffed. "So after you kill me, and Heaven sends me back," Gen paused, hoping her bluff carried confidence, "I get my family. Then, we hunt you down, send you back to Hell, because let's face it, that's where you belong—"

"Enough!" Schlosser yelled and the ground beneath her feet shook, just as it had that day on the field with Leucous.

Gen watched the demon start to pace and mumble to himself. Clearly, he was unhappy with her refusal to show fear.

Perhaps he hadn't thought about the possibility of my returning to Earth to hunt him down, Gen thought. *Maybe he's unsure whether that's a real possibility.*

"You should re-think this plan Roamer," Gen said sternly.

"I'm not a Roamer, not anymore." Schlosser stopped and made a beeline for her position, grabbing her by the throat. "I have waited far too long for this revenge and I will have it! Your death will be by my hand, Guardian." Gen could see the hatred in his eyes as he seemed to have to force himself to unclench his grip and let go.

"Speaking of Death," Gen paused trying to calm the tremor she could hear in her voice. "Do you know whose power you took? Because I do."

"I don't care." Schlosser smiled, and his stench burned Gen's nostrils. "It doesn't matter, finders, keepers." He almost sang the lyric.

"Until they find you." Gen peered into his eyes. The glowing green she saw in the others she now saw in his eyes. It might be the longer he holds the power, the more it takes over. "They've been chasing you, following their brother's essence, you must know that already." Gen let a slow smirk slide across her face. "Maybe it's not my family you should be worried about. Perhaps you should have made sure what you attacked was dead before you came back to Earth."

Schlosser stepped back. "I tried killing him, he was a tough one. But he just wouldn't die." The demon let out a sinister chuckle. "So, I chained his broken useless carcass up in the caves beneath the waterfall in Purgatory. No one will ever find him there. Not your family, not his brothers, no one."

Oh my God, Gen thought, *He's so cocky he just told me where he stashed Vermillion. I'm afraid he's right. Finding Vermillion in Purgatory would be a futile effort. There was no way the Horsemen would be able to sense him there, with nothing to track they would be aimlessly wandering in hopes of stumbling upon him.*

Gen wanted to allow for hope to emerge, but how could she when Schlosser just gave away his biggest secret. Telling her where he left Vermillion was equivalent to a murderer showing you their face. Killers only do that when they are assured no one will be left behind as a witness. Gen felt the scene shift, cracks in the image that surrounded them began to open, twisting the perfect trees into unnatural shapes. Whatever was coming, Schlosser had to release his grip on the scene to allow its entry.

A thunderclap overhead preceded lightning, wind picked up and the fake swampy pond all but disappeared before Gen's eyes. The true landscape behind the scene Schlosser was projecting revealed itself in small flashing images.

Large boulders were to her right, and off in the distance she could see what looked like miles of rocky cliffs dotted with caves along the ridgeline. Gen looked down to her left and realized she wasn't tied to a tree but to a gate, its old rusty spindles squealed in the swaying gale. The ground was covered in dirt and small stones mixed with dust and spun into tiny cyclones as Schlosser's demonic allies made their entry behind her.

Hell Fighters, Gen thought. *It's what it sounded and felt like when the Hell Fighter arrived the night of the school fire. I remember Michael's warning as we ran to take cover under the treelined canopy of the nearby forest.*

Gen's mind was swimming. *It seems to have taken a while for these Hell Fighters to arrive. Schlosser must have summoned them after he abducted me. He's not taking any chances. It may mean the rumor about the Hell Fighter is true, that they can't be absent from Hell for too long.*

Gen remembered Kelly telling her that Guardians believed a Hell Fighter's essence weakened the longer it was away from the source of its power. Schlosser's own punishment must be part of that source now, because Hell Fire was known to be spun from the tortured. The flames in Hell mix with the blood and burning flesh of the damned to create the Hell Fighter's lifeforce. Upper level demons then take the fiery elixir to Earth and thrust it upon an unsuspecting human. Once the Hell Fighter absorbs the human's soul, it will never be stronger, never more powerful, than it is during those first few years.

Gen heard the demons arguing, but in a language she couldn't decipher. Raised voices rode up and down like the waves of an ocean, making it impossible to tell how far away they were and just how many of them were behind her.

Maybe things aren't going to plan, Gen wished.

Looking straight ahead she watched a demon manifest in front of her. He wore a dark gray pinstriped suit with a long black trench coat with perfectly polished shoes. To say he was a fish out of water was an understatement.

Gen saw his weathered skin was creased with age, and he kept what little hair he had short and combed neatly into place. He was tall, thin, and stood bone straight, as if his spine were incapable of bending. Gen felt his black beady eyes inspecting her, practically boring into her soul.

"You didn't say which family this one came from." The demon spoke and with it the arguing stopped.

"I'm not dead yet, demon," Gen said to him. "I'm one of the O'Mara's."

"That's an old and powerful clan." The demon looked to his right and spoke to someone over her left shoulder. "Are you sure about this?"

"Shut the Hell up, Torin!" Schlosser's voice boomed from behind her. "You don't know a damn thing about anything. Now do we have a deal or not?"

Torin looked dismayed at Schlosser's outburst, as if he found the entire situation unpleasant.

"I have the last bottle of serum," Torin replied. "As I told you, each vial has a diminished effect. It will stop working soon, and when it does, your newfound powers will be traceable. Then whoever you're running from will know where you are."

"Just give me the damn vial and you can take her soul when we're done with it. That was our deal. After this, you and I are done." Schlosser walked past Gen and over to Torin.

Torin glanced at Genevieve before retrieving a small amulet of liquid from his trench coat. "Don't chew her up too badly or she won't be worth what I've already given you. If that happens, I'll return and demand a refund."

Schlosser laughed. "Don't worry, we won't harm the merchandise too much."

Schlosser grabbed the item Torin held out and gulp it down hungrily.

So that's how Schlosser's been evading the Horsemen, Gen surmised. *He's using something to mask Vermillion's power.*

Torin turned away as if to take his leave, and Gen understood this was the demon who would steal her soul. "I will get a message to my family, demon. They will know your name if you let this happen, Torin. I promise you that!"

Torin turned and looked back at Gen. "I have survived for millennia, not because I take sides, but because I make deals and keep them. That's all I do."

"You might want to make a new deal then, because I will get out of here. Then me and my family will find you, all of you!" Gen tilted her chin up trying to project the threat to whoever was still standing behind her.

"I'm afraid you're wrong, Guardian," Torin answered over laughter from the other demons. "No Guardian has ever escaped the gates of Hell and returned to tell about it."

With that, Torin left as the Hell Fighter who had arrived unlocked the Chain of Chaos from behind her, temporarily freeing Gen's body.

Fear ripped through her. *Gates of Hell!* Gen agonized. Her heart went into overdrive and her head spun with the truth of Torin's statement.

The dust, the large boulders, and caves she saw when Schlosser's powers released their grip on the scene, they were all glimpses of the desolate wasteland.

Gen's body shot forward clamoring to get away from the demons. She only needed a few feet to attempt an escape or at least surround herself with her shield. She took two, maybe three steps before pain ripped down her back. She fell to her knees and someone kicked her from behind forcing her down onto the ground. The Chain of Chaos was now lodged along her back. One of the demons pulled on the chain and Gen screamed in pain as her body was dragged, facedown, back across the stone-milled terrain.

She watched in horror at the site of her own blood mixing with the rancid dirt to make a brownish-red sludge that marked the trail they pulled her along. Struggling to breathe, she inhaled the dust being kicked up in her face as she was hauled back toward the gate she had been tethered to. Her chest was heaving, gasping for air, but sandy grains filled her lungs with dry desert soil making her choke and cough. She thought of Kelly's encounter with Sonoran; she remembered all the blood she had been covered in as she cradled Kelly's limp body.

At least no one is here to see me go through this, Gen found the only solace available to her in that moment.

As she was violently pulled up to her feet, staggering and unsteady she nearly bounced off Schlosser as he stood in front of her laughing. His wounds were now temporarily sealed and no longer oozing. The smell of death abated, he stood as tall as the Horsemen, with his hulking frame towering over her. She was terrified, but there was a strange sort of dreaminess to the scene now.

Maybe, if I'm lucky I'll lose consciousness soon, Gen hoped.

With force, the Hell Fighter yanked his weapon free from her back. Gen heard the clanging of the chain as it bounced to the ground. Her skin was flayed and ripped open as her shirt, now torn, hung loosely from her body.

324

Sweat from the Hell Fighter dripped onto her seeping wounds and stung as the venom burned away more layers of her skin.

She was screaming and flailing, but the Hell Fighter held both arms behind her. She felt her anger stir inside and the ground rumbled underfoot. Gen's rage felt like a tidal wave rising from her feet getting stronger as it struggled to free itself, she knew if relinquished she wouldn't be able to control it.

Her mouth flew open and Gen released a guttural howl. The rage unleashed was so strong it shook and cracked open the ground surrounding them. The demons stumbled backward away from her, including the Hell Fighter who lost his grip on her arms. Gen instinctively lurched forward tackling Schlosser. Gen's surprise attack took Schlosser down to the ground easily. She began swinging wildly at his face and the sides of his body. Each jab split Schlosser's worn and remolded flesh exposing the demon's true decay underneath.

Time seemed to slow and Gen saw her swinging arms and bruised hands land punches that wounded Schlosser in an onslaught of bloody succession. The moment felt like a living nightmare as demonic fluid and green puss splattered and hung in the air all around her. She felt as though she were watching someone else attack Schlosser. Gen witnessed her own anger spinning her helplessly into a torrent of fiery wrath that seemed to consume her.

Oh my God, Gen ached. *I'm drowning in my own rage, taking everything and everyone down with me.*

With sorrow, Gen watched herself continue to rampage against Schlosser's weakened body. She felt like a ferocious animal caught in a trap, unable to defend or help herself against the wildfire of violence.

This is what Harry warned me about, Gen reeled. *This is what he meant when he said my anger would fester and turn. My hurt at losing Gabriel didn't just linger, it manifested into something else. What have I done?* Gen felt her own heart thundering in her ears. *I'm broken.*

A silver shimmer caught Gen's eye through the brown haze of scattered dirt and dust. In the chaos of the attack Schlosser dropped the façade, now only dried up landscape could be seen. She was exhausted, the unexpected assault left her wounded body covered in a layer of sweat. It took her mind several seconds to comprehend the glimmering silver color. By the time she understood it was her wedding band she heard the Hell Fighter recover and stomp toward her from behind. She had expended all her energy. Drained and severely wounded, she was too weak to attempt an escape.

No! Gen thought about Gabriel. *I can't leave this world without the ring, it's all I have left of us.*

Gen launched herself forward, stretching her right arm as far as it would extend and felt the cold of the ring against the burning skin of her scuffed-up palm. Grasping the wedding band, she pulled her elbow in just as Schlosser pushed and kicked at her stomach. Gen was thrust off Schlosser, rolling several feet away from the demon. Closing her eyes Gen thought of her husband.

I'm sorry I wasted so much time, Gen thought in regret. *Gabriel, I hope you know how much I love you.*

Hearing the thundering footsteps of the demons as they reached her position, she could do nothing but kick toward them as their hands wrapped around her neck. This was her last chance to be free, she used it to slip the silver band around her left ring finger.

As she was being carried back to the gate, she heard Schlosser bark, "I'm done playing games. Put her down, I'm ending her right here."

The Hell Fighter released his grip and Gen fell to the ground in a heap. He then pulled her head back by her hair. She was on her knees, her face forced to look up at Schlosser as he wielded a sword above his head.

Oh God, Gen thought. *This is it, this is the vision we all saw in Gerry's dream that night in the hospital.*

"Now you die, just like I said you would." The demon's face was torn and shredded in several places. Soaked in his own blood, Schlosser's body was vile. He seemed to be rotting right there in front of her.

Damn coward, even with all the powers he's accumulated he has another demon holding me down, Gen thought. *He wants to ensure I'm in no shape to fight back when he brings the blade down on top of me.*

"I'll be sure to say hi to your family for you," Schlosser taunted. "Your sisters in particular will be ripe for the picking after your death."

Schlosser grinned, then he took a deep breath and thrust the blade down.

Gen closed her eyes. *I forgive you Gabe,* she said silently. *Now I hope you can forgive me too.*

Gen felt the power of the ring burst to life. The sword had already begun its descent toward her, but it was now halted in mid-air. The breeze turned cold and she saw an image take shape behind Schlosser's left shoulder.

The dust settled in mid-air as the world around her stood still. There was no sound, the demons stood frozen as her husband appeared above her.

"There's nothing to forgive," Gabriel said. "I'm the one who left, had to leave."

"I don't care, not anymore," Gen told him. "None of that matters."

"I can't free you from this," Gabe said, pain reverberating through his voice.

"How are you here?" Gen asked.

"You brought me here. The ring allowed me to feel you again, but you brought my consciousness here."

"I can't get out of this. It's the wasteland, there's no escape. But, I'm so grateful to be able to see your face and speak to you. Please Gabe, take care of my family, help them when I'm—"

"You can get out. You've had the power this whole time," Gabriel interrupted her.

"What do you mean? The anger?" Gen asked him. "I'm afraid I depleted that."

"No, anger is just one way to release your power, an emotion, a passion, something once expended, recedes."

Gen watched Gabriel's aura begin to glow, the once crisp vision of him started to fade as if he were being pulled back.

"Please, don't go. Stay with me Gabriel, please!" Gen pleaded.

"Come home, Genevieve." Gabriel's voice dulled. "Tap into the one source they can never take from you, the one thing that's yours in abundance."

Pain clarified Gen's consciousness as the image of Gabriel turned to dust. She returned to herself as the Hell

Fighter that held her down pushed her slightly forward spraying her back with venom.

The one thing he cannot take from me, Gen heard Gabriel's voice reverberating through her mind.

Thinking of her husband, of her family, of Harry, she understood. *It's love.*

Gen heard Schlosser's malevolent grunt cut through the air, he had thrust with force. The Hell Fighter was holding her in place by her hair, but her hands and feet were free.

Gen moved her right leg forward, digging her foot flat into the ground, now she was on one bended knee. As she felt the weapon crashing toward her, she thrust her arms up and caught the blade in mid-air just inches above her turned-up face.

Schlosser gasped in shock. Gen's wedding band glistened off the blade. She pushed back with all her strength and stood. Twisting the sword between her palms she jerked it to the right and continued pushing the blunt end back toward Schlosser. Gen's maneuver worked and she managed to send the weapon flying away from them.

Turning quickly Gen took her left wrist—her mark still ablaze from being exposed—and swiped the Holy light across the Hell Fighter's arms as he reached for her. The demon howled and staggered backward as his skin caught fire and he began to swat at the flames.

"Now, you're going to follow me," Gen said to Schlosser.

Gen projected her shield, sending the Hell Fighter further back away from her. She watched realization come over Schlosser; he knew she was about to escape.

"Don't let her leave!" Schlosser bellowed, but it was too late.

Gen used her aura to leave the wasteland and escaped back to Earth.

CHAPTER TWENTY-FOUR

Gen felt the rocky terrain beneath her feet and was engulfed by the smell of fresh grass, green trees, and wild lavender.

I made it, she thought to herself in relief. But it was short lived as the pain from her wounds rolled through her like a freight train.

"I need everyone, quickly, he's coming for me!" Gen wasted no time in yelling aloud to her siblings. She could sense them again and knew they could feel her too. "Kell, I need a sweatshirt and weapons, whatever you can grab on your way here."

The world seemed to calm as if she were in some sort of pause as she took in the actual landscape of where she first encountered Schlosser. Not much had changed since she was here last. The grass was lush now, the trees a bit fuller, and the purple color of lavender rambled through the brush, but overall it looked mostly untouched.

She closed her eyes when she realized she could feel Gabriel. She couldn't hear him, nor see him, but somehow, she could sense him.

It's been so long Gabe, Gen said as she tried to focus her energy to clarify the signal. *I nearly forgot what the connection felt like.*

An unpleasant odor washed over her, there was only one thing that smelled that rancid.

"You should have tried a different hiding spot," Schlosser said.

Gen's eyes opened, standing less than ten feet away, Schlosser leered at her.

"Who says I'm hiding?" Gen scoffed.

Schlosser didn't respond, instead he raised his arm and threw several round shaped globes toward her head. Gen assumed they were Hell Fighter venom. She thought it fortunate that the Hell Fighter did not accompany Schlosser.

Gen felt her exhaustion like a blanket tightly woven across her entire body. She hadn't projected her shield when she arrived because she wanted to be sure her family would sense and hear her when she contacted them. As the deadly bombs neared her position she flinched and moved to duck out of the way. Her reflexes were slow, and she realized she couldn't move as quickly as normal.

Her blood-soaked back burned from the venom that lingered on her bruised and battered body. Judging the speed and distance of his position, Gen knew the objects were coming too fast, at least two were going to make contact. She prepared herself for the pain. She knew this much venom would explode on contact. Judging by the larger than normal size of the amulets the fluid would be enough to ignite parts of her body on fire.

Gen closed her eyes and braced for impact.

Where are they? Gen's weary mind pleaded as her eyelids lifted and the field came into view once more.

The vials had exploded in mid-air sending small flames of oozing black sludge away from her and back onto Schlosser's face. The demon howled in frustration. Gen looked down but nothing had landed on her. She was so tired it took several seconds to register the warmth of Deb's shield wrapped around her.

"How?" Schlosser yelled. "You had no time to project your shield."

"Who said it was my shield?" Gen smirked.

Looking right, Gen spotted Deb, then turning to her left she heard Kelly's voice.

"Hey stinky!" Kelly toyed. "Looks like someone kicked your ass real good!"

"Shut the Hell up," Schlosser spit. "You can all go to Hell now."

Gen watched Schlosser jab at Kelly, but she was too quick for him. Her sister swung her blade down on top of his arm and pulled the blade back slicing him deeply. Schlosser howled and defensively ripped his arm back toward his body. The puss and blood that sprayed out fell to the ground and burned the grass below.

Before the demon could recover, Kelly pivoted her body to stand between Schlosser and Gen. Jumping several feet in the air Kelly kicked him hard in the chest. The lumbering demon stumbled back several feet and fell at Tom's feet.

"The only one going back to Hell tonight is you, Roamer." Tom towered over Schlosser's crumpled body.

Gen watched in glorious reprieve as her brothers loomed over the fallen demon. Everything became murky, like a foggy haze she was trying to see through as Kelly and Deb approached.

"Oh my," Deb gasped. "Your back, it's so bad, how are you standing?"

Kelly took a peak and winced at the site of Gen's wounds. "We don't have time to heal you, Gen."

"We have to," Deb pleaded. "She's sure to pass out soon if we don't do something."

"Kelly's right," Gen said. "There's no time, he's sure to be sending more demons if they aren't already enroute."

As if on cue, Gen saw a portal open behind her brothers who were now engaged in battle with Schlosser. Even in his weakened state the powers he stole from Vermillion made him a formidable opponent.

"You were right," Kelly observed. "The portal just opened, something else is coming."

Kelly pointed to the portal and yelled a warning to her brothers. Deb started to speak, but Gen was slow to react as she didn't want to take her eyes off whatever was coming through Hell's doorway. All of Gen's movements took effort, everything hurt. The thumping achiness rolling through her was becoming unbearable.

"What if I take her back to the house myself to heal her. It will take longer to do it alone, but—" Deb stopped mid-sentence causing Gen to glance right. Her sister's face registered shock at whatever was behind Gen's left shoulder.

"Holy crap, he is here!" Kelly's hushed tone made Gen spun her head left. Pain shot through her neck at the sudden movement. Gen wasn't sure how much longer she would be able to stand upright.

Legs trembling, Gen felt warmth emanating from behind her. Turning fully around, she nearly collapsed at the site of her husband as he stood in front of her.

"You're going to need to go help your brothers, this field is about to be overrun with demons." Gabriel gave the warning without ever taking his eyes off Gen.

You're here, Gen thought as she felt her eyes well up with tears. *You're finally home.*

Gabriel stepped closer to Gen. "I can close the wounds, stop the bleeding, but that's about it. You're going to have to fight through the rest, can you do that?"

"Yes." Gen's one-word answer was all she could muster in her emotionally stupefied state.

Behind them, Gen heard the arrival of other demons but refused to turn away from Gabriel to see what had come. Her sisters ran off toward the milieu. She focused her eyes on her husband as he reached his arm behind her and pulled her into his arms. Gen choked down the grunt of pain that wanted to escape her lips.

"I'm sorry," he whispered.

Placing the palm of his hand on her forehead Gabriel sent a wave of energy through her body. The surge made her spine arch backward, but he held her firmly upright. Cool relief replaced the burning sensation as she felt her skin come together. When he was done, Gabriel leaned in and kissed her.

The desire to grab hold of her husband and leave this place was overwhelming.

"Keep the enemy in front of you as best you can. Your wounds are sealed, but still sensitive," he told her.

The sound of clanging metal and guttural grunts snapped her back to the reality of their situation.

"I will do my best," she answered as she turned to survey the area. Gasping she threw her hand out and grabbed hold of Gabriel's arm. "You need to go, now."

The field was covered in demons and more continued to pour through the portal Schlosser had opened.

"What?" Gabriel adamantly shook his head as he spoke. "I'm not going anywhere."

"You have to," Gen pleaded. "We need Michael, please go get him and Harry."

"Gen, I can help," he said, his eyes pleading for her not to send him away. "You don't understand, I'm a much different fighter now than I ever was."

"I know, you would have to be to survive in the Pit for forty years. But this is part of my plan. Michael needs to be here, we're stronger together. Schlosser is going to try and start a war here today. We need everyone."

Understanding crossed his face and she knew he would agree. Gen grabbed a dagger she assumed Kelly left for her and prepared to enter the fray.

"I'll be back as soon as I can. Whatever you do, stay alive."

She turned back to him and smiled. "For you, I would do anything."

She didn't watch him go, but after turning to help her siblings she felt him leave.

Fully taking in the scope of the scene nearly took her breath away. The landscape was a plethora of demonic monsters. Schlosser was toward the back of the enemy line yelling at the Hell Fighter Gen assumed was the same one from the wasteland. Schlosser was pacing back and forth as he waved his arms all around.

Something is not going his way, Gen thought.

Her siblings were engaged in fierce battle, several demons lay dead or dying throughout the field. The O'Mara's had already done well, but the newest wave of demons through the portal were Gutter Demons.

Before she reached the nearest demon, she heard Deb speaking telepathically. *We faced these demons at the Church. Michael told me not to waste movement on them. They're fast, but they only know one technique, swarming. Go for any spot on the neck or the thigh area. If you stab in the leg, be sure and pull your weapon vertically, not horizontally.*

The ones with little color will be stronger; they're older, Tom added. *The younger ones will be easier to kill, but be warned, their blood is slick like oily water. Try not to step in it.*

Gen watched as three Gutter Demons surrounded Greg. She raised her blade and sliced two of them along the back and side of the neck. The Gutter Demons' blood splattered, and Gen managed to narrowly miss getting hit by it. But swiping the blade against her jeans she felt the frigid liquid and was surprised it didn't burn.

"Their blood doesn't burn," Gen said aloud almost without thinking.

"Heads up Gen," Greg said to her. "More incoming, stay behind us as much as you can, we don't want anyone messing with whatever mojo Gabriel did on your back."

Gen hesitated, but then stepped back. She was already slightly winded from the brief encounter, so she was grateful for the reprieve. The field had devolved into chaos, Kelly was on one demon's back slicing another Gutter Demon with her blade. Deb was back-to-back with Tom as the two of them faced off against four smaller Hellions. Gen hadn't realized Hellions had even come through the portal until now.

Hellions are here. Gen spoke to her siblings. *Kell, you know their Hell Fighter Masters will show up eventually.*

I'm keeping an eye out, Kelly told them. *So far, I only see one arguing with Schlosser on the other side of the swamp.*

Gen watched the portal continue to bring forth Hell's darkness.

Anything we can do to shut down that portal? Gen asked as two Gutter Demons spotted her standing alone slightly beyond the battle line.

Kill the being who opened it, Kelly replied.

Gen looked around for a second weapon but there was nothing on the ground. The body count was increasing but given the number of demons coming through the portal, it felt like the momentum was shifting in Hell's favor.

The closest demon running toward her threw a vial. Fortunately, his accuracy was off, and it sailed over her head disappearing into the thick brush behind her. She countered by throwing her weapon at his neck. It landed right where she aimed. Still running, the demon grabbed at his throat and pulled the weapon free. As blood gushed from his wound he slowed and then collapsed feet from her position.

Undeterred by his fallen comrade the second demon kept coming. Gen had no other weapon, so she turned away and ran toward the closest heap of dead bodies. The Gutter Demon was fast on her heals. She slipped on a patch of oily blood as she neared the crowd and slid past her intended target. Regaining her footing she pulled a small dagger out of the chest of a dead demon and stood her ground waiting for the second demon to reach her, but he never did. Xavier had thrown a katar killing the demon instantly.

Gen ran toward his corpse and took the katar for herself. Wielding both weapons, Gen pushed further into the battle. She did her best to keep an eye on Schlosser who remained off the field. He was obviously content to let others die for his cause. The concern for Gen was how long her family could keep up against this onslaught.

The deeper she got, the harder it was to keep track of Schlosser's movements. The chaos of the battle devastated the landscape. Small trees had been trampled, bushes were shredded, and lavender burned under the poisonous decay of the damned.

Gen spotted Frankie luring several demons up the small hillside toward the highway above. Before the Gutter Demons reached his position, Dan and Tom sprung from either side of the cluster of demons. The element of a surprise ambush combined with their expert use of their whip swords sliced most of the Gutter Demons' heads off. The cracking sounds coming from their weapons turned heads. Her three brothers had killed more than a dozen demons, yet the field continued to fill with more.

"We may have to fall back," Kelly yelled from deep within the center of the battle.

"No!" Gen yelled. "The Horsemen aren't here yet."

"Gen, are you sure they're going to come?" Xavier asked.

"The longer he stays in one place using Vermillion's power, the more likely they are to track him," Gen answered.

"Gen, these numbers are ridiculous," Tom conceded. "We can't keep this up much longer, we're nearly overrun now."

Gen felt a blade scrape open her arm and screamed. She whipped around but Gutter Demons surrounded her. She continued to slice and stab. For every demon she killed another would take its place. The hostile sounds of violence drowned out her anxiety as adrenaline kicked in and she focused all her energy on staying alive. They swiped at her, their blueish gray skin stained red from her blood as they ripped small chunks of flesh from her body.

She felt the power inside of her stir and knew if she could harness it, she may be able to get the upper hand.

Don't waste movement, Gen heard Michael's instruction ring through her mind as if he were standing next to her.

She took a deep breath, lowered her body, and took aim at their thighs. She stabbed and yanked the weapon vertically. Working quick and methodically with her movements, she only turned when she aimed for the next leg. She felt them slicing, stabbing, and grabbing at her, but she pushed the fear back into the recesses of her mind and continued to circle and bring them down one, sometimes two, at a time.

When she finished, all six Gutter Demons that surrounded her were dead and she was standing in a thick puddle of cold blue blood. Looking up she saw her siblings all in equally precarious situations. Most of them were surrounded by Gutter Demons, except Deb, she was facing another Hellion. This one was much larger, a giant of a beast, standing on hind legs he would have been nearly twice Deb's size. He snorted and swiped at her, but she was spry avoiding the blow. Gen ran toward her sister sensing none of them alone were any match for this demon.

The thunderclap of war reverberated through Gen's ears as she struggled to reach Deb. The clanging of metal, grunting of conflict, and hissing of fire sounded like a freight train running through Gen's head. She neared Deb's position, but her vision blurred and suddenly she saw two images of her sister. Gen understood the disorientation was probably from severe blood loss, the adrenaline all but wearing off.

Gen opened her mouth to yell out to Deb but stopped short when the beast kicked back and stood on two legs letting out a series of terrifying growls. As it came down it knocked Deb to the ground, pinning her beneath him with one paw, he snarled as he hovered above her.

"No!" Gen's knees gave out and she fell to the ground screaming.

Schlosser laughed as he locked eyes with Gen, she knew he was silently declaring victory.

The Hellion raised his giant paw and swung it down toward Deb.

No, Gen silently pleaded. *Please God help her.*

The cascade of light that surrounded the Hellion nearly obliterated her view of Deb.

What's happening? Gen questioned as she struggled to get back on her feet.

Reaching her hands up in front of her face Gen shielded herself from the emanating brightness. Though it seemed like minutes it was only seconds for her eyes to adjust. Through the haze she saw a form take shape, as the light receded, she caught the glimmer of a sword just before it entered the beast's exposed chest. The squeal from the wounded animal caused the field to momentarily standstill. The sound of war temporarily abated as she heard the heaving of her own chest laboring to breathe through the trauma.

The beast pulled himself away, but the sword kept coming. With a precision she should have recognized, the Hellion was bludgeoned and brought down to the ground in pieces. Deb scrambled to her feet, her eyes wide with shock.

That's when Gen saw him, the sword bearer was facing away from her, wearing no shirt, just cargo pants and combat boots. His large muscles flexed as he swiped away the Hellion's blood from his face. The light that burst over the field had come from his mark. The entirety of his back was ablaze in the image of a Shield of Trinity. It was Michael, he had finally returned.

CHAPTER TWENTY-FIVE

Gen's world seemed to slow to a standstill. *He's really okay*, Gen thought. *Thank God he's alright.*

She watched her brother hold out a hand toward Deb, then Gen heard his voice.

"Are you alright, Deborah?" Michael asked.

"Yes," she answered in barely a whisper, her voice in danger of cracking.

"Thank you," Michael said to Deb.

"For what?" she asked perplexed.

"For projecting your shield on me at the church. If you hadn't, I wouldn't be here."

Before Gen could rush toward him, Michael switched gears and launched into combat mode.

"Make your way toward each other," Michael ordered sternly, he was speaking aloud but, they were all open, so his words reached them. "No one fights alone, get back-to-back quickly. You need to battle outward, don't let them get too close, the swarming technique is most successful when they can smother and oppress. Use any leverage necessary to push them back."

Michael moved toward the battle but continued to speak to them. "Once you're together move counterclockwise, that will confuse them and give you an advantage."

Gen watched him pull a Goedendag out of the heart of a dead Hellion. Weapon in each hand he plowed through the crowd toward the center. Kelly was still in the heart of the battle, though she was jumping on and off demons' backs, she was the furthest from them.

Michael stabbed quickly into the Gutter Demons that dared attack him. He pulled his blade up as he pushed the demons back with the blunt end of the Goedendag, clubbing the demons backward.

Gen noticed he didn't yell or exert himself more than needed, every movement was deliberate and amazingly accurate. Demons seemed to fall at his feet, within minutes he was nearly tangled in a heap of dead bodies.

Michael stomped on the fallen. Using the bloodied remains of the Gutter Demons he gave himself a height advantage. He walked across the dead, swinging his sword and thrusting the dagger end of the Goedendag. Nearly every strike he launched landed with brutal force. Michael swung down upon the thronging masses, clubbing, slicing, and jabbing as he went further into the battle.

Gen was mesmerized by Michael's fighting prowess; she nearly missed the voices coming up fast behind her. She turned expecting to be attacked when she saw Harry.

"Oh, my dear girl," Harry said with a look of grave concern. "What have they done to you?"

Tears sprung from Gen's eyes. "Harry, I'm so happy to see you."

Harry pulled her into a warm embrace. "I'm relieved you're alright and I'm so proud of you."

"What? How can you be?" Gen pulled back and shook her head as she surveyed the slaughter playing out in front of them. "This is all my fault."

"Nonsense," he said abruptly. "This is Hell's doing, not yours."

Before Gen could retort she realized Jared and Gabriel were standing alongside Harry. Gabriel's creased brow betrayed his concern for her physical condition.

Michael yelled toward them and their attention turned back to the field. "Jared, get to Kelly, she's alone out there."

Jared looked quickly at Gabriel. "There's no way I'm not helping."

"Agreed," Gabriel answered.

"Gabriel you should stay with Gen and Harry," Michael ordered. "The Hell Fighters will sense their vulnerabilities and head straight for them."

"I'm not going anywhere, they're safe, Michael," Gabriel answered.

Gen felt a warped sense of relief. She was glad to know Gabriel and Harry were with her but heartbroken that her siblings were still in so much danger; the battle was far from over.

Gen kept watch over the scene and saw that most of her siblings had found each other. Dan was back-to-back with Tom, while Frankie had doubled back to pair up with Deb. Off in the distance near the embankment to the highway, Xavier and Greg teamed up while Jared fought his way to Kelly.

There was something about the way Jared was fighting that caught Gen's attention. Though Jared had only just left her, he was surprisingly close to Kelly already. Between him and Michael they had killed dozens of Gutter Demons, clearing temporary paths in the field.

How? Gen thought to herself. *How did Jared get through that quickly?*

Gen felt Gabriel's hand at the small of her back, the power of the ring allowing him to intuit her inquiry. "I'll explain later," he whispered. "A lot has changed for us since being sent to the Pit."

Gen wanted to ask more about it, but there was no time. She saw Schlosser leering over the field, clearly angered by the sudden shift in Heaven's favor.

"The upper level demon refraining from the fight doesn't look happy," Harry said.

"No, I think he senses the tide turning," Gabriel surmised.

"That's Schlosser, he's a Roamer Demon that I killed six, maybe, seven months ago," Gen told them. "He's back for vengeance, it's what he'll do now that worries me."

"What do you mean?" Harry asked.

"He's not going to stop," Gen said as she looked at Gabriel knowing her answer was going to add to his already elevated level of concern. "He's not going to give up until I'm dead. He's already sold my soul to a trader named Torin."

"That's not possible," Harry answered. "Roamer Demons don't have the power to remove a soul, let alone a Guardian's soul."

"He seems to have a lot of allies on this field for a Roamer Demon," Gabriel commented.

"He stole the powers he has now," Gen explained.

"Even so, only a few entities have the power to steal a soul," Harry countered.

"He'd need a soul catcher," Gabriel said.

"A what?" Gen asked feeling the ache in her head as she tried to keep up with the conversation.

Before Gabriel could answer he was thrust into battle as several Gutter Demons swarmed them from behind. Gen maneuvered in front of Harry, but she barely engaged one of them when Gabriel swiftly killed the other three.

"I don't understand," Gen heard herself say.

"I promise I'll explain later," Gabriel told her. "What is the game plan here?"

"It's not working," Gen said simply. "They should have been here by now."

"Who?" Gabriel asked.

The sky above grew gravely dark as a malevolent wind swept through. The trees strained against the torrent of debris that was churned up and tossed about. Gen saw Schlosser turn his back to the field and swing his arms up to the sky as if he were cursing Heaven.

"I have a bad feeling," Gen said.

"He looks like he's calling for something," Harry added. "How many more things can he raise from Hell?"

"He's opening another portal," Gabriel told them.

"Oh no!" Gen strained to keep from losing all hope. "They should have been here by now!"

"Who's coming?" Gabriel's voice was tinged with impatience.

"The Horsemen," Gen told them. "Schlosser attacked Vermillion, stealing his powers he used them to return to Earth seeking revenge."

Gen watched their faces as the words penetrated. Harry seemed shocked, but Gabriel stood stoic.

Maybe the Pit has changed him in more ways than I realize, Gen thought.

Gen gleaned the outer edges of a second portal opening behind Gabriel's shoulder. As she circled around him for a better look, she saw a battalion of Hell Fighters come through the doorway.

Oh no, Gen agonized. *We've run out of time. Kelly can't beat back this many Hell Fighters.*

The Hellions bucked, thrusting their heads in the air, greeting their masters with a series of sinister howls.

"Get back!" Michael yelled. "Kelly, Jared, and Gabriel get to the front with me now!"

Gabriel reluctantly stepped forward, but Gen grabbed his arm.

"No Gabe!" she said to him. "Don't go. I can't lose you, not again."

"I'm immune Gen," Gabe answered. "That's why he called us forward. I'll be alright, you're never gonna lose me Gen, never."

Gen watched in frightful terror as Gabriel moved into the battle.

"What about Michael?" she yelled.

Gabriel didn't turn back. He spoke to her telepathically instead. *His injuries, they were severe.* He told her. *We had no choice, we had to share our blood with Michael. He's immune now also.*

"Tom, make your way to Gen and Harry," Michael yelled.

"I'm on it," Tom replied as Gen saw him move toward their position.

Gen turned back to Harry and realized he had picked up a weapon; he now held a small dagger in his left hand.

"Hopefully, you won't have to use that," Gen said.

"Hopes and Hail Mary's," he said to her. "That's all we need."

Gen wanted to share in her Angel's optimism, but it was difficult. The battle waged on, the arrival of the Hell Fighters seemed to tilt things back in Hell's favor. Gen winced as she was forced to watch the others taking punches and stabs through gritted teeth while waiting for the Horsemen to show up.

Schlosser locked eyes with Gen, he spoke and somehow—though she was yards across the field from him—she heard him. "It's over, you're about to lose," he said in a grimly vicious tone. "You should have let me kill you at the gate, you could have spared your family, but now …"

Gen looked on in horror as Schlosser waved his arms across the field that spread between them.

"Now, you've doomed them all to your fate, Guardian." Schlosser's wide smirk was visible to her even at this great distance.

Gen was forced to watch the engagement from behind the fighting lines. Deb and her brothers kept the two groups divided. Nothing was getting past them to reach Gen and Harry. The Hell Fighters couldn't get past Kelly,

Jared, Michael, and Gabriel. This brought relief, but at great cost. Exhaustion had to be setting in.

It's not typical for us to fight this intensely for such a long time, Gen thought.

Gen could see they were all injured. The field was covered in her loved ones' blood. Shame made Gen's head fall downward and as she looked at the ground, she realized her own blood had formed a puddle at her feet. Cold settled in her joints, her mouth had a salty taste that made her thirst insatiable.

"Harry," Gen whispered. "I don't think I'm going to …"

Harry caught her as she started to sway. "Don't say that," he said firmly as he wrapped an arm around her. "You're going to make it, Genevieve. You are the glue holding this family together."

Gen leaned into Harry, but Xavier's deep throttled scream sent a shot of adrenaline coursing through her. She pushed off Harry and stood straight. Her eyes cascaded the field looking for Xavier. She spotted her brother holding his left side as blood covered his torso and soaked into the ground below his feet.

"This isn't working," Gen said out loud to them. "The Horsemen should have been here by now. The energy from this engagement should have been enough to draw them to us."

"*The* Horsemen?" Michael asked from deep within the trenches.

"Yes, Schlosser stole one of their powers to free himself from Hell," Gen answered.

"How have they not been able to find him before now?" Michael questioned.

"When Schlosser took me," Gen halted as the frightful memories of being held prisoner at the Gate assaulted her. "Another demon showed up, a trader named Torin, he gave Schlosser an elixir. Torin said it would mask the signal, but that each vial would have a diminished effect."

"That's why he's not fighting," Kelly interjected. "He knows the more energy he expends, the weaker he'll get, and the faster the elixir will wear off."

"We need to draw him into the battle then," Jared added.

"We could try that," Michael paused before continuing, "or we could bring down his cloaking shield."

Gen's mind spun, something familiar tickled the back of her mind. She was so weak every solution seemed just beyond reach. She felt as though her mind were running aimlessly through a labyrinth, every muddled thought leading her astray.

Finally, she heard Kelly's voice clarify an answer. "Antonio!" she yelled. "He can drop the cloak, just like he did that day at the restaurant."

"Except we can't call him." Deb's fragile voice sounded like heartbreak to Gen.

"Why not?" Gabriel asked.

"There's no way to just call an Arch Angel," Kelly sarcastically snapped.

"Of course there is," Gabriel stated. "You just need to ask the Angel you know."

"What?" Kelly's emphatic yell nearly caused her to fall over the dead Hell Fighter that lay at her feet. "Harry can call Antonio?"

"Are you offended or excited?" Jared matched Kelly's sarcasm with a bit of his own. "By the way, I don't think you're Antonio's type."

"How do you know Antonio?" Kelly asked in disbelief.

"Doesn't everyone know Antonio?" Jared answered with a quick wink. He killed the Hell Fighter nearest him as a new throng raced through the open portal.

There's no time left, Gen thought in anguish.

"I think we need to fall back," Tom yelled. "Xavier's really hurt."

Gen felt her chest heave in pain. *No!* Her silent scream was a crushing emotional blow.

A bright light which had been creeping along the horizon, pushed in, swooping straight toward them. The Hellish wind died down and the Gutter Demons all but stopped their swarming seemingly confused by the change. The air warmed and comfort rode the calming breeze that now surrounded them.

Michael stabbed a Hellion bringing him down to the ground, but before he could finish the kill, a Hell Fighter pulled the beast from the field, tugging him back toward the portal.

"Something's coming that some of them are afraid of," Tom said.

Antonio appeared next to Harry. "What is happening?"

Harry touched the Arch Angel on the shoulder. "There's no time my friend. You see that hulking coward of a demon across the battlefield? The one with the seeping wounds and glowing green eyes? We need you to drop his cloaking shield."

Seeing Antonio peer across the field, Gen thought he looked dismayed at the scene playing out before them. He caught site of Kelly and Jared and spoke to them.

"You watch out for her, Jared," Antonio said as he pointed toward Kelly. "Someday, I may steal her from you."

"I will my friend," Jared answered through a crooked grin.

Antonio turned to Harry. "It's done. Call us if you need us, Harry."

Walking toward Gen, Antonio asked, "What have they done to you?"

"Oh, you know," Gen said through a half smirk. "The usual bloody beating as they tried to kill me."

She felt disappointed that they had to call upon him, this was her fight. It was bad enough her siblings were involved, the last thing she wanted was for someone else to get hurt.

Antonio reached out and placed his hand on her shoulder. A warm white light enveloped her.

"That should help," Antonio said in a tone that felt like warm milk. "I'm sorry this happened to you."

"Thank you," Gen said as she was able to stand steady on her feet once more.

"Di nulla, Genevieve," Antonio said. "I must leave. I cannot be here when Heaven finds Jared and Gabriel. I know nothing." He winked at her, and for a moment, she felt all was right with the world.

Antonio left the field as quickly as he appeared. To Gen, the scene seemed to burst to life once more, but something had changed. Hell Fighters were no longer coming through the portal, Hellions were exiting hastily at the heels of their masters.

"They're leaving willingly?" Deb asked.

"They know it's over," Gen said through a smile that matched her optimism. "They know something else is coming."

Gen watched Schlosser running around cursing the Hell Fighters nearest him for the betrayal of attempting to leave him.

"His tactics don't seem to be working," Harry snickered.

"No," Gen said. "These things are smarter than Schlosser."

Gen saw the outline of the portals start to shrink. Before she could inhale a sigh of relief the Hell Fighters started running for the opening. Anxiety washed over her.

I really hope this works, Gen thought. *I've never known a Hell Fighter to run from anything.*

Gen's mind felt clearer and she watched the scene devolve into chaos wrapped in a thickening darkness. Schlosser ran to the portal pulling the Hell Fighters back, thrusting many of them back out onto the field. Schlosser trampled Gutter Demons as he yanked as many beasts as he could reach out of the portal.

Off to the side of the battle the three Horsemen Gen and Kelly had seen at the library appeared. Their majestic stature, long flowing coats, and glowing green eyes peered out over the landscape.

"About freaking time!" Kelly huffed.

The portal continued to shrink, the opposing side was writhing in disarray.

Gen's eyes narrowed in on Leucous, but he was busy looking toward Schlosser.

"Whose fight is this?" Raven's voice squawked like the bird named after him.

Gen watched Schlosser step forward yelling as he waded through the crowd of demons attempting an escape.

"Get back on the field and fight demons!" Schlosser screamed.

"Answer our question," Sonoran yelled. "Who's bringing forth the Hell Fighters?"

"This is my fight, my right to vengeance," Schlosser answered. "These Guardians are mine!"

"Enough!" Leucous yelled in reply.

"If you don't leave, you'll pay. All of you!" Schlosser threatened.

What now, Genevieve? Michael asked telepathically.

Gen took a few tentative steps forward and stopped when Harry's hand grasped her shoulder.

"Are you sure about this, Genevieve?" Harry's voice sounded solemn.

Gen glanced back over her shoulder and onto the field. The carnage spanned hundreds of feet across. Dead bodies, smoldering demon parts, and blood cascaded the landscape.

"Yes, I'm sure."

"Then I'm going with you." Harry dropped his hand from her shoulder and took steps toward the battle.

"I don't think—" Gen was interrupted.

"It wasn't a request," Harry said to her. "I'm the highest-ranking Heavenly entity here. If you're going to speak with the Horsemen, then I'm going with you."

Gen gave Harry a half-hearted smile and turned back toward the path to the Horsemen. Gen seemed to gain strength from Harry's mere presence, and they made their way down the small incline they had been perched on and walked forward.

Schlosser burst through the few remaining demons he had managed to keep from fleeing the field and faced Leucous.

"You want in on this fight? Fine, but she's mine!" Schlosser screamed as he pointed toward Gen. "You try and take her, and you'll feel my wrath."

Leucous barely glanced at Gen before turning back to Schlosser.

"You bore me with your infantile little demon vengeance. You don't know what wrath is," Leucous remarked. "Sonoran, show this pathetic Roamer Demon who's really in charge here."

Sonoran sneered in agreement and began walking slowly through the smattering of demons standing between The Horsemen and Schlosser. She quietly raised her hand, barely touching each demon as she cat-walked her way toward Schlosser. Each demon that felt her touch burst into flames and burned to the ground. Like living firecrackers, the demons exploded one by one as she sauntered through them.

Blackened clouds hung thick in the air as the Gutter Demons screamed in frightful terror at the assault. Her pale cloak billowed in the wind around her, seemingly immune to the splatter and fiery embers of the Gutter Demons' flesh as it rained down upon her. Several of the demons ran away, attempting to flee her assault, but the cloaking mechanism The Horsemen now had in place kept them from fleeing the field.

This is why they think she's Death, Tom said to them telepathically.

She's certainly playing the part right now, Michael added.

"Stop!" Schlosser yelled. "They are not the enemy here, demon." Schlosser pointed at Gen. "She is!"

Leucous finally turned and locked eyes with her.

"We don't have your brother, we never did." Gen said to Leucous. "Schlosser took your brother's powers and left him for dead."

"That's not true!" Schlosser bellowed. "She's a liar and a cheat. I'm here to kill her, if you stay out of my way, then I'll help you find what you're looking for."

"You'd be a fool to trust him," Kelly yelled as she stepped toward Sonoran. "Besides, you already invaded my mind and my sister's as well. You know we don't have your brother."

Sonoran turned toward Kelly. "I saw you die, Guardian." The Demon sauntered toward Kelly blowing up Gutter Demons in her wake. "Who sent you back?"

"She's correct," Raven said from behind Sonoran. "I read the other one's mind in that church. They know nothing about our brother. They didn't know who we were, or who it was we were looking for."

"That Guardian killed me unprovoked!" Schlosser spit the accusation as Gen and Harry finally made their way to within feet of Leucous' position.

"I don't care about your petty disputes," Leucous said to Schlosser. "If you did happen upon our brother, and harmed him in any way, you will perish for it." As Leucous stepped toward Gen, he paused and glanced back at Schlosser. "There will be no coming back from where we send you."

"There's no need for that," Gen said to Leucous.

"You want mercy for the Demon that was about to kill you and all your family?" Leucous asked Gen.

"No," Gen answered. "I want justice."

"Justice, you want justice!" Schlosser screamed. "You are a fraud and a liar!"

"I did kill Schlosser," Gen said as she peered into Leucous' eyes. "He was tormenting a charge of mine, a pregnant woman. She was harmless, defenseless, his attacks were for his own enjoyment, nothing more."

Leucous gazed down upon Gen before speaking. "I don't care about your charge or your fight. We're here for our brother and we're not leaving without him. So, I ask you, what are you prepared to offer, Guardian?"

"I'll tell you where Vermillion is," she said. "But we want something before you take Schlosser away with you."

"You want something other than his demise?" Leucous asked.

"Yes."

What's going on, Gen? Deb asked.

Let them kill him, who cares? Kelly added.

"And what does justice entail?" Leucous asked as he peered over at Harry for the first time.

"He's to be marked," Gen said. "Then we'll tell you where Vermillion is. That's the deal."

Leucous chuckled. "You think I need you." The demon stepped toward Gen, but Harry stepped between them.

"Your war has not yet begun Horseman," Harry told him. "Starting it prematurely would be a mistake, and you know it."

Leucous glanced between Sonoran and Raven, both of whom Gen saw acknowledge the truth of Harry's words with a small nod of their heads.

"Fine," Leucous said. "Do what you must, but this is not the last we'll see of you, Guardian. When called upon, we'll purge the Earth of all that plagues it. The Angels of the Four Winds will stand against us, and thus it shall begin."

Gen felt a tremor under her feet, something inside was awakening, but she worked to tamp it down.

Gen looked at Leucous. "I assume you can hold him down."

Leucous raised his arm in the air and Schlosser was violently forced to his knees. The Demon yelled and thrust against the invisible restraint, but he was unable to move.

"Let's go," Gen said to Kelly and Deb.

Gen walked toward Schlosser and Kelly and Deb joined her. They reached his position and encircled the flailing Roamer Demon.

"Schlosser, you are guilty of terrible sins against humanity," Gen declared above the maniacal grunts of her enemy. "You will be marked and forced to feel the weight of all that you have wrought upon this world, for all eternity."

Gen placed her hand on the right side of his neck, where a glowing light burned his skin. Schlosser yelled out in pain, but relief would not come. Deb raised her hand and placed it on the left side of his neck. The light continued to work its way around Schlosser burning him on both sides.

His body began to violently shake. Kelly placed her hand on the back of Schlosser's neck and a Heavenly glow burst into the air. Shards of luminescent rain fell upon them enveloping the demon and lifting him off the ground. In a sweeping, terrifying motion, the demon flailed in the air and was then thrust down upon the ground between them.

Moaning and shaking his head, he struggled to sit up. As he lifted his face in the air, his neck revealed a ring of scar tissue outlined in black. Barely able to breathe, he sat in a heap on the ground.

"You wanted to bring destruction upon the weak," Gen said to him.

"What is this?" Schlosser's question was nearly drowned out by his continuous moaning.

"We aren't Angels," Kelly said to him.

"We're Guardians, remember?" Deb followed.

"What have you done to me?" Schlosser hissed at Gen.

"You're feeling your own demise, demon," Gen told him. "Tell all the things you encounter in Hell, if they come for the humans, then we'll be coming for them. Tell them we're the physical manifestation of God's wrath. We're Heaven Sent."

Schlosser's lungs labored to breath in relief, but none came.

"It's done," Gen said to Leucous. "Your brother has been left in the caves beneath the waterfalls in Purgatory. Schlosser stole his powers, but was unable to kill him, so he left him there never to be found."

Leucous violently pulled his arm toward his chest and Schlosser's ragged body was dragged painfully through the field until it lay at Leucous' feet.

Sonoran waved her hands over the field killing every demon that remained.

"Vermillion owes your family a debt," Leucous said. "It's up to him how he repays it."

With that, the three Horsemen took Schlosser's body and disappeared from the field. Gen turned to look at Gabriel and saw Lacey standing behind him. Gen wanted to ask when Lacey had arrived but was unable to form the words. As her head swam with questions, Gen's vision blurred. What little energy she was blessed with during the battle had been expended during Schlosser's marking. She could make out Gabriel running toward her, but not what he was saying. Suddenly, she sensed the ground racing up to meet her and knew she was about to pass out. Darkness enveloped her.

CHAPTER TWENTY-SIX

Deb sat on the breaker wall looking out over the ocean smashing toward the sandy shore. With the dust finally settled, she went searching for Marcus. At a minimum she owed him a thank you. If it weren't for him, Kelly wouldn't be here, alive and well. That wasn't her only reason though, selfishly she wanted to understand her feelings for him and if those feelings were truly reciprocated.

She had left the house looking for Marcus after she knew Gen was going to be okay. She had left her sister in Gabriel's care.

Where are you? Deb's mind reeled in exhaustion.

She had gone to all the usual places: the river, the old mill by the creek, and now here. Marcus was nowhere to be found.

"I need you Marcus," Deb whispered as she folded her legs up in front of her. As she wrapped her arms around her legs, she let her head rest against her knees, shielding her face from the bay breeze that whipped up from the shoreline.

The rushing sound of water breaking and crashing down upon the beach soothed her aching joints. Despite the relative calm that had settled back down upon their lives, Deb's soul was restless. Something wasn't right, she felt off. Confusing dreams had become commonplace and with it sleep was elusive.

Why are my emotions all over the place? Deb questioned. *Why am I dreaming of this beach, over and over again? I've never been here with Marcus, have I? If so, how could I have forgotten?*

Frustrated, she unraveled her cocooned body and hopped down off the wall and onto the cold sand. Kicking off her shoes she made her way toward the water's edge.

The moon cast a long narrow shadow across the choppy water. Like a spotlight she followed it walking over broken seashells and small pebbles along the way. Her feet became scuffed against the rocky terrain, without looking down she felt the line between the high tide mark and the sandy shore. The sand went from dry cool grains to hard wet surf. She struggled to make sense of what her mind was trying to tell her. It was as if something were blocking her from seeing what was right in front of her.

The smell of the ocean enveloped her and when she felt the wet foam and slimy seaweed beneath her feet she stopped. The next wave brought a splash of cool water over her toes. She felt the sucking pull of the sand underneath her feet as it was dragged back out with the tide. Something inside clicked into place and she saw a memory flash before her. She was standing at this very shoreline, her left hand enclosed in someone else's. She peered left, the image was blurry, but there was a male standing next to her wearing only shorts. He was tall with broad shoulders and a crew cut. His sandy colored hair rippled in the sun, but his face was obscured in a fuzzy light.

"Who are you?" Deb said as the male turned to face her. Before there was any clarity the image broke apart and fell away.

"Deb?" The familiar voice behind her sent chills up her spine.

She turned and found Marcus standing a few yards up on the beach away from the water.

"Marcus," she said nearly breathless. "I've been looking for you everywhere. Where have you been?"

"I've been trying to keep a low profile," he said.

"A low profile, why?" she asked. "Are you in some kind of trouble, was it for helping us?"

"I'm fine Deb." He smiled at her. "How are you? How's your family?"

"It's still raw, but we're healing. And you?"

As Marcus walked closer, Deb felt the memory echo wash over her again, bringing comfort and familiarity.

"Are you alright?" Marcus asked as he stepped closer.

"For some reason, I am now," she answered.

He smiled again, but there was something about the encounter that seemed different, distant even.

Before her mind could form any follow up questions, Marcus tucked a piece of loose hair behind her ear. Instinctively, she put her hands on his chest and he leaned in for a kiss.

Deb felt his hungry mouth engulf hers. She let go of the pretense of not wanting him and allowed her body to react to his. She felt his hands on her arms pulling her closer. His desire for her was primal and raw. Deb responded to the kiss, but it felt forced, like something inside of her was trying to come to the surface and stop her.

Deb heard a wave crash behind her, sending water spiraling toward them. This time the water washed up the sides of her leg wetting the tops of her rolled up pants. The cold snapped her free of her emotions and she pulled back from Marcus in a gasp.

She stared at him, trying to reconcile everything she was feeling on the inside with the way she just reacted to him physically. She felt desire coursing through her, her heart raced with an almost overwhelming need to be with him, but something was missing.

What's wrong with me? Deb pleaded silently.

"I'm sorry," Marcus said sensing her apprehension.

"It's okay, I wanted to kiss you. I mean, I do want to kiss you," she huffed and turned her head away. It was a romantic moment ruined by her muddled thoughts. After what seemed like several minutes she said, "Can I ask you a question?"

"Of course, anything," Marcus answered.

She focused on his face. "Have we ever been here before?"

He looked up and around the beach as if he were seeing it for the first time. Shaking his head, he answered, "No, I don't think so. I mean not that I remember, why?"

Deb felt her head shake in response. "No reason. How did you find me?"

"Just lucky I guess." He smiled. "I know you love the water, the riverbank, the ocean. I visited a bunch of places before I found you here."

Deb read his body language and knew he had just lied to her, but about which part she didn't know. She seemed to see Marcus for the first time the way her sisters did. There was something underneath his facade, like a veneer covering something troubling.

Fear cascaded through her body, not that he would hurt her, but that she could no longer trust her own feelings.

"I should go," she said to him.

"Alright, I hope I didn't upset you."

"No," she answered through what must have been a thin smile. "I just need to get back."

She walked past him toward the sea wall retrieving her shoes along the way. She turned back before leaving. "Thank you, for all that you did for me and my family. Being grateful doesn't seem like enough, but I don't know what else to say. If it weren't for you, Kelly would be ..." Deb stopped short unable to actually say the words.

"You're welcome. I'll always be here for you."

She watched him leave the beach before she could respond and felt her heart break a little.

What did I just do? she thought. *Why is it that when you're gone, I miss you? When you're near, I want you. But when you touch me, it feels all wrong.*

Heading home Deb arrived in her bedroom relieved to find the house quiet. She fell into bed tossing and turning, nightmares plagued her in fitful slumber. She saw the beach again, with the same man as before, his somewhat rugged face just out of focus. Each time he turned she saw a glimpse of something that seemed familiar but then her mind would lose it and she'd forget what it was. There was something she was certain of though. The person from her dream on the beach wasn't Marcus.

Deb's dreams were not so much dreams as distant memories. The happy depictions flooded through her as her mind tried to keep up. She chased each thread to a dead end. Sometimes she felt as though she could nearly place them, but they remained out of reach.

Rolling over, she kicked off the sheets. The chilly air from the open window roused her to give up on sleep and get out of bed. Her chest heaved as if she had just run a marathon. Her legs were shaky, and her face was damp from tears she hadn't known were shed.

Sitting up, Deb swung her legs over the side of the bed. Leaning over she reached for her robe and heard paper crinkle. Flipping the light switch on she moved the blankets and sheets looking for the source until she finally found it under her pillow. It was a note from Marcus attached to a small envelope.

I don't know what happened on the beach. The kiss felt so right, yet your face, you looked as though you'd seen a ghost. I need to take off for a while, work some things out, but I'll be back. I'll always be there if you need me Deb, please know that. Inside this envelope is my grandmother's wedding band. It means a great deal to me. If you feel about me, the way I feel about you, then it will fit, and I will come for you.

I don't know that I have the right to ask, but I want you in my life forever and I hope you feel the same.

I love you, Marcus.

She felt the small hard object in the envelope and peered inside. The shimmer of a simple gold band gleamed up at her. She took the band out and stared at it.

Oh my, she thought. *Do I dare try it on?*

"Woman!" Jared sarcastically yelled. "You are driving me crazy, fill that bag up already and let's go!"

Kelly giggled over at him. "I don't know what to pack or how much."

"I already told you, clothing is optional, but not preferred." Jared winked at her.

"That can't be true for the entire time!" Kelly folded her arms across her chest in mock anger. "Just tell me how many days and the average temperature."

"Fine. Three days." He huffed. "You need a bathing suit, one pair of jeans, a top, a sweatshirt in case it gets chilly at night, and those sexy red high heels, that's it."

"That can't be it for three days!" she squealed as she raced around the room jamming clothes into the single overnight bag Jared had negotiated her down to.

"Here's your map," he said when she finally finished packing.

"Finally!" she exclaimed. "Ok, so where are we going?" She let the bag drop to the floor and opened the folded-up piece of paper he handed her. Inside was a badly drawn map of three locations. There were stickers haphazardly placed next to each site with numbers marked next to each.

Kelly felt his eyes on her and looked up. "I don't know what to say …" she smirked, "where am I wearing the bathing suit?"

Jared laughed. "You didn't look close enough."

Kelly looked down again. "You're taking me on a three-day tour of Columbus, Ohio; Sydney, Australia; and Montreal, Quebec?"

"Yes," he said gleefully. "I thought the stickers would be a big enough hint."

When Kelly turned the page a little to better see the pictures she gasped. "Cheeseburgers, these are cheeseburgers!" Throwing herself into his arms she finally understood. "You're taking me to the three best cheeseburger joints in the world!"

Jared hugged her tightly. "Are you ready?"

"I'm so ready." She said. "It's the second-best thing you've ever given me."

"The first better be that ring on your finger," he quipped.

"No," she said as she peered up and into his deep brown eyes. "The best thing you ever gave me was your heart."

Gen felt the warmth of someone sleeping beside her. A strong arm was draped across her small frame. She sensed the brightness of morning splashing over her face even before she dared open her eyes. She knew the windows were open, she could hear the snapping of the curtain's fabric as it billowed in the whipping wind that had swooped in to greet her.

She inhaled deeply and smelled a mix of Gabriel and fresh cut grass as it wafted over her. *I'm not dreaming, he's here, he's right here holding me.* Her mind shook off the remnants of the dream she had been in. She didn't want to move as if she thought he might suddenly vanish.

Her mind sifted through the last several days, bits and pieces of it came back in disarray. She had been hurt badly, inside and out. She remembered walking toward Gabriel on the field, but then blackness enveloped her. She remembered her sisters standing above her in the living room, their arms raised over her bruised and battered body. She remembered the crushing sensation of pain as she struggled to heal. A memory of Gabriel feeding her soup and then talking quietly until she fell back to sleep warmed her.

How long have I been out of it? she thought. *I have no idea how long it's been since the battle.*

She felt her husband stir and turned toward him. Gabriel groaned and mumbled to her sleepily. "It's okay," he told her. "You're home." She heard his breathing get heavy almost immediately, he was already falling back to sleep.

Gen rested her head against his chest and listened to his beating heart. She had heard it a thousand times, but due to the long absence it somehow all felt new again. She slipped her hand beneath his shirt and rubbed his bare skin, feeling new scars where unblemished skin had once been. She heard him moan in response and fully wake.

"Hey," he said to her. "You're awake." She felt him lift his head and look down at her. She looked up and smiled at him.

"Yes, but somehow this still feels like a dream."

"It's not," Gabriel told her. "I'm really here, with you, in our old house no less."

He squeezed her and kissed the top of her head. Her heart filled a little and broke at the same time. *He'll be gone soon.*

Gen pushed up and off his chest, turning to leave the bed.

"What's the rush?" he asked.

"How much time do we have before you need to go back?" Gen asked. "I know it can't be long."

Gabriel's eyes followed her around the room as she proceeded to get dressed.

"Let's just say I'm overdue."

"That's what I thought." Gen sighed heavily. "I am assuming my siblings are all downstairs waiting for a debrief."

"Um ..." Gabriel got up slowly and got dressed himself. "No one else is here."

Gen stopped short. "What do you mean? Where are Kelly and Deb?"

"Kelly went off with Jared for a few days before he had to leave. When she returned, she grabbed some clothes and said she was going to stay with Dan."

"And Deb?"

"She's been staying with Harry."

"Wow, I don't know what to say."

"Say you'll get undressed and get back in bed with me."

Gen laughed, the thought had crossed her mind, and not for the first time.

"How about something to eat first?"

He smiled at her and it sent her head swimming in thoughts of being alone with him. *But I won't have that for long.* Gen smiled through the painful thought. *The mind was cruel sometimes.*

After eating something small they went out to the screened-in porch off the kitchen. She had managed to paint it before everything happened and in the breezy morning air, she still smelled remnants of it.

"The garden looks amazing," Gabriel said. "I keep looking at it, wondering how it can be the same yard, the same street, the same place."

"I know," Gen said to him. She took the lightweight throw she had carried out with her and draped it over them. They were on the small loveseat that sat against the far wall. "I can't imagine what it must be like to realize forty years has gone by."

He draped his arm behind her and pulled her a little closer. The smell of the coffee from the mug he held in his other hand hit her. It was like she was transported back in time. *How many times have we sat out here and talked about our future, Gabe?* she thought.

"A thousand maybe," he said.

"What?" Gen asked confused.

"We must have sat out here a thousand times and talked about our future."

"The ring," she whispered. "That means you know what I was thinking upstairs."

"Before or after you were thinking of making love to me?" he said with a grin.

She elbowed him gently and he chuckled.

"We need to talk," she said. "It's not like we can pretend you're back, though I really want to do that."

"I know." He looked over and she felt his heartache echo her own.

"Where do we start?"

"I will tell you everything, you deserve to know." He paused. "But you need to understand, there's a cost, a price I'll have to pay."

"I don't understand, Gabe. What do you mean?"

"The Pit, it's a place you pay for the things you've done wrong." He shifted in his seat pulling back his arm so he could face her more fully.

"I know. Kelly explained it as a sort of penance." She watched him nod.

"You're not allowed to tell anyone about it, while you're there. You can only tell your story once you have paid for your sins in full."

"You're saying that even if the ring had stayed on," Gen glanced down at her wedding band, "and we were connected, you wouldn't have been able to tell me anything about it?"

"Correct."

"But I would have felt you?" she asked.

"I think you were feeling me. My pain anyway. That's all there is in the Pit. Pain."

Gen's heart ached a little. She placed her hand on top of his and squeezed. "If you tell me about it now, before it's done, what's the price?"

"I'm not sure, but I can guess it would be more time." Before she could say anything, he added. "It might not be just me that has to pay it, Gen."

Gen understood. "It might punish Jared too." She watched him nod.

"And Dmitri," he added.

"Dmitri." Gen sucked in a breath. "So he is with you, even though we all saw him after you were gone."

"Dmitri is part of the reason Jared and I were able to come at all."

"What do you mean?" Gen was confused. "How?"

"Dmitri's knowledge of all the realms is unparalleled. He figured out how to smuggle the two of us out. We didn't even know it was possible, let alone that we could make it out without getting caught. He's back there now covering for me, but—"

"Don't tell me anything else." Gen interrupted him. "You have your reasons. I trust you. You can tell me when you come back to me for good."

"Are you sure?"

"I am," she said. "I don't know how my ring came off. Honestly, I don't remember. I'd been searching for you for weeks on end. I wasn't eating, I wasn't sleeping, and I felt this anger that wouldn't go away."

"Gen, that might have been my feelings mimicked onto you. It was probably me you were feeling." He shook his head back and forth. "I was angry all the time, you almost have to be to survive in that place."

"I was so scared something bad had happened to you." Gen's mind raced back to that time and tears sprung from her eyes.

Gabriel looked at her heartbroken. "I'm so sorry, Gen."

"When I woke, the ring was on a thick chain hanging from my neck. I didn't dare put it on, fearful I would know you were gone. I couldn't bear it. Instead I stayed in this denial, hunting down leads and driving everyone nearly mad as I did so."

"I felt the moment the ring came off. It was like someone had stabbed me in the chest. I hadn't been able to speak with you, but somehow, despite the heartache, I knew you were okay and then…" He paused as Gen got up and knelt in front him. "Then there was nothing. Gen, I had to live in that Hell hole not knowing if I would ever see you again."

"I'm sorry, sorry for both of us," Gen said as she looked up into her husband's war-torn face. "I know we're almost out of time. I'm grateful you stayed, that you figured out how to come for me when I was in trouble, but we've paid enough of a price. We've both been in a sort of prison for far too long."

Gen stood and opened the glass door into the house. Turning back she held her hand out to him. "Let's go back to bed."

ABOUT THE AUTHOR

Jennifer Rothstein lives in western Massachusetts with her husband and their two cats Brady and Mr. Thumbs. Jennifer is a business professional but is pursuing her MFA in Creative Writing. Atonement is her debut novel and the first in the Heaven Sent Series.

Visit her online at www.JLRothstein.com or via social media Facebook.com/JLRothstein. Follow her on Twitter @jlrothstein1 or Instagram @ jlrothstein1

Made in the USA
Monee, IL
22 March 2021